True Blue

True Blue

Luanne Rice

Bantam Books

True Blue

ISBN 0-7394-2713-X

Bantam Books are published by Bantam Books, a division of
Random House, Inc. Its trademark, consisting of the words
"Bantam Books" and the portrayal of a rooster, is Registered in
U.S. Patent and Trademark Office and in other countries. Marca
Registrada. Bantam Books, 1540 Broadway, New York, New
York 10036.

PRINTED IN THE UNITED STATES OF AMERICA

For Tracy Devine

And in memory of Mim

Acknowledgments

With love and thanks to Irwyn Applebaum, Nita Taublib, Micahlyn Whitt, Matthew Martin, Anna Forgione, Johanna Tani, Andrea Cirillo, Mia Onorato, Lauren and Melissa Monteleone, Heather McNeil, Br. Luke Armour, O.C.S.O.; my fishing partner, Bouner, and his sisters Whiller and Nuggledean; Paul, Twigg, Joe G., David, Richard, Dan, Georgie, Cora, Steve, Martha; the loving and omnipresent spirits of Helen, Val, Miss Davis, Granny Crawford, Aunt Florence, Uncle Lote, and Lucille; and Bobby Monteleone, for keeping the faith.

True Blue

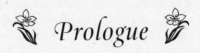 Prologue

ZEBULON MAYHEW OWNED the sky, and Rumer Larkin ruled the earth. That's how they had divvied up the universe when they were five, and the split had worked just fine this far, into their fifteenth year.

Crawling behind Zeb out his bedroom window, Rumer pulled herself across the strip of roof that ran below the front windows, and then used the dormer's peak to haul herself up to the very top.

"Wait for me," she called to Zeb as he ran along the edge of the sharply slanted roofline, arms out at his sides.

"You're too slow," he said, but he did wait, throwing a quick grin over his shoulder and holding out his hand. Grabbing it, Rumer felt sparks in her blood, making her tremble and hold on a little tighter.

"What are we going to see tonight?" she asked, following him as they balanced their way across the steepest part of the roof between the crooked brick chimney and the unicorn weathervane.

"Larkin, you're hopeless," he said. "If it doesn't pounce or hop, you don't remember anything about it. What's the date?"

She hesitated, waiting for him to let go of her hand. He didn't, and she hoped he didn't notice her fingers shaking. He was tall for fifteen, towering above her, his blond head silhouetted by the Milky Way. "August twelfth," she said finally.

"Right. The Perseid meteor shower—do I have to remind you every year? We're going to count shooting stars, and I'm not letting you down till you get at least twenty."

"Twenty!" she said, secretly thrilled because she knew it would take hours to count twenty shooting stars.

"There's one!" he said, dropping her hand to point. She turned just in time to see a trail of white fire blazing across the sky. "I'd show you the crab nebulae or Saturn or Jupiter, but I know you don't care."

"The sky's your domain, Astro-Boy."

"Rumer the bunny girl," he teased back.

They settled down on the rooftop, at the opposite end of the house from the chimney. From up there, Rumer could see Long Island Sound, white-edged waves of black rippling along the half-moon beach. To the north was the rest of Hubbard's Point, about a hundred cottages nestled together on the hill and in the swale. They lived on the Point itself, which jutted out into the Sound, the dead-end street populated by the grand old dames whose fathers and grandfathers had founded the beach area.

Next door was Rumer's family's cottage, built the same year as the Mayhews' and almost identical in design. While most people lived at the Point only in summer, Rumer's and Zeb's families had lived there year-round. Once, when she was seven, she had slept over at Zeb's and sleep-walked straight into his parents' room, the way she sometimes did at home.

"Another!" Zeb said, jabbing her side. "You're two behind now."

"I'm looking," Rumer said, but instead she looked through the sheer curtains into her family's bathroom window and watched her sister shaving her legs. "Maybe I'd better tell Elizabeth to pull the shades," she said.

"You'd be amazed at what I see you Larkin girls doing," Zeb said. "Even if she pulls the shade too, you can see through the crack."

"You look?" Rumer asked, her mouth dropping open.

"What do you expect? Our houses are about five yards apart, and your blinds don't close the whole way. Of course I look. Hey, another meteor!"

Rumer glanced over, assessing him. Did he mean he looked specifically at Elizabeth, or at Rumer too? Why did it seem, suddenly, to matter so much? They were friends, that was all. But Rumer's mouth felt dry, and her hand ached to have Zeb hold it again.

"Five," Zeb said, pointing. "Six."

"Elizabeth," Rumer called. She couldn't stand to have her eighteen-year-old sister not know what she was showing: everything. Her night-gown straps had slipped off her shoulder, and her boobs were half hanging out.

"What are you doing?" Zeb asked, watching Rumer beginning to scuttle across the roofline like a rock crab in a tidal pool.

"Warning her."

"I'm telling you—don't bother."

"Why, so you can watch her?" Rumer teased, but her heart began to pound when he didn't say no. The stars spun around, and a soft wind blew through the pine boughs. She held her breath, waiting. Even in the darkness she could see Zeb turning red. A sound caught in her throat, and she realized she was remembering the school Halloween party last fall, when she and her sister had worn identical witch costumes and Elizabeth—sweeping across the school stage as if it were a Broadway theater—had won "most beautiful."

"You're my best friend," Zeb said quietly, and suddenly Rumer knew he could hear her crying.

Rumer nodded, squeezing her eyes shut.

"More than Paul and Andy," he said, naming two of their other closest Hubbard's Point friends. She didn't reply. "Did I say something wrong?" he asked.

She shook her head.

"Okay, then. Let's get back to the sky. What's the score—me seven, you none? Come on, if there were rabbits up there instead of in the old briar patch we call a yard, you'd be going crazy."

But Rumer couldn't just let Elizabeth continue, knowing that she was on display. Crawling across the roof, she left Zeb behind. He was going to be an astronaut someday, and he liked to get all the star practice he could. Rumer's feelings were churning around, a combination of protectiveness and jealousy and hurt and love, and somehow she slipped when she should have grabbed.

"Whooooo!" she called, bare feet and fingernails scrabbling for a hold on the shingles.

"Give me your hand," Zeb said, reaching down.

"I can't," she said, sliding slowly.

"Come on! Give me—" he said, and then he began to slide too. They sped up, side by side, gliding down the Mayhews' roof, over the moss and lichens, under the trees and stars. But while Rumer managed to grip the gutter rim as she tumbled past, Zeb flew straight off the roof into the azalea bush below.

"Zeb!"

He didn't answer. It took all Rumer's strength to hold on, start to haul herself to safety inch by inch. Her heart was pounding. She had killed him.

"Ouch," he said, pushing himself up. "My leg . . ."

"You're alive," she called, breathless.

"You're still up there? Hang on, Rue."

A tall pine grew alongside the house. The space between the branches and roof loomed darkly before her, but she had to get down to Zeb. Taking a quick breath, she swung out, scraping her face and hands with hundreds of sharp pine needles. Making her way to the trunk, she scrambled down branch by branch, pine tar sticking to her skin, and dropped the last six feet to the ground.

Inside their houses, blue light from the TV sets came through the screens. She could hear Mary Tyler Moore's laugh track. Their parents had gone out for dinner together, and they weren't home yet. Zeb had broken his ankle—she saw his foot twisted around, jutting out at an odd angle, and felt sick.

Rumer had helped a hurt rabbit the previous week, an abandoned dog the week before that, a broken-winged robin in July, and two brand-new motherless kittens in June. She had a sense for helping hurt animals, but her feelings for Zeb were so strong, she couldn't even touch him. Instead, she crouched down and stared into his blue eyes.

"Zeb," she whispered helplessly, wanting so badly to lay her hand upon him, to fix his ankle the way she had sometimes healed cats and squirrels and rabbits, afraid that she'd somehow hurt him more if she did.

"What happened?"

The voice came from behind, and Rumer didn't even have to look. From the way Zeb struggled to sit up, not wanting to be seen as weak by the most beautiful witch in Black Hall, Rumer knew that Elizabeth had come outside.

"Tried to catch a falling star," Zeb tried to joke.

"I heard someone calling my name," Elizabeth said, "but when I looked out the window, all I saw was you two rolling off the roof. Are you okay, Zeb?"

"He's fine," Rumer said, but she could see that he wasn't. His face was turning white; she'd seen hurt rabbits go into shock before, and that was happening here. Even so, he propped himself up bravely on his elbow, to not look feeble in front of Elizabeth. So Rumer left him with her sister as she started across the yard to use the Mayhews' phone to call the Shore-line ambulance.

"If you'd wanted to impress me," Elizabeth was saying, and when Rumer glanced back, she saw her sister stroking Zeb's forehead, "all you really had to do was come down to earth. Why do you spend all your time chasing starlight? That's all it is, you know. By the time that light travels through space, the star might not even exist anymore. Earth, Zeb. That's where people belong."

"Yeah?" Zeb asked in a weak voice, as if he were taking her seriously. "Earth?"

"Earth," Elizabeth said, and at that moment Rumer hated her sister for having beauty so powerful it could blind Zeb to his own dreams, even more, hating Zeb for allowing himself to be blinded.

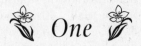 *One*

THE *FOR SALE* sign had been there, nestled in the ivy for so long, it had begun to seem part of the landscape, and then it was gone. Early June, Hubbard's Point was coming back to life, so everyone noticed. Taking their evening walks down the dead-end road to the Point, looking up at the old Mayhew place, couples would speculate—in voices loud enough for Rumer Larkin to hear—about who the new owners would be.

Rumer wondered herself, but only slightly. That house, no matter how often it changed hands, had had only one owner that mattered—and Zeb had sold it ten years ago, after his and Elizabeth's divorce.

Rumer knew there were two types of people who came to the Point. Those like her family, who stayed forever, and those who thought more about property values than the simple peace of the beautiful land. People like that came and went. The women of the Point—or *les Dames de la Roche*, as Winnie Hubbard called them—just watched without much comment.

It was dusk. The air was fragrant with honeysuckle and beach roses. Pale blue and white lace hydrangeas bloomed along the garage and stone wall. Pine and scrub oak trees, symbolic of Hubbard's Point, filled all the yards. The sound of her father sanding the bottom of his boat rasped through the air. Peering out the kitchen window, Rumer brushed wheat-colored hair from her eyes and knew this was the perfect time for the release.

She walked out to the mudroom, where the family hung their slickers and slipped off their boots. Wood for the fireplace was stacked against the wall—pine wainscoting darkened with time and salt air. Kindling was saved in a copper kettle, and two animal hutches, brought home from her veterinary office, stood in the corner.

They were covered with pieces of bright fabric—an old slipcover and curtain—to keep the birds and animals from being frightened, and Rumer knelt down to lift the cloth on the lowest hutch. There, huddled in back, was the small brown rabbit. Liquid eyes stared, whiskers quivering.

She had found him six weeks earlier, lying stunned near the angel statue on the border of her yard and the Mayhews'. The talon marks on his back had made her think an owl had caught him, lifted him into the sky. This little guy was fighter enough to squirm hard, wriggle free, and drop to earth. It had been a long fall, but she had set his leg, stitched his cuts, and he had survived.

"Oh, Rumer," her mother had said to her once when she was eleven and had stayed up all night watching over a baby blue jay who had fallen out of its nest, "Nature can be harsh—sometimes baby birds are born sick, and their mothers push them out. We just don't know. . . ."

"I know," Rumer had said stubbornly. "He was just trying to fly a little too soon. He's going to be fine. I'll take care of him, and then I'll put him back."

"He won't be accepted, Rumer," said Mrs. Mayhew—her mother's best friend since childhood. "Not after he's been touched by humans."

"Yes, he will," Rumer had said, undeterred, making him a nest in an old shoe box. "I'm sure of it."

"Well, just don't forget to take care of yourself as well. Okay, honey? Little girls need sleep too."

Rumer had listened, but inside she felt so thrilled and alive, as if she'd never need sleep again. But the next day, when she checked on the small jay, she found him dead in the shoe box. Her insides felt like ice, numbness spreading into her fingers as she gently touched the bird's wings, discovering the broken bones.

Zeb helped her bury him, she remembered now: by the angel statue between their yards. Kneeling there, digging the hole and smelling the fresh dirt, she knew that she wanted to learn everything there was about helping animals, and she whispered to Zeb, "I'm going to be a vet."

"No kidding, Larkin," he'd whispered back. "I've known that since you were five."

Holding the rabbit—now rehabilitated from his broken leg—in her hands, she walked outside. Crickets chirped in the tall grass. Across the water, seabirds cried on their way home to Gull Island. Pines whispered in the wind. The rhythm of her father's sanding continued. Down the street, Winnie sang scales. Stopping by the stone angel, Rumer set the rabbit down in a patch of glossy-green myrtle.

Pausing to sniff the air, he scampered straight into the Mayhews' yard. Rumer hid in the bushes, holding her breath, watching him go. I knew it, she thought. Although there were plenty of other rabbits around, he was part of the old family that lived under the azalea bush, in a warren deep in the rock ledge.

When she, Elizabeth, and Zeb were kids, their mothers had taught them all about the animals who lived on the Point, the trees and flowers that grew there, the fish that swam the waters, the stars that shined down on them every night. The Mayhews and Larkins had the Point's wildest, least-tamed lots, so they had the most nature to love and learn about right in their own backyards—behind the very same houses their mothers had grown up in.

Rumer glanced up at the house next door. No matter how many times it had changed hands, everyone still called it "the Mayhew place." Built on granite ledge, its shingles were still stained dark green, with cutout pine trees in the white shutters, the way it had been when Zeb had lived there. Funny how none of the three subsequent owners had bothered to change much.

Tall pine trees shaded the rocky land. Mrs. Mayhew's gardens were still the same: rich tangles of ivy and woodbine, rare wildflowers such as bloodroot and ladyslippers, hybrid lilies of gold and rust-red growing—with such heart-piercing tenacity—from out of the gray, glacial ledge where the rabbits made their home.

Now, gazing west at the beach and marsh, Rumer saw the crescent moon hanging low in the sky. Just below, to the right, was a planet. Mercury? Venus? She wasn't sure, but seeing it stirred something old and nearly forgotten deep in her soul, so bittersweet, she picked a honeysuckle blossom and licked the nectar to chase the other taste away even as she realized Winnie's singing had stopped.

Watching her charge, she saw two new rabbits venture out of their hiding place among the low azaleas. They sniffed the air, hopped through the yard. Rumer watched the tall grass move, and they encircled their friend, welcoming him back.

Just then the animals froze. They turned to statues, like the stone angel, and Rumer glanced over her shoulder to see someone tall coming up her hill, through the shadows. It was Winnie; Rumer could tell by her stooped grace, by the *shush, shush* of her long caftan against the grass and stones. Behind her, with hair as tangled as the ivy, was Rumer's neighbor and a student in the veterinary science course she taught at the high school, Quinn Grayson.

"Are we too late?" Winnie asked as the two joined Rumer. Although she didn't lower her voice, the rabbits weren't scared away. The creatures on the Point, humans and animals, knew each other so well, and at eighty-two, Winnie was the oldest of all. Quinn, crouching down, didn't say a word.

"Almost," Rumer said. "I let him go a few minutes ago—there he is, by the azalea. See him?"

"Being welcomed back by his family."

"Always."

"I'm sorry I was late. I was rehearsing, and I lost track of the time."

Quinn looked up. "And I was making a tea ceremony for Aunt Dana and helping with the wedding . . . instead of green tea, I made rose-hip tea from Point roses! She loved it, and it was so—"

"Test on pet first aid tomorrow, Quinn," Rumer said.

"I know, but I wanted to see you release the rabbit . . ." Quinn said. Although she was as wild and native as most of the animals on the Point, she was trying hard to have a normal junior year. At school to teach just one elective class a semester, Rumer looked after her the best she could, but what could she really say to a girl who had missed more school days than she had attended since last September?

"Well, mission accomplished," Winnie said in her straightforward and sensible way. "You've seen the rabbit safely home, and now you must return to your studies. Excellence, Quinn, is what we expect from you: The world has far too much mediocrity already. Go to your books and make us all proud."

"Dr. Larkin," Quinn said, smiling. "It always feels so weird, calling you that at school. You've always been just Rumer to me and Allie."

"You can call me whatever you want," Rumer said. "Now go on home. Forget about the wedding for one night, and study hard. . . ."

"I'd rather be lobstering," Quinn said. "I want to live life, not study it."

Rumer hid a smile. She remembered feeling that way at Quinn's age; she still did. "Well, for now you have to do both."

"Yes, darling," Winnie agreed.

Reluctantly, Quinn shook her head as if both Winnie and Rumer were too old to ever understand, and ran through the yards.

"Not the first complicated girl the Point has seen . . ." Winnie murmured.

Fireflies flickered in the bushes, and ghostly shapes shimmered in the twilight haze. Standing there, Rumer felt the old woman's hand on her shoulder. Winnie's white hair piled on top of her head made her look even taller than her six feet, and Rumer felt flooded with love for her neighbor and friend.

"Who do you think has bought the place?" Rumer asked, gesturing at the green house.

"Someone fascinating, I hope."

"With children," Rumer said. "Who'll climb the trees and love the birds and rabbits that live here."

"And stars and sky overhead," Winnie said, her trained voice rich and melodic.

Why had Winnie said that in that way? Rumer looked over, a question in her eyes.

"Nothing, dear," Winnie said, catching her glance. "Don't read so much into an old woman's musings. Now, are you ready for the wedding?"

Rumer nodded, brushing the hair from her eyes. Dana Underhill, one of the women of the Point, was getting married that Saturday to Sam Trevor—finally, after four years together. A tent had been erected in their yard, and Quinn's sister, Allie, had stopped by earlier to ask if they could pick some roses and lilies on the wedding morning, to decorate the tables.

"I am," Rumer said, although the last thing she felt like doing was go to a wedding. "Are you singing?"

"Of course! It wouldn't be a Hubbard's Point wedding if I didn't sing!" Winnie said imperiously, and Rumer smiled at her unabashed pride. *Winnie Hubbard has a very good opinion of herself,* Rumer's grandmother, Letitia Shaw, had once observed, making it clear she thought the quality perhaps too much of a good thing.

"We haven't had a Point wedding in a long time," Rumer said, still watching the rabbits, their small movements making the grass twitch.

"I'm not sure this counts as a full-fledged Point wedding," Winnie said. "Sam's from away. But I can understand how he fell in love with Dana, of course. . . ." Her voice grew softer and her gaze fixed on the green house as the scent of roses and honeysuckle embraced them. "The air here is an aphrodisiac. But you know the tradition: The boys of Hubbard's Point marry the girls of Hubbard's Point."

"Some do. . . ."

"Your ancestor blew it, of course. Running off with that ship's captain and dying together on the Wickland Shoal. So romantic, but missing the point. Everything she needed was right here!"

Rumer nodded, thinking of the old story. The legend of Elisabeth Randall and Nathaniel Thorn was famous—more so since Sam's brother, Joe Connor, had raised the treasure of the *Cambria*, the ship that had carried them to their deaths.

"But true Hubbard's Point marriages . . ." Winnie continued. "Beginning with my great-grandfather and great-grandmother, right down to your sister and Zeb."

"That one didn't last," Rumer said sharply, watching the rabbits.

"It was never the real thing . . ." Winnie began, and then seemed to change her mind. "He's coming, you know."

"He's what?" The pit of Rumer's stomach turned to ice.

"Coming. For Dana's wedding. He and Michael are renting my guest house. Zeb sent his check, and I cashed it, so I know it's true, they're really coming." She gestured at the green house, almost invisible in the darkness. "I think he would have liked to rent his old place, but the sale had already gone through. The timing is dicey—my spring tenants weren't out soon enough to suit him, but—"

"Why's he putting himself through it, coming back to Hubbard's Point after everything? And dragging Michael along with him?" Rumer asked, the words tearing out. The ice had melted and she was now boiling mad. She didn't want to lay eyes on Zeb ever again.

"Who knows?" Winnie said, holding her arms up to the sky. "Perhaps he finally heard his son calling all the way from the moon, or wherever it is he goes up there. Dana's wedding is only the excuse—I think it's a chance for him and Michael to spend some time together."

"Why don't they do it somewhere else?" Rumer asked. "Zeb's a fool if he tries to come back here."

"What about Michael?" Winnie asked dryly. "Don't you want to see your nephew?"

"I doubt he even remembers me."

"There's plenty of time for you to refresh his memory. You'll have the summer."

"The summer?"

"That's how long they're staying."

"You're kidding!" The shock struck Rumer like a lightning bolt, entering through the crown of her head, singeing the nerves along her spine. Her heart had been broken, her family nearly destroyed by what Zeb had done. Marrying Elizabeth: Rumer would never forgive either of them for it.

Elizabeth, Zeb, and Michael. They had been the star family, no question about it: a Broadway actress lured by Hollywood, an astronomer and mission expert, and their beautiful miracle child whom Rumer barely knew. The situation filled Rumer with emotions she hadn't felt in several years—the feelings had been unpleasant then, and they were no more welcome now.

"When do they arrive?"

"Before Saturday—in time for the wedding." Stretching her arms toward the sky again, Winnie turned to go. "It promises to be an interesting summer."

"Winnie, the eternal optimist," Rumer murmured.

"Precisely," Winnie replied, dead serious. "Is there any other way to be?" Turning, she swept majestically down the hill, leaving Rumer alone with the rabbits.

Crouching down, Rumer found that her hands were shaking.

Zeb was coming home.

Zeb and Michael.

She thought of the layers of love that covered her life, like clouds over an unchanging hillside. There was love, and there was love. Cloud upon cloud upon cloud. They arrived, obscuring the moon, parting to reveal the starry sky. Cirrus clouds came, a thin high screen softening the white moon, covering the constellations.

Nothing inside Rumer was soft. She was all hard edges, and had been since Zeb married her sister. Her breath seemed to scrape her lungs, her heart. Turning, she walked slowly into her house.

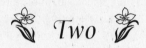 *Two*

THE ROAD ROLLED out before them, an endless ribbon of tar. Through the canyons of Utah, the plains of Kansas, the hills of western Pennsylvania, they followed the road back home. Funny, Zeb Mayhew thought, that he still considered Connecticut home—he hadn't lived there in many years. Transplanted to California, he spent a lot of his time in the sky. Elizabeth had often said his official address was the Milky Way, and she was only half kidding.

"Hey," he said out loud to the young man sleeping across the seat from him. Curled up into as tight a ball as a six-foot-two-inch person could get himself, he didn't react. Zeb reached across to jostle his shoulder. "Wake up. You're missing it all."

"Rhunngh."

"I mean it—open your eyes and see what's here."

This time Zeb got no response at all. The sleeper just hiked his shoulders around, reconfigured the backpack he was using as a pillow, and went down for the count. Zeb held on to the steering wheel tightly with both hands to keep his frustration in check. In the twenty-five hundred miles they'd driven so far, they had exchanged about eleven words—not a single complete sentence.

The June day was brilliant, clear, and fine. Speeding east on highway 70, Zeb leaned forward to look up at the sky. There in the field of blue, he saw bright objects shining out that no one else could see: satellites, planets, and stars. He had better than perfect vision, and he knew the sky the way other people knew their backyards. Narrowing his blue eyes against the glare, he searched for satellites he had launched into orbit, the space station where he had periodically stayed.

The sky usually calmed him, but today it made everything else worse.

His better than twenty-twenty eyesight was mocked by the fact he was on the ground, that his flight days were done.

Elizabeth thought this trip was mainly a bonding experience; neither she nor anyone knew that Zeb had something else on his mind. His bosses had told him to take a rest, to get as far away from L.A., Houston, Caltech's Jet Propulsion Lab, and the brand-new Laguna Niguel Mission Center and Observatory as possible.

They were giving him his own lab there. After the "event," he had hung up his flight suit. Come September, he had to shoot back to California like a rocket—with fanfare, press, and parties. The space world was cheering him on—he was about to become a mission specialist here on earth. He had a huge budget, a hand-picked crew, and high expectations. With America heading for Mars, Zeb was about to be in charge of interpreting all of that mission's satellite photos—and plenty of others as well.

But that wasn't for three months.

Right now Zeb had a different kind of mission in mind. Lying in bed every night, stripped of his defenses, he saw her in his dreams. He'd see the sun on her white-gold hair, a playful smile in her sea-blue eyes, and he'd feel her small hand in his as they climbed up to the top of the roof. In those dreams Rumer was still his best friend; she hadn't yet been gutted by his betrayal.

"Didn't you hear me?" he asked Michael.

No response; he thought of his times in space, wired to his colleagues with mikes and headsets, talking constantly as they flew around and around the world. There was always so much to say—observations, philosophies, stories to tell, lost loves to lament. He imagined how it would feel to be a hundred miles up, talking to his friends, looking down at this long, dark road stretching from sea to sea. The camaraderie up there had been something akin to the closeness he had once had with Rumer.

"Sea to shining sea," he said out loud.

What if it was too late? What was "too late" anyway? He thought of his own childhood and the happy summers they'd spent at Hubbard's Point. His mother had always been there—just like Mrs. Larkin next door. Taking the kids on picnics, nature hikes, rows out to Gull Island: Zeb had wished that for Michael, but Elizabeth had never wanted to be that kind of mother.

"The simple things in life are for simple people," she had said, laughing, a martini in her hand. "Like my sister." And thinking of her sister, Zeb felt a long, slow shiver all through his bones.

Elizabeth had never made any secret about the fact that her career came first.

Especially during the years before the divorce, before Elizabeth had gone to Betty Ford, Zeb had always been there. Ironically, since she'd gotten sober, he had seen his son much less. Elizabeth had become more available, often taking Michael with her on location.

Zeb hadn't seen him anywhere near enough after that. Although he had a house on the beach in Dana Point, it didn't compare to movie sets in Fiji or Paris. To make up for earlier missed opportunities at NASA, Zeb had logged a lot of extra time in the simulator, gotten assigned to some relatively routine but time-consuming payload deployments. The work had helped him get over missing Michael after the divorce, but it had also made it harder for them to schedule time together.

Glancing over at Michael, he caught his breath. He had grown and changed so much; it seemed that Zeb had turned away for a minute and missed it all. At first he and Elizabeth had split the holidays with Michael. But when Michael became a teenager, Zeb had had to sacrifice his times: Michael's friends were children of Elizabeth's friends in L.A., and that was where he'd wanted to stay.

Zeb had tried to respect Michael's wishes even when he'd been hurt by them. He refused to replicate the kind of man his father had been. As gentle as his mother had been, his father was just that hard. He had established one way of doing things: his way.

Zeb tried to make the marriage work. That was important to him. He made a mistake, but he'd done his best to fix it—especially after the baby was born. He tried to pick up the slack. As demanding as his career had been, he passed up many flights to stay home with Michael.

With Elizabeth on location and him alone with their boy, he had had plenty of time to think. He'd been racked by torment, like a Monday-morning quarterback running the plays of his life. If only I had, if only I hadn't . . . He thought back to the day he'd admitted to Rumer that he'd fallen in love with her sister; he could still see her face, first blank, hearing the unbelievable, then twisted with anguish. He could still feel the places on his chest where she'd hit him with her fists.

Alone with Michael then, alone with him now. Glancing over, Zeb thought of how hard it must have been for him, the only child in a loveless marriage. Zeb had had the same kind of childhood; he knew. At least Zeb wasn't like his own father.

When he was seventeen, Michael's age, his father was hardly ever around. Whenever he was, all they seemed to do was fight: "What are you doing, hanging around with women all the time? Your mother, the girls next door? You can do one of two things with your stargazing, you can become a fucking poet, or you can become a man. It makes me sick, seeing you turn into one of them. Up on the roof with Rumer, for chrissakes. What's wrong with the boys around here?"

"Rumer's my friend, Dad," Zeb had said, stunned.

"People will think you're queer. Always hanging around with the girls—even your hair looks like a girl. Why don't you cut it and be a man?"

Now, driving along, Zeb glanced over at Michael's ponytail. It was longer than Zeb's had ever been. He thought of the night he'd gone to bed, woken up to find his father had cut his hair while he'd slept. His father had been a pilot, stationed in Rangoon during World War II; coming home, he had flown for Pan Am. Serving his country, flying airplanes, had been his father's way of being a man's man. The fact that he was never home, never around to talk to, wasn't supposed to matter.

Zeb had relied on his mother. She had been great—from the start, she had recognized his love of the stars. She had given him a telescope and a guide to the sky when he was five. She had also seen his love of the Larkin girls, and never tried to make him feel ashamed of it.

"Never judge your friends by what makes them different," she had said. "Gender, color, none of that matters. It's who they—and you—are inside that counts."

Her only distress, Zeb thought, had come when he'd married Elizabeth instead of Rumer. While his father was pleased with Zee's beauty and glamour, sure his son's choice had made all the sense in the world, his mother had held back from ever really giving him her blessing. Rumer hadn't even come to the wedding; Zeb had had the feeling his mother hadn't wanted to either.

His father had been as taken by Elizabeth's fiery beauty as Zeb himself. What man wouldn't be? Side by side, the sisters were like silver and pewter: one shining so brightly, she could keep people from noticing the quiet and eternal beauty of the other. Zeb had been too young and dumb to understand that marriage partners had to be best friends too. His father hadn't taught him that.

Zeb's parents were dead now. His father had died in a plane crash—a small single-engine Cessna on a charter to Martha's Vineyard. That had been Zeb's first year away from Caltech, just months before he flew his first space shuttle flight. His mother's heart attack had taken her the week they found out Elizabeth was pregnant. So, separately, his parents had missed two of the most significant milestones of his life—and Zeb had never stopped regretting it.

Zeb shivered, thinking of his father crashing into the sea. He had been at the controls, flying two friends out for a golf tournament. One of them had survived, and he'd said to Zeb, "Your father died like he lived: doing what he loved, flying a plane, the king of the sky. He died like a man."

Like a man . . . Zeb held the wheel and wondered what that said about the reason he had stopped flying. His father would have laughed at him if he knew, considered the new lab small potatoes compared to a life of flight. All these years later, and he could still see his father shaking his head, disapproving of Zeb's life.

"Hey," he said to his son. "How about waking up?"

Michael shifted, burying his head deeper.

"Talk to me, Michael. Tell me your hopes and dreams. Ask me about the meaning of life. This is what fathers and sons do when they're driving cross-country—they exchange views on deep topics. Go ahead—humor your father."

"Tired, Dad," Michael growled.

"You can't be that tired. You've gotten about forty-eight hours of straight sleep. And you've got to be pretty well rested after stopping school in—what was it—early April?"

No response to that. Zeb's father would have killed him for dropping out. He would have ridiculed him, probably kicked him out of the house. Zeb could almost hear the derision in his voice: "If you don't want to go to school, fine: Get a job. Pay your own way. Stand on your own two feet."

Maybe Zeb should say that to Michael. Perhaps his father's way, the hard way, was the best. Shake his son awake and give him a strict talking-to. Tell him he was taking him to Connecticut, where his grandfather was a retired high school teacher of the first order, that his ass was in a sling—he just didn't know it yet.

"Horses," Zeb said instead, looking out the window at two chestnuts grazing in a field. If there was one thing Michael loved, and always had, it was horses. But right now, still, the boy didn't stir.

"Go ahead," Zeb said now. "Miss everything. Sleep your way across the country—sleep through life, buddy."

When Zeb was little, his dad had called him his copilot. He had taught him to look both ways at an intersection and say "clear"—just like on a runway. Somehow he thought he and Michael would have the road atlas open between them, plotting their route, taking side trips to the Grand Canyon, the stockyards, Graceland. All the way from Los Angeles, and nothing. A big void: a father-and-son black hole. Zeb thought back nearly eighteen years to a difficult premature birth in California, holding his wife's hand, praying that the baby be born alive, be safe, be happy. . . .

Traffic was light; a shadow crossed the hood of their car, and Zeb looked out the window to watch a red-tailed hawk soaring overhead, a rabbit squirming in its talons, until it disappeared into the forest. He thought of Rumer again, felt a shiver, as if the hawk were her messenger.

He felt a flash of anxiety—his hundredth of the day. The blast up in space had knocked him around, shifted everything from his mind to his heart. The violence of it had terrified him, made him think he was about to die. Life hadn't been the same after that: The explosion had torn a hole in him that only talking to Rumer could fix.

He knew it would never be the same; he knew he'd never get her back. But he had to try to make everything right . . . or at least okay. That was why he had to get home to Connecticut. He hit the gas, the needle edging past eighty, just to keep himself from turning off the highway, turning back.

Hubbard's Point, the land of the sisters. Zeb held the wheel and wondered what it would be like to see Rumer again, whether it would do any good for him to tell the truth once he got there, whether she'd be willing—or even able—to hear. Michael groaned in his sleep. High above, the blue sky curved to the horizon, dotted with invisible silver stars, paving their way home.

Three

QUINN GRAYSON sat in the back row of veterinary science—an elective intended to complement freshman biology—staring at her test paper and listening to all her classmates' pencils scribble madly. They were all on fire with inspiration. Every single kid seemed positively *inflamed* with answers—writing so crazily, as if they'd burst if they couldn't pour forth their knowledge about animal first aid.

Quinn tried to read the questions. Her eyes scanned the words. Her brain took in the meaning, but the questions stopped short at her heart. She didn't like thinking about puppies with heartworm, cats who had swallowed fish bones.

"Oh, no," Quinn gasped, seeing the diagram of a canary with a broken wing. Catching lobsters for food was one thing, but tending to injured pets was another. Rumer—Dr. Larkin—looked up from her papers.

"Is there a problem?"

"The poor canary," Quinn said, her eyes filling with tears. She had overdeveloped sensitivity. She thought of it as a condition, as real as asthma or a heart murmur. It had started the year her parents had drowned, and at times the feeling overtook her like a huge wave rising out of the sea.

The class snickered as Dr. Larkin rose slowly from her chair and started down the aisle. She was small and thin, dressed in a long, pale brown dress. Sometimes, when she came straight from her office as the town's vet, she wore a white lab coat. Quinn wondered whether she knew the kids commented on how plainly she dressed, as if she wanted to become one of the animals she loved so much.

"What is it, Quinn?" Dr. Larkin asked, standing beside her desk.

"It looks like someone's pet," Quinn said, pointing at the picture of a yellow bird, its left wing splayed in a very painful way. She closed her eyes. "Something . . . loved. I don't know how you can do it, work on hurt things. . . ."

Ryan Howland, the boy sitting in front of her, laughed. "It's a test, Quinn. You're supposed to answer the questions, not ask them . . . and besides, people eat the lobsters you catch. They *kill* them."

"I'm talking to Rumer—Dr. Larkin—not you," she said, and slid his chair slightly forward with her booted foot.

"Hey, stop that!" he said, turning to stare straight at Quinn, an angry yet injured expression on his face.

Rumer crouched down and looked into Quinn's eyes. Quinn knew she taught this class out of the goodness of her heart. Many families in Black Hall had pets, and Rumer wanted to teach the kids responsibility and care. She gazed at Quinn with "what am I going to do with you?" written all over her face.

"I should never have taken this class for my elective," Quinn whispered. "It's only because you're teaching it. I should have signed up for automotive arts instead. Cars don't hurt or feel pain—they just rust."

"The point of the class," Rumer said, smiling, "is to help the pets so they don't hurt either. Now, finish up, okay?"

Closing her eyes, trying to ignore what Ryan had said about killing lobsters, Quinn heard wind blowing through the trees outside. She imagined the breeze sweeping across the sea, from the Wickland Shoal, across Firefly Beach, up the bluff, over the marsh, across the three white steeples in town, into her very soul; she tried to think about the nobility of providing food for families.

She forced herself to focus on the next test question: *What are the benefits of having more than one pet at the same time?* Wasn't that sort of like her and her sister? Life without Allie would be unimaginable. Or maybe the question had to do with love: the importance of animals, like people, being together. Companionship, love . . .

Her mind jumped to her parents, sinking with their ship, together under the sea forevermore. . . . Daydreaming, unable to focus on pets, she stared at her paper. Sunlight poured over her shoulder from the large bank of windows; silvery dust motes danced in the air.

"Don't hear you writing, Quinn," Ryan whispered. "That because you don't know anything about warm animals? All you can handle are lobsters, because they're cold like you. You like dropping them in boiling water?"

"You don't understand. . . ."

"Tell that to the lobsters. You're just as cold-blooded as they are."

Quinn felt ice in her belly. She knew she couldn't argue with him, because he was right: *I am cold. I've been a changeling, a sea creature, since my parents drowned*, she thought but didn't say. On the other hand, she felt like attacking him—pulling his hair until he begged her for mercy. She loved the lobsters she caught and felt very proud to be playing her part in the food chain.

"I'm finished here today," she said calmly, with great dignity, as she pushed back her chair and walked to the front of the room, placing her unfinished test on Rumer's desk. Although she had other exams scheduled that day, she wasn't going to take them.

"What do you mean?" Rumer asked.

"I'm going lobstering," Quinn replied.

"Don't leave," Rumer said, holding her gaze. "Remember what Winnie said last night—be excellent."

But the rage and sorrow gushing from Quinn's heart were too huge for the classroom to hold, and she backed away. Their eyes met, but Quinn didn't speak. No one in the world—not even her fellow *Dame de la Roche*—knew what it was like to be Quinn Grayson on a daily basis, and for that, Quinn knew that Rumer should feel grateful.

❧

"So, she got kicked out?" asked Sixtus Larkin, hunched over as he lovingly sanded the rail of his pride and joy, a Herreshoff-designed New York Yacht Club 30. His hands were as gnarled as tree roots, but he worked with gentle precision.

"Suspended, Dad," Rumer replied, sitting on the rock ledge, looking up at him. The sloop was in its cradle, ten feet off the ground, recently uncovered after its long winter's sleep. Arthritis had taken hold of Sixtus recently, giving him a stooped back and creaky joints. Rumer worried, watching him balance on the rail, but took a deep breath and continued: "The principal heard that she left school property, and she won't get to finish the year."

With his leg propped up on the cabin top, leaning into each strong stroke of the sandpaper, her father chuckled. His skin, leathery from the sun and wind, was flecked with tiny bits of varnish. He wore ancient Top-Siders, white shirt, and khakis—all filled with holes, as if he'd just stumbled off the street. People might imagine that these were just his boat-painting clothes, Rumer thought, regarding him, but they weren't: He hadn't bought anything new in fifteen years, and he dressed like this all the time.

"Boy, Quinn's a tough one, isn't she?" he asked, sanding harder.

"I never think of her that way," Rumer said, rubbing her eyes.

Last night she had had a bad dream. It had left her writhing, lying in sweaty sheets, trying to remember what had happened. A green house, a rooftop, the sweetest feeling of love, then everything falling away, changing into something else: lies, betrayal, catching two people in bed together . . . she shuddered now, getting the picture. Zeb was coming: Old wounds were being opened.

"Well," her father continued, "in the lingo of teachers, she's what's known as 'a discipline problem.' Can't have kids walking out of class just because they feel like lobstering." He chuckled. "Personally, I admire her gumption."

"Me too, but I'm afraid to encourage her. She's on the edge enough as it is."

"She shouldn't have walked out of school, that's for sure. If I were still teaching, I'd have called her back, given her a talking-to."

"It's so much easier to be a vet," Rumer sighed. "I'm really out of my element at school. If it weren't for wanting to follow in your footsteps just a little, I never would have started the program. Give me a litter of feral kittens, and I'm fine. A roomful of teenagers, and . . . I don't know how you did it all those years."

"Sometimes I don't either," he said, smiling.

"I just finished talking to Dana—she and Sam have enough to do with the wedding Saturday, and now she has to worry about Quinn . . . and decide whether they should even leave on their honeymoon."

"Let Quinn stay with us. Between the two of us, we should be able to drill some sense into her. She's a bit of a feral kitten herself."

Rumer smiled. "She and Allie are staying with the McCrays. But we'll all pitch in."

"That kid is something special," he said, pausing to wipe the sweat from his brow. "Ever since she and her sister tried to sail to the Vineyard that time, I've had my eye on her."

"I know."

"Kids like that, who've had too much adversity young, have a real uphill battle. Quinn tries so hard, but she's something of a lost soul . . . she needs us to understand her."

Rumer nodded. Her father and Quinn had several things in common. Although Sixtus hadn't been orphaned, as Quinn had been, his father had died when he was a child. His mother had worked very hard, often leaving him and his twin brother on their own for long stretches of time.

"I might have stayed lost forever if I hadn't met my Clarissa. Your mother was the most patient woman alive."

"She was," Rumer agreed.

"I'm a better old father than I was a young father."

"Oh, Dad . . ."

Smiling, she stared up at him, leaning across the deck canvas. He was right, but she would never acknowledge that out loud. "He's haunted by demons," her mother would say when Rumer and Elizabeth would ask why their father seemed so quiet, so sad.

"Demons?" Elizabeth would ask, frowning as she watched her father go off on another of his solitary sails, leaving behind his wife and daughters. "You mean, like devils? Inside him, eating him up?"

Rumer would flinch, feeling her father's pain and also her sister's—Elizabeth could never understand why her father wouldn't take her along, why she couldn't cheer him up. She would put on skits so hilarious, Rumer's sides would ache from laughing, but her father would just sail away instead of watching.

"Not real devils," their mother would say, trying to soothe Elizabeth. "Just bad memories from his past. His father died very young, leaving his mother with too much responsibility. And Daddy had his own brother to look after. . . ."

"Like me and Elizabeth," Rumer had said.

"Yes, only you look after me, not the other way around—and you're my little sister," Elizabeth had laughed, hugging her and teasing her for being her caretaker.

"It's because I love you so much," Rumer had said, her throat aching as she wondered what she'd ever do without her sister. She had adored Elizabeth. She had protected her from their parents, hiding the fact that Elizabeth loved to steal their beer and drink it till she could block out her loneliness, hiding the times she'd gone over to Little Beach with boys and a blanket, the fact that she was a fast girl in a small town.

"You know," her father said now, "Quinn might not need school—education snuffs the spirit right out of some people. She'll wind up being an artist or a poet or an actor or a sailor—something that would scare the life out of most folks around here."

Rumer watched the rabbits coming out of their warren under the azalea bush next door. It was happening all through the yards on the Point: animals everywhere at dusk, their time to feed.

She found herself thinking of her sister—the untamed artist. Unable to keep their father from sailing away, to really connect with anyone but Rumer, Elizabeth had decided none of it mattered anyway. Drinking killed the pain, but it also drove her grades down. She had dropped out of school, left town, and in the process—almost in spite of herself—become a star. She had made their father more proud than any degrees, certificates, or veterinary positions ever could; Rumer suspected that he wasn't speaking about Quinn at all right now.

"Did Winnie tell you that Zeb and Michael are coming?" she asked, feeling cold, last night's bad dream rising up inside her again.

"She mentioned the possibility a while ago. I know, I know—don't look at me like that. I didn't believe her, or I would have told you. After all this time, who would think they'd come back here?"

"I know."

"Elizabeth didn't say anything when I talked to her last Saturday," he said. "She's on location in Toronto, then east to the Maritimes; she said she might hop down for a visit. . . ."

"She might not know herself," Rumer said. "They are divorced, Dad."

"That they are," her father said stonily, starting to sand again. Irish Catholic, he didn't like acknowledging Elizabeth and Zeb's divorce. Born in Galway, he and his family had moved to Halifax, Nova Scotia, when his father—on his deathbed, and never having mentioned it before—had instructed his wife to "sell everything and move to Canada."

Brave woman: single mother, pioneer that Una Wicklow Larkin was, she'd boarded her twin boys onto a ship and taken them across the sea. Sixtus revered the headstrong spirit of his mother and had passed it on to his two daughters.

"It'll be good to see Michael again," her father said.

"But not his father," Rumer said, shaking her head.

"Hmmm," her father said, fiercely working on the boat. He had a cane now that he rarely used. Sailing was the only way he could move freely through life, as freely and gracefully as when he was young, and Rumer knew he couldn't wait to get his boat into the water.

But right now her focus left her father and spiraled backward in time. Memories of Zeb flooded in so strong, clawing at her heart. Rumer wanted to run. She wasn't sure which had been the more excruciating: losing Zeb to her sister, losing her sister to Zeb.

All she knew was that after everything had happened, her entire world had exploded. Rumer could have sworn the sky was a totally unfamiliar shade of blue; the roses in her mother's garden had seemed to wilt. For a few weeks, Rumer had wished she would die.

Now, picking up her medical bag, she waved good-bye to her father and started down the hill. There really wasn't much more to say.

But there was so much to remember.

Driving in her truck, a basket of carrots and apples on the seat beside her, she wound her way through Hubbard's Point, under the train trestle, and onto the main road. Old memories seemed to gather and grow more solid. The marshes—greening for summer—stretched eastward and formed the estuary of the Connecticut River.

She remembered the sweet, bone-deep feeling of having a best friend. Zeb: the sense that they would do anything for each other, anything, for the rest of their lives. They had been connected by a golden thread that could never be broken. His force could reach her from wherever he was. And when his fingers touched her skin, she felt the fire in her heart and bones.

Her mind played over lazy summer meanderings, down the beach, across the creeks, over to the Indian Grave. They would crab for blue claws, race to the raft, keep each other warm at movies on the beach. She could see his smooth, tan skin, seal-silky. His tousled, sun-lightened hair, his amazing grin—the image still brought an electric jolt, like a dire warning to not go there.

Steeling her back, she ignored it.

Every summer had had its own character: Their fourth summer, they had learned to swim; their seventh, they had rowed out to Gull Island; the ninth had been the start of their paper route; their eleventh had been filled with swimming and fishing; by their fifteenth, Rumer had fallen in love with him with a sense of longing so fine, it became her constant companion. She brooded about him constantly. Listening to the radio, hearing love songs that reminded her of him, her eyes had filled with tears and she had thought that this lifetime was nowhere near long enough for all the things she hoped to do with Zeb.

He must have felt the same. When they were sixteen, their first kiss was a thrill that rivaled the meteor showers Zeb was always dragging her onto the roof to watch. Rumer couldn't remember when they had started, and she couldn't have imagined them ever ending. She had counted on him like clockwork.

She remembered the time he had sailed to Orient Point with a group of boys. They were late getting back. His father was due home from a long trip, and Zeb was supposed to have cut the grass. Rumer had pulled out the lawn mower and mowed his grass for him. He'd told her later that when he came up the stone stairs, carrying the sails, he'd been able to hear the engine, and he'd run up the hill to give Rumer a salty kiss, to take over the job.

The sound track of their friendship: the lawn mower, sails flapping, wind in the branches overhead as they stared at the stars. She had nurtured his love of the sky, and he had encouraged her to follow her dream and become a vet, his voice in her ears so soft and kind and funny.

All that music was gone now.

No promises had ever been made; Zeb had certainly never proposed to her. But somehow, deep down, she had always imagined that they would be together. Weren't there promises without words? To Rumer, those were the strongest kind.

They had the golden thread: They hadn't needed words. Promises made with silent kisses, with tentative touches, with the passion of their hearts. Clicking from childhood friendship to being in love had been a tough transition, but they'd been making it. Their connection probably could have survived anything, forever—except falling in love with someone else. Especially when the other person, for Zeb, was Rumer's sister, Elizabeth.

Another electric jolt, more memories.

Driving faster, Rumer wished they would fly out her truck's open window. She remembered their wedding day, nearly twenty years ago now. She had been invited, of course. Elizabeth had actually asked her to be the maid of honor.

"Please, Rue," Elizabeth had said, holding her hand. "I know it's hard for you, but it won't always be . . . we love you, you know?" she had pleaded, that "we," the "we" of Elizabeth and Zeb lodging in Rumer's heart like a splinter of ice.

"How can you ask me that?" Rumer had replied, her voice shaking, her skin clammy.

"Because you're my sister."

"That's your reason?"

"Of course. I'm not sure I can get married without you there."

"Then don't get married," Rumer shot out, the words zinging in the air. Elizabeth stayed silent for a long while—shocked, as if she'd been slapped.

"Put it behind you," Elizabeth said. "Please? Be my maid of honor. Be a part of our wedding."

"I can't," Rumer said.

"We're fighting over a guy? Let me get this right—you're holding a grudge about this, letting it come between us? He's the boy next door, Rumer. He's lived there forever—you've had all this time to make it clear you loved him, if you did. Just because you had a paper route together—"

"It was more than that," Rumer cried, "and you knew it!"

"I did not! Not really . . . I knew you had a crush on him, but you were just kids. You dated other guys—he went out with other girls. Nothing was ever serious between you, Rumer—no matter what you might have thought."

Rumer walked away.

The tears were pouring down her cheeks. She could almost taste the salt now, streaming into the corners of her mouth. She had felt a burning coal in her chest, pressed against her ribs. It hurt so terribly that she'd thought maybe she was having a heart attack. Walking fast away from Elizabeth, then running, she had really thought she might die. She had wanted to.

Elizabeth didn't know everything. Zeb hadn't told her their secret: It was serious between them. They had a magical connection. They had nearly made love. That last spring . . . they were going to lose their virginities to each other.

Something had gone wrong: Crossed signals, and they'd never had the chance again. Elizabeth had swooped down when Rumer wasn't looking, and Zeb had been all too happy to follow her away.

Running down the beach, past all the people who knew her, knew her family. Some of them had watched her and Zeb grow up together—they had been their customers on the paper route, the parents of their friends. Did they know about Elizabeth and Zeb? Rumer had felt humiliated to think so.

Picturing her sister's wide-open eyes as she had actually asked her—with sad, absurd innocence—to be her maid of honor made Rumer shake inside. How could Elizabeth do this to her? And how could Zeb? They had betrayed her.

Betray: The word was so huge, like something that belonged in the theater, in Shakespeare, in the opera, not at beautiful, peaceful Hubbard's Point. But, of course, the fact that it had happened here only made it worse.

During those summer weeks, while Elizabeth had gone about making her wedding plans, Rumer had been on the waiting list for the Tufts University School of Veterinary Medicine; in mid-July, she received her acceptance. She had wept to get it: Thank God she had finished up at college before it happened.

She hadn't been able to think anymore. She felt dull, stagnant. She stared at the papers on her desk, wondering what they were for, how they'd gotten there. Her heart felt sluggish, as if every beat might kill her. She slept all day. She stayed awake all night. She ate bowls of cereal with sugar and whole milk until the box was empty. She gained weight and didn't care. Washing her hair seemed like a chore.

It was the only summer of her life that she didn't swim in the sea.

Her jeans wouldn't fit. Her face looked thick, puffy, in the mirror. She never wanted to leave the house. She avoided the windows that faced Zeb's, living completely in the rooms that looked north.

Her parents were worried about her, but she couldn't hear their words. They were making plans to go to the wedding. Because their voices spoke about such things—her father giving Elizabeth away, her mother buying a mother-of-the-bride dress—Rumer couldn't bear to hear them ask her how she felt, whether she needed a doctor, whether she wouldn't like to take a swim?

And then the acceptance into Tufts arrived.

It was like a lifesaver thrown to a drowning girl. She had grabbed it with her last strength. She was going to become a veterinarian! The fact that she wanted to tell Zeb more than anyone in the world tore her in half. She cried over it, shuddering and quaking, all night.

She thought of nature, how they had fallen in love with it together. How the bodies of heaven and the bodies of earth had balanced them. How the sky was his and the animals were hers. How his arms had felt around her shoulders; how their bodies had felt almost coming together.

One time, almost, not quite, but leading to what would have been the sweetest time of their lives.

Rumer held on to that memory like a secret treasure. Her beautiful sister, the actress, didn't know what Rumer and Zeb had done. Next to Elizabeth, especially with all the weight Rumer had gained, she felt like an ugly, fat, bitter, lonely, defiled, vengeful person—guarding her secret treasure like a madwoman.

They had nearly made love; if they had met at the Indian Grave as planned, they would have.

She'd show them, she'd thought: Who cared about Elizabeth and Zeb anymore? Rumer was on her way. She didn't need Zeb Mayhew to watch her dreams come true. She was going to Tufts, the best school around; she was going to become a vet.

The week before the wedding, Rumer had driven her things to North Grafton, Massachusetts, and moved into the third floor of a Victorian house favored by students. On the actual wedding day, she reported to work at her new job at a local animal shelter.

Two days earlier, a shepherd-Lab mix had been left to die after being hit by a car outside Boston. The owner had found him, and the vet had stitched him up the best he could. Rumer's instructions had been to sweep the floors, swab down the stainless steel surgery tables. But, going into the kennel, seeing the dog staring up with cloudy eyes, Rumer dropped to her knees.

There, kneeling on the floor outside the cage, she placed her hand against the wire mesh. The vet told her the dog would probably die of his injuries but that the owners wanted to do everything possible. Holding still, she let the dying dog lick her hand. His tongue was so soft, nudging her with such heart-piercing friendliness, and she felt the dam break inside her.

She sat there for hours. The sun faded, and through the lone window in the concrete wall, she saw the moon begin to rise. Rumer sat on the cold, sterile floor until the dog died, until she was sure Zeb and Elizabeth's wedding was over. The events blended together in her mind, each of them bringing sadness beyond belief.

And when they were over, Rumer knew more than ever that she wanted to help animals, that when all was said and done, she could trust the kindness of a strange dog more than she could that of her sister and former best friend.

Animals had never failed her, and to the best of her ability, she never failed them. Turning into Peacedale Farm, she jumped out of the truck with her medical bag. Edward McCabe owned the place. He was a gentleman farmer with a serious nature. He had gone to Deerfield and Dartmouth; he belonged to the Grange, the River Club, and the Black Hall Reading Room. During the years Rumer had known him, he had had a series of long-term relationships that had sometimes led to engagements but never to marriage. Lately, those relationships had fallen away.

Rumer was the vet for all the animals on his farm, and she helped Edward administer an important scholarship in his mother's name. Their time together had always felt easy and natural; they both loved nature, hiking, riding, and all animals, especially Blue—the horse Rumer had owned since vet school and kept stabled at the farm.

Over the past year, Rumer herself seemed to have also become the object of Edward's considerable affection. The word "love" never passed her lips—she didn't want to do anything to jeopardize their very good working friendship, but recently she had sensed Edward wanting more.

"Blue," she called now, walking across the yard toward the field.

The old horse stood at the fence, whinnying softly. He was a big bay, his coat no longer as glossy and fine as it had been when he'd been young. Flicking his black tail, he tossed his head in greeting. Rumer broke a carrot in half and approached him, hand open, feeling him lap the carrot from her fingers, his muzzle so velvety. Putting her arms around his neck, she held him close and felt his love.

Then, scaling the fence, she climbed onto his bare back and rode into the field. He broke into a gentle canter, circling around the stone outcroppings and birch grove, heading down to the river. She thought of how long they had been together—long enough that she had brought Michael here to ride him sixteen years ago, when he was almost two, during his first visit east, on a thaw in his parents' and aunt's relationship.

"Old Blue," she said, leaning forward to whisper in his ear, her voice getting lost in the wind blowing through the valley.

"Ish-ish," Michael had said of the cod weathervane on the fish market, and "Boo," he had said of the then-young horse.

"His name is Blue," Rumer said, supporting the baby on the horse's back, his tiny hands holding tight to the mane.

"Boo," Michael said, pointing at the sky. "Da-da . . . boo."

"Yes, Daddy's up in the blue sky," Rumer had said.

Riding Blue down a bridle path cut through shoulder-high stands of mountain laurel and rhododendrons, Rumer felt her heart beating hard— as if she were running herself, not riding her horse. In spite of the breach between Rumer, Zeb, and Elizabeth, Rumer had forged a relationship with Michael. It was imperfect, filled with many obstacles, but Rumer had adored him.

Elizabeth had made it big on Broadway, and from there she'd taken the leap to Hollywood, in tandem with Zeb's ascension at UCLA. Michael had gone with them, of course. Never in Rumer's wildest dreams had she imagined that over a decade would pass without her seeing him. Their last time together, he had been seven years old.

Coming around the bend, they flushed a quail and her brood. Rumer pulled back, slowing Blue down. Sitting tall, her fingers loosely holding Blue's black mane, she rode him through the June twilight. When they climbed the rocky hill behind the barn, she smiled to see Edward waiting for them at the fence.

He wore khakis tucked into worn old riding boots, a soft green chamois shirt, and horn-rimmed glasses. His eyes were velvet brown, his hair mostly gray. Standing back, he watched Rumer dismount.

"How was your ride?" he asked.

"Great, thanks," she said. "How are you?"

"Better for seeing you, my dear," he said.

"Thanks," she said, laughing at the flattery. He had been raised by the very wealthy and blue-blooded daughter of a minor robber baron, and she had instilled in her son courtly manners that never failed him.

"I do have an ulterior motive," he said. "I've rounded up all the barn cats, and they're ready for their annual shots. Also, the inspector's coming tomorrow, and I want to make sure the dairy herd's immunization records are in order."

"Okay, great," she said. "Let's go to it."

They walked into the big red barn, shady and cool. The smell of straw, animals, and raw wood rose around them. Light slanted in through the wallboards, and pollen danced in the air.

Edward had corralled the cats and kittens in one of the feed bins, and when he lifted the lid, Rumer was greeted by a symphony of meows. These cats went back generations, to the beginnings of Peacedale Farm. All-black cats, tuxedo-black cats, tawny yellow cats, striped tiger cats: They mewed and writhed.

With Edward acting as her assistant, Rumer went through the annual summer ritual of examining them. The old cats already had cards documenting their names and health. Each new kitten got a card, a shot, and a name.

"Desdemona, Abigail, T.C. . . ."

"Listen to this guy," Edward said, holding up a tiny all-black kitten who was purring so loud, he sounded like rattling machinery. Rumer's heart caught, remembering that she and Zeb had once found a stray kitten on their paper route. His purrs had sounded like growls, like an outboard engine, and Zeb had called him "Evinrude."

"Evinrude," Rumer said now, giving him the shot and then rubbing his back to soothe the stick mark. In spite of the hurt, he just kept purring. "You're all revved up, aren't you?"

"Uh-oh," Edward said. "She's getting attached."

"Occupational hazard," Rumer said, her stomach fluttering at the strange, unbidden memory of Zeb. She kissed the baby and put him down in the straw. He scampered up a splintery wooden support into the hayloft to join his brothers and sisters. "Evinrude," she repeated quietly, feeling suddenly anxious.

"That's an original name," Edward said.

"Not really," she said. "Someone thought of it a long time ago."

He gave her a quizzical look, but she just continued staring into the hayloft.

"They have the life, don't they?" Edward asked, watching the kittens tumble in the hay. "Naps and milk."

"Hmm," Rumer said, wiping her forehead and heading into the cow barn. Now she became very businesslike, forcing herself to concentrate through the swirl of emotions in her chest. Checking each head of cattle, she made sure all the paperwork was in order. The state inspectors were rigorous, and she considered it her responsibility to make sure all the dairy cows were in fine shape.

"Well, that's about it," Edward said when she'd closed up her vet bag and walked out into the farmyard.

"I'll be back tomorrow," she said. "In case we missed any kittens."

"If all the kittens suddenly found homes," he said, a deep yet playful look in his warm brown eyes, "would you still come back?"

"Of course I would," she said.

"I know," he said, putting his arm around her shoulders, caressing her back. "To see Blue . . . you'll never go too far away from Blue, would you? That's my one sure way to keep you coming back."

"I love Blue," she said, her voice low as she took his hand, "but you're my friend, Edward. I come here to see you."

"If you say so, Dr. Larkin," he said. "If you say so."

"I helped you read the essays for your mother's scholarship, didn't I?"

Their relationship had been moving forward lately. Rumer liked him a lot, but she felt a little guilty because she knew Edward liked her more. Over the years she had dated many men in Black Hall; she had always had the sense of him patiently waiting.

"How about if I invite you to a wedding on Saturday? Will that prove it to you?" she asked.

"It might," Edward said, grinning.

"Okay, then," she said, and told him the details.

The declining sun spread yellow light across the fields and stone walls, covering the land with golden threads, filling Rumer with deep longing for something she couldn't name. Blue stood in the tall grass, flicking his black tail. From there she could almost think he was a young horse, ready to run until the earth ran out and the sky began.

Like a boy she had once known . . .

Climbing into her truck, she waved at Edward and drove away. As soon as she turned onto the shore road, her heart began to beat harder. She didn't know what she would find when she got home. Or, more accurately, *whom*. It was like living with some kind of countdown, the seconds ticking away until she had to confront the man she had grown to hate more than anyone in the world.

 *Four*

SOMETIME LATE WEDNESDAY morning, the sound of an engine woke him up. Startled, Michael Mayhew looked around. A locomotive was bearing down on them. No, they were racing a train. They were on some back road, driving parallel to the railroad tracks, past a salt marsh and a bunch of small houses. Glancing over, he saw his father was wearing sunglasses, bright sun flashing from behind a line of trees.

"Where are we?" Michael asked.

"We're there," his father said.

"There?" Michael asked, rubbing his eyes, taking in the nowhere of their surroundings, hoping his father was kidding. "This is it?"

Without responding, his father clicked on the blinker and turned right under a trestle while the train roared overhead. Michael saw the carved wooden sign: HUBBARD'S POINT. It had a simple, weathered look, and had probably been hanging there forever. He saw his father draw a deep breath, his eyes open wide, as if he had seen a ghost and wasn't sure what to do.

"We can turn around," Michael said. "It's okay with me if we go back to California."

"I'm not driving five more minutes with you, let alone five days," his father said. "That's more than you've spoken the whole trip."

Michael looked out the window. He knew argument was futile. He and his father were in an eternal standoff—his father only *wanted* to think they were going to start liking each other someday. It made him feel better. Fine, Michael thought as they drove up a hill along a winding road past a cemetery hidden in the trees.

"This is where we're staying?" he asked, noticing the size of the cottages: tiny. They were someone's idea of cute: brightly colored paint, little shutters on the little windows, kids' beach toys piled outside screen porches, signs over the front door with names like "Teacher's Pet," "Highover," "Glenwood."

"It's where we're staying."

"Do we have to?"

"Yes."

"I don't know why we had to come. I don't even know those people who're getting married."

"Dana Underhill and Sam Trevor."

"Whoever they are," Michael mumbled. He looked around—little Fords and Toyotas in all the yards. This was the famous Hubbard's Point, where his parents grew up? He had come here years before, when he was small, and he had dim memories of crabbing, fishing, riding a horse, playing hearts with his aunt, getting brushed underwater by a school of bluefish—the kind of strangely happy childhood stuff that becomes embarrassing to give much thought to as the years go by.

As they drove down the lane in their Range Rover, people glanced up. Some were standing outside, washing their cars or watering their gardens. Others were rocking on the porches, glancing up from their newspapers. Passing a DEAD END sign, they drove down a road with the sea on the left, a rock ledge rising on the right. Some kid ambled up the road, grinning, holding up a little fish as if he wanted applause.

"I have the strangest feeling we're not in L.A. anymore," Michael said.

"You made your point," his father said, parking in front of a one-story gray cottage set right on the water. The sound of opera filled the air— trilling, high, dramatic. Michael winced. He was about to ask, when, turning toward his father, he caught the look in his eyes.

His father, holding the wheel, looked . . . happy.

That was the only word Michael could think of. The tension was gone from his tan face, the anger had left his eyes, and a smile had come to his mouth. For a second, Michael spun back in time, to a father he used to know and had forgotten existed. The strangest thing was, Michael suddenly felt different himself.

"Dad?" he asked.

"That's Winnie," his father said. But the spoken words had broken the mood, and his father's face changed back. He gestured at the small gray house and the even smaller one beside it. "She lives there, and we're staying"—he pointed to the right—"there."

Michael stared. He couldn't believe it. There was no way two grown men were going to fit into that—that dollhouse. It was the size of their gardener's shed back home, only not as nicely painted. The weather-beaten shingles were bleached silver from the salt wind—couldn't this Winnie afford the upkeep?

As his father climbed out to get the bags, the singing stopped. A screen door slammed, and before Michael could turn around, he formed a picture of the woman he expected to see: someone big and fat, like his image of an opera singer, and dressed in a faded housecoat, like a New England person who would own these old houses.

The woman was tall, as tall as Michael and his father. She had snow-white hair swept up on top of her head, and she wore a long, loose-fitting, emerald silk dress over her strong body. Her eyes were made up as if for the theater—dark liner, green shadow. Dangling from around her neck was a large gold pendant in the shape of a cat—it looked incredibly familiar. She reminded Michael of his mother in a stage production of *Antony and Cleopatra*—only much, much bigger.

"My dear boys!" she called, sweeping across the lawn. Her arms were open, as were Michael's dad's, and they met in such a strong embrace, Michael heard the breath forced out of them.

"Zebulon Mayhew, you darling rascal . . ." the woman said, pushing back to smooth the hair out of his eyes. "You high-flying, globe-trotting, escape artist—where, where have you been? My God, you look exactly the same as you always have . . . you look . . ." Now, stepping back, she grabbed Michael and hugged him so hard, she half choked him to death.

"And *you*! Good Lord, Michael! All grown-up! The two of you—grown men! I simply cannot comprehend the truth of this situation. Michael, the last time I saw you, you were crouched down on my rocks with a piece of bacon tied to a string, trying to lure a lobster out from the crevice where he'd gone to molt. You were all of seven. . . ."

Michael laughed politely.

"You don't remember me, do you? I'm desolate," she said, stepping back. Even her expression was theatrical, as if she were playing the grande dame on some stage. In spite of himself, she had Michael's attention. "Positively crushed. And even after I wore the Pharaoh's Cat—"

"That my mother wore—"

"Yes," Winnie said, her smile widening. "When she *defined* Cleopatra at the Winter Garden . . . her tour de force."

"I remember that necklace," Michael said. He wanted to step closer, to get a better look. There were the ruby eyes that had mesmerized him as a child, the hieroglyphics intended to protect the wearer from the sphinx's curse. . . . "It turns into a pin, right? When you take it off the chain?"

"Right you are. I loaned it to Elizabeth for her performance; she told me you liked it so much, you didn't want her to give it back."

"It protected her against the curse," Michael said. The childish memory made him redden, and he wished they hadn't started talking about any of it. But, in spite of himself, he stared at the cat. His mother had pinned it to her costume.

"Ah, yes," Winnie laughed. "The dreaded sphinx—afflicts ninety-nine percent of all actresses who try to step into Cleo's shoes. Laryngitis, sprained ankles, opening-night nerves . . . but with the pin and your support, she was always fine."

"Elizabeth never suffered from opening-night nerves," Zeb said wryly. "Pretty much the opposite. She's always revved and ready—critics beware."

Winnie laughed. "I'd like to think she got some of that from me. She's my honorary niece, you know, along with her sister. Rumer, however, communes with animals in a way that no human can take credit for. . . ."

Michael felt her looking at him, and he backed toward the car, to get away and start unloading.

"You, young man, must be brilliant. With your parents . . ."

"You'd think so," his father said. "But Michael's decided he's had enough of school. As of April, he's officially dropped out."

Michael glanced over, expecting Winnie to look shocked. Instead, she was grinning, as if she had just met Pavarotti. "That explains the earthquake," she said.

"You have earthquakes in Connecticut?" Michael asked.

"Not ordinarily, but I did feel the earth move last spring. I attributed the seismic activity to an aberrant quake, but in fact it must have been shock waves from your parents' reaction."

"You might be right," his father said. To Michael's relief, seeming to want to change the subject, he turned to look across the street—up the hill at a dark green house nearly obscured by foliage.

"The old place has been sold again," he said, a question in his voice.

"Yes," Winnie said. "The sign came down a week ago. I don't know much about the new owners except that they want to make some changes. The realtor told me."

"Looks exactly the same as it always has . . . even the color."

"Why fiddle with excellence?" Winnie asked. "When something's been working for many years, only a fool would change it. A lesson all of us have learned the hard way . . ."

Her tone was mysterious, and something about it made Michael glance at his father. His dad frowned, looking away, seeming as uncomfortable as Michael had felt a minute earlier.

"In any case," Winnie said, looking over both their heads, as if unaware that she'd made both the Mayhew men squirm, "what the new owners must realize is that nothing at Hubbard's Point ever changes. It's why we love it so. . . ."

` "Dad—want me to carry these things in?" Michael asked, wanting to get away.

"Sure, Michael," he said. "Winnie, I think we'll unpack and take a swim. If that's okay with you."

"Okay? It's *de rigueur*, dear."

"And Rumer . . ." his father began, referring to his aunt.

"What about her, dear?" Winnie asked.

His father didn't reply. But when Michael glanced over at him, his father's face was turning red. He looked upset, or embarrassed, or somehow at a loss for words. Winnie was patient, and after a minute his father said simply, "How is she?"

"You'll see for yourself," Winnie said. "She knows you're coming. I'm sure she'll stop by to say hello. Lessons learned the hard way . . ."

His father reddened even more deeply. Michael waited for him to say something else, but two girls standing down the road had drawn his attention. He had caught sight of them, turned his head to see them better.

One was small and cute in a pink and white checked way—totally alien to Michael's L.A. frame of reference, and the other looked like a bizarre warrior: She had wild brown hair, huge sunglasses, big rubber boots, and bright orange oilskin pants. She glared at him, and then tapped the younger girl's shoulder. They both turned without another glance and walked away.

And Michael and his father began to unload the car as Winnie called over her shoulder, "Should you want to go crabbing after your swim, I'll be happy to supply the bacon for bait. Just stop by. . . ."

Michael looked at his dad, wondering what lesson they had all learned the hard way, but he decided not to ask.

"Who are the Range Rover people?" Quinn asked Rumer. It was early afternoon; she had stopped by school to raid her locker, and then she'd ridden her bike down Shore Road to Rumer's veterinary office. The windows overlooked the woods and a small parking lot. Her walls were covered with snapshots of people with their pets, posters for nature organizations, and several children's drawings of animals.

"The who?" Rumer asked. It was just before afternoon office hours, and she was standing in the exam room, counting the amount of rabies vaccine she had on hand. Down the hall, her assistant was in the kennel—probably playing with the strays or checking on the postsurgery animals. The sound of dogs barking filled the room.

"The man and the boy who just drove into the beach. Fancy car, California plates. They look rich and obnoxious," Quinn said.

"They're here already?" Rumer asked. She looked shocked, as if Quinn had just dropped a live eel on her stainless steel exam table.

"Yep. Are they who I think they are?"

Rumer didn't reply. She must have lost count of the vaccine doses because she went back to the beginning and began over again. Her assistant, a woman about Rumer's age named Mathilda, came down the hall with a bandaged cat.

"He's trying to chew his stitches," Mathilda said.

"They itch," Rumer said softly, examining the mangy old cat with gentle fingers. "Don't they, Oscar?"

"Hi, Quinn," Mathilda said.

"Hi," Quinn said, feeling self-conscious. Naturally, Mathilda was scoping Quinn out, wondering what she was doing here on a school day. She probably looked like a suspended loser: Instead of school clothes, she was in her old salt things, straight from checking her lobster pots—greasy oilskins, fish-scale-encrusted boots. Mathilda smiled, as if she wanted to make Quinn feel better.

Rumer swabbed the cat's wounds with some orange stuff, and then rebandaged them. Quinn kept her eyes on the cat so she wouldn't have to look at Mathilda. Sometimes she didn't know how to be around people trying to be nice to her. She didn't know the woman's last name, but she knew that she was divorced and lived in a small house out by the lake. People whispered about the tragedy she'd been through—it had to do with love, marriage, some man.

When Mathilda left the room with Oscar, Rumer looked up.

"So, what brings you here today?"

"I don't know," Quinn said. "I had to go to school to get my ruler out of my locker. Yesterday I threw back at least two keepers because I wasn't positive they were legal size." She reached into her pocket and wagged the ruler in the air.

"And you came by to show me?" Rumer asked, smiling.

"Yeah, I felt like it. Well, and something else . . . I'm sorry I walked out on my veterinary science test. I just wanted you to know, it wasn't personal."

"Thanks for telling me," Rumer said. "But you still have to make it up—in summer school."

"Summer school," Quinn said, shivering. "That would kill everything. I have my lobstering. . . . I don't want to go to school after June. In fact, I *can't.*"

"Quinn, there's no such thing as the easy way out," Rumer said.

"Lobstering's not easy!"

"I know, but it won't get you into college."

"Who needs college? It would just take me away from what I already have. . . . I can't wait to grow up and be a *Dame de la Roche*. I'm going to be like you and Winnie—never get married and stay at the Point forever."

"Hmmm."

"Even Aunt Dana's selling out! But at least she's marrying Sam and staying here. I feel sorry for the women who leave—like ol' Elisabeth Randall. And your sister! Are those guys in the Range Rover with her? I know they're coming—Aunt Dana told me."

"Sounds like them," Rumer said, her voice strangely calm. "Zeb and Michael. You used to play with Michael a long time ago."

"Must have been a long, *long* time ago. He doesn't look like someone I have much in common with."

"What time did they get here?"

"I saw them about two hours ago. Talking to Winnie in her yard." Quinn scuffed her toe, felt her heart kick over. She pictured Mr. Sargent, the principal, standing at the end of the hall, watching as she'd gotten her ruler from her locker. "Rumer?"

"Yes?"

"Do you think . . . if I apologized . . . you could talk to Mr. Sargent and get me unsuspended? I don't want to go to summer school. . . ."

"I don't have much influence with him, Quinn. I teach just one class, part-time. But I'll try," Rumer said as the outside door opened and closed. Quinn heard the sound of a big dog pulling on a leash—panting, his nails scrabbling on the hard linoleum floor.

"Okay—and thanks," Quinn said, leaving a trail of fish scales as she walked down the long hallway to the doorway where she'd left her bike.

Riding six miles to the train bridge, her emotions stabilized. Up the hill just inside Hubbard's Point, past the cemetery, down the hill toward home. She coasted past Sixtus, fixing up his boat. She almost stopped to talk to him—he understood her like hardly anyone else did. Her aunt had told her he'd lost his father even younger than Quinn, and that he'd had a rough childhood up in Canada. He had had a twin brother who'd died of pneumonia some years back.

Now, stopping by her house, Quinn caught sight of Allie. Allie had gotten out of school early today—she was two grades behind, and the ninth-graders had taken a morning field trip on board the nature center boat. She was watering the garden, to make sure it looked nice for the wedding. Quinn's spine tingled just thinking of how horrible it would be to lose a sibling—almost worse than losing their parents.

"Hey, Al," she said.

"Where were you, Quinn?"

"School."

Allie's eyes showed confusion—also hurt. She thought Quinn was ly-ing—of course she had heard the whole story of her getting kicked out.

"I really was there, Allie. I had to get my ruler."

"What for?"

"To measure the lobsters. Don't want to get arrested for taking under-sized—"

At Allie's look of alarm, Quinn shook her head fast. "No, no—just kidding, Al. I won't get arrested."

"Why do you have to get in so much trouble?" Allie whispered, tears sparkling in her eyes. They were tears of love—Quinn had no doubt. Their bond was strong and permanent; since their parents' drowning, they had taken care of each other. Quinn would say and do anything to chase her sister's tears away, but she didn't seem able to change herself.

"I try not to," Quinn said. "I don't mean to. I'm sorry if I embarrass you."

"It's not that," Allie said, sounding tormented as she wiped her eyes. "I just worry about you. I don't want life to be so hard for you."

"Neither do I," Quinn whispered, sinking down to sit on a rock, spot-ting that boy from California watching them from down the street. She felt like throwing something at him, telling him to mind his own busi-ness, but with Allie watching, she never would. She didn't want to upset her sister, but she didn't like being watched.

"Let them know you're wonderful," Allie said, her throat thick with emotion.

"What? Who?"

"The kids at school."

"Why should I? They think I'm weird. Why should I try to change their minds?"

"They don't think you're weird, Quinn," Allie said. "But they don't know you very well. You only let the people you're sure of know you at all."

"Who am I sure of?"

"Me, Aunt Dana, Sam . . . Rumer, Mr. Larkin, Mrs. McCray, Winnie . . . the ones who love you."

Quinn just stared at her rubber boots. Allie had left the hose running, watering the rambling pink roses that tumbled over the steep ledge, and the sound was soothing, like a waterfall.

"To everyone else," Allie whispered, "you're like a lobster."

"I love lobsters," Quinn whispered back.

"I know. But they have such hard shells and big claws. . . ."

"They can't hurt you," Quinn scoffed. "Not seriously."

"But people don't know that. All they see is the armor, the scary claws."

Quinn watched Allie move the hose, so now it was watering the bridal-wreath and basket of gold—spiky bushes of white flowers and low feathery green ground cover, all planted by their grandmother. She had died last winter, and Quinn felt a pang. Allie's words were ringing in her ears.

"You don't have to hide yourself," Allie said. "I want everyone to know you like I do."

"No one ever can," Quinn said, closing her eyes tight. "We've been through so much together."

"I know . . . but just don't make it so hard with the others. You don't have to."

"It feels as if I do," Quinn whispered, her eyes still closed.

When the last people had left with their animals, Rumer took a long time making her last rounds of the kennel. She had one cat—Oscar—who'd been mauled by a fox, a golden retriever who had been hit by a car, a highly protective stray mother cat and her kittens, and a litter of puppies who had been stuffed into a pillowcase and survived being thrown into the Ibis River. She petted and talked to all of them—the strays needed to get used to people, and the others missed their families.

"You're here late," Mathilda commented, looking up from washing the instruments.

"Yes, I just don't feel like leaving yet."

"Everyone ready to go down for the night?"

"Actually, there's a feeling of just getting geared up for the evening," Rumer said. "That mother cat has her eye on the golden—I think she's afraid he'll come right through the cage for her kittens."

"Poor guy can barely walk," Mathilda said.

"I know, but tell that to her instincts," Rumer said, making notes.

"Ah, instincts," Mathilda said meaningfully, glancing up from under her bangs. She was a large woman; she had once told Rumer that the kids in her neighborhood growing up had teased her and called her "fat girl." Her blue smock held the pin Rumer had given her as an award last year: "In honor of superlative care and compassion for the animals of Black Hall and everywhere." When Rumer ignored her now, Mathilda cleared her throat for good measure.

"What are you trying to say?" Rumer asked.

"Just that, given what Quinn Grayson had to tell you, your instincts

have to be going on a bit of a rampage. 'The Range Rover people'—
that's them, right?"

"Bingo."

"So, how do you feel?"

"Well," Rumer said, listening to the animals down the hall, "something like that. . . ."

"A kennel full of barking dogs?"

Rumer nodded.

Mathilda had been a friend as long as she'd been an employee: eight
years. Rumer had seen her through her divorce; she had helped Mathilda
find the courage to call the domestic abuse hotline, she'd driven her to the
lawyer, she had held her hand while Mathilda had cried, and she'd
bought her a rosebush to plant in her garden the day the divorce was final.
Now Mathilda settled herself on a stool in the corner, wedged her chin in
a propped-up hand, and peered out from under her bangs.

"What?" Rumer asked.

"Dr. Larkin. Rumer, my friend," Mathilda said. "I've been waiting all
this time to be here for you, and something tells me this just might be my
chance."

Rumer took a deep breath and closed her eyes. The air filled her lungs,
and tiny white stars spangled on the back of her eyelids. "I can't believe
the effect this is having on me," she said. "It's Zeb and Michael. My
brother-in-law and nephew."

" 'Brother-in-law'? I guess that's *one* way of putting it," Mathilda said
as if questioning that particular definition of their relationship.

"You're right. Ex," she said, correcting herself.

"Come on, Rumer!"

"Former best friend," Rumer said, conceding.

"Get out of town! How about love of your life? Till he took up and
married the movie star who just happened to be your *sister*!"

"When you put it that way . . ." Rumer said.

"No wonder you feel like a kennel of barking dogs. I think I'd feel as
if my skin were inside out! I remember the first time I saw Frank and his
new wife together—in the Pampers aisle at the A&P, wouldn't you
know? I swear, I thought I was going to vaporize on the spot."

"Did you?" Rumer asked, smiling.

"Damn near!" Mathilda said, giving a shiver. "But not so he could
see."

"Wouldn't give him that kind of satisfaction," Rumer said.

"Nope. You'd have been proud of me. I stood tall—gave my spine a
little talking-to and drew myself up from the inside out. Then I pushed

my cart straight on past, looked his new wife right in the eye, and gave her a serious wink."

"Really?"

"Sure," Mathilda said. "Why not? I know what she's in for, even if she hasn't figured it out yet."

"Men are like tigers," Rumer said. "They don't change their stripes."

"Damn straight," Mathilda said. "So no wonder you're all shivery over Zeb's arrival. Doesn't much matter whether the guy's a wife-beating boat mechanic or a world-famous astronaut. Once they've broken your heart, they're done for."

"It all happened so long ago," Rumer said. "I'm way past having a broken heart. It healed twenty years ago. I became a vet, I'm following my dream, and I've never looked back. He's long since faded into the woodwork."

Mathilda just looked at her as if she were the saddest case in the world.

"What?" Rumer asked.

"Oh, Doctor," Mathilda said, patting her hand. "You're in trouble."

By the time she drove into the Point, up Cresthill Road to her house, the sun had started to set, and Rumer was again calm. The yards were a lacework of shadows, deep and profound. The rabbits had come out of their warrens up and down the road, hopping through all the yards. At this time of day, late sun shone in bursts of gold through the thick branches, the lighthouses had come on across the Sound, and Rumer felt the presence of old ghosts; she thought of Mathilda's word, "shivery," and shivered.

She felt her mother; Quinn's mother, Lily Grayson; and Elisabeth Randall. She had good women in her life and in her past.

Rumer stood still, gazing across the water toward the Wickland Rock Light. It flashed once, twice in the deepening twilight. Elisabeth—her grandmother's great-grandmother—had given up so much for love. She had abandoned her daughter Clarissa—Rumer's great-great grandmother—to run away with ship captain Nathaniel Thorn, and die in a gale when the *Cambria* wrecked on the shoal.

And Rumer's mother—she had loved Sixtus Larkin so much, Rumer had no doubt that she had saved his life. Rumer had once thought she and Zeb would be that for each other.

Looking up at the roof next door, she could almost see herself and Zeb as children, staring at the stars. Cassiopeia, the North Star, Arcturus, the Big Dipper . . . the stars told their story.

She had never thought she could hate, but that's the feeling she'd had when Zeb had married Elizabeth. She and her sister had had a code—they would never go after the boys the other liked.

In a way, before Elizabeth had turned her sights on Zeb, boys had seemed trivial when it came to the relationship of the two Larkin girls.

"I'm for you and you're for me," Elizabeth had said, linking arms with Rumer as they stood in the side yard. It was July, the year the sisters were fifteen and eighteen, just before Elizabeth would leave for her first off-Broadway part in *The Wild Duck.*

"Truer words were never spoken."

"No mere boy will ever come between us."

"As if one could!"

"Tell it, Rue!"

"I can't believe we're even having this conversation. If you like someone, all you have to do is tell me."

"He's off limits forever."

"And vice versa."

"Drink to it," Elizabeth had said, holding out her flask of blackberry brandy.

"I don't need to," Rumer said, trying to laugh it off. "Why do you have to drink anyway?"

"Because it makes more passion possible!" she exclaimed, swigging.

"You're passionate enough," Rumer tried to assure her.

"No such thing. That's why we'd better take this vow. Okay, where were we?"

"We'll never cross each other's line when it comes to boys."

"The weaker sex," Elizabeth chuckled.

Rumer laughed right along.

"Although, who needs such a vow?"

"What do you mean?"

"Well, we all know who you're going to marry. . . ."

"Who?"

"Starman. But, please, Rue—can't you be a little more original? A little more adventurous—I mean, the boy next door?"

"Zeb."

"Yes, Zeb. When did he first propose? When you were six?"

"Five," Rumer said, pushing her.

"At least promise me you'll lose your virginity to someone else. If you have sex with Zebulon Mayhew and no one else, you'll never know what you might have missed. Although, he is fairly hot."

"Yes, he is," Rumer said.

"Those biceps popping out of his T-shirt—not bad. And the other day I was standing upstairs and I saw him naked through his window. Wheeeeew! The boy next door grows up!"

"I've noticed," Rumer said, and her gaze traveled over to the bushes between their yards, hoping Zeb wasn't listening. The fact was, she had never imagined loving anyone else. They had the same history . . . they had loved each other forever. And regardless of Elizabeth's teasing, she thought he was the sexiest guy at Hubbard's Point or anywhere else.

"Just promise me you'll have sex with more than one person. That was fine for Mom and Dad, but not for us."

"I don't think it sounds so bad," Rumer said.

"What are you, a prude? Learn to make Zeb a little jealous along the way—all the boys at the beach like you. It wouldn't kill you to date them as long as you stay away from Billy Jones. He's mine."

"I know," Rumer had said, wondering what would happen. Although she and Zeb loved each other—she had no doubt—they had never gone on a date. Passing notes back and forth in the drawer at Foley's was about as far as they'd gotten.

"Right—time to take the vow." But then Elizabeth had caught the look on Rumer's face. "What's wrong?"

"Sometimes I think Zeb and I are *too* close," Rumer said. "More like brother and sister than—"

Elizabeth had laughed—a little bitterly, Rumer had often though later. "Believe me, Rue. He doesn't think of you as a sister. I've seen how he watches you—and when you went sailing with Jeff McCray that time, he spent the whole time on the beach, waiting for you to get back. When you played tennis with Halsey James last week, he got me to grab my racket and take the next court. . . ."

"See? Maybe he likes you."

"Hah. You didn't hear him! Bashing Halsey's backhand, cracking up every time he double-faulted. Didn't you see him nailing winners at me every shot? He practically knocked my head off! That was to show off for you."

"I wasn't sure," Rumer said, although she had hoped.

"He loves you—and not like a sister. Trust me. I was playing right next to him, and I saw the bulge in his shorts."

"Stop."

"You've never noticed?" Elizabeth asked, starting to slur her words. "When you're on the boat together, and he's in his swim trunks? Last week, when we all went over to Orient Point, you dove down to get that conch shell from the bottom, and Zeb turned into a flagpole."

"Maybe it wasn't me . . . there were other girls on board," Rumer said, embarrassed.

"Yeah, Lily and Dana Underhill, me—all with our boyfriends. No, you were the one—you had on that blue bikini . . . it's probably the first time he's ever really seen your boobs. Really, Rumer, when you dove down, you were hanging out—"

"I didn't mean to," Rumer said quickly.

"Well, you should do it more often. You sure got Zeb's attention— gave him a huge boner, dear heart. Sometimes I'm jealous," Elizabeth had confessed, sipping from her flask.

"Boys always look at you," Rumer said.

"So what? I'm talking about your connection with Zeb. I don't have that with anyone. They might fall in love with me, but they don't last."

You shouldn't give it so easily, Rumer had wanted to say. "When you drink, you stop caring what happens," she said instead, "and boys take advantage of you."

"No one takes advantage of me, get that straight right now," Elizabeth called, her voice booming as she tripped over a gnarly oak tree root. Mrs. Mayhew glanced outside, concerned, but Elizabeth just pulled Rumer away, out of sight. "Back to our vow . . ."

"To stay away from each other's boyfriends?" Rumer asked.

"Yesh . . . to make sure even *you* don't take advantage of me," Elizabeth laughed, slugging from her flask again. "Because I always come out on top. Always, always. Never forget that, little shishter. . . ."

"I never will," Rumer said, linking arms with Elizabeth and taking the vow.

But Elizabeth had been the one to break it, Rumer thought now. It had happened so long ago . . . maybe none of it had been real. The promise, the broken promise, the love, the poisonous hatred that had followed, nearly destroying Rumer in the process. She thought of what she had said to Mathilda back at the office: "Men are like tigers. They don't change their stripes."

But that wasn't true: Zeb had changed his stripes. He had gone from being the person Rumer trusted most in the world to someone she didn't even know. He had broken their amazing connection, thrown it away.

Her father was still working on his boat; she heard the rasp, rasp of sandpaper just beneath the music of wind in the trees and waves on the shore. Standing still, her feet rooted to the ground, Rumer looked fifty yards down the road and saw Zeb's car. The sight of it made her pulse pound, a drumbeat in her ears.

After a decade of knowing he was thousands of miles away—in California, or up in the sky—he was finally here.

The tiger who had changed his stripes.

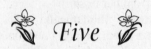

Five

ZEB MAYHEW couldn't sleep. He tossed and turned in the creaky old bed, smelling the Atlantic salt tang through the open windows and knowing Rumer was just up the street. It was like that childhood game: The more you try not to think of something, the more impossible it was. He kept telling himself to stay away, to let her be, but his mind was on fire.

Lessons learned the hard way . . . Winnie's words rang in his head.

He did it—he'd blown it. Put a stake through the heart of the gentle girl he had once loved. He had come home to set things right, to the place where he'd always been able to see the stars. He didn't dare hope she'd actually be his friend again, much less love him again, but he wanted, somehow, to make things okay. More than anything, Zeb wanted to see if Rumer could forgive him.

What did she used to say? That they were connected by a magical thread. It ran straight from her heart to his. All he ever had to do was grab on, feel his way to her. He thought of how often he had done that. He remembered touching her heart as he'd kissed her lips so tenderly, the two of them learning their way together.

He remembered that time in the dark, across the marsh, with his sleeping bag and the lantern, their secret time together, when he'd learned what it was to fall in love with his best friend. He had wanted her so badly, but he had respected her too much to do anything more than hold her and kiss her all night. He had thought there would be plenty of time for them to get to the rest of it, but he had wrecked it all.

"Shit," he said out loud.

Hubbard's Point felt familiar right down to his bones. He had the sense that if he walked outside blindfolded, he could find his way around every rock, every tree. If he went outside, he knew he would see her. Although it was late, all the neighbors' house lights out and everyone in bed, Zeb's instincts told him to get moving—he couldn't waste another minute.

The summer air was heavy. It was the middle of the night. A layer of fog drifted in from the east, across the sea to the water's edge. Winnie's cottage was built directly above the rocks—rocks where Zeb and Rumer had spent entire summer days crabbing. Elizabeth had always been above such activities—"Crustaceans and seaweed aren't my things," she'd say, watching Rumer and Zeb head down with buckets and bait.

Slipping outside, Zeb walked barefoot across the grass. He glanced up, toward Rumer's house. Then, instead of turning left, he went right, to the ledge. The rocks felt warm from the day's sun. He edged his way down to the water and checked on the tide: dead high. The small waves lapped his feet and ankles, luring him in. Glancing around to make sure he was alone, he tugged off his shorts and T-shirt and dived into the cove.

The water was June cold and sent a shot straight to his heart. It stripped the years away—age by age, he went back in time until he was fifteen. He could almost feel Rumer swimming beside him, her leg brushing his as she kicked by. Swimming along the Point, he felt the pure joy of being there. Nothing forgave like saltwater: It washed all the sins of life away, scrubbed a person clean. Life was one big promise just waiting to be taken. The stars were his territory; all he had to do was get there. Nothing could ever fall apart.

Turning onto his back, looking up, he saw only haze. Momentarily deterred, he stopped. There was one place—one foolproof place—where he could see stars. He knew it like he knew his own name. Kicking to shore, he shook off the saltwater and pulled his clothes onto his wet body, back on his original mission.

He cut through the yards just as he'd done as a kid. People here didn't care about property lines; the parcels of land blurred together, separated by raggedy lines of privet and bamboo. Generations of kids had made holes in the hedges to ease their passage. Zeb knew every one, and he made his way across the street, up Hecate's hill, through the privet hedge into his old yard.

The darkest land on Hubbard's Point, it was as tangled and overgrown as ever. Animals scooted into the brush at his approach. He heard the grass move and branches rattle. Glancing next door at the Larkins' house, he felt Rumer's presence—as if that magical tie had never been broken—and knew she was home.

Through the window he saw his ex–father-in-law. Sixtus was up late, sailing charts spread out on the dining room table. His back looked crooked, hunched over; his hands were old and gnarled. The strange thing was, Zeb still felt fifteen: None of the bad years had ever happened. He was just a Point boy with none of the disappointments and failures of manhood to hold him down, none of Sixtus's disapproval to contend with. He could almost forget that he had fallen from the sky.

Peering at his old house, Zeb knew a hundred ways to break in. He could have loosened the pane of glass in the kitchen door—pried up the molding with a stick—to reach in and undo the latch. He could remove a rickety panel of lattice on the south side and sneak up the basement stairs. Or he could bypass the house entirely, climb up the stepped chimney onto the roof. . . .

"The key's still there."

Her voice had a knife edge in it. At the sound, Zeb turned around. His heart thudded, stuck somewhere between the dreams of his youth and the reality of his life. Rumer stood in the darkness, her white shirt glowing like mist.

"Rumer," he said.

"I heard you were here," she said.

"We got here earlier today," he said.

"News travels fast," she said, and he winced at her tone.

He nodded; he could see her fairly clearly in the light from her father's lamp, shining through the windows next door. Her hair was pale as a field of wheat—silver and gold.

He moved, as if to give her a brotherly hug, but she took a small, definite step back. The fact was, she couldn't stand him. As close as they stood, he could see anger and unfamiliar hardness in her blue eyes.

"You came to visit your old house," she said.

"Yes. I hear it's been sold again. . . ."

"The sign came down last week." She eased backward in the grass. "You're here before the new owners—"

"I went for a swim," he said, "and the rocks were covered with fog. I wanted to see the stars, and I knew there was one sure way—"

She nodded, understanding. Their one sure way of communicating had to do with stars and nature, and no matter how she felt about him, she would help him with this.

"You still have a chance," she said. "The house is between owners—the old ones have gone, and the new ones haven't fallen in love with it yet. Like I said, the key is still in the same place. I checked the other day when I let one of the rabbits go. . . ."

"Still taking care of rabbits in the yards?" he asked, shaking his head as amusement came over him.

"Yes, I still am," she said. "It's my profession now."

"Call it whatever you want," he said. "But we both know it's your passion."

The truth of who they were, who they had always been, hung between them in the summer air. A light breeze blew up the hill from the beach, making Zeb shiver in his wet clothes. He stared across the space at Rumer. She looked like a young girl standing there, and as the wind picked up slightly, he realized how much he wanted to take her in his arms and make everything okay between them.

"Michael's with you?" she asked.

"Yes. Sleeping down the street. Catching up on his rest—tired himself out, not talking the whole way cross-country."

"It's the age," she said. "I've seen an entire classroom filled with mute boys. . . ."

"No more classrooms for Michael. Didn't your sister tell you? He decided to drop out."

From Rumer's neutral expression, Zeb couldn't tell whether she knew or not. Did she and Elizabeth ever speak? He wasn't sure. The bond between the sisters had always mystified him. Marrying Elizabeth, he had actually felt more, not less distant from the two of them.

"I'm sorry to hear that," Rumer said.

"Well, creativity runs in the family, right? Zee made it to Broadway without going to college—she says too formal an education kills the left brain. Stomps the artist to death. She supports him totally."

"Deciding not to go to college is one thing," Rumer said sharply. "If he discovers that's what he really wants. But not finishing high school . . ."

Mist lay heavy, even on the hill. Looking up, Zeb couldn't see through the veil to the stars. He knew if he could climb up to the roof, the sky would be his: The constellations would tell their story and help him make sense of his life. He almost wished it were September already, that he was into the adventure of getting his new lab up and running. Looking at Rumer, he knew their thread was broken forever. Suddenly his spirit felt much too heavy to climb the stairs or the chimney or the vines growing up the side of his old house.

"You want to go up?" Rumer asked, following his gaze.

"No," he said. "It's not my place. It doesn't belong to me anymore."

The beam of Wickland Rock Light passed over their heads, held down by the light mist. Rumer stood still, watching it go. Her eyes were steady, blue as the daylight sky. Zeb considered the phenomenon of being able to see stars in daylight, straight through the clear blue, yet being unable to see them tonight, in the very place where he had learned to love them so much.

"It is your place, Zeb," Rumer said in a husky voice. "It's always been, and it always will be. No matter what else has happened."

Zeb made no attempt to move or speak. Rumer stared at him, seeming to get a message he hadn't intended to send. He felt her dismiss him: She had moved on, and she wasn't going to waste much time going back. Starting to walk away, she turned again.

"Will you and Michael come for dinner tomorrow night? Give Dad and me a chance to see him before the wedding."

"Sure, Rumer. Thanks—"

"It'll be good to see Michael."

Without looking back, she walked away. Had she meant to sound so scathing—good to see Michael but not Zeb? He watched her walk through the tall grass, fireflies blinking around her knees, into the house next door. Down the hill, Sixtus's beautiful old Herreshoff sat in her cradle behind the garage, sleek in the shadows. Zeb stood there for another minute, in his own yard, thinking of everything she had said.

She'd been wrong about one thing.

It wasn't his place anymore; it wasn't at all—he had left it behind. The wedding was Saturday, a day and a half away. That left all of summer spreading before him like a strange landscape. The way he felt right now, he could drive away and never look back. His lab was waiting in California; he could get the jump on setting up his team. He had brought books and charts with him to start researching, but maybe this was the wrong place. Zeb looked up again just to check one more time. No stars.

He heard the door close quietly behind her. The sound made by the click of the lock did something to his heart—squeezed it hard. It sounded familiar: Living here so long ago, he had heard that sound a million times. Turning away, he looked at the other house—the green cottage where his family had once lived.

He thought of all the nights his father had come through the door, grouchy after hitting traffic on the highway from Kennedy Airport. His mother had counseled Zeb to leave his father alone, let him unwind and relax a little before bothering him with the worries on Zeb's mind.

Zeb remembered that the only person his father had ever seemed happy to see was Elizabeth.

"Hi, Mr. Mayhew," she'd say, dimpling and swinging on their light pole.

"Hello, Elizabeth."

"How was your flight?"

"Long. Really long. What I need is a swim and a drink, and then I'll be okay. What I don't need is a long list of everything that went wrong here at home while I was flying to Brussels and back."

"Well, *I'm* glad to see you," she'd say. "Nothing's wrong with me!"

"You can say that again," Zeb's father would say. "You're a regular movie star, you know that? Anyone ever tell you that?"

"Just you, Mr. Mayhew!"

"Well, when you get famous, you have to tell everyone the old man next door discovered you first."

"You're not old. . . ."

"Oh, come on."

"No, really. I think Mrs. Mayhew's the luckiest woman at the Point. Being married to a pilot!"

From their hidden perch on the roof, Zeb and Rumer would be listening, and Zeb would pretend to gag.

"Listen to her butter him up," he'd say. "Why's she wasting her time?"

"She's trying to soften him up for you and your mother," Rumer giggled, hardly able to contain herself, so amused by her amazing sister's guile. "She's practicing using her female wiles on him."

"Well, he sure thinks she has them," Zeb said. "He's practically following her inside."

"She doesn't mean anything bad," Rumer said. "I'm not sure she can stop herself though."

"She's pretty," Zeb said. "That's for sure."

Had Rumer been jealous to hear him say that? Zeb wasn't sure now. He remembered how she had tilted her head, as if thinking it over, then nodding—in total agreement. "She's beautiful," Rumer had whispered.

And she was. Even now Zeb couldn't deny the beauty of his ex-wife. She and Rumer were so different as girls. Rumer was small and thin, a tomboy with freckles and straight hair the color of cattails. Elizabeth was lush, gorgeous, with large breasts, wide hips, and full lips.

The thing was, Zeb had never wanted anyone but Rumer. Her plainness had seemed more beautiful to him than anything in nature. It was simple, unadorned, and yet somehow perfect. Elizabeth had always seemed *too*: too everything. Too loud, too sexual, too ambitious, too outrageous. But once she had turned her sights on something she wanted, she'd dial up the volume so high, it was impossible to ignore.

When his time came, Zeb hadn't even tried. His father had had a crush on her—Zeb had always been sure, and he'd sensed his mother's dislike for Elizabeth at an early age. Maybe it was a Freudian thing—after loving Rumer, he'd let himself fall for the sister his father preferred. And if that wasn't disgusting enough, Zeb thought, he'd also let himself fall for the same line.

He remembered it now, standing in the yard between their two childhood homes. Twenty years ago . . . he and Rumer had gotten very close the summer before. They had come together, letting their bodies nearly catch up with what their minds had always known: that they loved each other.

By spring, they were insane for each other. A winter apart at their respective colleges had made them crazy, and Zeb knew he'd do anything to have her. He'd cooked up a great plan.

Vernal equinox, first day of spring. Lots of things to observe in the field: migrating birds, bloodroot and trillium, snakes emerging from hibernation, spring constellations. He'd pitch his tent in the hidden lowlands behind the Indian Grave—the most private spot near Hubbard's Point. No one would find them. They'd have all the privacy and time they needed, and in the midst of new spring they'd make love.

He had laid the groundwork: a call to her dorm, getting her home to the Point, a note in the drawer at Foley's telling her where and when to meet. But she hadn't shown up. Zeb had waited, alone in his tent by the grave, the happy sound of spring peepers mocking him. Perhaps she just wasn't ready. Maybe he had rushed her. But he felt scorned and humiliated, and he wasn't sure he'd ever gotten over it.

Would they have possessed each other then? Would they have belonged to each other forever? Zeb was loyal. Rumer might not think so, but he was. Until he and Elizabeth divorced, she was the only woman he'd ever slept with. And from their first time, his fate was sealed: His own stupidity, his lust, had blinded him to the future. He'd landed in bed with Elizabeth Larkin, and that was that.

Now, standing in his yard, he couldn't stop himself from running through the torturous rest of it. The way he and Elizabeth had gotten together: A few weeks later, Elizabeth had invited him and Rumer to see her in a play. Rumer had come to New York. Zeb, still smarting over being stood up, had acted so aloof, she had laughingly decided to head back to Hartford to study for exams, "where people aren't mad at me for no reason," Rumer had teased. Elizabeth must have noticed. Because walking her home after watching her onstage in *Romeo and Juliet*, Zeb had felt her take his hand.

He had pulled it away, thinking of Rumer.

"What's wrong, Zeb?" Elizabeth had asked.

"Nothing," he'd said. "Except we're just friends."

"Like you and Rumer?" Elizabeth had asked.

Zeb hadn't known what to say to that. What did Elizabeth know? Had Rumer confided in her? The sisters seemed to know everything about each other, but Zeb had thought maybe Rumer would keep things about her and him private—even from Elizabeth.

"I thought you and Rumer were more like brother and sister than . . . you know," Elizabeth had said. "Maybe that's the problem?"

"What problem?" he'd asked, his heart pounding. So Rumer *had* talked about it. Maybe she'd blown him off at the grave for reasons he didn't understand. Maybe she didn't love him anymore. What if there was someone else?

"The fact that you can't seem to get together. It's just not meant to be, Zeb. When you start out as really close friends, it's sometimes too hard to take the leap. She's more like your younger sister, you know?"

"And you're older and wiser?"

"Hey! Watch the 'older' part." Leaning forward, she'd tousled his hair, letting her fingers trail down the side of his face.

"Sorry," he'd said, the heat rising in his neck as he tried to control the lust he'd always felt for Elizabeth. Looking down at the street—right there by the curb—he saw gold glinting amid litter. He bent to pick it up and realized it was one of the Larkin sisters' lighthouse pins.

"My pin!" Elizabeth exclaimed, throwing her body against his. "You found it."

"You lost it?" he asked, feeling her full breasts against his chest.

"I did," she whispered now. "Only now . . . who cares? You found it." Her breath was warm, but it made him shiver.

"Elizabeth," he said, warningly.

"It's hard to feel sexy over a little sister," she'd said, now touching his neck, his collarbone, as he pulled away. "And that's what she's been to you. Face it."

He didn't answer. His feelings toward Rumer hadn't felt brotherly at all. He remembered his arms around her, the intensity of her kiss, his wild desire to make love to her, but all that was melting away in the inferno of Elizabeth's attention. She was a blast furnace, the Queen of the Point. She brought out his base instincts; he'd been fighting them for years.

"See?" Elizabeth had asked smoothly, taking his hand again. "I'm not a shrink, but I think it's pretty plain that you're better suited as friends than lovers. Lovers are more alluring when they're unfamiliar, somewhat forbidden. Like you and me, Zeb."

"Excuse me?" he asked, jumping, watching her run her hand over her own breast, feeling for a place to attach the pin.

"Forbidden, I said. Just imagine what everyone would say . . ."

He closed his eyes, blood thumping in his ears. Forbidden, all right. It would kill Rumer.

Now Elizabeth's hands ran up under his shirt, and he shivered as she lightly raked his skin with her nails. On the other hand, what did Rumer care? After waiting so long, trying so hard, she had left him alone in the tent, waiting yet again. It seemed clear that their deep friendship was as far as they would go. Maybe that was best, not to ruin it.

He tasted copper as Elizabeth's hand rubbed his chest. His knees nearly buckled. Why couldn't this be Rumer? Shit, why had she pushed him away? He pulled Elizabeth close and began to kiss her, their mouths open and their tongues hot and moving, right in the middle of New York City, feeling that damn gold lighthouse dig into his chest.

"Elizabeth, sorry," he had said, dizzily yanking himself back, trying to forget the shocking sensation her nails had made on his body, wondering what the hell was happening. He was with the wrong sister—how could Rumer have drifted off without him noticing?

"You're forgiven. All you have to do is feed me."

"Feed you?"

She'd laughed. "I'm hungry."

"Oh," he'd said. It had sounded as if she'd meant something else.

"I just did a performance, and you just made it a perfect night by finding my pin. Now I need food. Not to mention wine. How about you buy me a burger and a bottle of merlot, and I thank you by listening to your troubles? You can call me Dr. Larkin if it'll make you feel better. I'll even give you my best advice. . . ."

"Maybe I could use some advice."

"Oh," Elizabeth had said, her laughter trilling into his ear. "I think you know what you want . . . you don't need me to tell you. After all, you're a man who shoots for the stars. You're going to be a pilot—a *space shuttle* pilot . . . and I think that's *so* incredibly sexy."

Her hand had slipped from his to his elbow, and then around his waist, under his shirt, her fingernails raising the goose bumps on his skin again. Zeb held her too. The thing was, he felt so lonely. He was at school in New York City, and with all these people around, he was a stranger to them all. Rumer was the only person he'd ever felt like himself with, and he felt the division between them. Elizabeth's words, her arm around his waist, had been like hot wires zapping him awake.

Looking back all those years, Zeb stood in his old yard and sighed. He had bought the burger; they had drunk the wine. People in the restaurant—Bradley's, on University Place—recognized Elizabeth from the play, and he felt proud and pumped up.

Was that the night he had sold his soul? Turned in his true feelings for some idea of what would bring him more? More fame, more notice, more attention, more approval? Especially from his father—even that first night, holding hands with Elizabeth Larkin under the table while the

Ricky Karsky Jazz Trio played on, Zeb had realized that his father would think he'd chosen the right sister, captured the prize.

Or she had chosen him. . . .

They had slept together, and their lives were sealed: He wouldn't leave her after that. His father had cheated on his mother, showing Zeb how not to do it. Especially after Michael was born.

Zeb gazed at the house next door. He wasn't going back to California; he wasn't going anywhere. He had come east to pay his penance to Rumer, and he wasn't leaving until he did. Winnie was right: He had learned his lessons the hard way. But now it was time to put them to the test.

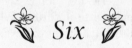 *Six*

THE NEXT DAY, the tent went up for the wedding. Michael stood in the shady road, watching the men hoist it. He had been to plenty of big parties out in California and Houston, and at the sets of his mother's movies around the world; this tent looked just about big enough to cover the buffet table at one of his mother's premieres. Blue and white striped, this puny one was obviously for the whole wedding: Round tables were being rolled in.

Walking past, Michael headed the long way down to the beach. He'd left his father holed up on the screen porch, doing preliminary research for the first project at his new lab. Books and papers were spread over the scarred wooden table; star charts and navigation tools were piled beside his chair. Satellite photos were stacked on a pile of books. No matter what his father said about wanting to drive cross-country with his son, Michael knew the real story: His dad had needed the car just to lug all his stuff.

Anyway, Michael was on his own today. The place looked vaguely familiar: His father had pointed out the side-by-side cottages where he and Michael's mom had grown up. An overgrown right-of-way led along the southern edge of his dad's old yard, all the way down to the beach, but Michael bypassed it in favor of the road. Knowing he had spent his first few summers here, he wanted to see what he remembered.

Around the bend, down a bicycle path that led past the tennis and basketball courts, along a rough stone wall that dropped steeply to the sandy parking lot. Reeds grew around the perimeter, right up to the edge of the boat basin. A quick memory flashed into Michael's mind: he and his aunt in an old rowboat, drifting around a small island where the swans made their nest.

He scanned the island and saw no swans. Boats filled the round basin, bows forward, rocking with the tide. Some of the boats looked sweet:

fiberglass, chrome rails, big engines; others looked like they could barely make it out to sea. And there in the scruffiest boat of all—wooden, looking ready to sink—was the girl he had spotted yesterday.

She was still in her oilskins. Dark glasses covered her eyes, and when she glanced over at him, her expression grew dark to match. Lobster pots were piled high on the boat basin's wall. Reaching for them, she dragged them closer—it took real strength to haul and stack them one by one in her boat.

"Need some help?" Michael asked, walking over.

"Wouldn't want you to get your hands dirty," she said.

He stopped short. What was she talking about? He was a man of the land. While his mother was on location last spring, he had replaced about half the shingles on the barn roof. He wore the jeans he had worn for that project: faded, torn, stained with tar. His shoulders were practically bursting the seams of his old Nine Inch Nails T-shirt; to hold his long brown hair back, he wore a red bandanna.

"Where do you want it?" he asked, hoisting one of the pots—surprisingly heavy, weighted down with bricks. "In the front or back?"

"Thanks," she said, ignoring his question and, taking the pot from him, expertly swinging it into the back of the boat. "I can take it from here."

"Have it your way," he said, shaking his head and giving what he hoped was an ironic little laugh. Did she think he was after her or something? If so, dream on. He had had girlfriends back home with younger brothers cuter than her. Starting to walk away, he realized the whole thing bothered him.

"Yes?" she asked, right in the midst of hauling another pot onto the boat.

"You got a problem?"

"Just your looks," she said.

His mouth dropped open—he couldn't help himself. Without intending to, he touched his hair. He was his mother's son, and she was considered one of the most beautiful women in Hollywood. He had never considered his looks to be part of his problem before. "My what?"

"Your . . . looks," she said slowly, one word at a time, as if he were not only very ugly but stupid as well.

"What about them?" he asked, anger rising.

"You've got to think them through," she said. "You can't come roaring up in a Range Rover one day—the speed limit in Hubbard's Point is fifteen miles per hour, by the way—and go walking around like Hippie Boy nineteen sixty-something the next. It's just incredibly annoying."

"What the hell is it to you?"

"I live here."

Michael stood on the seawall, unable to speak or move away. He was totally shocked by her rudeness, and his tongue was ready with about fifty comebacks.

"I have the right to be here," he said.

"It's not about the right, rich boy. It's about fairness."

"Explain your warped logic. I'm sure it's fascinating."

"Well, you and your father are renting Winnie's little house, right?"

"Unfortunately."

"See? You don't even want to be there—I knew it! What's a Range Rover person doing at Hubbard's Point? Especially in Winnie's cottage? You're used to mansions, right? Malibu, or wherever the beautiful people go?"

"Malibu."

"Well, you should have rented a place in Fenwick, across the river. They have huge houses and millionaires there—even a movie star. You should have left Winnie's place free for a family that would love it. Kids who like sand and rocks and crabs, you know?"

"Aren't we a little too old for sand and rocks and crabs?" Michael asked, smirking.

The girl reached into her bait bucket and, shouting like a ninja, sprayed him with a burst of fish heads. "EEEEEEEEEEYAH! Maybe you are!" she yelled.

"You're sick," Michael said, wiping fish entrails off his shirt as he backed away. "Why aren't you in school anyway? They kick you out for being a sociopath? Jesus Christ!"

"I'm not a *sociopath*!" she hissed, sunglasses sliding down her nose as she pulled the starter cord on her engine and revved it up. Casting off her lines, she gave Michael an evil stare. "And it's 'bow' and 'stern,'" she said. "Not 'front' and 'back.' I'd have thought you'd know that from spending time on people's yachts."

"I hate yachts," he said, watching her back the boat into the basin, Vs of wake rippling the smooth surface, reversing direction as she shifted the engine and began to move forward.

Michael watched her maneuver around the island very gently, as if there were still swans nesting there. And then, moving under the footbridge, she shouted something over her shoulder, then gunned the motor and zoomed through the narrow channel with a rooster tail of white spray flying out behind her as she left Michael in her wake.

❧

Rumer had set the table with her mother's china, wishing Clarissa Larkin could be there to help her through. It felt impossibly hard, having

Zeb and her nephew over for dinner. Bumping into Zeb last night in the dark had nearly given her a heart attack. She had thought she was prepared to see him; she had steeled herself from top to bottom.

But when she glanced through the privet hedge and saw him standing there, the ice in her veins melted all at once. She'd been gripped by old, undeniable joy—as if the cells of her body remembered their old love. But then her mind with its more recent memories regained control again, and the ice returned, encasing her heart for good measure.

Getting dressed proved to be difficult. She wanted to make the right impression on Michael. First she put on an Elizabethesque light blue sundress, then changed into a Winnielike caftan thing, then, cursing at herself for being idiotic, threw on what she had wanted to wear in the first place: jeans and a white cotton sweater.

Her mother's needlepoint pictures hung on the wall. They showed scenes from the Point: swans on the island, Mrs. Lightfoot's house on the Point, Wickland Rock Light, and then the series that Rumer had loved most when she was a child . . . she and Elizabeth had nicknamed them "The Unicorn Tapestries."

Clarissa Larkin had incorporated the Point legends into her work. She had begun some of these as a very young girl, living in this same house. She and her best friend next door—Leila Tournelle—had seen a unicorn one foggy night when they were ten. Pure white, with a flowing mane and a horn of pearl, it had stood among the azalea and laurel bushes, staring at them with gentle black eyes.

Leila had grown up to marry a pilot—Jacob Mayhew. Clarissa had grown up to run a small needlework shop by the Congregational Church in Black Hall. It was called Tapestry, after the lush and magical unicorn tapestries at the Cluny Museum in Paris and the Cloisters in New York.

Clarissa spent her days at the shop, needlepointing her own panels: the Point unicorn leading her and Leila amid oak, holly, pine, and flowering pear trees, its pearlescent narwhal's tooth pointing toward the lighthouse. Hubbard's Point rabbits nestled beneath the azalea bushes. The rich colors—the dark blue sky and green house—created a harmonious background.

It was into that shop, with Clarissa stitching one of her panels, that Sixtus Larkin walked one June day. He had come down from Halifax to teach school in Black Hall, and he carried under his arm a sampler his mother had made as a girl.

"It needs restoring," he said gruffly, spreading it out on the counter.

"It's lovely," Clarissa said in her gentle way, running her soft hands over the water-stained and moth-eaten canvas.

"Had it in my trunk . . . I nearly threw it out, but then I saw your shop and thought I'd come in and see."

"You did the right thing," Clarissa said, and as her gaze moved from his mother's embroidery up to his hurt and hollow blue eyes, both their fates were sealed. Clarissa had never stopped believing that the Point unicorn had brought them together, and although Rumer knew her father was more practical and scientific—even about love—she knew that if his Clarissa said it to Sixtus Larkin, it must be so.

The wind had swung around, blowing from the east. Rumer stood at the kitchen window, watching the road and the sea beyond, hoping the weather would hold for Dana's wedding tomorrow. Spotting the guys coming through the yard, she felt her heart start to pound.

Michael had grown so tall—he was over six feet, a young man. She watched Zeb duck through the privet hedge, say something over his shoulder to Michael, scowling at the ground. Getting no reply, Zeb pulled the red bandanna from Michael's head. The exchange was so swift and charged, she barely had time to register anything but Zeb's nervous eyes, Michael's shocked expression, the jolt she felt at seeing Zeb, and the overwhelming love she had for her nephew.

"You're here," she said, opening the door wide, looking past Zeb.

"Hi," Zeb said. Their eyes met just briefly. Rumer sensed him wondering whether to hug her or not, like last night, but she brushed past him. Here was Michael, her baby nephew all grown-up, right there in her doorway, and the sight of him made her eyes fill with tears.

"Michael, this is your aunt Rumer," Zeb said. "Do you remember—"

Rumer didn't give him the chance to answer. She stepped forward, stood on her toes, and gave him a huge hug. He had been so small, and now he was enormous.

"Oh, my God," she said, "Michael! I can't believe you're here. It's really you!"

"Yeah," he said.

"You remember me, right? Say you do—I couldn't bear it if—" She stopped herself, laughing, wiping tears from her eyes. "No, don't let me tell you what to say. I want to know what you really think. Do you remember being here?"

"Kind of. A little," he said.

"You said you remembered things on your walk," Zeb said.

Rumer could hardly tear her eyes off Michael, but now she looked at Zeb and saw him coaching his son, wanting Michael to say the right thing and not disappoint his aunt. Rumer laughed in spite of it all. Leila Mayhew and Clarissa Larkin had to be smiling down from somewhere to see their grandson standing in this house after so very long a time.

"How about a drink?" she asked. "Some iced tea—or a beer?"

"A beer sounds good," Michael said, cracking a smile.

"You're not beer age," her father said, coming through the kitchen. Although he had just showered, his hands were still speckled with brownish boat varnish. He stood apart, regarding Michael. "Are you?"

"What's the drinking age in Connecticut?" he asked.

"Older than you, I hope," Sixtus said. "Or else that would make me ancient, and I'm not ready for that yet. Come shake your grandfather's hand. Hello, Zeb."

The men exchanged handshakes, but Rumer wouldn't quite let go of Michael. She linked her arm with his, walking past the empty hutches in the mudroom into the kitchen. Zeb and Sixtus greeted each other warily; Rumer remembered the last time they'd seen each other.

It had been over a decade ago, at her mother's funeral. Her father had aged since then: As if seeing him through Zeb's eyes, she noticed his white hair, stooped posture, lined face.

Glancing at Zeb, she saw that he had aged too. Still tall and lean, his body was as hard as a young man's in jeans and a Brooks Brothers shirt. Sun lines creased his eyes and forehead, and he had gray hair at his temples. His eyes, on the other hand, looked exactly the same, as if he were still that same young boy who lived next door. Rumer stared, looked away, back again.

Zeb's sharp blue eyes were as bright as the sea and sky, the clearest blue imaginable. Rumer had always thought they looked as if he'd seen all the wonders of the universe and knew where they were hidden. Pushing the thought aside, she opened the refrigerator and pulled out an assortment of iced tea, sodas, and beer.

"You know the way, Michael," Sixtus said gruffly. His arthritis had been bothering him today; he gripped his cane with a clawlike hand, his back crooked like a staff. "Lead us onto the porch."

"There's only one door . . ." he said, looking around, and Rumer had to smile at her father making the boy feel at home, watching Michael walk through the living room onto the screened porch.

While Michael grabbed the binoculars and began to scan the beach, Rumer put out cheese and crackers, shrimp and crab. They all talked about safe subjects: the Point, how Winnie never changed, Dana and Sam and how they'd met, Sixtus supplementing his pension by tutoring kids in math, the weather, Zeb's new lab.

"A lab?" Sixtus asked. "You mean on terra firma?"

"Yep," Zeb said. "Old astronauts never die; they just wind up in laboratories, staring at pictures of stars."

"Instead of flying to them?" Rumer asked.

"That'll be the day," Michael snorted.

"The new observatory," Zeb said, "is really great. The funding's generous, the telescope's better than anything else in the world. . . . I'll be the guy who predicts the next big meteor shower. When you go online and some know-it-all tells you to set your alarm for three A.M. because you'll see twenty shooting stars a minute, that'll be me."

"But you won't be flying?" Rumer asked.

Zeb seemed not to hear, reaching across the table for some shrimp. His tone might have been joking, but his bright blue eyes looked serious—not laughing at all. Rumer realized he didn't want to talk about it anymore, so somewhat uneasily she turned her attention to Michael.

"Michael, your dad said you remembered things on your walk," she said.

"Yeah," he said, smiling. "You took me in a boat. There were swans on an island."

"Making their nest," she said. "You remember. How about Blue . . . do you remember Blue?"

"Blue . . ." Michael said, turning the name over.

"How's Zee?" Sixtus asked, and the first awkward silence of the evening befell them.

"Mom's fine," Michael answered. "She's doing a movie in Toronto."

"I know. But she'd better come home one of these days if she knows what's good for her," Sixtus said, and Michael laughed.

"Watch it, Dad—she's Michael's mother," Rumer said.

"She was my daughter before she was his mother!" Sixtus said. "You know how she got her nickname, Zee?"

"No one calls her that in California," Michael said.

"Yes, well, this is Connecticut. She was baptized Elisabeth, with an S, after your grandmother's great-great-great-grandmother—am I leaving out a 'great'?" he asked, glancing at Rumer.

"No, I think you got them all," Rumer said, sipping her iced tea.

Nodding gravely, Sixtus continued. "Anyway, the woman who lived at that lighthouse right there"—he extended a strong arm out toward the Wickland Rock Light—"ran off with her lover, some English sailor. Right, Rumer?"

"Right," Rumer said, but she could barely concentrate with Zeb sitting right there.

"Keep in mind, names were important to Clarissa Larkin. Her own name comes from the little girl left behind at the lighthouse. And your aunt here is named after Rumer Godden, author of many books her mother loved."

"Okay," Michael said, intrigued by the family history. Sixtus went on.

"Anyway . . . your grandmother names her firstborn baby—your mother—Elisabeth, after her drowned ancestor. And your mother—upon reaching the ripe old age of about thirteen—announces she's changing her name to Elizabeth with a Z. *Because,* she says, she intends to be as famous or more so than Winnie Hubbard, and she wants the critics to know *exactly* how to spell her name. Took on the nickname Zee to drive the point home."

"The missing Z in Elizabeth," Michael said.

Rumer saw the boy look from his grandfather to his father, but Zeb's face seemed to have frozen into a permanent frown. They were discussing the intractability of Elizabeth Randall Larkin Mayhew, and from personal experience, Rumer knew it was an uncomfortable place to be.

"So why'd she do it?" Michael asked.

"Maybe because it's theatrical," Sixtus said. "Added to her stage mystique. Or maybe to mollify me."

"Or maybe just because she wanted to," Zeb said quietly, still staring at the house next door as the gazes of both his son and his former father-in-law slid inquisitively in his direction.

"Huh?" Michael asked.

"The way she does everything else," Zeb said.

Rumer heard the bitterness. She felt it herself, but for Michael's sake, she wasn't going to give Zeb the satisfaction of pursuing the subject. Just then the phone rang. Her father started for it, but Rumer beat him to it.

"Hello?" she asked.

"It's me," said Edward. "I missed you today."

"I missed you too," she said. "I'd have come, but I got busy at the office. Now we have company for dinner."

"Really? Anyone I know?"

"My nephew, Michael," she said. "And his father."

"Oh, the famous Zeb," Edward said, his voice a little uneasy. "They're there right now?"

"Yep."

"Ah. Well, just wanted to say hi. And to say I'm looking forward to the wedding tomorrow."

"Tomorrow," Rumer agreed. "Say hi to Blue for me."

"I will."

When she hung up, she started for the kitchen. Zeb was watching her, his eyes sharp as a hawk's. As she left the room, she heard Michael ask, "Who was that?"

"Your aunt's boyfriend," Sixtus answered. "One of these days he's going to ask her to marry him, and then I'll have to fend for myself. He's got a big, beautiful farm up the river, with horses and cows. She's scoffed at marriage this long, and she might be able to resist Edward, but the vet in her'll never be able to resist that farm and all those animals."

Michael laughed. Rumer tried to hear Zeb's response, but from him all she got was silence.

Michael liked them, and that surprised him. Not that his mother ever said anything really bad about her family, but she had given him the idea they were—watching his grandfather set up the grill, he tried to come up with the word. "Dull" just about covered it.

"They're nice, Michael," his mother would say when he used to ask if they could go east and visit. "Very nice, and I love them. But 'nice' isn't enough. I'd die if I ever had to live there."

"You'd die?" he'd asked, confused by the idea.

"Not literally. I mean it hurts to spend time with people whose idea of fun is watching the tide change. You know?"

Michael had guessed he knew, but now, hearing his grandfather swear as he struck match after match to get the grill going, he wasn't sure. The whole place intrigued him. A cool wind blew off the Atlantic, so Michael held his hands out to shelter the flame, helping his grandfather light the match. The old man nodded his thanks.

"So, how'd you get your name?" Michael asked. "Sixtus?"

"I'm a twin," he said, arranging tuna steaks on the grill. "And when I was born, the doctor suggested to my mother that she name us after the last two English kings. Instead, she named us after two popes—Sixtus and Clement." He slid a narrow gaze Michael's way. "You have to be Irish to really appreciate that story."

"Oh."

"Which you are—Irish. Your mother take you to church?"

"Um, no."

His grandfather frowned, sliding a spatula under the steaks and turning them. "She should," he said. "Or you should go on your own. Things matter in this world beyond good movie parts and palm trees, or whatever the draw is out there."

"You mean in California?"

"Yes. She knows better than to not send her son to church. She knows better than to do a lot of things." The old man looked up again, and this time his expression wasn't so much angry as sad. "She's kept her distance for a good long time now. Time was, your father was like a son to me. Knew him from the day he was born. I'm sorry they got divorced."

Michael felt a thud in his body down near his stomach. He never thought about the divorce anymore, and he didn't think anyone else did either. His parents tried to do the right thing. He lived with his mother, but his father stayed in touch from wherever he was. With her being on location, he spent a lot of his time alone. In some strange, mysterious way, it felt good to be talked to like this.

"Well, the important thing is, you're here now," his grandfather said.

"Yeah. Till September, when Dad has to get to the lab."

"When you should be starting school . . . except that you dropped out."

"Well," Michael said, not wanting to get into it.

"You don't have to tell me anything. I've known a lot of high school dropouts in my day, and I know the right thing always happens—if they're supposed to stay dropped out, they do. But your aunt Rumer . . ."

At her name, Michael looked through the kitchen door. He had expected to see his aunt and dad talking, just like him and his grandfather. But to his surprise, his aunt was alone in the kitchen, mixing up the salad dressing.

"Your aunt won't let it rest," Sixtus said. "I'm telling you. She'll be all over you like sand on wet feet. She wants you to finish high school."

At the sound of an outboard engine, Michael looked off the edge of the terrace, down the hill to the beach and the boat basin. There, in her old boat, was the salty girl. She must have left her pots at sea, because they were no longer in the boat. His grandfather saw him looking, and laughed as he shook his head.

"Oh, boy. That's all we need, is to have you and Quinn hook up."

"Quinn?"

"That delightful curmudgeonly young lady I see you observing there."

"I met her—well, kind of—before. When I took my walk. She was in some kind of bad mood."

"She's always in some kind of bad mood," his grandfather chuckled. "We love her for it—or through it. Allowances must be made for the people we love, Michael. You know?"

Michael was silent, thinking that over. He had learned that the opposite was true: in his house, when someone screwed up, they were either out the door or shut off.

"Why's she always in a bad mood?" Michael asked, to change the subject.

"Well, it's complicated. But she lost her parents in a boating accident, right out there—" he pointed across the beach to the Sound. "A few years ago now. She's getting better a little at a time. You never get over something like that, but she has a lot of people loving her, pulling her through."

Michael nodded. He felt empty without knowing why.

"Good thing the summer's young," his grandfather said. "Young for you, young for me."

"Do you have plans?" Michael asked, but his grandfather just smiled and shrugged.

Michael nodded. He thought of Blue, and he thought of Quinn. He thought of his mother and wondered why she never came back here. And he thought of his aunt, alone in the kitchen as she fixed their dinner, and his father . . . why wasn't his father in the kitchen, talking to her?

Because when Michael had gone to the terrace's edge and looked down at the beach, he'd seen his father standing alone in the living room, staring out the window—not up at the sky, as usual, but straight across at the dark green house next door.

The breeze was getting chillier by the minute, and clouds of mist were billowing out of the east, obscuring the hillside. Rabbits scurried for cover, hiding in the massive gray rocks. A shadow moved, disappearing into the trees. Michael shivered, looking down at the boats: Quinn had climbed onto the seawall, heading toward home.

With the weather turning so fast and everything mysteriously unsettled, Michael found himself feeling glad, unexpectedly relieved—in spite of her nasty attitude—that she was back from wherever she had gone at sea, safe and sound.

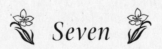 Seven

THE MORNING of the wedding, it poured rain. Quinn swore, feeling awful. The lobsters didn't respond to surface weather; they had to eat, and they came to the bait in her pots whether it was raining, snowing, or sunny. But for Aunt Dana's and Sam's sake, Quinn was upset. She had wanted this to be a perfect day for them.

She had gone out at five-thirty, before sunrise, to check her pots one last time. Pounding over pewter waves, she had gone from buoy to buoy, hauling lines and opening the pots with rain driving into her eyes. She had marked her school ruler at three and a quarter inches to measure the lobsters' carapaces and make sure they were all keepers. She threw back small ones and egg-bearing females. Even so, in this one run alone, she got twelve lobsters.

On her way back in, she swung left and headed toward the Wickland Shoal. Quinn's heart was wide open this wedding morning, and she had people she had to visit. Her first pass was by the lighthouse, where Elisabeth and Clarissa Randall had lived so long ago. She identified with the girl who had lost her mother so young, and she related to the woman who'd given up everything in search of adventure.

"That doesn't mean she didn't love you," Quinn said out loud to the ghost of the first Clarissa. "You know that, right?" And when she got to the spot where Joe Connor—Sam's famous treasure-hunting brother— had raised the *Cambria* a few years before, Quinn bowed her head to the love of Elisabeth Randall and Nathaniel Thorn and prayed that her aunt and Sam's would be just as intense but much more happy and lasting.

As a gray, rainy dawn spread westward from Block Island, the light-houses seemed less bright. Quinn glanced up, wishing there were a dawn star to wish on. Instead, knowing she had one more stop, she gunned her engine and sped out to the middle of the Sound.

This was her favorite place in the world. Although there were no markers, no graves, she knew it was the place of her parents' souls. Their boat, the *Sundance*, had sunk here six years ago. Quinn could see the spot from her bedroom window, on the hill at Hubbard's Point, but actually being here felt so different.

For two years after their death, Quinn had heard and glimpsed a mermaid. She knew it was odd, unusual, but she didn't care: It had been her mother staying close to make sure she, Allie, and Aunt Dana were okay.

Much longer ago, Rumer's mother had seen a unicorn, and Quinn remembered her telling her that at Hubbard's Point when it came to true love, the deepest kind, there was no such thing as magic: It was very, very real. Quinn had always believed the unicorn had been the spirit of Mrs. Larkin's own dead.

Scanning the Hunting Ground, Quinn looked for a sign. She wanted her mother to know that this was her sister's wedding day. Thinking of Allie, she tried to imagine how she'd feel if she had to miss seeing her get married.

"Hey, Mom!" Quinn said out loud. She looked for a splash, a rogue wave, the flash of a silver-blue tail, and the sea-silk of a mermaid's hair. Nothing. Perhaps she was now too old to see them. She had outgrown the need—something like that. But Quinn had come here for a reason, and no amount of rain could stop her.

Opening her sailing bag, she pulled out the bouquet of white flowers she'd picked that morning. She and Allie had been raiding Point gardens all week, gathering blooms for the wedding, but she didn't think Aunt Dana would mind that Quinn had saved a few for her mother.

"For you, Mom," Quinn called, spreading her mother's favorite white flowers on the gray waves. "So you know . . . so you're with us. Aunt Dana said you'd be her matron of honor if you were here . . . that Daddy would walk her down the aisle. . . ."

Her engine hummed steadily. Seagulls and terns wheeled overhead. In the distance, the Wickland Rock Light spread its beam one last time, then went off for the day. The land along the Connecticut shoreline was coming into view: Firefly Beach to the west, Hubbard's Point to the east. But there were no mermaids to be seen.

With one last glance at the path of white flowers, borne westward by the current, Quinn turned her boat around and headed back toward shore. She had lobsters to deliver; she was providing the wedding feast. As she approached the breakwater, she happened to glance up the hill, toward her house.

Two yards away, to the right, was Rumer's house. Movement caught her eye—for a second she was startled, remembering Mrs. Larkin's unicorn. But whatever it was disappeared into the fog. Thunder rumbled down the coast, and lightning flashed. Twisting the throttle, Quinn opened it up and headed into the shelter of home.

❧

"When it rains on a wedding day, the marriage will be happy and long," Sixtus Larkin said, standing under the tent in his morning coat.

"Marvelous," Augusta Renwick said, resplendent in lilac silk. She was Sam's brother's mother-in-law. Sam loved her; she treated him like a son. Her white hair was brushed and flowing, sprigged with actual lilacs. "Then Sam and Dana will be together till the end of time."

"This isn't rain—it's a biblical deluge," Annabelle McCray guffawed, her accent as southern as her picture hat. "I'm expecting a plague of locusts at any moment."

"The beauty, the absolute wealth of emotion, reminds me of the wedding scene in *The Marriage of Figaro*," Winnie Hubbard said, waving her arm as if to conjure the stage set at Milan's La Scala opera house. She wore Egyptian garb—an authentic burnoose, along with the Pharoah's Cat—in honor of the missing Elizabeth Randall, to please her son, Michael. A former opera star, she later helped to found a music school in Hartford. Although she taught only private students now, she retained her diva regality.

"Is there ever a time you simply live life?" Augusta asked. "And not relate it to some opera you were in once?"

"Rarely, darling," Winnie said, sipping champagne.

"Tell me about it," Annabelle said. "I'm her ever-loving neighbor. . . ."

"As am I," said Hecate Frost, dressed all in black as usual, her black cape lined with iridescent purple silk. "Winnie's singing is the music of our spirits. For better or worse, she sings the songs of our lives. My best visions come when she's singing arias from Puccini."

"Oh, gawd," Annabelle said. "Enough about your visions, Hecate. The children might believe you're a witch, but don't expect us to—"

"She *is* a witch," Winnie said, embracing Hecate, who had gone quite pale. "She and I were children here together, and she's had second sight since childhood. Annabelle, you're a newcomer."

"Second sight," Annabelle snorted.

"Only at Hubbard's Point would someone who's been here thirty-five years be considered a newcomer," Sixtus said, patting Annabelle on the back. "But that you are, Annie. A young newcomer, wet behind the years. You didn't grow up with Hecky's visions like Clarissa and Winnie. . . ."

Weddings made Sixtus uncomfortable. He couldn't help thinking of Zee's wedding day, of the cold, empty feeling he'd had in his chest. Walking out the door, on his way to the church, he had thought of Rumer, far-away at vet school, unwilling to come home.

His two daughters, closer than anything, torn apart by the boy next door. Sixtus had had moments of wanting to rip Zeb Mayhew apart—just to show him what it was like.

Sighing, Sixtus tried to focus on today's wedding instead of that old business. What was done was done. Elizabeth and Zeb were divorced now; Elizabeth had a very successful film career. Rumer was a vet—the best in town. There she was, across the crowd, laughing with Edward McCabe. Sixtus watched them for a moment, wondering whether Edward thought he was making her happy.

Rumer had learned to hide things very well. After all those years of wearing her heart on her sleeve for Zeb, she had figured out how to bury the real stuff quite deep. There it was: her radiant smile. No one could chase the dark clouds like Rumer when she turned it on. She wore a blue sleeveless dress, her mother's lighthouse pin near the collar. Her sun-lightened hair was prettily cut; it slanted against her fine cheekbones. Her brilliant laughter came floating across the crowd. Anyone would think she was having the time of her life.

The trick, Sixtus thought, was in noticing her eyes. His arthritis was hurting today, so he leaned on his cane, giving his aching bones a rest, watching his daughter. All of Rumer's secrets lived in her eyes. Her laughter, her smile, were just two parts of the story; the secret code, however, was in her gaze. His mysterious child . . .

Those blue eyes were quite anxious today, Sixtus thought. Surprisingly so, considering how many old friends were surrounding her. All her childhood buddies, her beach pals, her boyfriend the gentleman farmer, the Grayson kids she loved like nieces: all present. But now, watching Rumer's gaze slide slowly, surreptitiously, over Edward's left shoulder, Sixtus broke the code.

She was looking at Zeb.

He stood alone, sipping from a drink. With so many people he hadn't seen in all these years, what was he doing over there, by himself, in the corner?

Jesus, Sixtus thought: He's looking back at Rumer.

Rumer scowled and returned her attention to Edward. Zeb's eyes didn't waver. They didn't leave Rumer for one second.

"Oh, for Christ's sake," Sixtus said out loud, then limped over to the bar for a refill of his Jameson's. His knotted hands gripped the glass as his gaze slid down the yards to his boat on her cradle behind the garage.

Seeing the sailboat calmed the pounding of his heart. That was his lifeline, his hope, his guardian angel right now. Sailing on the *Clarissa,* Sixtus was pain free and moved as easily as a young man. Rumer didn't have to worry about him when he was on the water, sailing away. She could live her own life, pay attention to her own course instead of looking after her arthritic old father.

And God knew her life and course needed paying attention to.

"Another, please," Sixtus said to the young bartender, sliding his glass over.

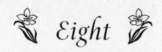

Eight

"HI, THERE."

Surprised, Rumer turned around. Zeb was standing there, tall and alert, almost aggressively smiling down at her and Edward. He wore a blue blazer and tie; even after all these years, it jarred to see him so dressed up here at the beach.

"Hello," Rumer said, her spine stiffening. Silence filled the air, stretching out like a tight rubber band.

"Aren't you going to introduce us?" Zeb asked.

Edward, always correct, stuck out his hand and shook Zeb's. "I'm Edward McCabe."

"Zebulon Mayhew."

"Ah . . ."

Rumer blushed, glancing up at Edward. Had he actually said that? From the satisfied look in Zeb's eyes, she could see that Edward indeed had, and that Zeb had picked up on it. Now Zeb would know that she'd talked about him.

"What's Rumer been saying about me?" Zeb asked, smiling ferociously.

Rumer nearly exploded—what a conceited jerk!

"What do you think, Mayhew?" she asked. "That I sit around telling everyone about your exploits in space? Or about our childhoods? They seem awfully long ago, don't they?"

"Not to me," Zeb said, grinning. "Being here at Hubbard's Point, I feel as if it was yesterday. You and me up on the roof, counting the shooting stars . . . that's what drove me to the space program. You know, Edward"—he smiled, tilting his head—"it's Edward, right? Not Ed . . ."

"It's Edward," Edward said.

"I'm sorry, *Edward*," Zeb said, smiling and sounding genuine. Still, Rumer's antennae were up, and her heart beat faster.

"All that early inspiration, hanging out with Rumer on the roof, made me realize that no career could keep me on earth. I was going to blast off as soon as I could. Honestly, I have Rumer to thank for that."

"Your future sister-in-law," Edward said, sliding his arm around Rumer's shoulders.

"Yep," Zeb said, sounding odd, but Rumer couldn't read his eyes.

Music had been playing, but suddenly it got louder. The wedding was about to start. Zeb's eyes held Rumer's. She had a crackling sensation in her chest, as if she'd just been struck by lightning. Edward squeezed her hand, holding her still. Very slowly, Zeb's gaze shifted toward Edward.

Zeb's fix on Edward had a definite tone, purpose—Rumer recognized it from the world of animals. She had last seen such intensity in the eyes of a bull mastiff staring through the bars at an injured ferret. The dog had the look of a hunter on the scent, of a wild animal who had spotted his prey.

Edward straightened his rep tie, adjusted the lapels of his blue blazer, and slid his arm back around Rumer's shoulders. She felt prickles on the nape of her neck, the way she had one time years ago, when doing research near Takkakaw Falls in British Columbia—turning around, she had spied a grizzly bear watching her from across the Yoho River.

The wedding music grew louder, but with Zeb standing right behind her, watching, Rumer could hardly hear it over her own heartbeat.

The wedding itself went off without a hitch. The girls, Quinn and Allie, walked their aunt from the house under a huge blue-and-white-striped umbrella to the tent. All three were barefoot; because the ground was so wet, it had already ruined the girls' shoes.

Dana's cream-colored gown glowed in the storm light. Winnie Hubbard whispered loudly that wedding planner May Cartier's work should be ensconced in the Costume Institute of the Metropolitan Museum of Art post haste. Sitting beside her, Zeb nodded gravely, trying to forget how Rumer was leaning her head against Edward's shoulder.

Look somewhere else, idiot, he told himself. *Like, watch the wedding*.

Sam and his best man—his brother, Joe—stood together at the makeshift altar. Sailing had brought Sam and Dana together, so the tent was decorated with bright spinnakers, signal flags, charts, and candles stuck in brass fittings. The flowers Quinn and Allie had picked from the yards on the Point were everywhere.

Rumer's arms were tan. Her sleeveless blue dress showed them off to really good advantage—her shoulders looked strong but slim. Zeb noticed her toned biceps, the thin silver bracelet she wore on her left wrist. *Doing it again*, he realized, forcing himself to pay attention to the nuptials.

Reverend Peter Goodspeed took his place at the altar. He was married to Clea Renwick, Augusta's middle daughter and already practically family to Sam. Sam, grinning, greeted his bride and her daughters. He took a vow to love and protect Quinn and Allie until the day he died, and when Peter then asked "Who gives this woman in matrimony?" the two girls, Quinn and Allie, spoke up solemnly, as if it were the question of their lifetime: "We do!"

Zeb tried to listen. There was a reading from *A Gift from the Sea*: "When you love someone, you don't love them the same way all the time. . . ." The language was beautiful; it rolled over and past Zeb, who hardly heard it at all.

He remembered his own wedding, where Zee—onstage, as if the wedding were her biggest role—had recited lines written for her by a young and brilliant playwright. Although she had not cried, Zeb had felt the tears welling up, his heart pounding out of his chest, knowing that the words were supposed to be about love and realizing at that moment that he didn't love the woman he was saying them to.

Glancing over now, Rumer saw him watching her and scowled. He felt a trembling inside, as if Hubbard's Point had just experienced a small earthquake. In spite of himself, he smiled. In fact, the deeper her scowl became, the more intense the quake felt.

The scowl increased, and she looked away. Edward seemed to have gotten the picture. He looked at Rumer and saw the tears. Then he glanced over at Zeb, alarm written on his patrician face. Reaching into his pocket, he removed a white square—a linen handkerchief that Zeb had no doubt was monogrammed, hand-stitched, and slightly starched—and dabbed at her eyes.

Rumer nodded her thanks, took the handkerchief out of his hand, and gave her nose a loud blow. Half the people at the wedding jumped. Edward, looking dismayed, leaned away from her.

Zeb just watched her, grinning.

Rumer held Edward's soaking wet handkerchief, wadded up in her right hand. She wished it were a rock; she'd throw it at Zeb's head. What was he thinking, baiting her from across the crowd?

She had just been having a moment: a sentimental summer wedding, gathered-together moment. Then she'd caught Zeb staring at her—grinning!—ruining the whole thing.

The music was beautiful: Kate Wolf's "Give Yourself to Love," and Bonnie Raitt's "Feels Like Home." Reverend Goodspeed nodded to the girls, who picked up white wicker baskets filled with rose petals and passed them around the congregation.

"Each of you take a handful," the minister directed. "Hold them over your heart and imbue them with your blessings and good wishes.

"Right offshore here," Reverend Goodspeed continued, "within sight of this very tent—two shipwrecks. Beautiful people who meant very, very much to the celebrants here today. Elisabeth Randall and Nathaniel Thorn, Mark and Lily Grayson . . ."

Zeb heard Quinn take a big breath, saw Allie slide her hand into her sister's and squeeze tight. "Those good people hit a storm—it might have been a clear night, there might have been moonlight, but they hit the biggest storm of their lives." Zeb's stomach dropped, thinking of his last flight, and again his gaze swept over to Rumer.

"We all reach that point," Reverend Goodspeed said. "And what I want to say . . ." He slid a gaze at Quinn, and she gave him a big smile and nodded.

"What I want to say," he continued, "is that I encourage you to love as if you're riding through the storm of the century. You surf the waves, ride the crests, sail through moonlit waters with ice in your rigging . . . but you love each other as you go. You love each other as if every day is the only day. . . ."

Reverend Goodspeed smiled, nodding to Sam and Dana as they slid the rings onto each other's fingers. "And so . . . by the power vested in me, I now pronounce you husband and wife. You may kiss the bride."

And their friends, neighbors, relatives, and children threw the rose petals they had blessed with their hearts, showering the newly married couple with all the love Hubbard's Point had to offer.

Edward leaned down, gave Rumer a soft kiss on her lips.

A cool breeze touched the back of her neck, and she knew someone else was watching her.

"Good wedding," Quinn said, standing by the buffet table to make sure everyone got enough lobster.

"Except for the shipwreck part," Michael said, eating shrimp from a giant clamshell.

"What do you mean?"

"Mentioning wrecks at a wedding, when we all know the odds are in favor of divorce."

"Not my aunt and Sam," Quinn said. "Besides, weren't you listening? The reverend was talking about storms, not really shipwrecks. He said storms are good—they hold a lot of love and passion."

"Oh. Okay," Michael said.

"You patronizing me?"

"Just this," Michael said. "What do you think you know about love and passion? No offense, but the Connecticut suburbs aren't known for that kind—"

"You are so pathetic," she said. "Hubbard's Point isn't the 'Connecticut suburbs.' It's magical here. Think I'm kidding? I'm not. We have ghosts, mermaids, unicorns . . ." At the sight of his expression, she nodded. "You've seen something, haven't you?"

"No."

"Yep, you have. You're not sure, and you don't want to sound stupid, so you won't ask. But you've had a visitation. . . ."

Staring up at him, Quinn felt her heart beating in a funny way. He had washed and brushed his long hair; it looked handsome and soft. His eyes were dark green—the color of Winnie's cove, lined with rocks and seaweed.

"What did you see?" she asked, the words jumping out before she could stop them.

"A shadow, that's all," he said. "It was in the side yard . . . something in the fog. Or maybe just the fog itself."

"This is Hubbard's Point, Michael. It wasn't just the fog."

As he turned away to get some more shrimp, Quinn realized that was the first time she'd said his name. Michael. It felt hard in the middle, gentle at the end. It made her think of a stone wall, flowing over hills and meadows, through woods, keeping things in, keeping things out, moss-covered rocks of granite piled on top of each other, solid in one way, fluid in another . . . for some reason, his name made her think of a stone wall.

Rumer and Edward leaned against the tent pole, watching Winnie prepare to sing. Quinn and Allie had hung garlands of flowers overhead, and they'd made wind chimes from shells and driftwood gathered from the tidal pools. Wind and the sound of crashing waves filled the tent with sea music.

"You seem awfully uncomfortable," Edward said.

"No, I'm fine."

"It's having Zeb here, isn't it?"

"Forget Zeb," she said. "Let's just enjoy the wedding."

"Your father doesn't seem very friendly today," he said.

"Oh, he's just thrilled to be the center of all those women. They love him."

Edward nodded, satisfied. "Would you like something from the bar?" he asked. "I think I'll get a refill."

"I'm okay," Rumer said, tapping her glass.

The minute he walked away, Zeb came over to stand with her. Heat spread from her chest up her neck, into her face, and suddenly the glass felt awkward in her hands.

"Here we are," Zeb said.

"What a brilliant observation," she said.

"Do you think so?" he asked. "See, to me, it's no mean feat—being here."

"You mean because you're such a renowned intergalactic traveler?"

"No," he said quietly. "I mean, instead of *here*, per se, we could—for example—be in a black hole. You know about those?"

"Only from what I read," she said.

"Yeah, well, I've been in one," he said, looking up at the sky. "It's not fun, let me tell you."

"No?" she asked, watching Edward at the bar.

"Nah. It's a collapsed star, for one thing. Who'd want to be in a collapsed star? Its gravity is so intense, even light can't escape. We're talking a cosmic tornado, if you want the truth—a ferocious, spinning, churning storm of star particles—swirling at one point two million miles an hour."

"And you were in one?" she asked skeptically.

"Yep."

"Then how'd you escape?"

"Good question," he said, clinking his glass with hers. "I'll tell you next time we talk. It'll be like the next episode—you won't be able to wait to find out, so you'll come over for dinner tomorrow night and I'll tell you."

"Think again," she said.

"Oh, because you'll be fine-dining, or whatever, with your prep-school Ivy League friend?"

"What do you call him that for? You went to Columbia."

"Yeah, but I don't wear it on my sleeve. That guy is so patrician, his face is about to crack. Where'd he get that lockjaw thing? Come on, Rumer—you never liked pretentious people like that."

"He's wonderful," Rumer said, staring Zeb straight in the eyes. "He cares about me, and I care about him. I keep my horse at his farm. We're dear friends going through life together—" She swallowed, seeing Edward talking to Annabelle.

"Then why aren't you married to him?"

"Maybe I don't believe in marriage," she said. "Look at you and my sister."

"We're not the best examples of the institution," Zeb agreed.

Rumer breathed out slowly. She watched Edward politely asking Annabelle what she wanted to drink, relaying the request to the bartender. Annabelle, enjoying the attention, touched Edward's arm and laughed. The sight of him brought Rumer peace of mind and heartsease. But when she turned back to Zeb, all her serenity fled.

He took a step closer. Their bodies were nearly touching. She could see his chest rising and falling, as if he were breathing a little too hard. She felt trapped in her head, unable to put words together.

The irony was, when they were young, they had never had anything like this between them. Their bodies had moved in unison: swimming, biking, climbing trees. Words had flowed and flowed; they'd told each other everything. Finally Rumer glanced up at him—he was wearing a navy blue suit and a dark tie with white dots on it. On closer inspection, the dots were the phases of the moon.

"Can't take you out of the sky for long," she said cautiously.

He laughed, obviously relieved that she had broken the silence, brushing the tie with his hand. "A birthday present from Michael," he said.

"That's interesting," Rumer said. "It means he came around."

"In what way?"

"Well, when he was little, he didn't want to acknowledge that the moon existed. He didn't want you to go up there. I remember sitting with him on the rocks, on the darkest nights, and him crying because the sky was so far away. He couldn't bear thinking of you flying away from earth, getting lost in the sky."

"Now he wishes I'd go up there and stay," Zeb said.

"Not that I know anything about kids, but in my father's book, he says something about that being par for the course."

"Sixtus wrote a book?"

Rumer nodded proudly. "He doesn't call it that—he'd say it's a bunch of pages stapled together—but yes, it's a book. Not published or anything . . . the teachers passed it around. When I started teaching my vet course, I had about twenty copies made. They flew out of the faculty room."

"I'll have to see that," Zeb said, gazing across the tent at Sixtus in his morning coat, tall and hunched, surrounded by Michael, Quinn, Allie, and the McCray kids. "Maybe he's going away to write another one. To a desert island somewhere—or a cabin in Maine. That would explain it."

"Explain what?" Rumer asked.

"The getaway look in his eyes. He's on his way somewhere. . . ."

Frowning, Rumer looked over at her father. The pain from his arthritis was quite bad this year, and he hardly ever went anywhere.

"All he seems to want to do is stay home and work on his boat," she said. "He's been sanding and painting all month. I think maybe he wants to sail in the Classic Boat Parade in July," she said.

"Maybe that's it," Zeb said.

Rumer tried to let herself relax. She remembered their friendship had been deep and long, and they were standing in the place it had been born: at Hubbard's Point. The memory made her miss it all the more. Her heart was racing so fast, she wondered whether he could feel the air moving two feet away.

"You're wearing your pin," he said.

Rumer glanced down, touching the pin her parents had given her for her middle school graduation. They had had two made of gold, replicas of the Wickland Rock Light, for her and Elizabeth.

Their mother had told them the pins were slightly different—the girls had never been able to find the distinction. They had examined them under magnifying glasses, in bright light—nothing. They had counted the steps, the bricks, and the panels in the Fresnel lens. It had delighted their mother to see them so entranced; no amount of begging could ever convince her to reveal the difference.

"What do you want from me?" she asked after a moment.

"You should know," he said huskily. They were standing close. The wind was steady, and a section of Rumer's hair blew into her eyes. Very tenderly, Zeb reached over, as if it were the most natural thing in the world, and tucked the hair behind her ear. His touch sent shivers down her neck, and she pulled away.

"What?"

"To be your friend again."

She felt a freight train in her chest, plowing down the tracks. Still trembling from where he had touched her neck, she wanted to punch him, knock him back, and show him how crazy he was.

"That's impossible now," she said. "And you should know it."

"We grew up together," he said. "We know all each other's old secrets."

"There are new ones, Zeb. The old ones don't matter anymore."

Edward had spotted them talking. He froze, holding his drink and Annabelle's in his hands. Rumer's heart fell at his expression. He actually looked stricken, as if he'd caught Rumer betraying him. She smiled, gesturing him over. She couldn't wait to reassure him that he had nothing to worry about. Her smile faltered, but she kept beckoning.

"You're wrong, Rue," Zeb said quietly. "The old ones matter more than anything."

"If that were true," she said, struggling to keep her voice steady, "you had a funny way of showing it."

"I was young and stupid," he said.

The words kicked her in the chest. What was the point of him telling her this now? Glancing across the tent, she saw Michael talking to Quinn. He was tall and handsome, with a combination Elizabeth and Zeb in everything about him.

"I made a huge mistake."

"No, you didn't," Rumer said, staring at his son.

"Rumer," Zeb said, sounding insistent, and when Rumer glanced up, she saw Edward coming quickly across the floor.

"You did what you wanted to," Rumer said, "and it ripped our families apart. You and I were the least of it; I lost my sister too."

"We *weren't* the least of it," Zeb said quietly. "Not by a long shot."

But then as Edward joined them, Winnie took the stage, and a great round of applause rose from the crowd. She bowed, taking the accolade as her due. The orchestra began to play, and over the growing roar of wind, Winnie started to sing.

The clear, pure notes of "Cara di Amore" poured forth. They mingled with the wind, with the waves crashing on the beach and rocks. The storm was gathering force—the wind battered the tent flaps, and everyone huddled together as if to keep from being blown away. Edward took her hand and held it tight. Rumer wondered whether he could feel her trembling.

Rumer let the music wash over her—Winnie's voice, the wind, trying to push Zeb's last words out of her mind.

As soon as the singing was done, she found Dana and hugged her, saying she hoped she, Sam, and the girls would be happy forever.

Then, her heart pounding, she grabbed Edward's hand.

"Come on," she said. "I'd like to go. . . ."

"Where?"

"To the farm."

He laughed. "You have a sudden, undeniable urge to see Blue and a barnful of wild cats?"

"No, Edward," she whispered, throwing her arms around his neck. "I want to see you. . . . I want to be with you."

They didn't even take time to say good-bye. Rumer saw Dana watch her run down the hill through the rain; she gestured with her bouquet.

Rumer waved back, one hand on her heart to let Dana know how much she appreciated the thought. Dana wound up, signaling that her aim was good, that if Rumer stayed, she'd be sure to catch the bouquet. As Edward turned his Mercedes around in the cul-de-sac, Rumer blew kisses to Dana and noticed Zeb watching them leave.

"Such a lovely ceremony," Edward said. "I saw May's Bridal Barn touch in so many things. The gown, the floral pieces, the candles . . . did I ever tell you that my mother was one of Emily Dunne's earliest customers? She used to recommend her to many of her old friends from Pittsburgh."

"Uh-huh," Rumer said, reaching across the seat to caress the back of Edward's head.

"Sam must be a good man to take on raising Dana's two nieces. . . ."

"He certainly is," Rumer said, hiking over to kiss his ear.

"Luckily, they all seem to get along."

"Edward," Rumer said, loosening his tie and unbuttoning the top button of his British-made shirt. "Haven't you noticed that I'm seducing you?"

"I have, my dear," he said. "It's all I can do to keep my eyes on the road."

"Then let's not talk about Dana and Sam anymore, okay?"

"Okay," he said, gripping the steering wheel with both hands and letting her slowly and softly unbutton the rest of his shirt.

When they reached the farm, Edward dropped her at the side door of the house. She let herself into the kitchen, and she watched from the window as he opened the barn door, drove the dark green Mercedes inside, and sponged some mud from the door panels. Then he walked into the cow barn, checked the livestock, and turned the overhead light on to chase the rainy day's darkness.

Orazio, the old sheepdog, lay in the corner on the stone floor. Rumer crouched down to scratch his ears. He had an eye infection from where he'd gotten clawed by one of the cats. She went to the cupboard, found the ointment she had prescribed, and applied it.

When Edward came in, standing on the mat to brush the mud off his feet, Rumer felt her heart skip. She focused on Orazio, to buy a little time. Edward seemed to want to do the same; he washed his hands at the sink, hung his jacket in the closet, and turned on the classical music radio station.

Still kneeling by the dog, Rumer felt his hands on her shoulders.

Now, turning, she leaned into his arms. Her heart was pounding so hard, she thought he must be able to feel the velocity through her dress. He traced her shoulder blades with his fingers, then leaned down to kiss her lips. Their mouths were open slightly, shyly exploring each other with their tongues.

"Will you tell me something?" he asked, stopping after a moment.

"Of course. . . ."

"What's the reason for this?"

"The reason?" she asked.

"Yes. We've been . . . together, I guess you could say . . . for a long time. We've gone out to dinner, to parties with each other, and you've never wanted to come home with me before."

"We were always with other people. Either you were just getting over someone, or I was," she said, her heart aching, feeling bands around her chest. The tightness was so constricting, squeezing her heart. She wanted to break free, get rid of the pain, stop feeling this way.

"Are you sure that's not what's happening now?" he asked.

Her heart lurched, but she shook her head. "No, Edward. It's only you. The storm got me churned up, feeling this way. . . ."

"And weddings are so romantic," he said, interlacing his fingers with hers. Now, pulling her close again, he kissed her lips. Together they walked to the stairs.

Ascending, she noticed that the walls held family pictures. The treads were covered with needlepointed panels—so delicate, she almost didn't want to step on them.

"Mother did those," he said, pointing down. "Of the wildflowers on the farm."

Rumer nodded. Her mouth was dry. She had the urge to stop in her tracks, turn around, run downstairs and out the door. But Edward was right behind her, his breath in her ear, his hand on the small of her back. She had started this; *it's for a reason*, she told herself.

His bedroom was in the front of the house, overlooking the country road and the meadows to the east. Rumer skirted the iron bedstead, looking at the books in the glass-front mahogany bookcase, the watercolors of the red barn hanging on the wall, some sepia-toned portraits in silver frames propped on the dresser, a lace bureau scarf covering its highly polished surface.

"My sanctuary," Edward said proudly, looking around.

"It's lovely," she said, her heart catching at the word, but even more at his vulnerability—everything here was so pristine and proper, just like Edward himself. She took his hand, walking over to the bed, covered with a white and blue quilt.

They began to kiss, lying down on the bed, fumbling with each other's clothes. Rumer's eyes were shut so tight, she felt tears squeezing out from behind the lids. She had an engine inside her chest; it had been running full blast for the last twenty-four hours. If Edward hadn't been her date, would she have grabbed a stranger—some scientist from Yale— from the crowd at the wedding? Pushing the horrible thought from her mind, she kissed his neck.

"You're so dear to me," he whispered with great propriety, as if they were having tea.

"Edward . . ." His name ripped from her throat, and she rolled over.

Crying, she pulled away. Edward put out a hand to touch her—to soothe her, maybe. But Rumer was in a frenzy, wanting something she couldn't name, wrestling with angels she had known forever. Edward was here, he was safe, and as much as she wanted to be made love to right now, she knew that it had absolutely nothing to do with him.

"I'm so sorry," she said, backing away, tears blurring her vision.

"It's okay," he said, of course being gallant, letting her off the hook. "This isn't the right time. . . ."

It wasn't, Rumer knew, the realization coming over her: It wasn't now, and it never would be.

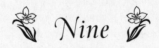 *Nine*

"IT WAS A good wedding," Sixtus said on Monday morning, leaning on his graceful old boat and accepting the mug of coffee from Rumer. She had been so rattled by those moments with Zeb at the wedding and what had almost happened with Edward that she had spent Sunday alone, walking the beaches.

Now, on her way to the office—she had two spayings scheduled for that morning—she had a few extra minutes to have coffee and catch up with her father. Later, she would go to the farm with a peace offering: She had filled a bag with lily shoots she wanted to plant along Edward's wall.

"You disappeared pretty quickly," her father said, flexing his hands. "I've barely seen you since—"

"Mmm. How are you feeling this morning, Dad? How's the pain?"

"Pain's fine," he grumbled. "You and Edward hightailed it away from the wedding as if you'd a mind to elope yourselves. That's what I said to myself. . . ."

"That's not what happened," Rumer said. "I spent yesterday alone."

"Good," her father said, "because—"

Rumer shot him a warning look, and he stopped. "Ahh," he said. "Why don't we stay on safer subjects than my daughter's happiness, now and in the future? Like Dana's wedding . . ."

Although early, the day was already hot. Locusts sang in the trees, and haze hung in the rosebushes. Rumer had booked a chimney sweep—for their house and Edward's—and he had arrived first thing to clean their flue after a long winter's use. They could hear him whistling on the roof. It sounded joyful, a harbinger of summer, and Rumer's heart was in sore need of lifting.

"It was a beautiful wedding," Rumer said quietly.

"So beautiful it drove you into solitude," her father grumbled, switching gears when he saw by her expression that he was going too far. "Winnie hit her famous high note. Eighty-two, and still singing like Maria Callas. Every time she does it, I think she's going to shatter every window at the Point."

"That and the high wind."

"Winnie beats high winds every time."

"The kids were amazed," Rumer said, glad of the small talk. "Right at the end, I happened to look over at Michael, and his mouth was wide open."

Her father chuckled. "Takes a lot to amaze him," he said.

"I know, after seeing his mother in the movies," Rumer said. "And getting calls from his dad on the space station." Just referring to Zeb made her remember how he'd brushed the hair out of her eyes at the wedding. She shook it from her mind. "Michael's had such an exciting life."

"And you haven't?" her father asked gently.

"Sure I have. College, vet school, interning and treating animals in Appalachia and the Rockies, setting up my practice and doing what I love in my favorite place on earth . . ."

"That is an amazing gift, Rumer. To do what you love. Do you know how rare that is? It takes a person of great integrity and strength to discover the right path in life and not to be lured off it. Not to settle for less than they want or deserve."

"Do you think I've done that?"

"Every day of your life. In all ways but one."

Rumer winced. Her father opened his mouth to continue, but then caught the raw look in her eye and hesitated for just a second.

"Perhaps Michael will turn out to be a true Point boy," Rumer said, taking a sip of coffee, watching two white Long Island ferries crossing paths far out in the Sound.

"We'll have the summer to see. That's how long they'll be here," Sixtus said.

Rumer sipped her coffee. The caffeine delivered a punch, and her pulse was racing again. An entire summer of avoiding Zeb. Her mind flipped to Edward, but instead of the familiar ease of mind that came from thinking of him up there in the hazy hills of Black Hall, she felt a jolt of shame about her behavior.

"All I can think about is how short summer is—just one hundred days—and how much there is to accomplish," her father said.

"It's summer, Dad," Rumer said, laughing. "Isn't summer about what there's *not* to accomplish?"

"We'll see. . . ."

The sun had risen over the eastern bay, shining hotly through the white pines and oak trees. Sixtus set down his coffee mug and picked up his paintbrush. Squinting in the bright sunshine, Rumer checked her watch and then looked up. The chimney sweep had arrayed his brushes on the roof; they looked like a line of bristly crows.

"You must be almost finished teaching your vet class—in the home stretch," her father said. "These last days of school were always my favorite. Launching a new group of seniors . . . has Edward chosen the recipient of his mother's scholarship yet?"

"Dorothy Jackson," Rumer said.

"She must like cows," he chuckled.

"What are you getting at, Dad?" she asked.

"Absolutely nothing, darling. Cows are lovely animals; chickens superlative birds. But over the years, Edward has proven himself rather single-minded, hasn't he? He only chooses applicants with a bovine bent— grow up on a farm, want to be a farmer, or hit the road. . . ."

"His mother wanted to preserve Black Hall's agrarian heritage," Rumer said. "All those beautiful farms are disappearing so fast . . . they're being subdivided, sold off into little lots. We take them for granted—even the Black Hall Impressionists all used to go up there to paint. They're part of us all. . . ."

"I don't deny that," he said. "Not at all. Just that . . . farms are Edward's passion, not yours. Maybe it's time for him to administer his mother's scholarship on his own."

"You don't like him, do you?"

"If you loved him, it would be different. But I think you should get on with your life," her father said. "And be happy."

Rumer blinked, stung. Happy . . . she had always wanted that, and she had always wanted to be loved. "I'm not sure it's for you to say how that should work for me," she said.

"No, I'm just your father," he said. "I only know you better than anyone else in the world."

Rumer stood there, feeling unsteady. Just then they heard a car engine. Cresthill Road was a dead end, and quiet at this time of day. Most residents rode their bikes or walked up to the post office for the mail and newspapers. Turning their heads, Rumer and her father saw a large Jaguar slide into sight. It parked at the foot of the hill of the Mayhews' old house, and two people got out.

"The new owners?" Rumer asked.

Her father nodded, not speaking.

They watched as the couple—perhaps in their early forties, both tan and blond—climbed out of the car and began to walk up the crumbling stone steps.

"It's welcome time," her father said. Laying down his painting things, he wiped his hands on his khakis and led the way. He and Rumer walked through their yard, under the bramble-laden archway, past the stone angel, into the Mayhews' old yard. Two rabbits, including the recently released one, grazed as they approached.

"Hello there," Sixtus called, and the rabbits bolted into their hole under the azalea bush. "Welcome!"

The couple stopped, startled. Rumer noticed the man's polo shirt and cleanly pressed chinos, his hair slicked back in the Wall Street look of a few years back. His wife was expensively coiffed and clad. She wore a large diamond ring. Without knowing quite why, Rumer's heart sank a little.

"I'm Sixtus Larkin, your neighbor," her father said. "And this is my daughter, Dr. Rumer Larkin."

"Hello," the man said. "I'm Tad Franklin. My wife, Vanessa."

"Very nice to meet you. We're happy to know you!"

"You're a doctor?" he asked.

"A vet," she said.

"Oh," he said, dismissing her. Rumer got that sometimes from people who didn't have pets, didn't love animals, who thought that veterinarians were somehow not real doctors.

Rumer smiled, shaking the couple's hands, wondering why they were looking over her head instead of into her eyes. "Welcome to the Point."

"The Point's quite a place," her father chuckled. "As I'm sure you already know. If you ever have any questions, or if there's anything we can do to help you find your way, just give a holler. We don't stand much on ceremony around here. If you see an open window, just call in!"

"What kind of work are you doing on your house?" Tad Franklin asked, squinting as he pointed up on the roof.

"Work?" Sixtus asked.

"Improvements," Vanessa said, gesturing at the varnish on Sixtus's hands.

"Oh, this?" He laughed. "I'm getting the boat ready to go in the water. That's all. Happens every year. And up there"—he gestured up at the roof—"that's Tim Hanson, the best chimney sweep around. I recommend him highly."

"Why do you ask?" Rumer heard herself saying. "About improvements?"

"Well, we're planning some ourselves," Tad said. "Naturally."

"Naturally?" Rumer asked, her heart sinking a little more, wondering what there was to improve.

Now the Franklins fell silent. Perhaps they had just decided Rumer and Sixtus were nosy neighbors and they wanted to keep their plans to themselves. Rumer could even understand—sort of. She felt absurdly proprietary about the land; she had grown up here, and every ounce of love she had had sprung from the soil. What kind of "improvements" could they possibly make anyway? A new deck, maybe. Or perhaps they—after all these years—would change the color. Paint it white or gray, instead of dark green.

Taking their cue, she and her father shook the Franklins' hands once again, wishing them well. Then, limping through the tall grass into their own yard, Sixtus led Rumer back toward the old boat.

"That Jaguar's not a good sign," her father said in a low voice.

"Why not?" she asked, intuitively agreeing with him.

"They have a lot of money to spend on 'improvements.' "

"But let's hope they don't see a lot to improve," she said, kissing her father good-bye for the day, trying to push aside how upset he'd made her by his comments about Edward.

Zeb sat at his makeshift desk, surrounded by satellite photographs, documents, charts, and books. Although this trip to Hubbard's Point was supposed to be a vacation, he had set himself the large task of organizing his last ten missions. NASA was giving him a great opportunity: After all his years of service in the sky, they were letting him establish his own department at the newest research center in California, between Scripps and Caltech. The least he could do was show up prepared.

His mind wouldn't cooperate. Concentrate, he told himself. The words ran together; the photos looked like Rorschach ink blots.

Let's see, he thought, staring at ink blot number one.

Right there in the satellite photo, an image of Rumer materialized. Rumer at the wedding in her sleeveless blue dress, her arms taut and tan. Now other images came through: the way she had cried during the vows, the defiance in her eyes as she'd driven off with her stuffed-shirt boyfriend.

"What a jerk," Zeb said out loud as ink blot number two revealed the man's smug smile.

He worked for a few hours, taking calls from people on his staff. One reported a problem with the lenses of his new telescope, and Zeb spent twenty minutes on the phone with the manufacturer in Switzerland. What the hell was he doing? He felt so detached from the new observatory, his great new lab. He got so frustrated, he almost pulled the phone out of the wall.

Trying to direct this operation from so far away was crazy—and why was he here anyway? That was the real question. Work had always served him well. It was his personal life that dragged him down. Rumer obviously wanted nothing to do with him. Maybe he could leave Michael here with Rumer and Sixtus, and he could get straight to work. So what if he was a burned-out refugee from the astronaut corps? The observatory would welcome him with open arms. His life would be a lot less complicated that way.

A knock startled him. Michael had gone out somewhere—had he forgotten they didn't need a key here at the Point? Crossing the room, he opened the door. Sixtus stood there wearing his paint clothes, stooped over, smelling of varnish. Cradled in his arms was a big pineapple.

"Here," Sixtus said, thrusting the pineapple into Zeb's hands.

"What's this for?"

"It's a symbol of welcome. Perhaps you've forgotten. All the seafarers in Clarissa's family used to bring pineapples home from the South Seas, and their wives would stick them over the front doors as a sign they'd returned safely, that friends were welcome to stop by."

"I remember," Zeb said stiffly. "I thought you said welcome at dinner the other night."

"That was just for Rumer and Michael. This is between us. I figured we have some stuff we need to get straight."

"Come on in," Zeb said, standing aside. His ex–father-in-law limped past, straight out to the screened porch. After a lifetime of living here, he knew this cottage—like every other one on the Point—as if it were his own. Wincing as he settled into the wicker rocker, he let out a sigh.

"You okay, Sixtus?" Zeb sank into a chair next to him.

"Goddamn arthritis," he said. "Used to be fine on summer days; now it's there all the time."

"I'm sorry. That must be tough."

"Tough on Rumer." Sixtus scowled. "She does too much as it is; next thing, she'll be helping me tie my shoes."

"I'm sure she wouldn't mind," Zeb said.

But Sixtus's scowl just deepened as he stared at the twisted hands in his lap. Then, lifting his eyes, he gazed at the bay.

"There's Quinn, pulling her pots," Sixtus said, watching the small lobster boat go from buoy to buoy. The young girl was expert at her job: She'd hook the buoy, haul the line, check the pot, throw back the small ones, bucket the keepers, and move on. Zeb and Sixtus watched as if it were a ballet being put on for their enjoyment. After a moment, Zeb's gaze drifted to the rocks, where he saw Michael sitting still, watching as well.

"What can I do for you?" Zeb asked.

Sixtus rocked slowly for another minute, in no hurry to answer. When he did, he looked Zeb straight in the eye.

"What are you doing here?" Sixtus asked.

"We came for Dana's wedding."

"Bullshit," Sixtus said. "No offense, but bullshit. Dana Underhill's not the first Point friend to get married. You and Elizabeth were invited to Lily Underhill's wedding, and you didn't come—didn't come to her funeral either. You didn't come to Halsey's wedding, or Paul's, or Marnie's. So what brings you back now?"

"Time for a vacation, Sixtus," Zeb said. "Everyone needs a break sometime."

"Too bad you couldn't have taken one while you were still married to Elizabeth."

"You think that would have saved our marriage?" Zeb asked. "Me taking more vacations?"

"Might have helped. Couldn't have hurt. Every time I talked to her, it sounded like you'd rather be up in the stars than home with her and Michael."

"I never wanted to go away from Michael," Zeb said. "I signed on as a mission specialist, I had to do what they told me. That was my job."

Had Sixtus noticed the omission? If so, he didn't let on.

"Being away was just a condition of the operation, Sixtus. You don't just call from the space station and say you want to get off."

"What were you doing there in the first place? You weren't at NASA to be an astronaut—you were a specialist in interpreting satellite photos. At least that's what you told Elizabeth."

"Circumstances change. People change, Sixtus," Zeb said, not wanting to blurt out that he'd gone in part to get away from the man's daughter. "Did you think I'd say no when they offered me the chance to fly?"

"Maybe you should've."

"The marriage was in trouble before—"

Sixtus didn't speak, but his lips tightened. Zeb knew this was rough territory for the old man, and he regretted saying anything. At least he'd held back from saying "It was in trouble before it started." Everyone knew that.

"Look," Zeb said, wanting to make peace. "You know I grew up wanting to be an astronaut, right? You must know that—your daughters teased me about it constantly."

"Yeah. Astro-Boy, they called you."

"Rumer anyway. You want to hear this, Sixtus? I don't want to bore you, but maybe it'll help us get past you thinking I ran away from Elizabeth."

"It's not boring me, Zeb. Go on," Sixtus growled.

Zeb closed his eyes and thought back many years. He remembered how Guy Chamberlain, his NASA guru and one of the first space pilots to focus America's vision on the stars, had changed his life. "Well, I applied to the agency, and they hired me. I thought that was enough of a dream—I traded in wanting to be an astronaut and got practical. . . ."

"The satellite photography."

"Right. And then, one day, this old astronaut—Guy—told me, 'Zeb, anyone who wants a reason to go into space can find one. That's what the station's for: missions. Ecologists, oceanographers, even economists go up.' "

"Economists?" Sixtus snorted with disbelief.

"Sure. They study the western plains—the production of grain—to forecast for the Chicago grain and corn futures markets."

"They could do it just as well from solid ground."

"Maybe so, but they want to see firsthand. And so did I," Zeb said, his defenses rising.

Zeb had been among the eight groups of pilots and mission specialists added to NASA since 1979—his class of fifteen had joined in 1987. With his better than 20/20 vision, his 140/90 blood pressure, and his height falling just under six feet, he was an acceptable candidate.

He joined other civilians as well as military applicants to the Astronaut Candidate Program. Classes at the Johnson Space Center in Houston included shuttle systems, basic science and technology, math, geology, meteorology, guidance and navigation, oceanography, orbital dynamics, physics, sea survival, scuba diving, space suits, and his beloved astronomy.

Completing military water survival, he became scuba qualified in preparation for extravehicular training. He had to swim three lengths of a twenty-five-meter pool in flight suit and tennis shoes. His instructors exposed him to problems associated with high—hyperbaric—and low—hypobaric—atmospheric pressures in altitude chambers. In a modified KC-135 aircraft, he experienced periods of weightlessness and was exposed to the microgravity of space flight.

He had formal training in the SST—single systems trainer. He worked on all areas of shuttle operations: prelaunch, ascent, orbit, entry, and landing. He became proficient in payload operation, deployment, retrieval, maneuvers, and rendezvous. Zeb Mayhew was making his dreams come true. He was becoming an astronaut. He told all this to Sixtus, still loving to tell the story. He had loved space; he had once loved his work. When he was finished, he leaned back, looking Sixtus in the eye.

"Nice story," Sixtus said. "You're well trained."

"It might not mean anything to you, but it does to me."

"So, what you're saying is, you weren't trying to escape her? It just came with the territory?"

"Elizabeth?"

"Yes," Sixtus said, breathing hard, obviously going somewhere with this.

"It came with the territory," Zeb said, the old shame kicking in.

"So did Michael—he came with the territory too."

"You can think what you want, but I love Michael more than anything. I wanted . . ." Zeb trailed off, clenching his fists because he wanted to punch Sixtus in the mouth for even questioning his behavior as a father. "I want him to be proud of me."

"And I'm sure he was. Is."

"I had to work," Zeb said, pissed off at himself for defending his life to his ex–father-in-law. "The job was demanding, I know. The marriage was unhappy—from the start. What do you want me to say? But I saw Michael whenever I could. Zee filmed at sets far from L.A., and she'd usually take him with her."

"The jet-set life," Sixtus said mildly.

"You weren't there," Zeb said.

"No—you made sure of that."

Zeb bit his tongue—the frustration and fury were so great, he wanted to fight the old man here and now. It was your daughter, he wanted to say.

Zeb had given up more chances than Sixtus would ever know to make sure his son was safe and cared for. He had regularly driven Elizabeth to rehab after their breakup because he felt so guilty for marrying her in the first place. With Michael six, frantic with worry about his mother, Zeb had turned down chances to travel to Russia, for joint cooperation meetings, to other conferences too numerous to recall through the years.

"What do you want me to say? That I should have passed up every opportunity? That I should have stayed home, been a househusband?"

"Things might be different for your son if you had."

Zeb drew a deep breath. From the small porch, he could see his son watching the girl pull her lobster pots. Michael sat still, arms wrapped around his knees, at the edge of the sea. There were always stray days in the middle—when Zeb had a launch and Elizabeth had not quite returned, when Michael would be left with the baby-sitter. Now, watching

Michael, pain shot into Zeb's heart as he remembered his son sitting like that on their front steps, waiting for his parents to come home.

"You have mighty fine credentials," Sixtus said, twisting his knotty hands. "But your son is a high school dropout."

"I'm goddamn aware of that."

"What are you going to do about it?"

"I'm hoping that this summer helps. That something between us can open enough for my words to make a difference. I tell him how important education is, but he doesn't hear. Or even listen . . . I want him to get his diploma and a college degree, too. I'm hoping his being around you will help. You and Rumer."

Sixtus tilted his head. He stared down on the rocks, at his grandson sitting so still, and Zeb wondered what the old man was thinking. Michael's long hair blew in the wind, the red bandanna a badge of rebellion. Zeb felt disoriented, as if he'd just come out of an altitude chamber. He thought of his father cutting his own hair while he slept, and felt a kick in his gut.

"Degrees aren't what matter," Sixtus said after a while.

"You can say that," Zeb said, "because you have several."

The old man waved his hand, shaking his head. "You're not a stupid man, but that's a goddamn lame-brained way to think. You have several too, and look where they've gotten you!"

Zeb's anger kicked in so hard, it took all he had to contain it. Being at the Point was painful enough on several counts, without being insulted by Elizabeth's father. He jumped to his feet and began to pace.

"You're miserable," Sixtus continued, rising as well. "Anyone who feels like looking can see it. That frown line's as deep as a trench. You got the weight of the world on your shoulders, and not one of your goddamn degrees is taking it off."

"There's a new lab opening in September! Two hundred and fifty million dollars riding on it, and I'm in charge! Jesus Christ, Sixtus—you want me to leave the Point? I'll leave. I'll head west today—Michael can come or stay." Zeb began jamming his books into the box they'd been unpacked from. "I don't need this lecture—or whatever it is—from a man who despises me. I got enough of that from my father."

"Zeb," Sixtus said, his crippled hand on Zeb's arm.

"Get off me," Zeb said, shaking free and packing the books with even greater intensity.

"I don't despise you."

"The hell you don't."

"What gives you that idea?" Sixtus said.

"The way you sound when you talk to me. The fact that you blame me for marrying Elizabeth and hurting Rumer. For being a lousy father to your grandson, not making it so you could see him. That enough?" Zeb snapped.

"Whew," Sixtus said. He shook his head, looking up at Zeb with bright light in his watery blue eyes. "Sounds more like you despise yourself."

Zeb stopped dead. He dropped the book he was holding into the box, and it fell with a muffled thud. It was true. Sixtus was right, and as much as he loved everything here at Hubbard's Point, it all pointed Zeb straight to that one fact.

"It's a big waste of time," Sixtus said.

"What do you mean?"

"Self-loathing. I've tried it."

"When?"

"Ahh, when you were a little kid. The boy next door. Rumer was crazy for you and you for her, but Elizabeth looked to me. I was her daddy—and I wasn't there."

"Sure you were. My father was the one who wasn't there—being a pilot, flying wherever. You were always mowing the lawn, reading in the hammock . . . sailing."

"Sailing away from my wife and children," Sixtus said. "Airline pilots might fly farther, but small-town sailors have their escape routes too. I'd look back as I cleared the breakwater, up on the hill—I'd see you and Rumer sitting on the roof of your house, talking a blue streak to each other. And there Elizabeth would be, standing on the rocks, staring after me, crying as I left."

"Hard to imagine the Elizabeth I know crying," Zeb said, picturing the hard look in her beautiful eyes.

"Well, I left her enough so she learned she didn't like it. I think she arranged the rest of her life so it would never happen again. She hadn't banked on you shooting for the stars. . . ."

"I never misled her. And I always came back."

"To what, Zeb?" Sixtus asked softly.

"What are you trying to do?" Zeb exploded. "Get me to admit we were wrong for each other? Okay! I admit it. I made a mistake—I ruined our lives. Both of them."

"Not just both of yours," Sixtus said, softer still.

"What the hell? You want to blame all the hunger and suffering in the world on me, go ahead. Jesus—"

"There was a third life," Sixtus said. "Rumer's."

Zeb stopped.

"She wants no part of me," he said. "I've tried to talk to her."

"Yeah, you have?"

"Yes. It's one of the reasons I came back."

Sixtus nodded, knowing.

"You think you're gonna wipe the slate clean, get forgiveness from her in one fell swoop?" he asked.

"No, I don't think that," Zeb said, although deep down he knew he wished for it.

"You've got to look at this realistically," Sixtus said. "She was in love with you. You realize that?"

Zeb shrugged. Of course he knew she'd been in love with him. Just as he had been in love with her, for more years than he could remember, for their whole lives. The problem was that because they had been so young and because love had come so easily to them, he had undervalued it. He hadn't known it was the real thing, something precious and irreplaceable he would never find again.

"What's the difference?" Zeb asked. "She's with Edward. What's his problem anyway? He's got the stiffest goddamn upper lip—"

"What he has," Sixtus said, "is a poker up his ass."

"I thought you approved," Zeb said. "At dinner the other night, it sounded as if you were giving them your blessing."

"The hell I am. I try, for her sake, to get along with him. Try with all—or most—of my might. The thing is, he lets her keep her horse at his farm. She's gone out with lots of men over the years—I guess Edward waited and saw his chance. It's obvious he's wanted her this whole time. But who wouldn't?"

"Yeah, who wouldn't?" Zeb asked in a low voice.

"Damn right. She's a beautiful, vibrant woman. All that giving she does—to her goddamned old father, to every goddamn animal that comes along . . . she deserves something better than Edward. Something real."

"What are you saying?" Zeb asked, looking up.

"Ahh, never mind. What the hell business do I have venting my spleen to you of all people? You're where the whole problem started. She'd kill me if she knew I was over here," Sixtus said.

"I'm sure she would."

"Draw and quarter me," he said morosely. "Hang me out to dry, you got it?"

"Yes, I've got it."

"The point being, you're not gonna tell."

"No, I won't."

"I regret saying one goddamn word to you. My daughter doesn't need my help in getting men to love her—believe me, I've watched a parade of them come through over the years. The ones I mentioned before—a doctor, a lawyer, another vet, a professor, a sailor . . . now this farmer."

"Edward."

"Yeah, Edward. When none of 'em, not a one, can make her happy. She's an extraordinary girl, and she needs an equal. Know what I mean? She needs a person who can keep up with her. That's what I'd tell her if she wanted advice on fixing her own life."

"Good advice," Zeb said.

"Yes. Just like I'm telling you to get over yourself. Take off the hair shirt and quit being a martyr. Make up for lost time, young man."

"What?"

"You have the summer, Zeb."

"For what?"

"You know—don't be thick. I don't want to have to spell it out. I'm old, and you're young. I spent lots of years making mistakes that I've learned how to avoid. I'm going to give you this advice for free."

"What is it?"

"When God hands you a gift, take it."

"What gift?"

"The truth. The truth of who you are and what you feel. You get one true love in this life, Zeb. Only one."

"Like you and Clarissa?"

"Yes. I'm lucky because I found her and I knew right away. Others aren't so fortunate. They find the real thing and throw it back because it's not bright enough. Then they spend the rest of their lives regretting and searching. It's like being a lost soul here on earth."

"Or up in space," Zeb said, remembering how the spacecraft would pass over Hubbard's Point and he would always watch, always wonder what she was doing. He thought of the black hole he had told her about, and his blood ran cold. He wanted to tell her what had really happened, how it had brought him back to earth. Talk to her about all the things he had seen—and felt—over the years. Would he have the chance?

"Don't waste your summer, Zeb," Sixtus said.

"She won't talk to me," Zeb said.

"Then talk to her. I swear, I'll deny I said it, but wear her down."

"Why are you telling me this?"

The silence between them crackled with tension. Zeb heard gulls crying from across the water. It sounded so much like his childhood, he had to brace himself against the table. He thought he knew what Sixtus was saying, but he wasn't sure: He couldn't believe the old man didn't hate him.

"Because I'm an old man. I'm getting crippled with this goddamned arthritis, and this might be my last hurrah—throwing my weight around where I think it might do some good."

"That's the reason?"

"I love them both so much," Sixtus said, his voice dropping. "Elizabeth and Rumer. The thing is, Zeb, you fell in love with the girl next door—and married her sister."

"I know."

"Two wrongs won't make it all right."

"What's the second wrong?"

Sixtus just stared at him.

Zeb closed his eyes. He had been too young to understand. He and Rumer were such good friends, doing everything together, bonded to the core—and then he'd been totally blinded with lust by Elizabeth. She had turned up the heat that spring—flashed him with that megawatt sex appeal, and everything between him and Rumer had seemed pale in comparison.

Was Sixtus giving him permission—no, a directive—to try to win Rumer back? That seemed unbelievable. Zeb wanted to ask, but the words caught in his throat. What could the point be anyway? By September, if not before, he would be settled in his new position at the research center, three thousand miles away in California. Even if Rumer could forgive him, could forget what had happened, he knew she would never leave Hubbard's Point.

Perhaps to change the subject, take the pressure off himself, Zeb looked up at Sixtus.

"When are you planning to tell her?" he asked.

"What do you know about it?"

Zeb laughed. "You just accused me of running off on my family—taking to the sky. I know it from the other side, Sixtus. When a guy's getting ready to leave, I know the signs."

"It shows?" Sixtus asked.

"Yeah. It shows. Rumer doesn't know?"

Sixtus shook his head, leaning forward, his elbows on his knees. He looked old and defeated, the pain showing in his face.

"No, she doesn't."

"Then you'd better go home and talk to her tonight."

Sixtus narrowed his eyes, looking down to the shoreline. Quinn had looped the boat around, to get closer to Michael. He pushed up from the rocks, leaning forward to be heard above the engine. While his father and grandfather watched, he pulled off his shirt and dove into the water. He swam out to the boat, and Quinn helped haul him in. The two kids headed out toward Gull Island.

The sun was bright, illuminating the bank of yellow day lilies in front of Winnie's house. Zeb squinted, then looked up at the sky. Stars were everywhere. White lights in the brilliant sky. Zeb, the man who could see stars in daylight, remembered when he had flown among them, before he'd had his courage shaken out of him, and he thought of all the years before, here at the Point. He had lost so much wisdom along the way.

"Where are you going?" Zeb asked.

"That's the wrong question," Sixtus said quietly.

"It is? Then what's the right question?"

" 'Why?' " Sixtus said, staring at his hands. "That's the right one. . . ."

"Tell me, then."

"Because I'm old. Because I don't want her stuck with me forever . . . she's too good. She'd ruin her own life taking care of a dependent old father."

"You mean you're not coming back?"

"I might; might not. All I know is, I need this trip to do what I have to do next. Can't live in a nursing home wishing I'd sailed where I wanted to sail, crossed the Atlantic Ocean while I still had the health and strength."

Zeb nodded. He knew better than most about the desperate need some people felt to take long voyages, to travel to the edge of the world and beyond.

"You were like a son to me, Zeb," Sixtus said. The words and tone were rough and passionate, as if Zeb had broken his heart too. The men stood looking at each other as the seconds ticked past.

"Talk to Rumer," Zeb said.

"That I'll do," Sixtus said. "If you'll promise to look after her while I'm gone."

"The least I can do," Zeb said gruffly. "But you have to tell me: What's the second wrong?"

"Not being with her now . . ." Sixtus said. "But you already knew that. It's why you're here."

Zeb nodded, shaking inside. He paused, but then Sixtus reached across the table to shake his hand. His hand felt rough, his grip strong. They held on for a few seconds longer than customary, then let go.

Turning to leave, Sixtus looked stoop-shouldered and old, filled with pain both in his body and in his heart. Zeb watched his former father-in-law walk slowly up the incline to Cresthill Road, on his way home. He had felt earthbound by guilt, fear, and grief, but right now he felt the stirrings of something unexpected and long forgotten.

Something like hope.

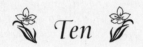 *Ten*

"Okay," Quinn shouted above the engine. "I'm going to go very slow. When I bring the boat around, you lean over and grab the buoy . . . now!"

She watched as Michael arched over the gunwale, his tan body long and strong, to reach for the orange-and-white Styrofoam buoy. Saltwater glistened on his skin, and Quinn found her eyes glued to his shoulders.

He hauled in the line but stopped when he got to the slick, seaweedy part just above the pot itself.

"Gross," he said, dropping it.

Quinn clambered around the console, swearing as she hooked the buoy again. Michael stood back, watching her pull hand over hand, right through the gunk. "It's nothing to be scared of," she said. "Just seaweed and algae. It grows on the line, on the bottom of boats. . . ."

"Sorry I dropped it," Michael said, watching as Quinn sprang the pot's door, reaching in to grab the squirming and clicking lobsters inside.

"Don't worry about it," she said. "You should see, in August, when the red jellyfish are here. Then the lines are covered with tentacles—I have to wear gloves, or I get stung."

"You like lobstering?"

"It's a living." She shrugged, banding the lobster claws.

He laughed as she steered the boat along the rocky shore. "As if you have to worry about making a living. You live with your aunt, don't you?"

"Yes, but I don't plan on being a burden forever."

"A burden—you're what? Sixteen?"

"Seventeen," Quinn said. "You?"

"Almost eighteen."

"Don't you work?"

Michael hesitated, as if he thought he should say yes, but he was honest and shook his head no instead. Quinn pulled the next three pots, and then Michael tried the next. He managed not to flinch at the seaweed, and when he reached inside, he did a good job of grabbing the lobsters by the carapace and not getting bitten.

"How long have you been doing this?" he asked.

"Three summers. I earned my first money when I was twelve—a hot dog stand. Then I had a paper route—a lot of Hubbard's Point kids start out that way. Then I worked at the parking lot in the green shack. And then Sam got me this boat, and I became a lobsterwoman."

"Pretty cool," Michael said.

Quinn gunned the engine just to see his long hair move in the wind. Now that she'd finished pulling her pots, she had time to consider the fact that he had swum out to her boat from shore. Why had he done that? Boys like him didn't like girls like her. He was so chiseled and handsome—she could easily see him being an actor like his mother. And he had that easygoing way people with money always had. . . . Quinn couldn't even imagine that.

"Well, I'm done for the day," she said, turning back toward the creek and boat basin.

"Can you show me around?" he asked.

"You mean a boat ride?" she asked.

He nodded. Quinn's stomach fluttered. Was he joking with her? Usually she drove boys away within the first ten minutes. Not only had Michael swum out to be with her, he wasn't in a hurry to go back.

"Okay," she said. "Where?"

He laughed, stretching out on the seat, his rib cage rippling under his tan skin. "You're the local," he said. "It's up to you."

"Local yokel," she said.

"I didn't say that."

She nodded, perplexed by the situation. About a hundred snappy comebacks zinged through her brain, but she said not a one. Instead, she pointed the boat west and opened the throttle. They zoomed past Tomahawk Point, the nature sanctuary, and several family beach communities. Then Old Bluff, the honky-tonk part of town with beach bars, miniature golf, a carousel, and lemon ice. Finally, on a cliff rising straight up from the Sound, was the Renwicks' mansion.

"That's Firefly Hill, Sam's brother's mother-in-law's house," Quinn said. "I guess that makes Augusta my stepgrandmother-in-law."

"Big house," Michael said.

"Her husband was a famous artist—Hugh Renwick. He was one of the Black Hall Impressionists—our town's famous for art."

"Cool."

"Firefly Beach—that stretch of white sand just below the house—is where they used to find gold coins. For years and years, the family would go walking along the beach, and they'd find these strange coins . . . everyone talked of the treasure, but no one knew for sure where it came from."

"From that ship . . . I know, my mother used to talk about it," Michael said.

"From the *Cambria*. It was an English barquentine loaded with the king's gold. No one knew for sure until Sam's brother, Joe, came up from Florida to excavate the site. He did, and he found a lot more than gold. . . ."

"Like what?"

"Well, like history," Quinn said, staring out to sea, to the spot where the *Cambria* had gone down. "You must know the story . . . you're related, right?"

"Yeah, to Elisabeth Randall, way back," he said.

"Well, her husband was the lighthouse keeper, right out there," Quinn said, pointing across the waves to the Wickland Rock Light. The pile of rocks sat in the middle of the Sound—so far from land, it might as well have been Alcatraz. Quinn never told this story without getting a lump in her throat, thinking of the original Elisabeth and Clarissa.

"Wow, that's where she lived," Michael said.

"Yep. In 1769. I know, because kids at Black Hall High School have to read Clarissa's diary and learn all about the *Cambria*. It's our local legend, but Rumer says it's a lot more—it teaches us about how people lived at that time, and how—" Quinn closed her mouth, unable to say the rest.

Michael sensed her emotion—she could tell by the way he gave her a worried glance. Probably he was one of those boys who couldn't stand a girl's tears, who wanted to jump overboard at the first sign of crying.

"What's wrong?" he asked.

"Clarissa's diary teaches us about ourselves," Quinn said as her eyes flooded. "About how we might feel to live on an island. To be lonely and abandoned. And to have our mother drown."

"Your mother drowned . . ." Michael said, moving toward Quinn.

"Yeah," Quinn said, staring out at the Hunting Ground, where her parents' boat had gone down. "She did. With my father."

"I'm sorry," Michael said. Although he didn't touch her, he sat so close she could feel his energy. Almost as if he'd just put his arm around her, Quinn closed her eyes and leaned her head back.

"Thanks," she whispered.

"I don't know much about Clarissa and Elisabeth," Michael said quietly. "About the *Cambria* . . . but I know about the lonely-and-abandoned part."

"But you're with your father now. You're together."

"We're staying in the same house for the summer," Michael said. "But we're not 'together.' "

"What do you mean?" Quinn asked, frowning. She knew that if she could have her parents back for five minutes, she'd never complain again. To be together with them, in their presence, hearing their voices . . .

"Together is more than two people in the same room," Michael said. "It's something that can get broken. And once that happens, I'm not sure it can ever be fixed. At least with us."

Although Quinn had cut the engine, the boat rocked on the small fair-weather waves. Sunlight glanced off the water, causing her to squint. At high tide, the lighthouse seemed almost to float. The tower loomed over them, casting a shadow on the Sound, and Quinn tried to imagine living there. Perhaps Michael was right; perhaps Elisabeth and the lighthouse keeper's "together" had been broken long before she sailed off with Captain Thorn.

"Does your family talk about the legend?" Quinn asked.

"Not for a long time," Michael said. "My mother and aunt have pins made to look like the lighthouse, and when I was young, I used to like hearing about them. My mother—or maybe it was my aunt—told me her grandmother told her about sea caves, where the girl—"

"Clarissa," Quinn said.

Michael nodded. "Where she used to hide."

"Sea caves?" Quinn said doubtfully. "I've never heard of those."

"It's probably just a story," Michael said.

Even so, when Quinn started up the motor again, instead of heading straight back to Hubbard's Point, she wheeled out into the Sound. They circled the island, staring at the lighthouse and the rock ledge on which it sat—at high tide, not much was visible. Seagulls and terns lived on the rocks; their cries filled the air like hungry ghosts.

Quinn shivered. She felt spirits the way other people felt breezes. Clarissa and her mother were here, talking to her. She glanced up at Michael to see whether he felt it too, and she was surprised to see him watching her, as if he were making up his mind about her. Quinn held the tiller, keeping herself steady.

She had the feeling someone had just thrown her a lifeline. Not the ghost of her mother or father, not even the ghost of Clarissa Randall. No, it was this too-handsome, too-rich, not-at-all-in-her-league boy sitting in the bow of her boat who couldn't—for reasons Quinn couldn't begin to fathom—seem to take his eyes off her.

Michael Mayhew had thrown her a line, and for the life of her, Quinn couldn't understand why. But it was too strange—feeling this kind of closeness. It had to be *pseudo*-closeness! No boy as cute as he was could be acting this way without some perverted motive.

"What's going on here?" she asked suddenly, her eyes snapping open.

"Going on?"

"Yes. Tell me right now. Because I don't have time for crap."

"What are you talking about?"

"I don't talk about my parents—to anyone!"

"Hey, I wasn't forcing you—"

"What do you know about it anyway? You have two perfectly healthy parents! Kids like you don't know what it's like. You say it's broken and can't be fixed, and I'm telling you you're lucky he's alive!" She pushed as far away from him as she could get without falling overboard.

"Why do you have to turn psycho every time—"

"Don't call me psycho," she said, shaking, not understanding why she felt so terribly undone. Why had she let her guard down?

"Okay, don't worry—I won't."

"Back off. I mean it!"

"I hear you, Quinn. Let's just head back to shore, okay?"

She nodded, firing the engine and wheeling the boat around, away from the lighthouse. Her palms were sweaty; never before had she brought someone besides Allie, Aunt Dana, or Sam this close to the place her parents' boat had sunk.

But as the fog of misery cleared and her heart slowed down, she caught sight of Michael's face. He looked befuddled, taken aback, as if he really didn't know what had hit him. Quinn had just laid a pretty heavy attack on someone who—maybe, just maybe—had only been trying to be her friend.

It was too much to take in. She opened up the throttle and sped faster, back to Hubbard's Point.

❧

Late morning sun streamed through the wide window, and the air conditioner hummed quietly, cooling the office. Outside the window, heat shimmered in the wide field. Four acres ran from the road to the woods. Dragonflies hovered over tall grass. The timbers of the fallen barn stood in the shade; a red-tailed hawk perched on a slanted cross-beam.

Rumer stood by the stainless steel exam table, sleeves rolled up, talking to an old cat.

Her work had saved her these last few days; with Zeb staying at the Point and with what had happened between her and Edward, she felt charged, as if lightning were striking from all directions. Right now, examining an old gray and white cat with a runny nose, she concentrated on her patient and forced herself to center.

"She's one of the reds," Margaret Porter, the owner said. "Five wild kittens born under our garage during Hurricane Gloria . . ."

"Wow, when was that?" Mathilda asked.

"Seventeen years ago," Rumer said, cleaning the corners of the cat's sharp yellow eyes. "I was in Alberta; I saw the news on TV."

"Brave old cat," Mathilda said with respect and awe.

"She's lived outside this whole time," Margaret said, holding the cat, whom her children had named Grey Kitten, steady on the table. "She and one other are the last left . . . her brothers and sisters were all bright orange—'the reds,' we called them. They let us feed them on the porch, set out saucers of cream to keep their coats full. We used to try to bring them into the house for the winter, but it didn't work—they always escaped."

Rumer petted the cat lightly; she knew that ferals sometimes hated human touch, but Grey Kitten began to purr and push into her hand for greater pressure.

"Oh, she's a love," Margaret said. "She gets more affectionate all the time. It started after her second sister died. . . ."

"As she loses her littermates," Rumer said softly, "she appreciates you even more, as her family—as her tribe." She cleared her throat, thinking of her own childhood, of how she had adopted Zeb as one of her own tribe, how lost she had felt when he went away. Holding Grey Kitten in her hands, she felt her bones and sinews, as if most of her fur had worn away and her skin was barely holding her together.

"She has a bad cold," Rumer said, "that won't seem to clear up. . . ."

"It's just gotten worse the last few times I've brought her to you—even after the antibiotics."

"Is she eating?"

"Not as much as usual, but yes."

Turning toward the medicine cabinet, Rumer pulled out pills and ointment. Margaret held Grey Kitten, petting and soothing her. To write out her instructions for care, Rumer reached for a black fountain pen—a gift from Edward on her last birthday. She felt off balance just touching it.

She hadn't seen Edward since Dana's wedding and the aftermath. Visiting Blue, she had gone once at dawn and once late in the day, when she knew Edward would be at the Grange. She had told herself she was just very busy, that those were the times that worked best in her schedule.

Everything seemed to have changed between them, and she wondered why she had ever crossed the line, trying to create love out of something that wasn't there.

Mathilda placed the medication in a bag and left the exam room with Margaret. A bell rang down the hall, and a moment later Mathilda returned, smiling widely.

"You have a surprise," she said.

It's Zeb, Rumer thought right away. He had said he wanted to talk to her, and he'd gotten tired of waiting for her to come over. Well, he might not like what she had to say, but since he was so eager, he'd have to hear it anyway. But when Rumer walked into the waiting room, she saw her father sitting in a maple armchair, reading *National Geographic*.

Now that she'd made up her mind to let Zeb have it, she felt strangely deflated. "Hi, Dad," she said. She walked over to kiss him. "What brings you here?"

"I've come to take the doctor to lunch," he said.

"You lucky girl!" Mathilda said. "I wish my dad lived closer so he could take me to lunch."

"Why don't you come along, Mattie?" Sixtus asked. "I packed up a picnic, and I've got more than enough sandwiches for you to join us."

"Oh, Sixtus," she said. "I appreciate that, I really do—and I know my father would thank you. But I'd better stay here and man the office."

"Well, next time," Sixtus said.

"Thanks, Mat," Rumer said, grabbing her purse and following her father out the door.

Sixtus drove a few miles along the Shore Road, then took a left. The lane led them past wildflower-filled fields, salt marshes, and estates encircled by stately walls of local gray stone, to a dirt parking lot overlooking the mouth of the river. Ospreys circled overhead. People launched their boats from a ramp slanting into the shallows, and Rumer and her father ate bluefish salad sandwiches and watched the action.

"Stopped by school on my way to your office," Sixtus said. "Heard that Edward addressed the seniors, gave his speech about how his mother went to Black Hall High, how proud she would be to know Dorothy Jackson."

"He's very involved with that scholarship."

"His talk sounded wonderfully stirring; only twenty kids fell asleep," her father said.

Rumer gave him a "watch it" look, eating her sandwich and watching an osprey dive; it came up with a wriggling silver fish in its talons.

"Let's see, what else? Oh, yes. They had a faculty meeting about Quinn; she's not going to be happy."

"Summer school?"

"Yes," he said.

"She'll never go for it."

"She doesn't have a choice if she wants to graduate next year. Dana and Sam will talk her into it—they'll be back from Newport and the Vineyard in a few days. That'll be enough time—summer school doesn't start for two weeks."

Rumer laughed quietly, imagining the task Dana and Sam had before them. The comfort and familiarity felt so good, and she and her father ate in silence for a while. But he kept glancing over in a way that made her think there was more to this than a father-daughter lunch. He held his hands in gentle fists. She knew his arthritis had been bothering him lately; she wondered whether he was in pain.

"What's wrong, Dad?" she asked.

"Wrong? What makes you think something's wrong?"

"You look worried—is something on your mind? Is your arthritis acting up?"

"Nah," he said, scowling. "No worse than ever. It's fine . . . I just wanted to brighten your day with my presence and a bluefish sandwich, and you think I've got ulterior motives? Jeesh," he said, shaking his head.

Rumer smiled, sipping her iced tea. The moments passed as they watched two men back their boat trailer down the ramp, their old Starcraft loaded with fishing rods, a tackle box, and a bucket. One of the men broke up a bag of ice, then wedged a six-pack of beer into the cooler.

"Talked to Zeb this morning," her father said.

"Zeb?" she asked.

"Yep."

"What's there . . ." she began. She was going to ask, "What's there left for you to talk about?" But she stopped herself; of course there was Michael. "How was that?" she asked instead.

"Well, he's got that new project out in California," her father said. "He seems quite industrious about it."

"I never thought Zeb would take a job that would keep him in an office," Rumer said. "Or even an observatory. I wonder what happened."

"You could probably ask him."

"Hmm," she said.

"If nothing else, you both love Michael," her father said. "And the boy clearly needs help. He's struggling. I'd like you to help Zeb with him."

"I'll try," Rumer said. "But what about you? You're the teacher . . . and his grandfather."

"Michael is on my mind," her father said, seeming to purposely evade the actual question. "He'll be here for so short a time—just till summer's end. Then he and his father will head west again."

"Did Zeb talk about being here?" Rumer asked, the question hard to get out.

"Yes. I think he's glad to be here. Happy to see you again."

Rumer scowled. Her father was peering at her as if he could see straight into her mind. "What a joke," she said. "Let him tell himself that if he wants to. I don't believe it. He wanted to 'talk' to me, but I don't think there's a point to it. What else did he say?"

"Well, he suggested something to me. Something I'd been neglecting."

"That must have gone over well with you—coming from Zeb."

"Yes, well, I did give him a hard time about it. But at the end of the day, he was right. Quite right."

"About what?" Rumer asked, and when she looked across the seat, she saw her father smiling at her. His weathered face was deeply lined, filled with the sort of kindness and caring that originates deep within. The smile wavered slightly, then widened.

"About you," he said.

"You and Zeb talked about me?" Rumer asked.

"Yes, Rumer. Among other things, about the fact that I've been less than honest with you."

Something about her father's eyes—a new brightness in them, perhaps—or about the way he'd been working on the boat so hard—with a different intensity than other years—made Rumer's heart skip a beat. Her father was about to tell her something that she didn't want to hear.

"What's wrong, Dad? Are you sick? I mean, aside from the arthritis?" Her throat hurt just to say the words.

"No, Rumer. I'm well. Very well."

Relief flooded through her, and she relaxed. "Then, what?"

"I'm going away."

"Away?" She frowned. What could he mean? How far could he go? To visit Elizabeth on the set in Canada? With a group of retired teachers to the Rockies or the Grand Canyon or New Orleans? She had seen the Elderhostel mailings he received, stacked neatly in the corner of his desk. "Where?"

"To Halifax, where I spent my childhood. And then to Ireland, where I was born."

"Why wouldn't you want me to know that, Dad? Is it because you think I'd want to come and you want to go alone? It's okay, you know. I can understand why you'd want that . . . it sounds like a pilgrimage."

"In a way it is."

"To trace your roots? To visit the important places?"

Her father nodded. She loved him so much. He had always been the wisest, kindest person she knew. Since her mother's death they had lived together, and she'd watched him slowly come back to life over the months and years. It pleased her a great deal to think of him doing this for himself.

"Dad, why would you think I'd be upset? Why—" she began, then stopped herself. "Is it because of Zeb? Are you leaving because he's here and you don't want to see him?"

"No. I've been planning this trip for a while. Since before we knew for sure Zeb was coming."

"Then why wouldn't you tell me? I'm happy for you, Dad."

"Because I'm sailing, Rumer."

She didn't understand. She heard the words coming from her father's mouth, but they didn't sink in. Did he mean on an ocean liner? Then suddenly she knew.

He meant in his boat. Looking at the mouth of the river, the Sound beyond, she saw several sails on the horizon.

In her mind, she now saw his boat behind the garage at the foot of the hill. The *Clarissa* sat there proudly, a stately sloop from another time, bright work glistening in the late afternoon sun. Her white hull gleamed, her deck shone. That morning, Rumer had seen a family of sparrows lined up on the wooden boom, singing loudly. The craft was graceful, classic, lovingly restored over the last years—in spite of the arthritis crippling him a little more every day—by her father.

"Sailing by yourself?" she asked.

"Yes, Rumer."

"From here to Nova Scotia," she said. "And then to Ireland . . . that's the North Atlantic, Dad. The storms get bad out there—the waves are so big. . . ."

"My boat is sturdy," he said. "A Herreshoff."

"But the arthritis," she said. "You have so much pain, Dad. How will you do it? How will you manage—to react quickly, when you have to?"

"This might be my last chance," he said. "I've given it so much thought, honey. I don't want to die without sailing the Atlantic."

"Then don't go alone," she said, taking his hand across the table. "Charter a bigger boat, with a captain. Please, Dad."

"The *Clarissa*'s big enough, sweetheart. I wouldn't be the first man to cross in a New York 30."

"Then take someone with you."

"This is my dream; I'm going alone," her father said, smiling into her eyes. Reaching across the seat, he held her hand for a moment, then squeezed her fingers and, as if he had already started to leave, gently slid his gnarled hand away.

"Your dream," she whispered.

"If I leave to follow mine," he said quietly, "maybe you'll stay and find yours."

"I live my dream," she said, "right here in our house, with you, with my work. . . ."

"That's not enough," he said. "Taking care of an old man, trading your life for mine . . . I won't have it. No, Rumer: I want you to take something from life, something really wonderful, all for yourself."

"It's all right here, Dad," Rumer said, watching the summer heat shimmer above the estuary's green rushes and blue water. "You know that. Stay."

"Sometimes a person has to visit where he came from to find out where he's going," he said. "Life never stays the same—as much as we love today, tomorrow's coming fast. You understand?"

Rumer shrugged, but deep inside she did understand. Was that why Zeb had come back to Hubbard's Point? To look back so he could know where he was going next?

Shaking her head, Rumer knew it didn't matter. What Zeb did was none of her concern. But knowing that her father was about to take off on such a dangerous journey filled her with worry. Her father had been the most solid part of her life; she couldn't imagine what she'd do without him.

"You'll be fine, Rumer," he said quietly.

"Oh, I know that, Dad," she said. "I just hope you will—"

"I'll have your mother with me," he said gruffly. "In spirit, in my heart. She'll look after me. And you'll have . . ."

"Edward," she said.

"No comment," her father said.

"Good," Rumer said.

She thought of the farm, of the smell of loam and livestock, of Edward's warm brown eyes, the feeling of his arms around her shoulders. But she still felt empty at the thought of her father leaving.

"Will you be home for dinner tonight?" he asked.

"Probably. But I think I'll go up to the farm for a while. Ride Blue, see Edward, plant some flowers along his front walk . . ." Working in the earth always made her feel safe and balanced. Her hands were shaking, and she tried to hold them steady in her lap. What was happening to her?

"Taken Michael up there yet?" he asked.

"No. I wonder whether he'd remember," she said. "I think it would kill me to learn that he doesn't."

"One sure way to find out," her father said.

"I wish they'd never come back," Rumer said.

"Don't say that," her father warned, shocked by her bitterness.

"It's taken all this time to get over it," she said. "And now they're here, and you're leaving. . . ." Tears sprang to her eyes. "Sorry, Dad," she said brushing at them. "I'm just feeling sorry for myself."

"Everyone needs a little of that now and then," he said. "But I promise you, Rumer, all will be well."

And then it was time to head back for afternoon office hours. She kissed her father's cheek, and together they drove through town. The ground of Black Hall felt so solid beneath their wheels, and Rumer tried not to think of huge waves, of gale winds, of a relatively small boat on a marvelously huge sea. They drove past the white churches and green marshes, the fish store with its great cod weathervane.

Rumer's hands were still trembling; her heart shifted in her chest. Zeb's arrival had changed everything. Rumer had felt the air was charged since the initial jolt of seeing him; in spite of the hot, sunny day, she felt it now. She thought of what her father had just said, about visiting the past to see the future, and she went spinning way back in time.

Michael had been two.

Elizabeth called Rumer in the middle of the night—it was three o'clock in Connecticut, midnight in Los Angeles. Slurring her words, crying, Elizabeth had been drinking.

"Michael won't fall asleep," she sobbed into the phone. "He just cries and cries."

"Is he sick?" Rumer asked, alarmed. "Does he have a fever?"

"No, it isn't that . . . he's upset. He's always upset!"

"Why, Elizabeth?"

"All the yelling."

Rumer gripped the phone, half wanting to hear everything about Elizabeth and Zeb fighting, half wanting to hang up before her sister said another word.

"You're happy, I suppose," Elizabeth said, sniffling. "Nothing would make you happier than to know Zeb and I aren't getting along."

"No, Zee," Rumer said. But her heart was beating hard, the way it did when she was trying to convince herself of something false. Even when her brain was attempting to accept something she found unacceptable, her heart would know the truth.

"Sure. You *want* us to hate each other, don't you? Want our marriage to end so you can say 'I told you so,' so you can have him!"

"Elizabeth, stop," Rumer said. "You're wrong. But forget all that—is Michael still upset? Where is he?"

"Say what you want," Elizabeth said, sobbing as the ice clinked in her glass. "But I know how you feel. I see it in your eyes when we get together—it's not the same between us, Rumer. You've turned against me.

Even now you sound so cold! You think I stole him from you, when you two were never more than friends."

"It's three o'clock in the morning, and—"

"You never used to mind when I called you late!"

"Listen! You said Michael was crying. Never mind about us," she said, relieved to get off the subject of her sister and Zeb. "Tell me about Michael."

"Now you're going to say I'm a lousy mother."

"Shush, Zee. Just tell me—"

"He's sitting in his crib, holding on to that dumb stuffed horse you gave him."

"He is?" Rumer had asked, remembering the delight in Michael's eyes as she'd pressed the toy into his arms.

"Whatever. He's holding it, rocking, saying boo, boo, boo . . ."

"He's saying Blue . . ."

"Oh, whatever it is, it's driving me—"

"Elizabeth," Rumer said, interrupting her. "Let him come stay with me for a while. Will you? Sounds like you could use the break. . . ."

"I'm leaving for Scotland next week," her sister said, "to start filming."

"Well, would Zeb mind? Would he let Michael come stay with me?"

"Zeb," Elizabeth said, her voice rising as if she wanted her husband—in the next room, out on the terrace, somewhere just out of earshot—to hear, "would be relieved, I'm sure. Says he can't leave Michael alone with me for a minute. . . . I'm the lousy parent. He's just wonderful—an astronaut, a national hero."

"Elizabeth," Rumer said. "Calm down. Can Michael hear you?"

"He's the hero, and I'm—what did you call me, Zeb? A drunk?"

"Elizabeth, stop," Rumer said, seething with frustration, wanting to transport herself bodily through the phone line. Mixed in was the old anger at both Elizabeth and Zeb bubbling up again.

"I'm only having a few," Elizabeth sobbed. "To take the edge off . . . I'm under so much pressure. I lost Best Supporting Actress last March, and you have no idea how bad that is—I should have won. You saw me in *Down Under*, didn't you?"

"Elizabeth," Rumer repeated, picturing Michael's face buried in Blue, wanting to grab him up into her arms.

"I was great," Elizabeth said. "I know when I'm doing my best work, and that was it . . . now I'm heading off to the Outer-fucking-Hebrides to work with the same director, and he's treating me so differently—as if I let him down. Zeb couldn't care less, Michael's all upset—how can I leave him with his nanny when he's like this?"

"Michael wants to come out here," Rumer had said softly. "He does, Elizabeth."

"He what?"

"He's calling Blue," Rumer said. "My horse. Michael loves him."

"Blue—Auntie's horse?" Elizabeth asked, her mouth just brushing away from the receiver as if speaking directly to Michael.

Rumer had heard him squawk: "Yak! Boo! Boo!"

"Huh," Elizabeth said, her tone changing dramatically. "He's saying he wants to see the horse?"

"Boo!" Michael yelped in the background.

Elizabeth laughed—it was forced, Rumer remembered now. As if her sister had actually found nothing, nothing at all, that was funny about the situation. "You were my husband's first love," Elizabeth said, "and now you're my son's."

"Don't think like that," Rumer said sharply.

"Hmmm," Elizabeth said, ice and glass clinking again.

Nine days later, with Elizabeth filming in Scotland, and Zeb down in a Houston lab, examining satellite photos of strip-mining in West Virginia, Rumer and Michael couldn't be pried apart.

Rumer would take him on long rides through the countryside, to see her horse. The time had flown too fast, and every second with her nephew had become precious beyond words.

Remembering that now, driving through town with her father, Rumer thought of what he had said: "If I leave to follow my dream, maybe you'll stay to find yours." Her eyes filled with tears, thinking of her father sailing away. But the thought of Michael so near, right now, soothed her heart, and she wondered whether her dreams were closer than she'd thought.

❧

Michael was walking up the road, covered with salt spray and smelling like lobsters, when he saw his aunt coming down the hill with a box filled with small plants. She looked confused, as if she just happened to find herself in her own yard and forgot how she'd gotten there. Quinn had gone to market with the lobsters and Michael's father was home, waiting for him.

"Hi, Aunt Rumer," Michael said.

"Hi, Michael."

"Going somewhere?"

"Yes," she said, balancing the low wooden box on the bed of her truck, looking over at him and seeming to make up her mind. "I have to take this flat of petunias to my friend Edward's farm and plant them in his garden. Would you like to come?"

"Sure," he said, casting a glance at Winnie's cottage. His father was sitting on the porch, staring out to sea. Anything was preferable to another evening of trying to talk to each other. Michael climbed into his aunt's truck.

They drove along the shore, past some wide green marshes and a fish market. Even though the sea was miles away, everything seemed salty. The old weathered shingles on some houses, pristine white clapboards on others; the oxidized green copper flashing along the rooflines; the ship weathervanes; the seascapes in the art gallery windows; the white churches. A lot of the gardens were overgrown, filled with flowers of white and green and blue, as if the colors of the sea had poured over the rocks and into the land.

"That's where Quinn's parents used to work," his aunt said, pointing out a yellow Victorian house on the main street.

Something old and weird stirred in Michael. He glanced at his aunt, remembering times when he'd go to stay with her. The memories were good but distant. She had taken over when his parents were busy . . . he had flown with a nanny from California to Connecticut . . . and she would pick him up in a truck just like this one.

His aunt drove out of town, along the river, and into the countryside. Stone walls crisscrossed green hills, and deer grazed in laurel thickets. They came to a fork in the road and went left. The truck began to slow down, and then his aunt turned into a gate that said Peacedale Farm. Just before climbing out of the truck, his aunt handed him an apple. Smiling, she caught his eye. "You'll need this," she said.

Michael nodded, lifting the box of plants out of the truck for her. She set them down by a long flower bed running beside the white house. Then they walked across the wide driveway, his aunt's boots crunching on the gravel. Michael was barefoot from his time on the boat with Quinn. The stones hurt the soles of his feet; he was about to tell his aunt he'd wait for her in the truck, when he heard a horse whinny.

There, standing across the field, was a dark brown horse. Its ears lifted, and it stood there, nostrils quivering as it smelled the air. Butterscotch light covered the stony field, buzzing with swallows and dragonflies. The horse tossed his head, and Michael's throat began to ache.

"He remembers you," Rumer said, her hand on Michael's shoulder.

Michael walked across the stones to the white rail fence. He broke the apple in half and held one part out in his open hand. The horse cantered across the field, stopping eye to eye with Michael.

"Blue," Michael whispered as the horse's velvety nose brushed his forearm. The horse ate the apple half as Michael petted his neck and looked into his dark, mystifying eyes.

"You knew each other a long time ago," Rumer said.

"He's still alive. . . ."

"He sure is," his aunt said. "He might be old, but nothing's stopping him. Right, Blue?"

Michael hung on to the horse. Strange memories came into his mind: him crying for the horse, begging to be allowed to see him, a door closing on him. He heard his mother's voice, telling him he could get hurt; it wasn't good for him. Now he looked up at his aunt.

"Why couldn't I see him all this time?" he asked.

"Your mother didn't want you to," she said.

"Why?"

"Because . . ." his aunt began, sounding choked up. She stopped herself, as if she weren't sure what to say. Michael could see her grappling with something, trying to decide. He was just a kid—there were certain things she probably didn't think she could—or should—tell him.

"Please tell me," he said.

"I can't, Michael," she said sadly. "She's my sister, and she's your mother. . . ."

Michael waited, but she couldn't seem to look at him. He felt his own breath coming faster. He knew that something had happened between his aunt and his father a long time ago. No one ever talked about it, but he knew it had to do with the reason he hadn't been allowed to visit Aunt Rumer, or even talk about her, as if even the mention of her name were too powerful for any of them to handle.

Just then the door to the house opened. A man walked out—Edward, the guy his aunt had been with at the wedding. Lean and kind of regal, like a duke or something, his whitish hair curled over his collar. His tall brown riding boots gleamed like fine wood. A workman came out of the barn to meet him. Seeing Rumer and Michael, Edward waved to them.

"Hello, you two," he called. "Rumer, Albert's showing me some water damage in the hayloft—come find me, okay?"

Aunt Rumer didn't reply. She just stood there, her shoulders shaking. Edward hesitated, waiting for her to reply.

"Okay," Michael called out so his aunt wouldn't have to. Edward waved, then headed into the barn.

"Aunt Rumer?" he asked.

"Thanks for doing that," she said, her face still hidden, as if she'd been crying.

"Are you all right?" Michael asked.

"I'm fine," she said, still looking away.

Climbing the fence, he swung his leg over the old horse's back. Michael grasped the mane, giving the horse a light nudge and galloping into the field. The salt air stung his eyes, fresh from the sea.

Quinn would love it here, he thought. He imagined flying by, sweeping her onto the horse's back. He thought of all the years gone by when no one mentioned his aunt's name—where had he thought she had gone?

Had he thought she had died? Or that his parents hated her?

He had loved her. He remembered that now.

When he turned around to wave to his aunt, to thank her for bringing him back to Blue, he saw her standing by the fence, her head resting on folded arms, crying as if she had a broken heart.

Eleven

THE NEXT DAY, it poured rain. Standing in her office, Rumer listened to drops pelt the roof and the leaves on the trees outside. A car had lost control on the wet pavement, hitting a collie. Rumer and Mathilda had been in surgery all morning, saving his life. Now, having been behind schedule all day, they were just catching up with the last appointments.

"Quite a storm," Mathilda said as the rain fell harder. "There's nothing like the smell of wet dogs to make me long for a sunny day."

"I hope my father's outside right now," Rumer said. "And imagining what this will be like, sailing through Georges Bank."

"He always seemed like such a *sensible* father to me," Mathilda said, clucking softly. "Or perhaps that's just because he has such a sensible daughter."

"Thank you, Mattie," Rumer said. "I'll tell him you said that."

They treated a colicky spaniel, a basset hound with an upper respiratory infection, and two cats with ear mites. The phone rang frequently; the answering machine picked up. Mathilda would play back all calls, keeping a stack of messages for Rumer to return after office hours. Escorting in the last patient of the day, Mathilda cleared her throat. "Dr. Larkin," she said. "You have a visitor."

Glancing up from her notes, Rumer saw Edward standing there. Her mouth fell open with surprise. Mathilda hesitated, as if she weren't sure what to do, then backed out of the room to leave them alone.

"I've come to pick up heartworm medicine for Orazio and Artemesia," he said.

"I didn't realize you had run out," she said. "You know I would have brought it to the farm."

"Do I?" he asked stiffly. "I also thought you'd have stayed to say hello last night. The young man acknowledged that you'd heard me saying I'd be in the barn."

"My nephew, Michael," she said. Her mouth felt dry.

"Yes, we met at the wedding."

"You know how young people are, Edward," she said, knowing she had to say something, to come up with a story; feeling ashamed for using Michael as her excuse. "When he finished riding, he wanted to head straight home . . . to have dinner, and to see Quinn."

"Would a quick hello really have taken so much time?"

"No," she said, the guilt snowballing. "I'm sorry."

"I've barely seen you," he said, his voice low. "Since—"

"I've just been so busy," she said hurriedly. "With all the summer people at the beaches, there seems to be twice as many animals. And yesterday my father told me he's leaving on a long sailing trip . . . it really shook me up."

"Is that the kind of friend you think I am?" he asked, stepping closer. He touched the side of her face with his finger, gently stroking her cheek. "One you can't call when you're feeling shaken up?"

"Of course not," she said, breathing harder. "You're such a good friend, Edward." Her stomach churned. His physical closeness was making her feel terribly uncomfortable, reminding her of what she had almost made happen between them. She had never used anyone that way before, never treated another human being as someone to fill her own need, give her comfort, help her to avoid painful feelings—but she almost had last week.

"What about dinner?" he asked.

"Dinner?" she asked, swallowing hard.

"Yes, tonight. We could go to the Renwick Inn, listen to the rain falling on all those willows by the river."

"Sounds romantic," she murmured.

"Then say yes," he said. "I'll go home and change, and you can do the same, and I'll pick you up—"

"Excuse me," came Mathilda's voice. She knocked on the door, then poked her head around. Her eyes were bright, filled with a question.

"Oh, you must want to leave," Rumer said. "That's okay—I'll close up myself."

"No, I still have to mop the kennel and play with the overnight guests," she said. "But I thought you should see this important message that just came in."

Rumer reached out, and Mathilda passed her a yellow slip of paper: *Meet Zeb at Foley's, 5:30, urgent.* The corners of her mouth twitched. She stared at the words, trying to appear calm.

"What time did the caller . . . ?" Rumer began.

"Five minutes ago," Mathilda said.

"Is there a problem?" Edward asked.

"Well," Rumer began. Her palms felt sweaty. What could the message mean? Rumer had made it very clear that she didn't want to stir anything up, listen to Zeb's explanations about the past and rehash all their family miseries. Was he persisting anyway? Or was it something to do with Michael—or with her father's trip?

"Rumer?"

"I'm not sure," Rumer said, feeling the color rise in her neck, spreading into her face. Edward was staring at her. She felt torn, wanting to tell him the truth yet not wanting to face whatever he might have to say about meeting Zeb.

"The doctor wants you to call him right back," Mathilda said sternly.

"The what?" Rumer asked.

"Oh, professional courtesy," Edward said. "Absolutely. Don't keep your fellow vet waiting."

"Listen, would you mind if we had dinner another night?" Rumer asked. "I've had a crazy day, and I just want to go back to the Point after work. I'm sorry. . . ."

"Don't worry," he said. "Just finish up here and take care of yourself. You've seemed so stressed and overworked lately." He held out his hand for the bag Rumer had filled with heartworm pills and treats for the dogs. They kissed, and she promised to call him the next day.

"The doctor wants me to call him right back? The *doctor*?" Rumer asked Mathilda as soon as Edward had left.

"From what I remember you telling me," Mathilda said, "Zeb Mayhew has a Ph.D. in astronomy or astrophysics or theoretical mathematics or something like that. That makes him a doctor, doesn't it?"

"Yes," Rumer said, peering at Mathilda. "You weren't listening at the door, were you?"

"How can you ask such a thing?" she asked, her hand on her heart as if horribly wounded.

"Because I was just about to say yes, I'd have dinner at the Renwick Inn with Edward, and I haven't heard the phone ring in the last half hour."

"Okay, so the call came in earlier, while you were giving Bootsie McMahon his rabies shot. I was transcribing the messages, and I just thought you should have all the information about all your options before you nailed yourself down for tonight."

"Having dinner with Edward wouldn't be nailing myself down. . . ."

"Whatever you say, Doc," Mathilda said, starting to smile.

"You sound like my father," Rumer said.

"I've heard worse," Mathilda said, beaming now.

"Was it really urgent?" Rumer asked, staring at the piece of paper. "What do you think he wants?"

"I don't know," Mathilda said, pointing at the clock, "but you'd better scoot—it's five-fifteen now."

Taking a deep breath and pulling on her slicker, Rumer yanked her hood over her head and hurried out the door. Her meadow glistened, green and silver under sheets of rain. The graceful maples spread their leafy branches over the rolling acres, and birds sang as Rumer walked to her car.

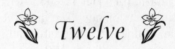# Twelve

THE BUILDING THAT housed Foley's store was as large and plain as a barn, inland and across Hubbard's Point from where Rumer and *les Dames de la Roche* lived. Sage-green paint had flaked from its weather-beaten shingles, giving it the look of old bronze. Rumer parked her truck in the sandy lot. Habit made her kick off her shoes; in summer, it was sacrilege to enter Foley's with anything but bare feet.

Covering her head, she ran inside. Vast and airy, the store was filled with groceries, books, magazines, bait and tackle, rafts, and tubes: staples for the shore. In the back was a soda fountain with a Formica counter and tall vinyl-covered stools.

Around the corner, just behind the pay phone, were four old tables and chairs. The wood surfaces were scuffed, scarred with coffee cup rings, carved initials, and burn marks from when smoking had been allowed. It was five-thirty, and Zeb wasn't there yet. Rumer rarely had time to come here anymore, but she didn't hesitate; she went straight to what had always been her favorite table—in the corner. She settled into the oak armchair to drink tea and listen to the rain on the roof.

Sipping hot tea, she looked at all the hearts and initials. So many Hubbard's Point boys and girls had fallen in love, wanted the world to know: TR&LA, SE&CM, DM&SP, ZM&RL.

Rumer still flinched to see their initials. Zeb had carved them almost as a joke, before they'd ever gotten together. They had been about sixteen; he had done it one day after finishing the paper route, saying best friends deserved memorializing too. . . .

Rumer closed her eyes for a minute, asking herself why she had agreed to come here. Foley's belonged to their past—she and Zeb had often stopped in for lemonade or hot chocolate. She shopped at the store, but she had avoided this table for years. Slowly, as if compelled from within, her fingers trailed across the oak surface, down to the drawer pull in front.

The table had one wide, deep drawer. Perhaps it had originally been intended for a desk but had somehow wound up at Foley's. Who had been the first Hubbard's Point girl to leave a note inside for the boy she loved? Over the years, the drawer had become a place to leave "secret" notes—telling someone how you felt about them, asking them to meet you at Little Beach or the Indian Grave, even—in a few celebrated notes—proposing marriage.

Holding her teacup steady in one hand, Rumer read the notes with the other. She refused to be affected—this kind of romance was too old fashioned, too nonsensical, for a woman of science like herself. As a young girl she had thought the drawers to be magical; she no longer did.

Still, once she started reading, she couldn't stop.

It was a tradition to spend an afternoon once in a while, going through the love notes. Mr. Foley—grandson of the original owner—prided himself on never throwing any of them out.

Time took care of it somehow. The notes settled—packed together in the drawer. Sometimes the authors came back to take them; other times, the recipients did. Others seemed to last forever. The oldest dated back decades, still stuffed into the drawer, an informal written history of this place that meant so much to everyone.

"Hi, Rumer."

Hearing Zeb's voice, Rumer looked up. He stood there in a dripping yellow slicker, khaki shorts, and sopping wet sneakers.

"Hi, Zeb."

"You got my message."

"Yes, what's going on?"

Without replying, Zeb gestured for the waitress to bring him a hot chocolate. Then he shook the water off his hair, spraying Rumer in the process.

"Hey," she said, brushing the drops off her skin.

"Oh, sorry," he said. "Just drying off."

"Well, dry off over there," she said, pointing at an empty space ten feet away.

"Oh, come on, Larkin. A little water won't hurt you. You're a vet—haven't you ever given a shaggy dog a bath? They shake and shake—"

"Shaggy dog. That's about it," she said, looking up at his messy blond hair falling into his blue eyes. Those eyes were giving off sparks, and she shivered. "What did you want to talk to me about?"

"Before I tell you, just let me drink a little of this," he said, pausing to lick half the dollop of whipped cream from the top of his steaming hot chocolate. "I really caught a chill out there in the storm."

"Your Range Rover has a leaky roof?" she asked.

"Nah," Zeb said, hunching down, his elbows resting on the table. "I've spent the day on my trusty bike."

"Your bike?"

"Yeah—my old Raleigh. Winnie had it in her garage. Guess she thought it was too good to throw out. Anyway, I'm not discussing business with you or riding back home till I finish this hot chocolate."

"Fortification," she said, and he laughed. "What's so funny?"

"That's what you used to say when we had our paper route. I'd be complaining about having to get up at five in the rain, and you'd bribe me with promises of fortification: You'd take me to Foley's and buy me hot chocolate when we were done."

"We had some cold, wet mornings. . . ."

"Saved up a lot of money . . ."

"Till you got us fired."

"Wasn't me!" Zeb protested, laughing hard.

"Are you kidding! Whose idea was it to single out poor Mrs. Williams—"

"She was mean to you—you went blue-crabbing on her stretch of the creek and she confiscated your shoes and Good Humor money."

"That *was* serious," Rumer scowled. "I had to go without a Creamsicle that day."

"See? I was looking out for you."

"But you didn't have to desecrate her paper."

"Dear Abby speaks. . . ."

Rumer hid a smile: To get back at Mrs. Williams, Zeb had started writing messages in her paper every morning before leaving it on her step. He would find the Dear Abby column, draw a balloon coming from the mouth of her picture, and scrawl some advice of his own: "Be nicer to everyone," "Having a bad day? Keep it to yourself," "Sure, you have a headache; you're tense, irritable: but *don't* take it out on others," and finally—the one that had gotten them fired—"Burn, baby, burn."

"The amazing thing was, it took her so long to report us," Rumer said.

"Maybe she thought the balloons were really part of Dear Abby's column. I printed very neat, to make it look official."

"She knew!"

"Yeah, you might be right. I think maybe she just liked the extra attention. You know? Is she still around?"

"Dead, Zeb. Fifteen years, at least."

"Damn," Zeb said, pounding his fist on the table. "I've been thinking I should apologize."

"You're a little late. . . ."

"Don't rub it in, Larkin. . . ."

They smiled in spite of everything, a memorial silence of affection and memory for old Mrs. Williams. Zeb got up to refill their tea and hot chocolate cups. When he returned, he clinked his with Rumer's.

"Okay," he said.

"Okay?"

"I'm ready to state my business. The reason I set up this meet."

"You make it sound like we're spies and can't be seen talking."

"That's truer than you think, Larkin. I want you to be the bad guy."

"The bad guy?"

"Well, that's not exactly it . . . I guess I was thinking good cop/bad cop."

She took a deep breath. "Just tell me, Zeb."

"Okay. It's about Michael. He needs help. . . ."

"Is he okay?" she asked, her heart skipping a beat.

"As okay as a high school dropout can be. Half the time I want to shake him, the other half I want to sit him down and make him tell me what I did wrong."

"So, why don't you?"

Zeb's face was very stoic, trying to smile, as if he wanted to make a joke. But then it twisted, and the smile left his eyes. "Because I'm afraid of what I might hear. What he'd tell me. That he has the two most selfish parents in the world, that I haven't been there for him enough. . . ."

"If he needs to say it," Rumer said steadily, "you should be ready to listen."

"Thanks," he said. "Very understanding of you . . ."

"No problem, Zeb. Anytime you want me to take your or Elizabeth's side against Michael, you'd better ask someone else."

He pushed back, nearly tipping his chair over. She saw the anger in his eyes, the furrow between his brows and the tension in his knuckles, and forced herself to sit still.

"Zeb," she said. "Sit down."

"Forget it," he said. "I was wrong to have expected—"

"No you weren't. Not when it comes to Michael. What can I do?"

Reluctantly, Zeb lowered himself back into the chair. His face seemed to have changed during the last few minutes, as if the emotions he felt were knocking him out. He looked tired, defeated—ten years older. The lines around his eyes and mouth were pronounced, and his lips were a thin straight line.

"I want him to go to summer school," he said. "I know Black Hall has a session—I heard him talking about it with Quinn. Also, your father mentioned it to me. I think, in the back of my mind, I hoped that coming here would be good for Michael. That Sixtus would take him under his wing."

"But he's sailing away," Rumer murmured.

"Yes," Zeb said more clearly, watching her reaction.

Rumer shrugged to shake off her worry and concentrate on Michael. "Anyway, with Dad gone, you want me to help?"

"Yes," Zeb said. "Michael likes you—he came back from seeing your horse the other day happier than I've seen him in months. I think he'd talk to you . . . and I think he'd like you to be proud of him."

"What about you and Elizabeth?"

"He's lost to us right now," Zeb said. "I can't explain it, and it's killing me, but he wants nothing to do with either one of us. It's as if we've let him down in too many big and small ways over the years."

"Do you think you have?"

Zeb sat very still. Color rose to his cheeks, but his blue eyes were as bright and clear as Rumer had ever seen them. "He's a child whose parents never loved each other," Zeb said quietly, and Rumer felt chills run down her neck and out of her fingertips. "That couldn't have made a very safe place for him to grow up. . . ."

"Zeb," she said, holding out her hand as if she could stop his words, keep him from saying any more about his marriage to Elizabeth.

"We never did, Rumer," he said. "Never, from day one. It was all a mistake. . . ."

"Stop!" she said. "We're sitting here talking about Michael! It can't have been a mistake, don't you understand?"

People looked up from what they were doing—shopping, sitting at the soda fountain. Rumer felt her heart racing, watching Zeb stare into her eyes and not look away. His hands inched across the table, as if he were thinking of taking hers. Their forefingers touched, and then she pulled hers away.

"Rumer, listen to me," Zeb said.

But she shook her head, composing herself. "I'll help you with Michael," she said calmly. "Anything you need, anything that will help him. I know my father would do the same. By the way, you know his plans?"

Zeb opened his mouth, floundering, as if he wanted to change the subject back to Michael. Then, resigned, he conceded, "He told me yesterday. Said he wanted to let it sink in for you before he started spreading the news."

"Are you encouraging him, by any chance?" Rumer asked. "Because if so, I wish you wouldn't."

Zeb gave a wry laugh. "Not that he'd take encouragement from me, but he doesn't need it anyway. He's on it, Rumer—this is his mission."

She shook her head. "I know he loves to sail, that he's been feeling nostalgic for old places. But I never expected him to put those things together and sail to Ireland—via Canada! It's crazy."

"So is flying to the moon," Zeb said. "But people have done it."

"It's a little different, don't you think? Astronauts have all that equipment and support. . . ."

Zeb fell silent for a moment, as if mulling that over. But then he looked up. "So will your dad. He has a great boat; he has your support . . . if you give it to him."

"Stop, Zeb," Rumer said, shaking her head. "I'm not there yet. I just came to Foley's to find out what you want. . . . I'd almost rather get lost in the drawer than talk about my father crossing the Atlantic in the *Clarissa*."

"Ah, the drawer," Zeb said, his face darkening.

"A lot of our old friends are in here," Rumer said, ruffling the papers and remembering a time when she and Zeb had left each other notes there, too.

"Look," Zeb said. "Here are the initials I carved." He traced the oak surface with his fingertips, going over and over the ZM & RL. Rumer's skin tingled as if he were touching her instead of the table.

"The kids are still using the drawer," Rumer said, changing the subject.

"Still and forever," Zeb said, reaching into the sea of scrap paper. "Here's one: 'Want to go to the movie on the beach Tuesday? I'll bring the blanket and bug stuff . . . you bring you.'" They laughed.

"Smooth operator," Zeb said.

"A lot of summer love in this drawer," Rumer said, feeling that unwelcome shiver again.

"Summer love is hard," Zeb said, watching her.

"Why is that? It seems as if it should be the opposite—sunny, happy. . . ."

"That's why it's hard, Rumer. The set-up is never like reality. People fall in love at the beach, but they can't take the sea and sand with them into winter. It doesn't travel well. Sometimes it doesn't travel at all."

Rumer closed her eyes. Zeb and Elizabeth? Or was he speaking of him and her instead? Ice filled her veins. She wanted to get off this topic and end this visit. She was just about to drink the last of her tea, when she heard the sound of bare feet slapping down the aisle of Foley's wooden floors.

"Look—it's the vet!"

"Yeah, that's Dr. Larkin—she takes care of our dog."

"Tell her!"

Looking over her shoulder, Rumer saw a young girl flying toward their table. Wet brown hair streaming behind her, her mouth open and eyes distressed, she was trailed by three other ten-year-old kids. Rumer had seen them around the beach, and recognized one as Jane Lowell's daughter, Alex.

"Dr. Larkin, there's a hurt sea hawk!"

"Hurt how, Alex?"

"I think he swallowed something sharp. He's choking, and there's blood coming from his mouth."

"Where?" Rumer asked, already hurrying down the aisle toward the door.

"In the cemetery. We went there to tell ghost stories in the rain, and we were sitting under the big tree, where it's sort of dry, and we heard this awful sound coming from the graves. . . ."

"I thought it was a ghost," one of the other girls said.

"I have my bike, Larkin," Zeb said, pulling his slicker off and throwing it around her shoulders. "Climb on."

Rumer followed Zeb to the bike rack. The rain was warm and steady. Her feet were tough from walking on the beach and rocks. Zeb pointed the bike toward the road, and she climbed onto the bar. Surrounding her with his arms, he began to pedal, heading for the train bridge. Their faces were close together, his breath warm on her ear. She closed her eyes and concentrated on keeping her balance.

Woods grew along the right, and when they came to the dirt road, they turned in. Zeb's wheels whirred beneath them, kicking up sand and pebbles. Tall maples and oaks formed a wide canopy overhead, protecting them from the rain. They reached a clearing—about four acres in size—of small green hills covered with perhaps thirty graves.

The kids pedaled in behind them.

"Over here," Alex Lowell called, heading toward a low hill. A huge dead oak stood at its crest, its branches bare of leaves. Rumer climbed off, and Zeb dropped his bike in the grass.

Rumer and Zeb ran up the rise, and she gasped at the heart-wrenching sight. An adult osprey was lying on its side, blood streaming from its mouth and a gash on the side of its neck. At first Rumer thought it was dead, but suddenly it thrashed, squawking, trying to rid itself of whatever had lodged in its throat.

Great wings, black and brown with white underneath, beat the air. The bird choked, cawing like a raven, then lay still again, its breast rising and falling.

"Can you save it?" Alex asked, crying.

"What happened to it?" another girl asked, her voice strained and thin. "Something cut its neck."

"Stand back, okay?" Rumer asked, patting the girls on their shoulders. She knew how traumatic it was for them watching the bird suffer. Stiff and shaking, they went to stand underneath the tree.

Rumer looked at Zeb. He was staring at the osprey, helpless, with a sort of horror in his eyes; she remembered that as a child he had hated the sight of blood. Blinking, he took a breath and glanced down at Rumer.

"Tell me what to do," he said.

"Maybe you should stand with the girls," she said. "Or take them back to Foley's—keep them from watching."

He shook his head. "You need help with this, don't you? I'll be your assistant, okay?"

Rumer nodded. She knew there wasn't time to argue. Peeling off his slicker, she handed it back to him. "We'll need to hold him steady. If you can get this around his body, keep him from beating his wings, trying to fly away—otherwise he'll injure himself. Or us."

"Okay," he said, gathering the slicker into his hands, holding it out toward the bird.

Rumer held his arm, making him wait. She inched forward, trying to see what they were dealing with. The hawk's eyes were yellow and wild; his curved beak was sharp as a blade. Blood had stained his white feathers rusty-red, still pumping out scarlet and wet. A silvery filament emerged from the side of his mouth. Her gaze ran down his neck, and then she saw it: the shiny metal protruding through the feathers and skin from inside his throat.

"He swallowed a fish," she said softly. "That had swallowed a hook."

"I see it," Zeb said, staring at the glinting metal.

Rumer held her breath. She had never tried to do anything like this without first sedating the animal, but there wasn't time. He was killing himself, ripping the fishhook inch by inch down his own throat, trying to get it out.

"This won't be easy," she said in a low voice, watching as the osprey went through another wrenching round of convulsion. "Do you have a toolkit on your bike?"

"Better than that," Zeb said, pulling his Leatherman tool from his pocket.

"Does it have a wire cutter on it?"

"Yes."

"Okay, then," she said, taking the tool from him. She licked her lips; her mouth was dry.

"Talk to me, Larkin," he said. "What is it?"

"I don't want to hurt him worse than he is now."

"You're a surgeon, right? Have you ever operated in the field?"

"Yes, but never without anesthesia . . ." She gazed at the bird; were his eyes more cloudy than before? "If I don't do this, I'm afraid he'll die."

"Rumer, you became a vet because you love animals. Of course you don't want to see him die—so let's save him. Okay?"

Rumer looked up at the dead tree. She knew this was a favorite spot of ospreys; they would catch fish in the tidal creek, then fly into this dead tree to devour the prey. The ground surrounding the trunk attested to it: fish bones, crab claws, and skate tails lay scattered around. Then she looked down at the injured bird and nodded.

"Okay," she said.

Zeb opened the slicker as if he were spreading wings. Crouching behind the osprey, he made one swift move to wrap the bird in the coat. Rumer's heart was racing—although the bird was weak, he reacted with terror and began to beat his massive wings. Zeb tried to hold him steady, turning the body toward Rumer so she could get to the hook.

The osprey was snapping, twisting his neck from side to side, losing more blood as he did so. Rumer's hands darted in; the hawk's bill was rapier sharp, and she knew he could take off a finger with one snap.

It happened so fast, she could hardly believe it: She grabbed his neck, opened the wire cutters, snipped the hook's barbed end; pulling the fishing line, she withdrew the smooth shaft from his throat. Up close, she could see the cut: about a half-inch long, the left anterior of his neck.

Her ministrations had enraged the hawk. Zeb was holding him tight, but with the hook gone, the bird was gathering strength and fighting hard. He twisted his head from side to side, trying to gouge Rumer's eyes. He was a tornado in Zeb's arms, a wild animal wrapped in a bloody yellow rain slicker.

"Let him go," Rumer said, jumping back.

Zeb dropped the osprey, who seemed to ripple every feather in his body and rise—weaving at first, then straight as an arrow—toward the tidal creek. The girls squealed and cheered in the background, then ran for their bikes to try to follow him.

Rumer's heart was pounding. She had never saved an animal's life in so difficult or dramatic a way before. She looked up at Zeb, facing skyward, watching the hawk disappear over the tree line. He put his arms around her, pulling her close to his body. She tilted her head back, feeling wild pleasure. He stroked her back, his lips brushed across the side of her face. She felt his breath hot on her skin, the most incredible celebration of life.

"You did it, Larkin," he whispered. "You saved his life."

"We did," she corrected him.

"I can't believe it! That was amazing! How he flew away . . ." Zeb said.

"Did you see? Wasn't it great?"

"I thought he was too badly cut; I thought you'd have to stitch him up."

"I would have if I'd had my bag—he'll heal on his own. Wild animals survive terrible things."

"They do?" Zeb asked, holding her tightly again so she could see straight into his blue eyes. He looked injured himself, as if he had survived something she couldn't begin to imagine. His gaze held her for a moment, and she stayed in his arms, holding her breath.

"They do," she said quietly. Then, feeling the blood rushing through her body, she forced herself to breathe and took a large step backward, leaving plenty of space between them. She fought the feeling as if it were a fever, as if she had to cling to every bit of strength she had. "Let's go, okay?"

"Rumer . . ."

"I have to get home," she said shakily.

"Five more minutes, okay?"

"I really have to—"

"Look, I just helped you, right? We saved an osprey's life—you'll be known far and wide, among veterinarians and bird lovers everywhere. You owe me this, Larkin. Take a quick walk with me."

Hesitating, Rumer shrugged and followed. This was the Hubbard's Point cemetery, with headstones dating back to the Revolutionary War. As children, she and Zeb had come here to visit the dead—although they didn't know many of them, they knew that they were their predecessors at the Point, that they should be loved for that reason.

As teenagers, Point kids had held séances here, played touch football in the clearing, lost virginities behind the bushes. As Rumer walked along beside Zeb, flushed, out of breath, she felt the history they shared uniting them.

Up the rise, Mrs. Williams lay beside her husband under a stone carved with angels and seagulls.

"Don't blame Rumer—it wasn't her idea," Zeb called to the woman whose paper he had defaced.

"I could have stopped Zeb from doing it though," Rumer said softly, acknowledging Mrs. Williams's grave.

"Think she forgives us?"

"I hope so," Rumer said.

"I want to be forgiven," Zeb said huskily, taking Rumer's hand. She knew, suddenly, that his words had nothing to do with Mrs. Williams. Continuing along, they paused at Zeb's parents' graves. Rumer said a silent prayer, and she saw Zeb doing the same.

They stopped for a moment at Rumer's mother's grave. It was on the outer edge of a circle radiating out from her ancestor Isaiah Randall, and her headstone was carved with the Wickland Rock Light and the words "Clarissa Larkin, beloved wife and mother, may her light continue to shine."

Rumer was always struck by those words, because they were so true: Her mother's light would shine forever. Remembering the voyage her father was about to take, she said a prayer for her mother to guide him. Zeb bowed his head. Rumer wondered what all the parents would think to see her and Zeb there together.

When they got back to his bike, the rain had nearly stopped. A few big drops fell down from the trees, but overhead, patches of blue gleamed behind the clouds. Zeb wheeled the bike down the path onto the paved road. It was ancient—black, dented, with the old baskets they'd filled with papers on either side of the back wheel.

There on the narrow road, Zeb stood aside, and Rumer climbed on again. She eased onto the bar in front, balancing her weight so the bike wouldn't topple. Zeb held the handlebars, his chin resting on the top of her head. And then, as they had done so many mornings so long ago, Zeb and Rumer rode through Hubbard's Point, past all the houses waiting for their papers.

Rumer watched the sky for the osprey. She didn't see him. Perhaps he was already fishing again; or perhaps his injury was too serious for him to survive. One of the hardest parts of being a vet was not being able to guarantee, or even know, the outcome.

Feeling Zeb's arms around her, she closed her eyes and almost wanted the ride to go on forever. *Not knowing the outcome*: It was one of the hardest parts of life. Twenty years ago she had taken for granted the idea that she and Zeb would grow old riding bikes together.

"Thank you," she said. "For saving the osprey."

"Do you think he'll be okay?"

"I don't know. I hope so."

Zeb's eyes narrowed. They clouded slightly, or was that a film of tears? He stared at Rumer without looking away, and she felt that her heartbeat must be showing through her skin. The truck keys felt hot in the palm of her hand. Zeb touched her arm with one finger, and it felt like fire.

"I want him to be okay," Zeb said.

"So do I."

"And I want us to be okay—friends again," he said. "More than anything. Keep watching, Rumer. When you least expect it, I'm going to prove to you what I mean."

"It doesn't matter," she said.

"Yes, it does," he said. "Just watch, okay? You'll know it when you see it!"

Rumer nodded, her hands shaking. She got into the truck. Overhead, the sky was clearing. Zeb held his bloody slicker. He stared at her, his eyes as intense as she'd ever seen them. Trembling, she backed out of Foley's lot.

When she looked into her rearview mirror, Zeb was just standing there, not watching her truck, but gazing at the sky, as if he hoped to see the injured sea hawk fly across the clearing blue.

Thirteen

THE FIRST MOVIE of the summer was *How the West Was Won.* It was the same every year: With all the great new movies available at the video stores, they always dragged out the archaic reel-to-reel projector with films such as *The Moon-Spinners, The Guns of Navarone, Flubber,* and *Mary Poppins.*

Mr. Phelan, the beach cop, would set up the screen: a huge white sheet hung between what looked like football goalposts on the beach. They would set the projector on the boardwalk and wait for dark. Mrs. Lowell of the Women's Club would sit at one end, selling tickets for fifty cents.

Most of Quinn's friends considered themselves too old for movies on the beach, but not Quinn. Movies on the beach helped her to unwind—especially tonight. A letter had arrived, hitting her with the news that she had to go to summer school. A big fat drag, to put it mildly.

She got to the beach early to dig her pit: Scooping out sand, she dug a big hole for her butt with a sandy backrest to lean on. Then she spread out one blanket underneath with a second to pull over her for warmth. Allie had gone to buy Good Humors, and now she ran over with them and snuggled under the blanket with her.

"What'd you get me?"

"Toasted almond."

"You're the best!" Quinn said, ripping open the paper. "What're you having?"

"Pink lemonade."

Quinn savored the ice cream, considering how Good Humors were like people. You were what you ate: She was crunchy and nutty, like a toasted almond, and Allie was smooth and pink, like pink lemonade.

"You hear about the osprey?" Allie asked.

"Yeah, Rumer and Mr. Mayhew saved its life," Quinn said.

"Well, here comes Mr. Mayhew's son," Allie said, gesturing toward the footbridge. "Maybe we could all celebrate together."

"Oh, great," Quinn said. "I just lost my appetite."

Michael Mayhew was striding down the ramp, his long hair held back by the red bandanna. In spite of herself, Quinn's heart skipped a beat. She tried to concentrate on eating her ice cream, but all she could think about was what a jerk she'd been the last time they'd been together, out in her boat.

"He's nice," Allie said. "He talked to me while I was picking flowers. I wonder if he knows about his dad helping Rumer save the osprey."

"I'm sure he'd be thrilled."

"He likes nature," Allie said. "I can tell."

"Maybe you should go out with him," Quinn said. "Then you can have a Point wedding."

"Quinn, you're turning red."

"Shut up—I am not."

"Quinny . . ." Allie said, laughing. "It's okay if you like him. I can tell you do."

"That's bullshit. But how?"

"Well, by how mad you get every time he walks by. You act like you hate him."

"Which I do."

"I don't believe you. It's like that January, when Steven Baird made you take your coat off and he threw it up in the tree."

"He hated me!"

"No, Quinn. That meant he liked you—you're so dumb about boys."

"How do you know all this stuff?"

Allie shrugged, daintily eating her pink lemonade. "I'm not sure. I just do. There he goes. . . ."

Together the sisters watched Michael Mayhew walk down the sands, away from the movies, toward the dinghy beach. Allie's words had sent all the joy flying out of Quinn's toasted almond. She ate it anyway; it tasted like sand.

Quinn had punk and Off! to keep the mosquitoes away. Although no food except Good Humors was allowed on the beach, she had smuggled in a few Slim Jims and a bag of red licorice. She offered some to her sister, but Allie was still slowly licking her pink lemonade.

Settling in, waiting for the movie to start, Quinn wondered why she felt so uneasy. To the left, Long Island Sound glistened like black diamonds under the twilight sky. Straight ahead, the evening star and the crescent moon hung over the marsh and the path to Little Beach. She hoped the injured osprey was safe in his nest over there.

"You could catch him on the way back," Allie suggested.

"Catch who?"

"Quinn! You're not fooling me. You know who—Michael."

"Yeah, well, why would I want to catch him?"

"I don't mean catch him like a lobster—I mean call to him. You know? Maybe he'd like to watch the movie."

"I doubt it."

"Just try."

"Why should I?"

"Because you've been here a long time, and you know the ways of the beach. You could try welcoming him. As a matter of fact, I'm getting out of here so I don't hold you back."

"Do me a favor, and don't leave—"

Quinn sighed. Allie threw back the top blanket, kissed Quinn's head, and walked away. Now Quinn was stuck waiting by herself, shivering like mad—and not from the sea breeze. Her stomach felt as if it were on a mad elevator ride: up to the top, down to the bottom. She felt like barfing.

And then, walking back along the tide line—just as Allie had predicted—came Michael Mayhew. He wore slouchy jeans and a black T-shirt, the bandanna covering his long hair. Quinn's heart picked up the pace—torn between wanting to duck down into her foxhole so he couldn't see her and facing the reality that Allie hadn't been all wrong about her liking him, she was momentarily frozen.

"Hey!" she heard someone call, and then realized it was her own voice.

Looking around, he changed direction and walked up to her.

"Hey," he said back, towering over her.

"Did you hear about the osprey?" she asked.

"Yeah," he said. "I was looking for it."

"You were?" she asked, surprised and impressed.

"Yeah, my dad told me about what happened."

"He and Rumer saved its life."

"I know. He's pretty happy about it."

"Yeah?"

Quinn tried to breathe. She felt almost like passing out, just from making small talk. It felt very strange to be having this kind of back-and-forth conversation with someone—it felt alarmingly *normal*.

"Coming to the movie?" she asked next, almost shocking herself to death.

"The movie?" He frowned, looking around. "That's what this is? They're showing a movie on the beach?"

"Yep. Run up to your house for a blanket, dig a pit, and watch the show."

Michael stood there, feet planted in the sand, staring at the boardwalk as if he'd never seen a projector before. Mr. Phelan was threading the tape through the spools; his wife held a flashlight so he could see better. Darkness was coming fast—the movie would start in a few minutes.

"Or . . ." Quinn said.

Michael looked down into her eyes. What kind of abyss was she getting herself into?

"Or you could sit here with me," she finished.

He didn't reply. He stood very still for a moment, gazing at her more deeply than anyone had ever done before. Quinn felt herself start to blush, but the feeling turned to a glow that warmed her all through. She pulled back the top blanket, and Michael crawled into her sandpit.

"Welcome to my cave," she said.

"Thank you," he said, sitting up too straight for comfort.

Very gently, with a hand seemingly not her own, Quinn touched the middle of his chest, easing him onto the sandy backrest. She felt the tension start to leave his body, through her fingers, as if they were a magnet pulling it out. He shivered, his eyes never leaving hers.

"Keep this beside you," she said, handing him two of her lit sticks of punk, the thin trails of smoke taken by the east wind.

"To ward off evil spirits?" he asked, joking.

"Yes," she said with perfect seriousness. "And to welcome the good ones."

"Really?" he asked, sticking it into the sand beside him. Now punk surrounded them, the sweet smoke filling the air like incense. Quinn considered his question, "to ward off evil spirits?" and thought—if he only knew. Hubbard's Point was an *axis mundi*—a place where the worlds met.

The dead danced here—sometimes, on midsummer nights, she saw her parents holding each other on the rocks, turning around and around to music only they could hear. Rumer's mother had seen unicorns as a child, hiding in the fog as they walked among the cedar trees; when she followed, they led her to the cemetery, where her mother's ghost was standing on the hill with her ancestor and namesake, daughter of the drowned lighthouse keeper's wife, Clarissa Randall.

"Evil spirits?" he prodded, still in a joking way.

Quinn took a deep breath. She understood—based on her experience of losing her parents—that where very good existed, evil was never far away. Michael wanted to laugh about something Quinn never made light of.

"You're not kidding, are you?" he asked.

"I never kid about the spirits," she said.

He nodded; she could see him trying to figure her out.

"I'm glad you've never lost your parents," she said. "If you had, you'd understand."

Offshore, the lighthouse beam played across the sky.

"I've lost them," he said. "I told you on the boat the other day. . . ."

"I know you think you have," she said in the softest voice she had ever heard herself use. "But it's different when they die. Believe me, it is."

At Aunt Dana's wedding, Quinn had considered the name Michael and thought "stone wall." Now, looking into his eyes, she thought "lost boy." The feeling behind the words melted her heart—and she fought it. Allie was coaching her from a distance: *Be nice to him*, Quinn could almost hear her sister say.

"You going to lose it on me again?" Michael asked. "I'm waiting for you to start yelling."

"Huh. Very funny."

"Glad you think so."

The night breeze turned cool, and Quinn pulled the blanket up a little higher. She thought of how her parents used to spread this blanket on the beach and sit with their daughters for hours on summer days. Now, years later, it was ratty and moth-eaten.

"I'm not laughing," Quinn growled.

"Not yet," Michael said. "But the night's young."

"If you hate me so much, what are you doing in my pit?"

"You invited me. And now I want to watch the movie."

"Right," Quinn said. "The movie."

To her absolute shock, beneath the blanket's soft surface she felt Michael Mayhew reach for her hand.

She had never held a boy's hand before. It felt big and strong, and when he squeezed hers, she felt the blood gush from her heart all through her body. It was a first for Quinn, holding hands at the beach movies—or anywhere—and she was so busy registering her amazement over how right it felt, she was bowled over with the shock of a second first: Michael kissed her.

Quinn saw stars. She felt a primordial rush, like having high tide all through her body. The sensation filled her, then washed away, back and forth like the sea caressing the sand. Michael's mouth covered hers, hot and wet, as if they shared one skin.

"What's going on?" she whispered.

"I'm kissing you," he said. "Would you like me to explain it to you?"

"You're crazy," she said.

"Yeah, maybe."

"The movie's starting. . . ."

"Sometimes people kiss at the movies," he whispered.

"Not me," Quinn said as he slid his arms around her neck and she let him kiss her again.

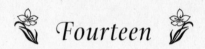

Fourteen

HE HAD TOLD her to watch for something.

He said she would know it when she saw it.

For twenty-four hours, since they'd saved the osprey, Rumer found herself on high alert. Almost in spite of herself, she found herself watching for him. Every time a car drove by, she would look up. Hearing bicycle wheels on the sandy road, she'd crane her neck. It was crazy, and she told herself to stop doing it.

At work, she made a report to the state wildlife office, filling out forms about what had happened with the osprey. Every question carried her back to Zeb. He had invaded her mind, and although she fought to banish him, the feeling of his arms around her shoulders was too intense and real to push away.

"What was it like?" Mathilda asked between patients, ruffling the wildlife forms.

"It was like trying to operate on a waterspout," Rumer said. "That bird had more energy than a hundred cats. His talons and beak could have done us in—"

"I wish I'd been there."

"Well, I had an assistant," Rumer said. "Sort of."

"You did?"

"Zeb, if you can believe it."

"Dr. Larkin! You're holding out on me!"

"It was nothing," Rumer said. "We happened to be talking together, when the kids came running up to tell us about the osprey. What choice did he have?"

"Did he do a good job?"

"Not bad," Rumer said, picturing Zeb's steady hands, the way he'd held that angry hawk without flinching.

"Maybe we should promote him to vet-for-a-day," Mathilda said, referring to the program Rumer had started two years ago, allowing high school kids to work in her office for a day to see what it was like to care for pets.

"Not a chance," Rumer said. "But would you mind taking over for me this afternoon? I want to see Blue; Edward and I are going to go riding down by the river."

"No problem," Mathilda said. "But I still think that any guy who subdues an injured sea hawk ought to be welcomed into the family." Then, as if she'd just realized what she'd said, she bit her lip. "Open mouth, insert foot," she said.

"Yes, we tried that already, didn't we?" Rumer asked. "Welcoming Zeb into the family . . ."

"We're back to the question of the stripes," Mathilda said. "Can a tiger change them?"

"I don't know," Rumer said. "And even if he can, would I be able to forgive and forget?"

"Forget, no," Mathilda said, giving her a hug. "But forgive, maybe."

Rumer nodded. She was itching to run out to the car, drive up to the farm, and ride Blue. Edward would be patiently waiting for her, the horses saddled and ready to go. Rumer pictured him there, working in the barn, taking care of his livestock. She wanted her heart to melt at the thought, to distract her from worrying about what Zeb wanted her to watch for—she wanted Edward to save her from the feelings that were welling up inside, making her flush and breathe too hard, just thinking about Zeb.

Rumer was at work, and Sixtus was out for the day. Zeb stood in the yard, wondering whether his work would show up in the moonlight. He held the spool, slowly unwinding as he reached from one branch to the other, in an oak between their yards, the first tree Rumer had ever climbed. The sound of feet on the stone steps made him look down.

"Uh-hem," Winnie said, clearing her throat.

"Caught me trespassing," Zeb said.

"Yes, I did, didn't I? Up a tree in Rumer's yard in the middle of the day . . . well, you'll have to pay a forfeit."

"What's that?"

"You must talk to me. Right now . . . put down whatever you're doing and humor an old woman."

Zeb laughed, climbing down. As old as Winnie might be, he knew she would go on forever. She held out her hand, and he kissed it first, then held it as they stood in the clearing between Rumer's and his old yard.

"You're as beautiful as ever," he said. "And forever young."

"Darling, I shan't be singing at the Met again anytime soon. Or even at the Bushnell. Gone are the days of Moshe Paranov and Dr. Nagy, my two beloved friends. They did so much to bring opera to Hartford. Previously, Connecticut was Siberia as far as that went. They hired me, and, oh, it makes me so sad. I'm the last . . ."

"But you're still here, Winnie," Zeb said, moved to see tears running down her wrinkled cheeks. He put his arm around her thin shoulders. "I know it's hard."

"You understand, don't you?"

He nodded. "To have lived a life; to have amazing connections with people you value—cherish—and to have those bonds broken."

"Our careers are oddly alike," Winnie said, drying her eyes with a lace handkerchief. "We both attained a measure of fame for doing work we loved. I've been worried about you, you know."

"Why?"

"Because you've come to earth after a decade of flying to the stars."

"Yep," he said, holding her tighter. "I have."

"I flew to the stars myself," she said. "Onstage in New York, Milan, Venice, even Hartford . . ."

"Was it hard for you to . . . alter your career?" Zeb asked, choosing his words carefully.

"How diplomatic of you," she laughed. "You mean when my voice could no longer draw audiences and I had to teach instead? Yes, it was hard."

Zeb just stared at the sky, seeing bright diamond stars within the daylight blue.

"Will it be difficult for you to administer a lab?" she asked. "To be the one studying the flights instead of flying?"

"Yes," he said, his stomach falling. "It will be."

"Perhaps you'll tell one of us," she said, "what happened to you up there."

"Someday," he said, still seeing constellations up above. "Maybe someday."

"Life goes on, Zeb. I could choose to be despondent, no longer performing for packed houses, but here I am, on terra firma, here at Hubbard's Point."

"Where everyone loves you," Zeb said.

"The same is true of you," she replied.

"Not everyone . . ." Zeb said.

"Ah, Rumer," Winnie said, nodding. "Our dear Dr. Larkin."

"I'm sure she wishes I'd just blast off and go back to where I came from."

"You came from Hubbard's Point," Winnie chuckled.

"I mean California," Zeb said. "Where the lab is."

"Seems you have work to do right here. The children told me about the osprey you and Rumer saved. Now when I watch them fish in the cove in front of my house, I think of my dear friend Zebulon Mayhew, and his newfound healing touch."

"Thanks, Winnie."

"And it's obvious," Winnie said, touching the spool in Zeb's left hand, smiling directly into his eyes, "that your work here is not done."

"It's just something stupid," he said, feeling embarrassed that she'd seen him.

Winnie shook her head. "No, darling. It isn't. All the great operas tell stories of doomed love. Missed chances, dire illness, broken hearts, betrayals . . . I have sung them all."

"Any advice for me?" Zeb asked.

"Of course," Winnie said, her eyes sparkling.

"I'm listening."

"In opera, the greatest loves end in tragedy. At Hubbard's Point, that doesn't have to be so. Your love for Rumer began in Act One, the years of your childhoods. Whatever foolish things you did with Elizabeth, that's Act Two. Over and done with."

"And now . . ."

"Now, this summer, is Act Three," Winnie said, touching his hand, then the wooden spool.

"What do I do?" he asked, really wanting to know, needing the wisdom of this old woman who had loved both him and Rumer for so long. He had told himself that all he wanted was forgiveness, but the other day, holding Rumer after they had released the hawk, he had known it was much more. He waited for Winnie to speak.

"What you do, dear boy," Winnie said quietly with perfect seriousness in her green eyes, "is not turn back. Don't let her talk you out of it. And don't be afraid. . . ."

"Don't be afraid of what?" he asked.

"Of a grand gesture or two," she said, tapping the spool and kissing his cheek. "Now, I have two voice students about to arrive. I must depart. . . ."

"Thanks, Winnie."

When Zeb looked up to see her go, he caught sight of the osprey, wheeling overhead, flying in wide circles. He hovered in the air, borne by the breeze. He made it look so easy—just floating in the air, lazily flying over the beach and sea. But Zeb knew the bird was hunting, fighting to stay alive, riding through all the dangers hidden by the beautiful day.

Watching Winnie disappear behind the hedges of her own yard, her bright caftan sweeping behind her, Zeb grabbed the lowest branch and pulled himself back into the tree. The thought of Rumer filled his heart, and with desire and hunger for her growing stronger by the minute, he resumed moving from limb to limb, continuing what he had been doing before Winnie had come.

ॐ

By the time Rumer got home from work that night, all she wanted was a swim and a cup of tea. Her head was throbbing. Even riding along the river on Blue with Edward beside her on Liffey, it took all her effort to concentrate on what Edward was saying. She watched every raptor soaring overhead, wondering what kind of recovery the osprey was making, feeling the thrill of holding Zeb after the release.

Now, pulling up in front of her house, she saw the yellow machinery and the crowd gathered, and put her head down on the steering wheel.

"Rumer, just look!" Annabelle cried. "Contractors and workers have positively invaded Cresthill Road! It started late this afternoon—panel trucks, dump trucks, vans, and a backhoe all rumbled under the trestle and down to the Point like an army on the move."

"It's true," Winnie said, standing in her flowing white, green, and orange gown, flanked by two of her voice students. "As dramatic as Annabelle is making it sound, it was even worse to see."

Hecate sidled through her shady yard like a timid animal afraid of the light to peer around her garage. Annabelle's daughters, dressed in beach things, crossed their arms and shook their heads.

"Where's my father?" Rumer asked, but she glanced around for Zeb. The workmen were in his old yard, talking to the new owner.

"Sixtus drove to Hawthorne to buy charts for his voyage."

"Do you know what's going on?" Rumer asked, watching the activity at the old Mayhew house next door. The new owner stood in the top yard, pointing at various spots while the contractor took notes. Obscured by the thick trees and overgrowth, it was hard to see what he was doing. All the rabbits had run for cover and were out of sight.

"That is the question," Winnie intoned. "What, precisely, is going on?"

"Big doings," Annabelle reported. "I looked through that truck window and saw a veritable forest of rolled-up blueprints."

"Has no one told them of the hammer law?" Winnie asked.

"They're not hammering yet," Rumer said, her heart sinking as she watched the workmen unloading shovels and pickaxes.

"Perhaps not yet," Hecate said, "but they will . . . and soon . . . all those tool belts."

"Dad said this would happen," Rumer said. "When we met the new owners, they seemed awfully interested in 'improvements. . . .' "

"Improving. Such an overrated occupation," Hecate purred, shaking her head and rolling all her Rs. "When nature has given us such beauty and the senses and capacity to enjoy it."

Winnie's car, an orange Volvo, was parked in the road, and the women gathered around it as if for warmth. Rumer leaned forward, her front pressed against the driver's door, and Winnie left her students to come over and place a hand on her arm.

"Darling, your bosoms. Never squish them," Winnie admonished as she pulled Rumer back. "Now, will you walk up the hill and do reconnaissance with me? Since the property lies between you and Hecate, I think you should both come."

Rumer glanced down toward the water at the cottage Zeb was renting. She wished he were standing with them now, but seeing no activity, she nodded and led Winnie and Hecate up the crumbling stone steps lined with bluebells and day lilies.

"Mr. Franklin," Rumer said, reaching the top. "I'd like you to meet two of our neighbors, Winnie Hubbard and Hecate Frost."

"How do you do?" Hecate asked.

"Charmed," Winnie said, holding out her hand as if she expected him to kiss it. When he didn't—and didn't seem to recognize her as a local celebrity—she got straight to the point. "What, exactly, are you doing?" she asked.

"Doing?" he asked, seeming shocked to be asked. "I'm consulting with my contractor."

"So it appears," Winnie said. "But do you realize that no work can be done until after Labor Day?"

Mr. Franklin laughed. "No offense, Ms. Hubbard, but I don't believe that's up to you."

"It has nothing to do with me," Winnie said. "It's the hammer law—an ordinance here at the Point."

"People summer here for the peace and quiet," Rumer explained. "To get away from the noise of life and find time to think."

"And to create," Winnie said. "There are many artists here . . . writers, musicians . . . we need peace for our creations to grow. A refuge from the noise and bother of the outside world."

"I heard someone down there singing before," the new owner said, gesturing down the hill. "Loudly. Isn't that noise?"

"Singing is not *noise*!" Winnie said.

"It's music," Hecate said kindly, as if the fellow were dimwitted.

"This is my property now," the man said. "If I want to build, I'll build. Nothing personal, it's just how it is. We're not going to sleep in there till some improvements are made, so that's what we're going to do. I've applied to the zoning board for everything we plan to do—don't worry, we'll dot the i's and cross the t's. I'm a good guy—everyone who knows me will tell you. I go by the book, but we don't want to waste the summer. . . ."

"You're not going to swing a hammer this summer," Winnie warned.

"Surely, Mr. Franklin," Hecate said, "you can enjoy this lovely cottage the way it is—for a night, for a weekend. Perhaps you will fall so in love with it, you'll find all this expense and bother unnecessary."

"Not one night in that firetrap till we make some changes," he continued as if the women hadn't spoken. "My wife saw bats flying out the attic vents. The ceilings have water damage. The closets smell like mildew."

"Pshaw," Winnie said. "What did you buy an old house for if you don't like old houses?"

"Bats are lovely," Hecate said. "They keep the mosquitoes under con-t*rrr*ol."

Rumer took a step back. She had spotted the rabbits peeking out of their hole beneath the azalea. Perhaps they had heard her, Winnie's, and Hecate's voices, ventured to the aperture to investigate. Crouching down, Rumer eased her hand into the cleft. She felt soft breath and delicate whiskers brush her skin.

When she glanced up again toward her own house, she saw something gold glinting in the trees. Blinking, she stared, trying to make it come into focus. But then the sun moved, or a shadow shifted, and it was gone.

Winnie was still arguing, and Hecate had started soothing. Rumer closed her eyes, knowing in her heart that they were fighting a losing battle. The man had made up his mind. Perhaps the hammer law would keep him quiet till Labor Day, but after that, changes were coming. Looking through the tall grass to her father's boat sitting in her own yard, past the tree where she'd seen a flash of gold, Rumer felt like a ship in a rocky sea.

❧

After seeing Winnie, Zeb had jumped on his bike to ride the hills of Black Hall. Wearing himself out till his lungs burned and muscles ached, he had done all the paved roads and half the dirt roads, wishing the hills were even higher. Overshadowing all the things that were on his mind was the idea of what Rumer would think when she saw what he'd done.

So many things made him think of her.

That morning he had received from Caltech a FedEx delivery of NASA satellite photos taken on his last flight and a request for his interpretation. He had opened the envelope, slid out the photos, and laid them across his desk. The images were blurred, undefined. They showed the North Pole taken from the Terra satellite. It had been the payload on his last flight, and just seeing them brought back memories of the explosion. The photos were of seals—hundreds of thousands of them stranded by encroaching ice—and Zeb thought immediately of Rumer.

What Rumer would say if she knew . . .

He had examined the data with the sound of waves splashing Winnie's rocks in the background. The juxtaposition of fear and peace was jarring—terror up in space, creatures stranded and starving at the North Pole, a summer day at Hubbard's Point, a surprise for Rumer.

The explosion in space had been Zeb's wake-up call. How could he come that close to death and not see his life pass before his eyes? And what kind of life was it anyway? He had thrown away his only love so many years ago: hurt her so badly, left her hating him for what he'd done.

Because of Zeb's own stupidity, he had lost Rumer once. Now, riding his bike back to the Point, he knew he'd do everything in his power to get her back. By the time he coasted down the far side of Cresthill Road, the moon was rising over Winnie's cove, and the stage was set for her surprise. Her car was in the road at the foot of the hill; all he had to do was knock on her door, drag her out of her house, and—

"Zeb?"

Her voice shocked him. He had just been thinking of her so intensely, it was as though he'd conjured her out of his fantasies.

"Hi, Rumer," he said.

"I have to talk to you," she said.

"Funny—I have to talk to you," he replied. "I was just going to come find you."

She stood in the shadows. A pine bough waved across the light coming from Winnie's windows, making it hard to see her. Zeb's pulse kicked in: Silhouetted from behind, her body was so pretty and fine. He saw the curve of her breasts and hips, and exhaled. As she got closer, the light caught the sparkle in her eyes, and he saw her smile, and his heart began to pound.

"Did you see it already?" he asked.

"See what? Oh, the thing I was supposed to be watching for?"

"Yes," he said, happy that she had remembered.

"Actually, no. I've been too distracted by what's going on up the hill. Did you see when you rode in?"

"No—what?"

"You missed all the heavy equipment at your old house. The new owners have bigger plans than we thought."

Zeb looked at her. He had known her so well for so long that he couldn't miss the signs—the tension behind her blue eyes, the hesitation in her walk, the hitch of laughter in her voice as she tried to be a good sport. Leaning the bike against Winnie's garage, Zeb wanted to take her in his arms but held himself back.

"What do you want me to do?" he asked, craning his neck to see the machinery. "Sabotage the construction site?"

"Now, that's an idea, Mayhew."

"Come on," he said, grabbing her hand. "Let's see what we can do."

"You're kidding, right?"

Peering at the sky, ignoring her question, he asked, "How are the stars tonight?"

"Pretty bright," she said. "Even though the moon's rising fast and they're dimming the higher it gets."

They crossed the street and cut through Hecate's yard, filled with fireflies. The branches hung low, brushing their heads. Rumer preceded Zeb, the tall grass swishing against her long legs. They climbed over an old wall, its granite quarried fifty yards down the rocky shore from Winnie's.

"You planning on us shinnying up the chimney?" he asked.

"Not exactly. There's an easier way."

"I hope we don't land in jail."

"Come on," she said, ignoring him and leading the way through the grass.

He didn't have to follow her; he knew exactly where she was heading. The full weight of their time together and apart on this planet hit him, and he felt a jolt in his bones. She stood aside, and he stared at the place he knew so well: under the flat rock just beneath the azalea bush, beside the hole that led to the rabbits' warren. Crouching down, he inched his fingers between the rock and the soft earth and came out with the key. His heart was racing as his eyes met hers.

"It doesn't belong to me anymore," he said. Maybe they should forget the roof, the stars; his eyes darted into her yard next door. There it was, the surprise he had set up. He wanted her to see, but he didn't want her to turn away from his eyes.

"I know."

"I don't belong inside."

She paused. He watched her gaze between the houses, to the Wickland Rock Light. She stared for a few seconds, as if the beacon were giving her a message.

"I think we do," she said. "For tonight only."

"Tonight only?"

"The house doesn't really belong to anyone right now. The old owners have sold it; the new owners don't love it yet. If you want, I think it's okay to go up on the roof—this one last time."

They walked to the door. Zeb felt the key in his palm—the metal was thin, worn by time. He wondered whether the lock had been changed. The screen door creaked as he pulled it open. The wooden steps groaned beneath their feet. Across the small screened-in porch to the kitchen door: a burglar's paradise. Large-paned windows in the door, a single lock. Inserting the key, it turned easily, and they were inside.

The house smelled exactly the same. The spicy perfume of salt air, cinnamon toast, musty cushions, well-worn rugs braided by his mother. They were still there, covering the dark pine floors. The subsequent owners had changed nothing.

"God, it's like going back in time," he whispered.

"As Winnie always says," Rumer whispered back, "why mess with perfection?"

They crossed the living room, went up the old wooden stairs. Zeb counted: one, two, three, four. The fourth step still creaked loudly—his perpetual downfall when trying to sneak out as a teenager.

"The new owners want to change this?" he asked.

"Shhh," she said. "Let's not talk about them tonight. . . ."

In the upstairs hall he passed his parents' room on the left. Looking in, he saw the same iron bedstead where they had slept, covered with a thin chenille spread. In the dim light, he had memories of waking up from a bad dream, standing in this very doorway to watch his parents sleep.

Years later, he and Elizabeth had slept there a few times. Time flashed, and now when he looked at the bed, he saw himself where his father had slept and Elizabeth where his mother had—closer to the window, overlooking the beach. It had never felt right to Zeb—staying with Elizabeth next door to Rumer. Their trips here had been brief and uncomfortable.

Rumer walked first through the door of his old room. All of his old collections were gone, thrown out long ago: insects, shells, starfish, vertebrae. His meteorite. One had fallen to earth here—right at the dead end of Cresthill Road, as if the land itself exerted a pull so strong, it reached into space. He had picked it up despite his mother's fear it could be radioactive, and displayed the small, craggy rock on a shelf he had made from driftwood boards.

Now, excited and stirred inside, Zeb unlocked the window and climbed out. Half turning, he offered Rumer his hand and helped her over the sill. They eased their way across the long, shallow stretch of shingles below the dormers, then up the steep side to the upper roof.

"Don't slip," Rumer said.

"Or I'll break my ankle again?" he asked.

"Just watching out for you, Zeb," she said, sounding breathless as they balanced their way along the peak. They inched along the shingles until they reached the midway point between the crooked brick chimney and unicorn weathervane, and then sat down.

From there, the sky was the clearest Zeb had seen it since coming east. This house was on the Point's highest land, and climbing to the roof had brought them above the marine layer of fine sea mist. Rising in the east, a big gold moon balanced over the cove. Above, the sky was paved with stars.

"I used to look up," Rumer said, "and wonder where you were. . . ."

"Really?" Zeb asked, staring into the Milky Way's white cloud.

"Did you think I wouldn't?"

"I thought you wouldn't, Rumer. After what I put you through—"

"Tell me what's new on the ground," she challenged him. "The work you've found that will keep you here on earth."

He found himself thinking of the photos he'd examined earlier, the report he'd made to the lab at Caltech. "I looked at some pictures today. NASA Terra satellites spotted an ice sheet," he said. "In northern Russia."

"And they wanted you to look at the photos?"

"Yes."

"What's so unusual about ice? Especially in northern Russia—it must always be icy up there."

"Not like this," Zeb said softly.

Branches crackled in the yard below; a creature moving through the brush, Zeb thought. Seeing Rumer tilt her head, listening with interest for whatever animal it might be, made it hard for him to say the next part, wondering why he was telling her at all.

"The thing is," Zeb said, "the photos show about four hundred thousand baby seals trapped by the ice."

"Trapped by the ice?" Rumer asked. "Seals?"

"Yes."

"How did it happen? Do they know?" she asked, visibly upset.

"Their path to the Barents Sea was blocked. Abnormally high winds created an icy bottleneck at the White Sea's northern entrance . . . the seals should have started their journey a month ago, but they can't get through."

"You can see this?"

"The photos show a sharp contrast between the clear waters and the large ice sheet."

"Zeb, what will happen to them?"

"They're starving," Zeb said, picturing the photo, knowing that not even the best vet in the world could save them.

He didn't have to look to know that Rumer was close to crying. His chest tightened, hearing her choke back a sob. She had always been like this: If a bird fell from its nest, she'd climb the tallest tree to put it back. If a swan got tangled in fishing line, she'd cover her head to protect herself from its strong wings and set it free. He had seen her with the osprey, and he knew she'd do anything to save the seals.

"What can we do?" she asked.

"Nothing," Zeb said. "That's the problem. We can see the way it is, but we can't fix it. All this satellite technology, the ability to see anything in the world, and no way to help. That's what I thought when—" He broke off.

"When what?"

He didn't want to tell her. It didn't take much for him to hear the explosion ringing in his ears again. He'd been clenching his teeth so tight, his jaw ached.

"That's why you're so lucky—to be able to do what you do. Help animals; save their lives. Like with the osprey . . ."

"We don't know if he survived," she said.

"I know he did," Zeb said. "I saw him today."

"You did? When?"

Zeb tried to breathe. Here he was, sitting beside the best friend he had ever had, surrounded by stars and the smell of honeysuckle, feeling the real magic of a summer night in Hubbard's Point.

"This afternoon," he said, pointing. "When I was doing that. . . ."

Rumer turned her head. She gazed down the rooftop, across the hedge, into her own yard. The moon had risen over the houses across the street, and it was caught in the tall dark pines. Its light, filtered through the boughs, had done its job: The branches of the old oak tree between the houses were a filigree of golden threads.

"What is it?" she asked, breathless.

"I did that for you," Zeb said, taking her hand. "Because I want you to believe in us again."

"Believe in us . . ."

"The way we used to be," he said. "When you said we were connected by a golden thread."

"Zeb . . ."

"And that it could never be broken," he said.

Rumer couldn't speak. Staring at the tree, moonlight dancing on the web of fine brass wire, she seemed to spin back in time. Her hand felt warm in his, and she glanced up to meet his eyes.

Now, looking over the unicorn weathervane, he saw Arcturus in its transit. From this angle on the roof, the star appeared to be speared on the creature's horn. He thought of the opposite perspective, looking down at Earth from space, and felt his throat tighten. Glancing at Rumer, he wanted to tell her.

"There were so many times I flew over . . ." he began.

"Flew over Hubbard's Point?" she asked.

"Yes."

"You could see it? You could tell?"

"I knew. I could picture this house; and yours next door."

Rumer's mouth dropped open.

"But most of the time, I'd be concentrating on other things. We'd be way up there, and I'd look out the spacecraft window. There were the stars, the moons, the planets . . . and then there was Earth."

"It looks different?"

He nodded. "This beautiful blue and white planet . . . yeah, it looks different." He stared up, remembering how it had felt to gaze down.

"Out in space, it's just like the moon or a star."

"Except it's not," Zeb said, hearing his own heartbeat. What was that? he wondered. In his space suit, everything echoed through his helmet, and he'd fall asleep to the sound of his own pulse, comforting and steady. But here on the roof, talking about flight with Rumer, he was hearing the rhythm of his own life.

"It's not?" Rumer asked.

"No . . . it's everything," Zeb said.

"I know," Rumer whispered.

"That little sphere, so far away, yet containing everything I love . . . trees, oceans, music, art . . . I never stopped thinking of our magical thread."

"Made of gold," Rumer said, staring at the moon.

"And people. Michael . . ." Zeb said. His heart was pounding, and he pressed his face close to hers and whispered, "You."

Rumer shivered, suddenly turning, surprising him, pressing her face into his shoulder. He could feel her breath against his skin, and the physical intensity made him shiver with thunder.

"Rumer . . ." he said.

She didn't move, but he could feel her mood change. A chill filled the air, surrounding them. "Why?" she whispered.

"Why what, Rumer?"

"Oh, Zeb. I never thought anything could break it. . . . I swore that could never happen. But it did—it's broken forever, and nothing can fix it. There's someone else now. Edward . . ."

"Rumer, please . . ."

"Why did you have to marry Elizabeth?" she asked, tearing away from him, sliding down the roof and into the window below. He couldn't see her, but he heard her running through the empty house. The screen door slammed behind her, and she flew through her yard and her own kitchen door.

The moon rose higher in the sky, and now Rumer's yard was in shadow. The bushes were dark, lifeless. The gold thread had vanished into the black.

Fifteen

SIXTUS CALLED OLIVIER de Cubzac at the Hawthorne Boat Works and arranged to launch the *Clarissa* that Friday morning. Since Olivier was racing in Newport, Sixtus oversaw the operation. Having launched his boat every summer since he'd first bought it in 1966, he expected—and got—no surprises. They wheeled the yacht just fifty yards down Cresthill Road, eased it down the abandoned tracks, and slid it into Long Island Sound.

"Why don't you store it at the Hawthorne yard instead of behind your garage?" one of the crew asked, handing out the bill for Sixtus to sign.

"Because I'm cheap," Sixtus said. "Because Hubbard's Point has this nice old marine railway that no one uses anymore, and it's free. Used to be a quarry here about a hundred years ago, and they laid these tracks for putting boats in and hauling rocks out."

"Hundred years ago," Richard Struan, the crew chief said, examining the rusty old tracks. "Just a little older than your pretty boat here. When was it built, Sixtus?"

"Nineteen-ought-five," Sixtus said. "Just past the turn of the last century. Found it sitting in a side yard in Silver Bay, just starting to rot. Her owner had died, and his wife was too broken up to care about some old boat." He shook his head at the memory and the idea of the *Clarissa* being "some old boat."

"So you took it off her hands . . ." Richard said, chuckling. "For a song."

"Yes, for a song," Sixtus said, the guilt just below the surface. He had needed to replace some starboard-side planking and completely redo the brightwork on the blackened rails. The sails and most of the running rigging had needed to be updated. The rudder was cracked, the keel chipped. The mast step and bronze mast support had needed replacing. The cockpit would require refurbishing. Sixtus had acted as if he were doing the woman a big favor, taking it away for three thousand dollars. In fact, he had been buying one of the prettiest boats on this planet for a mere pittance.

"Well, it belongs with someone who loves it, that's for sure," Richard said. "The former owner is probably smiling down on you from heaven—wishing you Godspeed on your journey."

"I hope so," Sixtus said, secretly hoping the owner wasn't hurling down bolts of wrath for having taken advantage of his wife. He felt a new pain in his shoulders and wondered whether he was feeling the man's retribution.

When the crew left and he had sailed the *Clarissa* to the dock, Sixtus forgave himself and fell in love with her all over again.

"It's just you and me, sweetheart," he said. "We're going to keep each other safe the whole way to Ireland, now. Rumer would never forgive us if we didn't." As he talked, he began to feel as if he had his wife back. He had changed the boat's name—even though some friends had warned him it could bring bad luck—from *Ceres* to *Clarissa*.

"God's not going to punish me for being loyal to the only woman I ever loved," Sixtus had scoffed. "Besides, I taught the myth of Ceres for forty years, and she and Clarissa have one thing in common: daughters. The way they love their daughters to the depths of the earth; in Ceres' case, literally. Plus, both their names begin with the letter C." Talking on and on, Sixtus had realized he was trying to assuage his own superstition. In the end, devotion to Clarissa had won, and he'd given Rumer the go-ahead to swing the champagne bottle and christen the boat.

Remembering all that now, Sixtus set about writing a checklist. He'd be leaving on the dawn tide Saturday, and he didn't want to get stuck off-shore without supplies. Hearing the put-put of a passing engine, he stuck his head up and saw Michael and Quinn checking her lobster pots.

"What's going on here?" Sixtus boomed across the water.

"Hi, Six!" Quinn called.

Michael waved.

Motioning them closer, Sixtus leaned on the coaming. It took him five seconds flat to get the lay of the land: They were in love, and they were in deep. Sixtus let out a long, low whistle, thinking of what Quinn's aunt and Michael's father were in for.

"Why aren't you at school?" he asked.

"Got work to do," Quinn said.

"What about summer school? You too, Michael."

"I'm helping Quinn," he replied, but by the surprised expression crossing Quinn's face, Sixtus considered the possibility that she knew nothing of Michael's dropout status.

"Lobster fishing is all well and good, but you've got to think of the future. You think you'll both be happy ten years from now, going out to pull pots in the dead of winter? With snow falling and the lines frozen and your hands blocks of ice?"

"Sure, why not?" Quinn asked happily.

"Besides, it's not snowing today," Michael said. "It's eighty degrees and beautiful. This beats sitting in a classroom, Grandpa. Even you can't say it doesn't."

"That attitude, young man, will get you through dinner and not much further. *Carpe diem*: 'Seize the day.' Well, fine: But what about tomorrow and tomorrow and tomorrow? You've got to look *ahead*, both of you . . . to the horizon and beyond."

"The horizon is yours, Sixtus," Quinn said, respect in her voice. "You're the one sailing to Ireland."

"I wouldn't be if I hadn't graduated from high school," he said.

"How do you figure that?" Michael asked.

"You might have noticed that this is a classic boat. Well, I'm navigating by sextant and compass—I need math to do that. I need every bit of education I have to get me across. English, history, science . . ."

"Why do you need English to sail across the sea?" Quinn asked.

"To amuse myself; to keep myself strong. I can recite poems I committed to memory fifty years ago, quote *Macbeth* to myself in moments of tedium."

"I can just see you, Sixtus," Quinn laughed.

"Yeah, Grandpa—you're probably where Mom got her acting talent from."

"Don't steer me off the subject of summer school," Sixtus warned. "You two are signed up to go, and you're going. Got it?"

"Grrrr," Quinn said in a stunningly real imitation of a tiger.

"Growl all you want, but you're going," Sixtus said, turning his back on them to get back to work.

When they got in from lobstering, Michael and Quinn reeked of the fish heads they used for bait. Michael watched as she secured the boat in its slip, learning the difference between bow, stern, and spring lines. She moved with grace, as if she'd been on boats her whole life, and he found her competence incredibly beautiful. Neither languid nor sophisticated like L.A. girls—just the opposite. She was down to earth, real, and totally New England.

"What was Sixtus talking about out there?" she asked, gathering her equipment together. "You needing summer school?"

"I'm between situations right now," Michael said.

Quinn laughed. "You mean you got kicked out too."

"No," Michael said, thinking back to the day he'd decided to just leave his books in his locker, walk out of school between French and English, and not go back. He had felt an emptiness inside, bigger than space. "I mean, that phase of my life is over, and the new one hasn't started. One door has closed, the other hasn't opened yet. I'm in the hallway."

Quinn tilted her head, sunlight striking her wild auburn hair. "I have no idea what you're talking about. I hate to tell you this, but you sound like one of those unhappy wife doctors."

"What?"

"Like on *Oprah*. Allie's always watching her—she wants to be a psychologist when she grows up. If I'm around, I sometimes watch too. Is that how people in California talk? Like doctors on *Oprah*?"

"Shhh," Michael said, just holding a finger to his lips. Maybe she didn't know that it hurt him to have her make fun of him like that. He lay on the seawall and turned his head while she finished on the boat, feeling the hot concrete beneath his cheek. He had just been trying to be open— she inspired that in him like no one he'd ever known. He didn't have it with his parents, he didn't have it with his friends, and he'd never had it with a girlfriend. Even now his feelings stung, but he couldn't resist turning his head back to look at her.

She was right there—leaning out of the boat to put her face close to his.

"I'm sorry, Michael," she said. "I was just playing, but Allie always says I play too hard."

"That's okay," he said.

They grabbed the pail of lobsters and the leftover bait and began to walk home. Trekking across the sand, over the footbridge that crossed the tidal creek, and up the right of way behind the yellow house, Quinn pointed out the huge boulder overhanging the path. "Indians used to cook under there," she said. "Back before there were any houses here. An archaeologist came once and found traces of ancient smoke. She uncovered arrowheads and other stone tools."

"They must have hunted and fished here," Michael said, surveying the wooded land, the sparkling water.

"Like us," Quinn said as the lobsters scrabbled against the plastic pail. "I'll live here, just like them, and I'll die here. Someday I'll show you the Indian Grave. . . ."

"Stop," Michael said sharply. "Why do you always talk about death?"

"Because it's part of us," Quinn said softly. "Part of our lives."

"That's not true," Michael said, suddenly wishing she would just walk away and leave him alone.

"It is," she said with terrible sadness in her eyes. "When you lose your parents as young as Allie and I, you have to make peace with that fact in order to go on. It's sad, but it doesn't scare me anymore."

The path came out at the dead end of Cresthill Road. With the Point on their right, they walked past two shingled cottages to Winnie's guest house. They stood in the road, and Michael felt torn between wanting Quinn and her death talk to disappear and wanting her to come inside so he could kiss her. Desire won, and he opened the door.

They stood in the tiny old kitchen. The pantry at his Malibu house was bigger than this. He watched as Quinn opened cupboards, found a big black iron pot, and started filling it with water. She put it on the old enameled stove, lighting the burner.

"What are you doing?" he asked.

"Cooking you a lobster. Do you have any butter?"

He got some from the refrigerator. "It's too early—not even ten in the morning."

"Lobster is the perfect morning meal," she said. "Full of protein. Sam sometimes goes spearfishing out at the breakwater and catches blackfish. We have them for breakfast, and he says it's brain food. . . ."

The pot hissed as the heat spread. Michael leaned against the rickety old table, and Quinn came into his arms. He kissed her.

They kissed slowly for a few moments, until the water began to boil and the pot lid started to rattle.

"I want to show you something," she said, holding his hand as they looked into the bucket. The lobsters had quieted down, lying together in the bottom.

"What?"

"It's about the food chain, the cycle of life. Everything happens for a reason, Michael, the way it's supposed to . . . you know those fish heads we used to bait the traps?"

He nodded.

"Well, they were tautog. Blackfish—swimming free out by the break-water. Allie and I caught them two nights ago. We caught them with sandworms. Those sandworms lived on nutrients in the sand . . . do you see? One thing feeds another, which feeds another . . . these lobsters are going to feed us."

Michael released the lobster; it dropped into the pot and almost instantly began to turn red. Quinn put hers in. She set the butter to melt on the stove and held Michael in her arms. Feeling the warmth and solidity of her body, he pulled her tighter, wanting even more connection.

They hugged for a few minutes, till Michael's heart went back to normal. The buzzer went off; the lobsters had turned scarlet and were done. Then Quinn grabbed an old blanket from the back of the wicker sofa and spread it on the porch floor. They carried everything out there and set it all out, lying down among the pot and plates and melted butter.

Michael had never eaten boiled lobster before.

"It's the only way," Quinn said. "At home, within sight of the sea. From respect, you nod to the water, and then you bless the lobsters."

Michael thought of the black-tie opening-night parties his mother had taken him to with lobster thermidor, lobster Savannah, lobster cocktails, lobster Newburg—fancy dishes with the lobster all picked out and dressed up.

This was basic, primal—life itself. Quinn taught him how to take the lobster apart with his bare hands, crack the shells easily, push the sweet meat out with his fingers. He felt like a man using all five of his senses, feeling the pleasure of life for the first time: the sunshine warming their bodies, the crashing waves filling their ears, the unfamiliarity of love pouring through his veins. He watched Quinn suck the meat from all the small legs, and he let her feed him a claw dripping with melted butter.

They kissed with a passion Michael had never felt before. Everything seemed so perfect and natural. Gazing down the rocks, Michael saw his grandfather's boat rocking at the dock. He had been afraid to think of his grandfather sailing across the sea, but he wasn't anymore. Something about being with Quinn had given Michael a new courage that he didn't quite understand.

"I want to do things . . ." he said.

"Like what?"

"Big things."

"Like your father? Going into space?"

"You think that's big?" he asked, his heart falling a little.

She shook her head. "No, but most people do."

"What do you think is big?" he asked.

"Oh," she said. "That's easy. Love."

"What do you know about love?" he asked, his heart beating hard and fast.

"I've lived it," she whispered. "Since I was very young. First with my parents, then with my sister, with my aunt and Sam, with everyone here at the Point. It's all that matters. . . ."

"I want it," Michael said, yearning for love more than he had ever dreamed possible. He thought of living in this cottage, lobstering for the rest of his days. Quinn could be his wife; they could make their lives together.

"Why did you leave school?" he asked after a minute.

"They kicked me out," she said sadly. "I did something I shouldn't have . . . lost my temper."

"I've seen your temper," he whispered, stroking her hair.

"Yeah . . . it's bad. But I wish—" She paused, swallowing. "I wish it hadn't happened. I mean, I wish I could go back to where I was before I had to leave . . . in September I'm supposed to be a senior."

"What would it take?" he asked.

"Summer school," she said, the words ringing dreadfully.

"Why don't you go?" he asked.

"Because I love summer so much. My lobstering business, the beach, spearfishing, everything. I can't stand the thought of being in a classroom—even if your grandfather wants me to."

"I'd go with you," Michael whispered, holding her a little tighter.

"What?"

He couldn't believe he'd said it, but suddenly nothing had ever made more sense. Knowing Quinn gave him a desire to have a future. She had set him on fire, to be the best man he could. And getting to know his aunt again, seeing how much having an education meant to her and his grandfather, made Michael feel that maybe he'd been selling himself short.

"I'll go to summer school with you," he whispered. "When does it start?"

"I think it started already," she said.

"Maybe my grandfather could get us in. Talk to the teachers he knows, get them to help us make up the stuff we've already missed."

"We'd go together?"

"Why not?"

"I've never gone to summer school before," Quinn whispered, "and I've never had a boyfriend."

"Two new things." He grinned.

"I don't change easily," she warned him.

"I know that," he said, pulling her down beside him on the scratchy old blanket, the wood floor hard underneath their bodies. He kissed her tenderly, knowing that every second was precious, that she was delicate, that life was taking them on a ride that could end anytime, anywhere. Michael Mayhew had plans: Oh, he had plans.

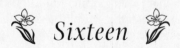

Sixteen

TWO SUMMER DAYS passed, and the morning of Sixtus's departure dawned with sunlight and fair breezes. Sixtus woke up early. His body creaked, moving around the house. Arthritis was creeping in; he felt a shiver at his core. He was so afraid of becoming dependent; he'd seen it happen to many of his friends. He'd die before he saddled Rumer with his care. Looking out the window, he felt relieved, knowing Rumer would have nothing to worry about weatherwise, watching her old man sail away.

But by eight there was a strange chill in the air and a dark line along the horizon. While the *Clarissa* waited at the dock, everyone from the Point gathered on the rocks to see Sixtus off. The group was loving and festive as always, but there was an ominous feeling in the air. Rumer stood beside him, oddly silent. He had told her to invite Edward if she felt like it, but the aristocratic farmer was notably absent.

"Dearest, what will you do for freshwater?" Winnie asked, sounding worried. "You can't drink the ocean. . . ."

"I've got a water maker," Sixtus replied, unobtrusively clenching and unclenching his fists, trying to work the stiffness out. "A desalinifier that'll eradicate every bit of salt and leave the sea tasting fresh as a spring. Thanks for asking."

"And food?" Annabelle asked. "What will you eat?"

"Oyster juice," Sixtus said. "I've got cans of it—full of protein, and it's easier than cooking."

"Sounds hideous," Hecate said, wincing.

Zeb walked over carrying a large carton, which he laid at Sixtus's feet. "Freeze-dried meals straight from NASA. It's what we used to eat in space."

Sixtus nodded, moved that Zeb would come to the party at all. Glancing over at Rumer, he could see her looking every damn place but at Zeb—avoiding his eyes at all cost.

"Look what Zeb brought me," he said.

"Delicious. Freeze-dried macaroni and cheese," she said, lifting one of the foil packets.

"Don't knock it, Larkin," Zeb said. "It hit the spot in orbit."

Sixtus sighed, and both kids looked at him. The feeling of trepidation was thick in the air—he had the sense of a storm building, although the marine forecast was for clear skies.

"What, Dad?" Rumer asked, sounding anxious. "Are you okay?"

"I want you two to . . ." he began sternly, then trailed off.

People—even impetuous children—don't set out to ruin their lives, but sometimes parents can see their children making enormous mistakes from a long way away, just like dark clouds bringing a storm across the sea. Sixtus would never understand why Elizabeth had set her sights on Zeb, for that was just what it was: After a lifetime of at best liking and at worst barely tolerating the boy next door, she suddenly went after him with a vengeance.

Zeb had been a late bloomer, Sixtus remembered. Small for his age, he had had a growth spurt his last year at Columbia. He had shot up four inches, lifted enough weights over the winter to give himself a big chest and shoulders, and announced his plans to go to graduate school at UCLA.

Sixtus had always believed Elizabeth had fallen in love with the "L.A." part of UCLA more than anything else. She had been acting in New York, getting plenty of parts off—and some parts on—Broadway. She had played Portia in summer stock in the Berkshires, Juliet in Montauk and Lower Manhattan, part of the company in *As You Like It* at Shakespeare in the Park, and now she was ready to move from the stage to the screen. Rumer had brought Zeb to watch Elizabeth in *Romeo and Juliet* at a theater off Broadway. When she returned to Connecticut, the spark had been struck, and Zeb and Elizabeth were on. The long day's journey into destruction had begun.

Sixtus sighed, wondering about the role he'd played in it all. He should have noticed as it was going on. Something—his own distance as a father?—had made a needy girl out of Elizabeth. She'd always had to have more of everything: attention, acclaim, love, even the boy meant to be with her sister.

"You want us . . . what?" Zeb asked.

"Never mind what," Rumer said. "He's just getting ready to say goodbye, and he knows how I hate good-byes—right, Dad?"

"That I do, my love."

"Hmm," Zeb said, remaining unconvinced. He watched Sixtus, expectation in his eyes.

"What's wrong, Dad?" Rumer asked. "Having second thoughts?"

"No, sweetheart. You wish I would, don't you?"

She glanced at the boat. "I wish I could lie and say no," she said.

"You were never one to lie," Sixtus said. "You're my truth teller. All I have to do is look into your eyes to know the whole story."

"Do you think you'll see Elizabeth when you get to Canada?" Rumer asked.

"I'd call it a dim possibility."

"In what way? She's there, shooting."

"Yes, but on a tight schedule—as she always reminds us."

"I hope you do see her; I know you'd like that," Rumer said, and Sixtus saw Zeb flinch.

Now, glancing around his party for Michael, Sixtus felt a rush of old sorrow for what had been lost between Rumer and her nephew. Once Elizabeth got sober and realized how much Michael and Rumer meant to each other, she had stopped Michael's visits. Always with a reason— never the real one: *He has a cold, he's coming with me to the set, we're going to Aix-en-Provence for the summer.*

"Okay," Rumer said, turning toward the *Clarissa.* "You've got the beacon on board?"

"The radio transmitter, yes," Sixtus said.

"You're not going to get lost at sea," she said. "But I want you to have it in case you need us—you might get lonely and want to call!"

"You're taking care of me the way I used to take care of you," Sixtus said, sliding his arm around her. This was the kind of care he could bear: love.

He remembered how she and Zeb would go off on adventures for hours, whole days. They would swim out to Gull Island, then across to Stony Neck State Park. Once they had rowed across Long Island Sound to Orient Point. Another time, they had ridden horses up Serendipity Hill at night to see stars from the peak. Sixtus and Clarissa's challenge had been to let them go, give them space to grow, protect them from afar.

"That's what she wants," Zeb said. "To take care of you." Rumer's gaze slid around as if she wanted to look anywhere but at Zeb. But finally she just gave up.

"I do, Dad," Rumer said, and Sixtus saw the first tears in her eyes. He looked down to keep from getting choked up himself. How long would it be before he became so arthritic he'd really need care?

"I'd feel better if you'd tell us you're actually going to *use* the electronics on board," Zeb said.

"Convince him, Zeb," Rumer said.

Sixtus shook his head and laughed. "I'm an old Irishman doing what a whole lot of my ancestors did before me—sailing across the sea. Only this time, I'm going in the opposite direction—*back* to Ireland. I've got a good sextant. You of all people, Zeb, should know the value of the stars. They're my map in the sky. They'll show me the way."

"They will," Zeb agreed, "but there are easier ways. GPS, INMARSAT . . . I personally placed satellites in the sky to help navigators on their boats."

Sixtus smiled. He understood the younger generation's reliance on GPS and computers—all they had to do was point and click, and the magic coordinates would come up onscreen. Such navigation was like following a cookbook—someone else's instructions—without a deep understanding of one's own.

"Zeb, thank you. Rumer—you know I wouldn't go offshore without electronics. I'll have the beacon on—don't worry. But that's my backup: I'm going to do sun lines. I'm going to shoot the stars . . . that's how I'll find my way."

"Just want you to be prepared," Zeb said.

"Well, don't take it personally if I don't use them, son," Sixtus said, slapping him on the back. "I'm sailing a classic Herreshoff, not some plastic soap dish. When it was built, a sextant was as good as it got. Expect miracles from nature, and you'll get them."

"Dad . . ."

"Dearest," Winnie said, coming over to join them. Her dark blue silk robe had huge epaulets on the shoulders—the nautical look in honor of his departure. Perhaps she had worn it in *H.M.S. Pinafore,* or perhaps she counted an admiral among her many admirers.

"What is it, my love?" Sixtus asked, noting the worry in her face.

"Reassure me, if you will, that that lovely boat of yours is seaworthy enough to cross the Atlantic."

Sixtus laughed, glad to be distracted from the looks flying between Rumer and Zeb, from the emotional tone of his good-bye to them.

"The *Clarissa*'s seakindly, Winnie."

"And boats like this have sailed across the ocean?" she pressed.

"They have," Sixtus said.

"Single-handed, Dad?" Rumer asked.

"Most certainly. I'm not a pioneer, sweetheart. I'm only doing what's been done before. In 1978, a man named Lloyd Bergeson sailed the *Cockatoo II*—another New York 30—single-handed to Norway."

"And he made it safely?" Rumer asked.

"He did," Sixtus said, his heart racing as he hoped she wouldn't ask the next question.

"What's wrong?" Zeb asked, stepping slightly away from Rumer and Winnie.

"Wrong?"

"You've got a cloud over your face the size of New England. What really happened to the *Cockatoo II*?"

"It sank on the return voyage. Don't tell Rumer that story, will you, Zeb? I remember how she was during your missions, watching the sky and afraid you'd be swallowed up."

"She hated me then," Zeb said. "I was married to Elizabeth."

"That's in the past," Sixtus said steadily.

"What do you mean?"

"Listen, Zeb. I was dead set against you and Elizabeth getting divorced—because it's against my religion. But there's an old saying: No amount of wishing can stop the cause of an effect."

"A simple law of physics."

"Physics, nature, the human heart," Sixtus said. "You can't stop a tidal wave, a hurricane, a falling tree. Get in the way, and you're done with. That's what you and Rumer brought to this Point so many years ago. Don't stop it again."

Turning his back, unwilling to say more to Zeb, Sixtus walked around the crowd, saying good-bye. Quinn ran over, gave Sixtus a huge hug.

"Be careful, please?" she asked. "Don't run into any whales or anything. I hear they're all over the Gulf Stream. And don't ram into any sunfishes—they're huge, and supposedly they love to sun themselves on the surface."

"Yeah, be safe, Grandpa," Michael said.

"I will."

"If you get lonely," Quinn said, her voice low with emotion, "you can do what I do. . . ."

"What's that, honey?"

"I close my eyes and think of my parents," she said. "No matter where I am, no matter how alone I am, I can always hear them. It's easiest by the sea . . . when I can hear the waves. Or even better, in my boat, where I can feel them . . . lifting me, supporting me, carrying me along. I think Clarissa will do that for you, Sixtus."

"*Clarissa*, my boat?"

"No, Clarissa, your wife. She's with you always."

"Oh, I know that, Quinn," Sixtus said, taking the girl's hand. He had always felt a great connection with her. It seemed amazing that one so young could know so much about real love and the human condition. Grateful that Michael had her for a friend, he kissed the top of her head.

"You belong in college, Quinn. To get there, summer school would be a fine start."

"We're going tomorrow," Michael said.

"What? To summer school?"

"We are," Quinn said. "We would have gone today, but we didn't want to miss your party."

"Why?" Sixtus said. "What made you change your minds?"

"We met," Quinn said simply. "And things started to make sense. . . ."

Michael didn't reply, but he nodded.

Sixtus hugged and kissed Quinn and Michael, then returned to the adults to say his good-byes. Annabelle McCray, knowing his love of Irish literature, gave him a book of Yeats's poems and a copy of Joyce's *Portrait of the Artist as a Young Man.*

Hecate, dressed in her customary black, gave him a small vial of fish bones, hydrangea blossoms, and cod liver oil. A cousin of the magical women at the Bridal Barn, she knew a thing or two about talismans and blessings.

"Forrr a safe trrrrip," she purred, closing his fingers around the glass bottle as Sixtus kissed her.

Winnie gave him a small tape player and a collection of opera cassettes. "Some of my favorites. Good sailing, my dear friend," she said, wrapping him in an embrace.

"Thank you, Winnie," Sixtus said, moved speechless by the love pouring out from his family and neighbors. Although Mrs. Lightfoot—the old woman who lived in the house on the Point and never left it—hadn't come, she had raised the American flag on the mast beside her house along with signal flags spelling out "bon voyage."

Looking down the rocky coast, Sixtus could see the tide turning, and he knew it was time to go. Music drifted down from the McCray cottage. The tune was Cole Porter, lush and romantic. If Clarissa were there, Sixtus would have grabbed her in his arms, swung her around the dock. Instead, he took Rumer's hand and began to dance with her.

"I'll miss you, Dad," she said.

"I'll be back before you know it," he said.

"Call me when you get to Halifax."

"Of course I will."

"Malachy Condon lives in Nova Scotia . . . let me give you his number," Sam Trevor said, walking over to hand Sixtus his card. "He's a great guy, an oceanographer who lives on his boat in Lunenburg. If you need anything at all, give him a call. He'll steam on out into the Gulf of Maine to meet you."

Sixtus accepted the card—partly because he knew it would give his daughter a little peace of mind to know he had someone looking out for him.

"Dad, I believe in you," Rumer said.

"That means the world to me, sweetheart," Sixtus said.

She was about to cry. Glancing around, he spotted Zeb standing with Winnie and called him over.

"Dance with her," he mouthed over Rumer's head.

Zeb nodded.

The song was "Every Time We Say Goodbye." "One of your mother's favorites," Sixtus whispered too softly for Rumer to hear. Now all he wanted was to be alone with Clarissa, sailing away on their long sabbatical. He hugged Rumer hard, kissed her forehead, and pressed her into Zeb's arms. She struggled to get away, as if she would climb on board and sail away with her father, but Zeb held her tight.

"Dance with me, Rue," he said. "We'll dance Sixtus right over the horizon."

"I don't want him to go," she wept into Zeb's shoulder.

"Remember the roof," he whispered back. "Remember what we said up there . . . you have to let him . . . it's his vision, his dream."

And it was, Sixtus knew. He wasn't afraid at all. The world opened before him: The sea was his road, and it lay at his feet while the wind blew at his back. He carried his gifts on board, stowed them below. The Cole Porter still played, and Winnie began to sing. *Les Dames de la Roche* stood on their beloved rocks of Hubbard's Point, waving as he cast off lines.

Sixtus pulled his white cotton sun hat on his head and raised the sails. The main filled, and then the jib, as the *Clarissa* sailed majestically away from the dock. His heart soared, beating fast. As perhaps only Quinn knew, he was alone with his wife, on their boat; he felt her spirit as truly as he felt the wind in his hair. She was his partner and sweetheart, his eternal guide. Their friends and family called and sang from shore, wishing them well.

Quinn started up her lobster boat, and she and Michael led him out of the cove. The voices grew more distant until all he could hear was the wind in the sails, the waves against the hull, and the throb of Quinn's engine.

"Don't forget," he called. "You two have made me a promise to go to school."

"And don't you forget you promised to be very careful and come back to Hubbard's Point safe and sound," Quinn called back.

"I won't. I never break my promises."

"Nor I mine," she said.

They had reached the red can buoy marking the north end of the Wickland Shoal, where Sixtus would bang a left and leave Hubbard's Point behind.

"We're ready to see you over the horizon," Quinn said, circling the *Clarissa* once with her lobster boat, then throttling back to let Sixtus swing the tiller and come about. The sails luffed, then filled again, the sloop pointing eastward past the Wickland Rock Light.

"Good luck in school, you children," Sixtus called, sailing away.

"Watch the waters off Point Jude," Quinn yelled. "They can get a little rough."

"I will!" Sixtus smiled, knowing she was referring to the time she and Allie sank in a big storm on their way to Martha's Vineyard.

He glimpsed the Point, all the shingled cottages with their bright shutters and tangled gardens, American flags flying in the wind. Hubbard's Point had been founded by the working class, by Irish immigrants, by people without money who'd had the foresight to put down roots by the sea that had brought them to the United States. He loved this land with all his heart, and he knew he'd be taking a bit of it with him. When his eyes fell on the Mayhews' old green house, he said a prayer for the new owners and what would be—that they would hold true to the spirit of the place—and he looked over to see Rumer and Zeb still waving from the dock.

He raised his arm in a final farewell. His hands hardly ached at all right now; the bones in his back creaked a little, just like the old boat, but the sun beat down on them and kept them from hurting too much.

"Don't forget we love you," Quinn cried out.

"I won't," Sixtus called over the widening expanse of blue water. "And don't forget that I love you too. Go to school, children, and learn everything there is to know!"

"We will, Grandpa," Michael shouted, the words sounding just like a promise he'd never break.

And with that, Sixtus Larkin rounded the headland and the buoy, sailing straight for the open Atlantic and into his destiny.

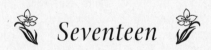 Seventeen

THAT AFTERNOON, after Sixtus had sailed away, after all the neighbors had dispersed, Rumer let Zeb walk her home. They went up the hill, past the spot behind the garage where her father had worked on the *Clarissa*. Wood shavings and patches of varnish and bottom paint lay in the grass—remnants of the hard work he'd done to restore the boat.

When they went inside her house, the curtains were blowing wildly in the fresh breeze. The music was still moving her. The unicorn tapestries looked more vibrant and alive than she had ever remembered. Zeb was there, right beside her, and as she stood barefoot in the cottage, all she wanted was to dance with him again, moving together with the music, the wind, and all the spirits of the Point.

"Would you like some tea?" she asked, her pulse racing.

"Sure," Zeb said, not taking his eyes off her. "That would be nice."

Holding the kettle under the faucet, Rumer's hands were shaking. Noticing, Zeb stepped in to take it from her. Did he know that he was the reason? He placed the kettle on the burner and turned on the heat. She still had the shimmery feeling of his arms around her shoulders, dancing. Stirred by wild desire, she slowly turned to face him.

Zeb stepped forward, putting his arms around her. So strong and tan, he made her glow as his hands stroked her back, pulling her against his chest. She stood on tiptoe the way she used to when he'd danced with her at block dances down on the tennis courts, and she leaned into his body. She shivered hard, from top to bottom, feeling the full crush of Zeb's hard body against hers.

The teakettle hissed on the flame, and Rumer was afraid it would start to boil before she and Zeb figured out what was supposed to happen next. This was her childhood kitchen; Elizabeth had fried eggs on this stove.

Her mother had cooked Thanksgiving turkeys in this oven. The Mayhews had come over for coffee a thousand times.

Images were flying through her mind: herself and her sister, padding barefoot across this floor with Santa mugs in their sticky little hands; herself and Zeb, as teenagers, filling plastic bottles with ice water for long sails across the Sound . . .

"Rumer," Zeb whispered, his mouth hot on her neck.

"What are we doing?" she said, reaching up to tangle her fingers in his hair, trying desperately to push out all the messy memories and scruples as she tilted her head back, felt his lips just barely brush against hers.

The kettle began to boil. It wasn't a subtle sound; it pierced the air like a siren, breaking them apart. Zeb stepped back. Rumer turned off the burner. Her heart was pounding, and she felt as disheveled inside as out—when Zeb touched her shoulder, trying to turn her around, she couldn't move.

"Rumer?" he asked.

"Isn't this strange?" she whispered.

"I think it's . . ." he began. "It's amazing, it's wonderful."

"It might be," she murmured.

"But . . . ?"

"I don't know. I'm not sure."

"On the roof the other night," he said, "when you asked me why I married Elizabeth . . ."

"Don't, not right now, Zeb—"

"Listen to me, Rumer. I didn't think you'd love me like that. We tried, that last year—I held your hand. We kissed, we went to the movies together . . . I asked you to meet me for the vernal equinox. . . ."

"The first of spring," Rumer murmured.

"And you didn't show!"

"I would have. I wanted to—you know that!" Rumer said, the words knocking the breath right out of her, pushing him away.

"Then why didn't you come? I was there, waiting."

Rumer closed her eyes tight, trying to remember. They had been in their senior years of college. Tests, papers, applying to graduate schools . . . but she would have done anything—absolutely anything—to be with Zeb. He had told her to come home for the weekend, and she had come. She had checked the drawer, waited for the phone call.

"You went to Elizabeth," Rumer said, and she felt like keening.

"I'm sorry," Zeb said. "You have no idea how much—but I went to her after you stood me up, when I thought you didn't want me that way. . . ."

"Stop it, Zeb," Rumer said. Her heart was hurting too much; her father had just sailed away, and too many memories of her childhood were coming back. This was her family kitchen; she and Elizabeth were sisters. They had stood right here, in this spot, and their mother had said, "You'll have many friends, but you'll only have one sister . . . each other!"

"Please, listen—"

"Not now!" she screamed. "Stop it—I don't want to hear."

"You'll listen to me before the summer's over," he said, his voice so low it was almost a growl. "You have to, Rumer. I know how you feel about me, because it's the same way I feel about you. You know what your father said to me today? You can't stop a storm from happening."

"Stop it, Zeb! Don't try to push me."

He moved closer.

"Maybe I want to protect myself," she said, breathless. "Maybe I just don't want to put myself into the same situation I was in twenty years ago. Loving someone who can't even see what's right in front of him."

"This isn't twenty years ago," he said.

"No, half our lives have passed."

"So, you want to ruin the other half?" he asked, grabbing her by the arms.

"I have a great life," she said, her voice shaking. "I love my work. I take care of animals, save people's pets. . . ."

"Save ospreys," Zeb reminded her. "With the help of someone who understands—" He had softened his grip, but he held her still, drawing her closer, bringing his face down to hers and brushing her lips with his.

"I don't trust you," she whispered.

"You're wrong not to," he whispered back.

"We used to kiss like this," she murmured as his lips caressed her cheeks, forehead, mouth. "And look what happened."

"I used to be stupid," he said.

"And you're not now?"

"No," he said, kissing her deeply for a long while, then pulling back slightly. "I got smart."

"What got you smart?"

"Realizing I'd lost you. That you were the only person I've ever wanted. Ever loved, Rumer."

"You . . ." she began. Her chest tightened. She wanted to ask him: You've never loved Elizabeth? She wanted to hear him say it; no, she *needed* to hear him say it.

"Go ahead," he said. "Ask me whatever you want."

"I can't," she said. Her mind was in full gear: the Indian Grave, the notes at Foley's, Elizabeth as Juliet, Zeb as Romeo . . . they had run away to California together. They had had a child. They had been a married couple—a family. "No matter what you say, Zeb," she said, "it can't change what happened."

"See, Larkin," he said, kissing the top of her head and taking a big step back, giving her the space she said she wanted, heading for the door. "That's where you're wrong."

"You're saying we can change what happened?"

"Yeah."

"How?" she asked. She might have sounded skeptical, but the word was a plea—her heart was racing so hard, she thought she might die on the spot.

"We can make it right," he said. "We have one chance—this summer."

"And we can make it right?" she asked.

"Yes, we can."

"How?"

"Love, Larkin. Love makes everything right—with all that compassionate work you do, don't you know that by now?"

But she didn't reply, and he didn't wait. She watched him walk across the kitchen, heard the door close softly behind him. She closed her eyes, saving the sense of his lips on hers, his arms around her shoulders. His presence filled the room long after he was gone. Rumer stood there for a while, letting her heart slow down to a normal rate. She didn't open her eyes until she heard thunder.

The rumble of thunder far away, coming across the calm sea, even though the sky was blue and there wasn't a cloud in sight.

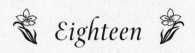

Eighteen

THE KIDS KEPT their word. Both Quinn and Michael enrolled in summer school. They did their homework most of the time. They studied for tests together. They helped each other write essays. They missed Sixtus and wished he were there to cheer them on.

Five days after her father's departure, Rumer picked them up after school to take them to the farm. She drove from her office to the Point, parking in front of Zeb's cottage. An osprey circled overhead, fishing in Winnie's cove. Rumer wished Zeb would come outside—maybe it was the hawk they had saved. She craned her neck, trying to see whether Zeb was home. She hadn't seen him since he'd kissed her in the kitchen.

Parked in the road, she closed her eyes. Last night she had dreamed of him. Sitting on the roof together, they had stared into the bluest sky she'd ever seen. Sunlight streamed down, covering the treetops in gold. She felt pure bliss, holding Zeb's hand. But when she turned to kiss him, he was gone; the only sound was Elizabeth's laughter ringing through the trees.

The kids climbed into her truck, and with one last glance at the osprey, Rumer drove away.

"How's school?" she asked.

"Good," Quinn answered, while at the same time Michael said, "Okay."

"That's a half-empty answer if ever I heard one," Quinn laughed, smiling across the seat.

"What do you mean?"

"Well, you know the old question . . . when you look at the glass, is it half empty or half full?"

"What's the difference?" Michael asked.

"Well," Quinn said. "It's a big difference. It tells you how you see the world. Are you positive or negative?"

Rumer felt her heart pounding. Quinn could so easily be speaking of her—Rumer had spent the whole week avoiding Zeb, thinking about what was wrong between them, trying to ignore the desire she felt inside.

"I'm a half-full person," Quinn said. "I didn't used to be. When my parents first drowned, I was half empty. Everything sucked. Sunny days were too hot, snowy days were too cold, if I ate ice cream, it was the wrong kind, if we went to the movies, it was never what I wanted to see. . . ."

Listening to Quinn, Rumer thought about herself. Her father had often said the students taught teachers more than the other way around, and once again he was right. Zeb was here, she dreamed of him every night, the summer was flying by—but Rumer kept turning back to the past, looking at the old hurt and betrayal, ignoring the magical threads of gold. Ignoring his very real kiss, his very real words.

She took them to Paradise Ice Cream for sundaes, driving the long way to the farm to stretch out the ride. Their music played on the radio, and Quinn sang along. Michael controlled the air-conditioning and the sunroof. They talked about their classes and homework.

Now, with the kids in her truck, she turned into the farm and felt a shock: Edward was sitting on the porch with a woman.

She had wavy blond hair and a periwinkle-blue summer dress, and Rumer recognized her from the Black Hall Art Museum. Annie Benz, the curator of American Impressionists—strong, smart, proper. Perfect for Edward, Rumer thought, feeling a strange shiver of relief mixed with regret. Edward must have gotten tired of the way she'd been treating him, and Rumer felt ashamed.

"Who's that?" Michael asked.

"A friend of Edward's," Rumer said.

"He's your boyfriend," Quinn said, squeezing Rumer's hand in a teasing way. "Aren't you jealous?"

"No," Rumer said softly. "It's okay with me."

"I don't blame you," Quinn said, thinking. Rumer could almost see electricity racing around her head; she brought sparks and energy to whatever she did. "Well, Edward is neither half full nor half empty. He's just 'half.' "

Michael laughed, surreptitiously glancing over. "How can a person be just 'half,' Quinn? Look at his farm—it's huge. He has horses, cows, barns, a big house, guys working for him. . . ."

"Things and money don't count when you're measuring a person's fullness," Quinn said. "Right, Rumer?"

"I can't say anything bad about Edward," Rumer said. They had reached the fence, and Blue came walking through the field to see them. Heat rose from the tall grass, dragonflies buzzing around his knees. "He's always been wonderful to me."

"How come you never married him?" Michael asked.

"Because she loves someone else," Quinn said, causing Rumer's jaw to drop.

"What are you talking about?" he asked.

"Hmm, nothing," Quinn said.

Rumer let it pass. She looked up at the couple rocking and talking softly on the porch. Had she and Edward ever looked so comfortable, so right together? She could think only of Zeb: straining like a horse at the gate, wanting to run, to sprout wings, to fly into the wild blue yonder, leaving a trail of thunder.

"Your father's sailing to Ireland," Quinn said, squeezing Rumer's hand harder. "You have that inside you! Rocking on the porch isn't enough for you! You have too much passion inside you for that. And I know . . ."

Rumer watched her eyes, wanting her to say more. But Blue whinnied, ready to be ridden. Quinn tore away, feeding him an apple, while Michael waited patiently to give her a leg up.

When Michael and Quinn had climbed onto Blue's back, riding together through the field, Rumer leaned on the fence and wondered about it all. Rumer had loved—really loved—only one person in her life. Zeb was here in Connecticut now, and what had she done? Pushed him away every time he'd tried to come close.

She watched the children hold each other, moving through the summer field. From here, looking through the haze, she could see Zeb in Michael. They had the same build, the same profile. Michael's hair was longer than Zeb's had been before his father had cut it, but it fell in a similar way, and had blond highlights.

Her heart blazed in her chest; her blood felt like flowing lava. She thought back to her and Zeb standing in the kitchen, feeling how much she'd wanted him to keep holding her, kissing her. She wondered what he had to tell her, and why it was so hard for her to hear.

Alert and intense, she watched the children disappear from sight and thought of Elizabeth keeping Michael from her all this time.

At first, when Rumer had needed a nephew-fix, she would get another vet to cover her practice and fly to California or ask Elizabeth to send Michael to Connecticut. They would have blissful days or weeks—vacations—together, until the day came when Rumer feared that Elizabeth was about to put an end to it.

Looking back, she realized that she'd been building lie upon lie. Inside, she had felt torn in half by Elizabeth and Zeb being together. Outside, she had tried to play the role of the perfect aunt—just to see Michael.

"Look what your auntie brought you!" Elizabeth had exclaimed the time Rumer had flown out with the stuffed horse.

"It's just like Blue," Rumer had said, putting the huge soft toy into Michael's arms. "Remember my horse? How I held you on his back, and you rode him around the field? You can name him Blue," Rumer had whispered, savoring the smell of Michael's hair, the softness of his skin. "Just like the real Blue . . . Bluuuuuuue."

"Boooo," Michael had said, as if remembering their time together at Peacedale Farm just months earlier.

"Yes, Boo," Elizabeth had said, drinking a vodka and tonic. She hadn't been with them at the farm; she didn't understand their connection. But Rumer was sure she'd seen Michael's eyes light up, his arms fly around his aunt's neck; she was positive her sister had seen Rumer's own joy— the way her eyes had filled with tears at the sight of the boy. " 'Boo' is just how I feel."

"Why, what's wrong?" Rumer had asked.

"I don't know what I was thinking when I married Zeb. You certainly had the right idea, getting rid of him."

"Elizabeth," Rumer had said sharply, her stomach in knots, not believing for a moment that she believed that, "please don't. Let's not talk about Zeb. . . ."

He was at Caltech analyzing satellite data; the next day he would leave for Houston. Rumer had chosen to visit Elizabeth and Michael now, on her winter vacation, when she was sure Zeb wouldn't be home. But she didn't want to hear Elizabeth talk about him, especially not in front of Michael. And she certainly didn't want to rehash the past. . . .

"Rumer, you're my sister. I don't have anyone to talk to . . . I'm so unhappy. . . ." She'd taken another big sip of her vodka and tonic.

"How could you be," Rumer asked, her lips against the side of Michael's head, "when you have all this? When you have him?"

"Booooo," Michael said, bouncing the horse.

"Booooo to your father," Elizabeth said, downing her drink, going to the sideboard to make another. The room was vast and airy, overlooking the Pacific Coast Highway and the Santa Ana Mountains. The sound of distant highway traffic and Elizabeth throwing ice cubes into a glass filled Rumer's ears. She could feel Elizabeth getting angry, and the energy scared her.

"If you don't want to hear about it," Elizabeth said, "then why did you come?"

"To see you and Michael."

"Really?" she'd said. "More to see Michael, seems to me."

"He's my nephew," Rumer said, sitting still, holding Michael and the toy horse on her lap. Her heart felt squeezed; she didn't want to hear this—and she didn't want Michael to either.

"I have a huge part in a huge film," Elizabeth said, starting to cry. "And no one cares . . . I'm having such a hard time, Rue."

"But why?"

"Marriage is nothing like I thought it would be. Especially to Zeb. He's in a bad mood all the time. Nothing I do makes him happy—all he ever wants to do is go to work or ride around in his car with Michael. The two of them go off on these long drives, and I'm here alone."

"You work a lot, Elizabeth," Rumer reminded her. "Seems like you're always getting a new role."

"Yes, and I made sure most of them were for movies filming here in California, so I wouldn't have to go far away from home. But now, I swear to you, Rue—next year I'm going to Istanbul, Kenya, Bangkok— as far away as I can get." Taking a big sip, she started to cry, choking on her drink.

"Don't drink that," Rumer said, trying to take the glass away from her.

Elizabeth tugged it back, spilling vodka on both of them. "You don't understand. . . ."

But then she put the glass down and went to Michael. Picking him up, she clutched him to her chest. Although he struggled, wanting to go back to his horse, she held on. Carrying him across the room, she stumbled on a pile of his building blocks.

"Watch out!" Rumer called, but it was too late.

Mother and baby went crashing to the ground. Rumer heard the bump of Michael hitting his head, his loud screams and cries: Terrified, she ran over to make sure they were both okay—no blood, no bruises. Luckily their fall had been partially broken by an armchair.

Taking Michael into her arms, Rumer examined his head. It looked fine, not even a small bump. She kissed him, handing him his horse, rocking him in her arms as he cried.

"Give him to me," Elizabeth said, holding out her hands. But Michael just pressed his mouth against Rumer's neck and sobbed.

"Let him be," Rumer whispered. "Just for a minute."

"How dare you?" Elizabeth snarled. "How dare you act so high and mighty? Don't you think people ever trip and fall? Are you trying to make me feel bad about how I mother my child?"

"No, Elizabeth," Rumer said, knowing nothing she said would get through anyway but frantic about Michael's safety.

"The hell you're not!"

"We shouldn't even be talking like this in front of him."

"You're jealous, that's what it is," Elizabeth said. "It's because Zeb married me, not you. Because I have his child . . ."

"Mama?" Michael asked, looking up with worry in his tear-stained eyes. He began to cry harder, reaching from Rumer to his mother.

"Look! Now you've upset Michael even more. Come here, sweetheart. . . ."

Rumer turned and quietly left the room. She wanted to pull her sister's hair out, slap some sense into her. Going to stand on the wide balcony overlooking the mountains, she forced herself to breathe. The worst part was, Elizabeth's words were true: She was jealous. What if Elizabeth sent her away, preventing her from seeing Michael?

Looking through the window, she saw Elizabeth hunched over, crying. Michael had left her to grab his horse, pull the big toy over to the plate glass window. He put his hand on the inside of the glass; Rumer put hers on the outside. At that moment, trying to touch each other's hands through the window, she knew she would do whatever it took to stay close to him.

Sliding open the door, she walked inside.

"I want, I want you to . . ." Elizabeth said, sobbing.

To leave, Rumer was sure she was about to say.

"Listen," Rumer said calmly, being very careful. "What can I do to help you? Do you need to talk? I'll listen. I love you; I love Michael."

"You love Zeb . . ." Elizabeth whispered through hot tears.

"No," Rumer said sharply, never taking her eyes off Elizabeth's for a moment. "He's your husband. He's my brother-in-law, that's all."

"You're sure?"

"Positive. What can I do to help you—right now?"

Elizabeth clutched her hand, crying silently.

Holding Michael, Rumer just rocked back and forth, trying to comfort him with her movements. Did he have to see his mother like this often? Her stomach turned. His eyes were wild, and his breath was coming in gulpy little sobs.

"Will you run into the kitchen?" Elizabeth asked finally, sniffling. "Get me some tissues and an ice pack—I have to go on camera later this afternoon, and I don't want my eyes to be puffy."

"Of course," Rumer said—and, swearing under her breath, did it. The nanny and the housekeeper, sitting at the kitchen table, drinking tea, watched her without a word.

She stayed with Michael while Elizabeth had her photo session, and again, the next day, while Elizabeth went to Century City to meet the press to promote a new movie. That afternoon, when the producer on her next project had called to talk to Elizabeth, Rumer lied for her. She said Elizabeth was swimming laps in the pool. Her sister was in truth passed out drunk. Rumer lost a little more of herself with every call, with every lie. But she got to be with Michael.

Night after night, Rumer had lain awake, thinking.

Finally, one day, while Elizabeth slept, Rumer called Zeb in Houston.

"Mayhew," he said into the phone.

"Zeb, it's Rumer," Rumer said, her heart kicking at the sound of his voice.

The silence was long and uncomfortable, but finally he cleared his throat and spoke. "Are you still in California?" he asked.

"What's going on here?" Rumer asked, ignoring his question.

"You mean because I'm not there? It's just work, Rumer. I would have been there to see you, but—"

"That's not what I mean!" Rumer interrupted. "You're as self-centered as Elizabeth—you both assume it's always about *you*. I'm talking about Michael."

"He's fine," Zeb said defensively. "He's the best baby who ever—"

"He's not fine," Rumer said. "He's in a tug-of-war. I don't know what's going on between you and Elizabeth, and honestly, I don't care. But if Michael has to suffer, I swear, Zeb, I'll take him away."

"You what?"

"You heard me—I'll take him away."

"Put Elizabeth on the phone right now."

"See, I can't," Rumer said. "She's asleep. Passed out."

That got Zeb's attention. He fell silent, and Rumer tried to breathe as waves of emotion passed over her.

"You know about her drinking, don't you?"

"Yeah. I know."

"And what do you do about it?"

"Christ, Rumer! I can't do anything about it! I've tried hiding her bottles, breaking her bottles, emptying her—"

"Zeb! Not about her! I'm talking about Michael! How can you leave him alone with her when she's like this?"

"He's never alone with her—Maria lives in. Before her, Katherina did. They don't last very long, but there's always someone."

"And you think that's enough?"

A long silence stretched out, Rumer's blood pounding in her ears. "No, it's not enough," he said. "I'm usually there. I gave up a chance to train on a new simulator last month so I could stay home. But I left this time because I knew you were coming. . . ."

"Me?" she asked hotly.

"Yeah. Rumer—"

"You mean you left because you knew I'd be here with Michael?"

"That," he said, "and other reasons."

" 'Other reasons'?"

"You think I'm made of stone? I didn't want to see you," he said, "any more than you want to see me."

"You're right there."

"So, then—you get it. I'm in a difficult situation with Elizabeth. I can't force her to stop, and I can't always be there. But I feel safe when you're with Michael—whether she wants to admit it or not, so does Elizabeth. So the answer, I guess, is for you to see him as much as you can."

"I'd see him every day if I could."

"You could practice in L.A.; vet to the stars," Zeb said.

"I live in Hubbard's Point," Rumer shot back.

"Don't be defensive. I know, you're the new generation *Dame de la Roche*. . . ."

"Like our mothers."

"Yeah."

Rumer had held the phone cord, her eyes squeezed shut.

"What about Elizabeth?" she asked, steering the conversation back where it belonged.

"We're not making it . . . we never—" Zeb began, and Rumer cut him off.

"Stop!" she said. "That's not what I mean! What about getting her help so you don't have to worry about leaving Michael with his mother. Because I swear, Zeb, if she stays like this, I'll try to get him away."

"I'd fight you till I die," Zeb said.

"Then don't let it get that far. Find a rehab for her, Zeb. If you need me to take Michael while she goes, I will. I'll take care of him. . . ."

"Okay, Rumer. I'll try. She's stubborn—she won't want to go."

"I'm stubborn too. I won't let Michael be hurt like this."

"I hear you, Larkin," Zeb said grimly. "I'll make it happen, okay?"

"I hope you do," she said, breaking down at the craziness of it all—at the layers and layers of memory and emotion among them all. "She's my sister, and no matter what, I want her to be okay. . . ."

"I know, Rumer," Zeb whispered. "I know that. . . ."

The years had gone by. Michael would fly east; Rumer would fly west. Elizabeth would stop drinking for a while, then start up again. When Elizabeth felt too much pressure, she'd go away and detox for a few days. There was a rehab in Phoenix; a twenty-eight-day program in San Francisco.

Michael had drawn pictures of Hubbard's Point and told Rumer he'd rather live there than in California. He'd ridden Blue, holding on for dear life, begging her not to send him away. The idea had broken Rumer's heart—"I'd never send you away," she had promised. "Mommy will get better, and you'll go home, but you can always come visit me and Blue. Always . . ."

But he hadn't. Elizabeth had never allowed him to visit again. She'd never given a reason; it was just never the right time. When Rumer wanted to fly west, Elizabeth was always too busy. Michael was growing up; he had activities, and if Rumer were to come, he would be too occupied to break away and spend time with her.

Rumer didn't often think these thoughts, but standing by the white rail fence that late summer afternoon, she was overflowing with them. When the kids rode over and dismounted, they said they had to get home to do their schoolwork. Rumer asked if they'd mind waiting a few minutes.

"Of course not, Aunt Rumer," Michael said, giving her a leg-up onto the horse they'd both loved so much.

When she smiled down into his almost-grown-up face, her heart cracked. She thought his did too; she could see it in his eyes, in the way they blinked and then held her gaze.

"Do you know . . ." she began, the warm breeze blowing his brown hair, tossing it around his face, "that I'd never purposely break a promise to you?"

"Yes," he said, standing very still. "I've always known that."

"I'm glad," Rumer said.

Quinn just watched, but she knew: Rumer could see in her young friend's eyes that she understood the depth of love between them. As Michael petted Blue's strong neck, Rumer rode away.

"Booooooo," she heard Michael call after her, as she rode the old horse into the green field. Perhaps Edward and Annie were watching from the porch; it didn't matter. Rumer cantered along the stone wall, over the rise, down to the river.

She watched the river flow as she rode Blue along its banks, and she still heard Michael's voice in her ears, the baby boy and the nearly grown man, calling their horse. And Rumer pictured Zeb, the only boy she'd ever loved, as she let her horse carry her along, the feeling growing in the summer heat.

❧

That night, Michael and his father had dinner at the fried-clam stand. They hit golf balls at the driving range, and Michael told him about riding Blue. When they got home, his father went for a swim on the rocks, and Michael sat down to study. The telephone rang. Thinking it was Quinn, he ran to pick it up. The connection crackled: a cell phone.

"Michael?"

"Mom?"

"Yes, it's me. We have an absolutely terrible connection. I'm in my trailer on the set in the most godforsaken place. Can you hear me?"

"Barely."

"Well. We'll do our best. This is the first chance I've had to call you since you landed in suburbia. Are you surviving? Are you dying of boredom?"

"I'm fine," Michael said.

"Do tell all. I got a message saying that your grandfather left on his trip. I couldn't bear to call back and hear the details . . . you know how I am with good-byes. Did he get away safely?"

"Yes."

"Oh, good. He's crazy as a loon, going off to sea like that, sailing up here to Canada, but there it is. That's your grandfather. He believes in almighty literature. If Melville and Joseph Conrad wrote about sailing the ocean blue, your grandfather wants to join the tradition. How's Aunt Rumer?"

"Fine."

"Probably lost, right? Absolutely lost without him. She can't be alone."

"She's okay."

His mother laughed. "You don't know her. She's spinning, I tell you. Positively off kilter. I love her dearly, you know that, but she has never cut the apron strings."

"Huh," Michael said. He pictured Aunt Rumer driving her truck to work every day. He thought of the animals she treated, of her saving the osprey. And he pictured her galloping across the field on Blue. "She's keeping pretty busy," he said.

"Well, she has to," his mother laughed. "To keep from mooning over your father."

"What?"

"Don't tell me you haven't noticed her swooning over him."

"I haven't."

"She was in love with him, you know. We never talked about it to you, but you're old enough to know now. It was really kind of a joke . . . shy little Rumer carrying a torch for Zeb. I mean, can you in a million years see them together? The veterinarian and the astronaut?" his mother asked, laughing again.

"Why not? You didn't want him."

"That's not nice, Michael," his mother said. Was she upset? Michael couldn't tell, but the laughter was gone from her voice.

"It's true."

"Truth is very subjective," his mother said. "It depends on who's telling it. You don't know the whole story. But the fact is, we outgrew each other. It's sad, but it happens. You'll learn someday when you fall in love. Have you heard from Amanda?"

Amanda Johns, the daughter of his mother's friend, the famous producer Buster Johns. Amanda was what people called "an exquisite beauty." She was a porcelain doll who'd already appeared in two movies and three music videos. She could sing, dance, act, and model. Michael had dated her during the spring, and his mother had been jumping up and down for joy.

"Not for a while," he said.

"Keep her on the string," his mother said. "She is perfect for you. When you've lived the life you have, you must remember that not everyone has. You'll meet many other girls in your life, but none with a background as similar to yours as Amanda."

"Background?"

"Yes. It's key, Michael. As you get a little older, you'll understand."

"What's the difference if we'll just outgrow each other anyway?"

His mother cracked up. "Touché!" she said. "Don't shoot me, I'm just the messenger. These are the true facts of life. You already know about sex . . . this part is much harder. So keep Amanda close—you don't want to lose her."

"Yes I do," Michael said, thinking of Quinn.

"What?"

"I don't care about Amanda Johns."

"Sounds to me as if you're fooling around with someone out there. Are you, Michael? Because listen to me—it's wrong for you. You're not a Hubbard's Point person, and you should be glad of it. It's small time. Have your fun, but let it go at that. Who is she?"

Michael was silent, holding the phone cord. Something told him not to reveal the truth about him and Quinn to his mother. She would try to crush it, he knew. Feeling protective of their love, he knew he had to say something else to throw her off.

"You and Dad had the same background. I've seen the houses you grew up in—right next door to each other."

"Yes, you're right. Background isn't everything, but it's important. If background was all that counted, I suppose your father might have married Aunt Rumer instead. Now, who is this girl? Go on, tell me."

"I think they'd have been happy," Michael said quietly.

Silence on the line. For a moment he thought the connection had been broken, and then his mother asked, "What did you say?"

"I think they would have made each other happy."

"They?"

"Dad and Aunt Rumer."

"Why in the world would you say something so ridiculous?"

"Because they look nice together."

"Together? When are they together?"

"They danced on the dock," Michael said. "At Grandpa's going-away party. And she's had us over for dinner."

"Your father's polite," she said. "That's all it is."

"Whatever."

"What do you mean, they danced?"

"Just what I said. Music was playing. They danced."

"How cute," his mother said. "What was it—one in the afternoon? Typical Hubbard's Point. I'm telling you, Michael—it's the most senti-mental crap I've ever heard. Leave my father his dignity, you know? Let him sail away without every old woman out there waving gingham han-kies . . . and Rumer leading the pack."

"It was fun," Michael said.

"Oh, forget I said anything. Listen. Just have a good time, and call your mother once in a while. The filming is interminable, and I need a distraction."

"Where are you?"

"I'm sitting in some Canadian fishing village at the end of the world. Nova Scotia, of all places—meeting your grandfather when he gets here. Fishing boats going in and out of the harbor all day long . . . the smell of lobster is enough to make me sick. Even my hair, my clothes, smell of lobster—it's appalling."

The word lobster made Michael think of Quinn. From his window he could see several of her buoys bobbing in the waves, his father swimming in the starlight.

His mother didn't understand what was important. Till this summer, neither had Michael.

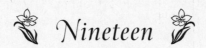

Nineteen

ZEB PULLED the old rowboat out of Winnie's shed, and together he and Michael dusted off the cobwebs, bought a new pair of oars and oarlocks, and launched it from the rocks in front. Although Michael would clearly rather have been with Quinn, he was a good sport while Zeb took him out to Gull Island and across to Tomahawk Point, reenacting some of his favorite excursions as a boy.

"It's nice here," Michael said one afternoon, rowing across the cove.

"A great place to grow up," Zeb agreed. "Do you think you could live here?"

Michael seemed to consider the question. "Yeah," he said. "Definitely. Could you come back?"

Zeb thought of what he had said to Rumer, how he had sworn that they could make it work. She hadn't spoken to him since. He was operating with the kind of faith that had flown men to the moon.

"Yes," Zeb said. "I could."

Zeb kept rowing even on days when Michael was busy. His back burned in the hot sun, and his muscles ached. He was trying to exercise the tension out of himself, waiting for Rumer. If he stayed out after sunset, he'd see Rumer's lights up on the hill. Once, he saw her pass by an upstairs window, graceful and mysterious as a shadow.

Another time he could have sworn he saw her watching him with binoculars. Standing on the porch, glass pressed to her eyes, observing as he rowed across the cove. His shirt was off, and sweat was pouring down his body. He flexed; he couldn't help himself. If she was watching, he wanted to look good. His NASA training had made him fit and strong; wanting to dazzle her with his muscles, he leaned in and rowed even harder.

When he looked up, she wasn't there anymore.

The next day, he saw her at the post office. Riding his bike, he had to get the papers and mail, and to pick up a quart of milk. Rumer had parked her truck there, on her way to school. The kids—Quinn and Michael—were huddled together in the cab, going over some assignment—Michael had been gone when Zeb got up, off to spend an extra hour with Quinn. As Zeb pedaled harder, coming up the hill, Rumer got into her truck with the mail and waved as she backed out, calling, "They're late for school—I'm giving them a ride!"

She had seemed singularly unimpressed with his speed, his muscles, and his prowess on a bicycle. She could not care less, Zeb thought. She had probably just been bird-watching with her telescope, hoping to spot the osprey they'd rescued, not watching him row at all. Or perhaps she'd been scanning the horizon for her father's gaff-rigged sloop.

Finally, getting impatient and because Zeb had promised Sixtus he would watch over her—he told himself—he decided to stop by her house and see how she was doing. After carrying the oars to the boat shed, Zeb started up the hill and heard a ruckus coming from her house. Rumer was in the yard, waving her arms and yelling at a man in a charcoal-gray suit, standing across the bushes in Zeb's old yard.

As Zeb got closer, he saw the look in Rumer's eyes: wild and furious. Her silver-wheat hair swirled around her face as she tossed her head, gesturing with her arms. The man had his arms folded in a defensive position, and Zeb suddenly noticed the work crew standing with power saws and pickaxes—just waiting behind him. An oak tree had been felled; it lay across the small driveway.

"Excuse me, but calm down," the man was saying. "What right do you have to tell me what trees I can cut in my own yard?"

"There's a squirrel's nest in that tree," Rumer said, her arm shaking as she pointed into the broken limbs. A clump of dry leaves lay at what had been the top of the small oak, and a grown squirrel was leaping from branch to branch, her chatters sounding like screams. "There are babies inside. They were born last week. . . ."

"Well, I'm sorry," the man said. "But I have the right to landscape my property."

"But the babies . . ."

"What's your problem? Mind your own business!"

"Look at her," Rumer said, watching the squirrel madly try to get to the nest.

"Rumer?" Zeb asked, standing at the foot of her steps.

She seemed not to see him. Pushing through the bushes, she walked to the fallen tree. The branches stuck out every which way, scratching her face as she moved closer to the trunk. The mother squirrel, sensing another attack, leapt onto her back and clawed through her sweater. Used to such things, the vet began burrowing.

"You can't just come into my yard," the man said. "Don't you understand property lines? Christ, lady. I've about had it with the goddamn 'hammer law' and all the other nonsense you people have cooked up to keep me from doing what I'm going to do. Get the hell away from that tree. . . ."

Zeb watched as Rumer dug into the greenery, trying to get to the dead leaves that formed the animals' nest. The mother squirrel scrabbled across her shoulders, screaming with grief as Rumer lifted her babies off the ground.

Crouching down beside her, Zeb's pulse was racing. He helped Rumer extricate the bundle of leaves, trying to protect her from the mother. Rumer just concentrated, her breath coming fast. Zeb's hands closed around her fingers, trying to keep her from reaching inside.

"They're dead, Rue," he said quietly. "Let them be. . . ."

"What if they're not?" she asked, turning to face him, her blue eyes shining in the light.

He realized that she could be right, and he had known her long enough to understand that she had to see for herself. Rumer was a vet now, not just a young girl who loved animals, but he could still feel the emotion pouring off her. Gently pulling the leaves back, she touched the still, gray babies curled up inside their nest.

"Oh," she said. They didn't move. Zeb's throat closed, hurting as he thought of all the animals living in the two yards—his and Rumer's. Their mothers had called the properties "the sanctuary." It wasn't official, but everyone in the neighborhood had come to think of it that way. All the nests, tangled vines, and tunnels had provided safety for multitudes of creatures.

Zeb helped lift the velvety squirrels in their nest of leaves into Rumer's arms. He started to follow her, but the man stopped him.

"It's crazy," he said. "All I did was cut down my tree, and she went ballistic. She should be thanking me—I'm clearing this whole lot. The property values around here will shoot right up."

"Property values?"

"Yeah. Do you know the view we could have from our windows when these trees get cut down? We'll be able to see to Block Island on one side, Firefly Beach on the other."

"You already can," Zeb said quietly. "Through the trees."

"Well, I want unobstructed. The property values will skyrocket—I'm getting rid of all these common oaks and pines and planting arborvitae. I have a landscape architect, not just some yard crew. The real thing, and he's going to make this a showplace. Wait and see—"

Zeb nodded. He started up the hill to Rumer's back door. Interrupted, the neighbor stopped in mid-sentence. "And you are . . . ?" He tilted his head as if wondering whether he had met Zeb, where he knew him from.

"A friend of your next-door neighbor's."

"You look very familiar. You're an astronaut, aren't you? I saw you on TV last month; they had a special on famous Connecticut natives—"

"Sorry," Zeb said as he started to walk away. "But I have to see my friend."

"Well," the man said, looking upset. "Well, hope you can calm her down. She's way out of line. If she tries to stop me again, I won't be happy—this is my yard . . . don't I have the right to do what I want? I hope she isn't going to make things difficult. I want to be a good neighbor."

"Can I make a suggestion?" Zeb asked, looking at the man, seeing the troubled look in his eyes. "Be careful with the animals around here. The people who live here are very attached to them. They used to call your yard the sanctuary. Even if you don't understand yet, you will. . . ."

"They're just rodents," he said. "Squirrels, rabbits—they're just nuisances, right? Except maybe to a *vet* . . ."

Zeb didn't even reply. He just knocked on Rumer's door and walked in. She was kneeling on the mudroom floor by the old rabbit hutches, peeling the dry oak leaves away from the nest one by one. The mother squirrel had climbed the house; she clung with all four paws to a screen in an open kitchen window, trying to get at her children.

"Are the babies dead?" Zeb asked, crouching down.

"Yes," Rumer said. Her voice was hard, her cheeks wet. She moved very slowly, as if every bone in her body hurt. "Even if they weren't, the mother wouldn't have come back to them once she smelled me. It's Animal Behavior 101, but your mother was the first one to teach me that."

"I remember," Zeb said. He could almost hear his mother's voice telling them to be careful, exploring in the bushes, climbing the trees—as kids they had been so curious about nature, and she had been afraid they would inadvertently drive animals from their nests.

"Are they in there?"

Rumer nodded.

"Let me see," Zeb said, pulling back the leaves.

There were four tiny squirrels, perfectly formed, the size of field mice. Their silver fur glistened in the kitchen light, their tails just beginning to fluff. Rumer held them in her hands, weeping. After a few minutes, Zeb took them from her. He carried the squirrels and the leaves from their nest outside and laid them on the rock ledge for the mother to see. She went wild, jumping down from the window. Screeching, she ran from one of her dead babies to another ceaselessly, over and over. Zeb left her to her grief and went inside.

Rumer was still on the floor. Leaning down, Zeb put his arms around her and helped her up. He remembered a time, twenty-five years ago, when while doing their paper route they had found a cat hit by a car. Rumer had jumped off her bike to hold the dead cat in her arms, and Zeb had crouched down to hold them both in his.

"Why did it have to happen?" she wept now. "If he had just said something, I could have climbed up and saved them."

"He probably didn't even think about it," Zeb said, picturing the oblivious look in the neighbor's eyes.

"I never cry at work," Rumer said. "Well, hardly ever . . . but just seeing that tree cut down, the nest broken. Hubbard's Point squirrels; they're probably descended from the ones your mother taught me about. And they're so small . . . they never had a chance."

"I know," Zeb said.

He held her while she cried and cried. "Do you think I'm an idiot?" she asked. "Caring this much about these things?"

"No, I don't. You're Rumer."

"What does that mean?" she whispered.

Zeb held out his hands. He led her through the house into the living room. A summer breeze blew through the open windows, smelling of salt and flowers. He had been in this room a thousand times, first as Rumer's friend, later while falling in love with her, still later as Zee's husband and Michael's father. Family pictures were everywhere, but as he looked into Rumer's blue eyes, the photos disappeared.

"Rumer," he said, cupping her face with his hands.

"Tell me what that means," she said.

"It means love," he said, his throat tightening. "Love for everyone and everything."

"But look at me," she said. "I'm all alone . . . I can't be with anyone."

"Neither can I," Zeb said.

He had never been able to be with anyone but her. How long had he known she was the one for him? Forever, it seemed. At least since he was a young boy . . . all through their teenage years. But something had taken him over, a lust for her sister that wouldn't go away, and he had blown it all.

"Zeb, what is it?" she asked.

"Nothing," he said, then changed his mind and reached for her hand. She let him hold it; they were both trembling.

"Tell me, Zeb."

Zeb couldn't contain his shaking. He got up and walked over to the barometer hanging on the north wall. Tapping it, he saw the mercury fall slightly in the glass. He wondered where Sixtus was on his journey, hoped he wouldn't hit any rough weather. Rumer had followed him; he felt the heat of her body standing beside him.

"Please, Zeb," she said. "Tell me what's wrong."

Zeb wanted to pull her close, hold her for the rest of the night. Didn't she know how long he'd kept his feelings inside? They'd been over it before, how hard it had been to go from friends to something more. Both shy, they had found the transition difficult. But they had been finding their way all those years ago.

They had conducted their courtship in an old-fashioned Hubbard's Point way, leaving notes for each other in the Foley's drawer. Before their first kiss, he'd been afraid she'd fall on the ground and start laughing. Rumer was just like a little sister. Then she was just like a best friend. You didn't have sexual fantasies about sisters or friends; it was incredibly rude.

Elizabeth was a different story. She was enough years older to make her completely off limits—yet at the same time, another girl-next-door. She was the dangerous Larkin sister—for years, Zeb had watched her undressing in front of her window. When she'd shave her legs in the bathroom, she'd make sure to position herself in full view of his room. She'd step out of the shower, taking a long time to dry herself off. Over the years, she'd driven Zeb crazy.

But nothing like Rumer. Rumer Larkin had gotten into his head, into his heart. She was part of him, the way salt is part of the sea. He knew her so well; he knew her by heart—he thought. While he could imagine kissing Elizabeth—ravishing her, in fact—he had been intimidated by the mechanics of touching Rumer. He had needed help to get from draping his old pal in seaweed to kissing her passionately.

That's where the drawer had come in. The old Foley's drawer, where every corny couple had at one time or another left love notes. As kids, they had loved to perch on the wooden chairs, howling with laughter at the sappiest letters. Later, when they were young teenagers, they had read more quietly, imagining how they'd manage to compose their own love letters someday.

Zeb had done it: His first effort had been a school-type essay, written for Rumer, about the best friend constellation. It had been about a boy and a girl (him and Rumer) who lived by the sea. After years of crabbing and fishing, casting their nets into the moonlit sea, one day they lost each other in a big storm. Thinking they were apart forever, the boy gave up hope. He went into his sea cave to die. The seas rose, the waves bigger than he'd ever seen, and suddenly he found himself surrounded by water. But there, glinting under the waves, were a few strands of starlight. They were the girl's net, and she pulled him back in, to safety, to her arms . . . they flew into the sky, and they live there even today, shining down from the stars above the rooftop.

She had loved it: He remembered how it felt to have her throw her arms around his neck. They clung together for a few moments; he nuzzled her neck, smelled her lemon shampoo. She tilted her head back; he kissed her lips in a long, slow kiss that took their whole lives to get to. They were sixteen.

Five years later, it was time for another leap. They were in their senior years of college—Zeb at Columbia, Rumer at Trinity. Their feelings had been building, taking them to a new place, wanting to make love to each other. Even now Zeb believed that Rumer had wanted it as much as he did. Both late bloomers, serious about work and about the committment, they waited until they could wait no more.

But Rumer held back. He visited her at Trinity once, and she was afraid her roommate would walk in. Another time, at Columbia, they were in his room with candles burning and jazz playing; Elizabeth called for Rumer, with some problem that only a sister could solve.

And finally, that first day of spring, waiting for her at the Indian Grave, she had never shown.

Rumer had stayed home, and Zeb had been there waiting.

Waiting in his tent for the love of his life, who didn't even have an excuse. She had checked the drawer and hadn't seen his note, she said. Why couldn't she at least have been honest and told him that she still loved him, still wanted him, but just wasn't ready?

If their courtship had gone more smoothly, would any of the rest have happened? He told himself he wouldn't have jumped at Elizabeth—even though she had jumped at him first. He told himself that if Rumer felt betrayed, it was only comparable to the crushing feeling he'd experienced when she'd let him down.

The years had passed—married to Elizabeth, the only times he had seen Rumer was when she'd come to California to visit Michael. One big happy family; at the sight of his beloved aunt Rumer, the baby would squawk like a chicken. Zeb had been polite, affectionate, but distant—letting all that old water flow under the bridge. All he knew was that last September, when he'd felt that explosion in space, his emotions had gone straight back to Rumer.

Next door, the new owner was standing below the window. He was talking to his landscaper, pointing out trees and bushes to cut down. "Those pines have to go," he said. "And that row of bamboo."

The chain saw started up.

Rumer went to the window and looked out. Zeb caught her from behind, pulling her with his arms around her waist. "Don't," he said. "The tree was struck by lightning . . . it's unhealthy. See the charred side? It's his anyway, Rumer. He has the right to do whatever he wants." ·

"But I love that tree," she said. "You and I used to climb it."

"Mom told us to be careful of the robins' nest. . . ."

"Should I tell him?" Rumer asked. "Do you think I could stop him?"

"No," he said. "He thinks he's increasing the value of everyone's property, cleaning up the place."

"Is that what he said?"

Zeb nodded. Looking out the window, he saw the excitement in the neighbor's eyes. He had just bought a new house; he was making it his. This was the man's right, his absolute right. But it twisted Zeb's guts, and he could feel Rumer shivering beside him.

"The value of our property . . ." Rumer whispered. "It has nothing to do with money. It's the land . . . this beautiful Point."

They stood by the window, gazing across the bay. People were leaving the beach for the day; just a few brightly striped umbrellas remained. The Good Humor man rang the bell, tempting the kids as they walked by. A few boats were fishing out at the breakwater, and several white sails dotted the blue water.

"This beautiful place," Zeb said.

Rumer sobbed, and she seemed surprised when he took her hand and pulled her to the sofa. Together they sat down, and he took a deep breath. The value of the land . . . the new neighbor had gotten Zeb thinking; he understood that Rumer's grief was for something much more than baby squirrels, the trees next door. It was for their childhood, their memories, the way things should have been.

"What is it?" she asked.

"The other day you asked me why I won't be flying anymore."

"I'm not even sure whether to believe you or not, Zeb. You love it so much."

"Not anymore," he said.

"Tell me why."

"Something happened up there last September," he said, stroking the back of her hand, "that brought me down to earth."

She stared into his eyes. "You looking down here, me looking up there . . . so many nights, when I dreamed, I left my body to go flying with you . . . up there. My old friend Zeb . . ."

"Up there," Zeb said, looking up at the blue sky, the golden clouds holding the first of the sunset light. "I felt very far away . . . that's what I remember thinking. Like, how will I get back? Will I ever see anyone again? I looked out the spacecraft window, down at Earth, and I swear, we were passing right over Hubbard's Point. . . ."

"What happened?"

"We had an explosion," he said.

Her eyes were wide, listening. She couldn't know that he was feeling the blast inside his body—as he did every time he thought of it. The Point was peaceful; he and Rumer were sitting side by side, and again Zeb felt the bottom fall out of the world.

His fingers closed around the sofa cushion beneath him. It was a subtle move; he hadn't even been aware he was doing it. But Rumer saw, and she reached down to hold his hand. Her fingers entwined with his—warm and secure. Without checking, Zeb knew his palm was sweaty. Rumer just held it, gazing at him steadily.

"There was an electrical fire," he said. "It wasn't the first one I've ever experienced; it wasn't even very bad. . . ." Even so, he could smell the wires burning, the plastic melting. Sometimes he felt as if the burning smell had gotten into his skin and hair, and nothing would ever wash it out.

"But it felt like an earthquake. As if we could get knocked out of the sky. As if we'd passed through a black hole."

"How long—"

"It lasted only a few seconds," Zeb said. "Our computer showed the fire was in the control panel, starboard side . . . Mel Davis, the pilot, took action right away. He was great—we shut everything down."

"Were there flames?"

"Not that we could see," Zeb said. "But we assumed it had to be bad—we'd felt the blast, and our instincts had kicked in. The thing is, it wasn't all that serious. There are procedures; we've run through them many times. We put it out right away—we were never in real danger."

"But you were up in space," Rumer said. "You must have been so scared."

"We're trained," Zeb said, his pulse racing, "to expect things like that. I've felt explosions worse than that in the simulator. But yes—we were in space. I felt very, very far from everything I loved."

He remembered how quickly he and Mel had taken action, put out the fire. Mel had laughed almost right away—Zeb ordinarily would have been laughing along.

"Michael?" Rumer asked.

"And you . . ."

"Me?"

"You and Michael," Zeb said, his voice thick. "Our groundspeed was so fast—we made that last orbit, and then we came down. But my thoughts were racing even faster. You and Michael . . . I couldn't wait to land, to check in with you right away."

"You called one day last September," Rumer said. "Dad told me. . . ."

"Yes. I was wishing you'd answered the phone, but Sixtus picked up . . . said you were working out in the field somewhere. I don't think I told him anything about the explosion—he thought it was just to catch up. That's when he told me about Dana getting married. I called Winnie to see if her house was available. I started thinking—I need to reevaluate everything. I need to figure out what was important. I need to set things right. It took some time, but I put the plan together."

"To come out here?"

"Back home, to see you," Zeb said, rubbing the back of his neck, feeling weary with how far he had come. "And to bring Michael here. I knew—I hoped—it would be good for him. This is my home . . . I've lived other places, but I've never really left."

"You couldn't," Rumer said, her voice raspy. "You belong here."

"I've done so much to push it all away. . . ."

"But you couldn't."

The chain saw whirred outside, slicing through pine branches. Zeb's stomach clenched. He thought of the new neighbor taking down the trees he and Rumer loved. He had to tell her how he felt, and he had to find out her side: The necessity had grown stronger every day, pressing his heart and strangling him. It was like a launch window—very little time to do a very precise thing.

Standing together, he and Rumer listened to the destruction of the tree they loved and watched the sunset. Yellow light spread over the beach and sea, and Zeb thought of launch windows. Once, during a June mission, the shuttle *Endeavour* had to lift off and rendezvous with the EU-RECA satellite in order to return it to Earth after a year in orbit. With a seventy-one-minute window, they reached it on the sixty-seventh.

Another time, they had to fire a Delta II rocket in order to launch a U.S.-Japan Geotail spacecraft into a looping orbit around Earth and the moon. It was July, nearly ten years ago, and they had had a two-minute window. In spite of the keplerian elements involved, they had succeeded.

"What are you thinking?" she asked now.

"About launch windows."

"What do they have to do with right now?"

"Well," he said, "they're a limited time in which something has to occur. Like the passing of orbiting spacecraft with which the shuttle must rendezvous . . . or the time of day that a satellite payload has to pass over a certain region of the earth. Or—" He swallowed, bowing his head. "A certain amount of time within which a person can correct all the mistakes he's made."

"Like selling your house," she said in a low voice.

"That's not the one I meant . . ." he said.

"Why didn't you keep it?" she asked, the words tearing out.

"I couldn't, Rumer. The divorce was a mess. Maybe if we'd waited it out, let the dust settle, we could have kept it . . . but Elizabeth didn't want it. She said anytime she wanted to come here, she could stay with you and your father . . . it bothered her to think of me owning property right next door. So we put it on the market, and it sold that very first month."

"Maybe you can buy it back," Rumer said with longing, looking out the window at the chain saws.

"I wonder what it would take," Zeb said.

"I don't know," Rumer whispered.

Zeb stared into her eyes. Summer was passing by; soon he was expected to return to California to start his new job. The launch window was getting smaller for him to say what he had to say. In that mission craft last September 30, choking on white smoke up there in space, he had known he had to get straight with Rumer. He stared into her blue eyes now: She was the one he had loved his whole life. Since they were kids, younger than Michael and Quinn.

"What happened that day?" he asked.

"Which day?"

"The first day of spring. We were supposed to meet at the Indian Grave, and you never came. . . ."

"I've told you—I came home from college planning to meet you, but I never got the word. Why have you never believed me?"

"Because I left you that note."

"In the drawer?"

"You know I did."

"I never got it, Zeb."

"Maybe you weren't ready," he said as if she'd never spoken. "Maybe I was rushing you."

She looked troubled, her eyes clouded as if trying to remember. From the front windows they overlooked the beach, cove, distant trees, and the path to Little Beach. Through those woods, at a secret spot, there was a hidden trail over the tidal creek to the Indian Grave. Zeb's pulse raced, waiting for her to speak.

"I looked for a note," she said softly, shaking her head. "I waited for you to call. I didn't know where you were. I waited up all night. You could have called me. You could have walked over and told me. We could have held hands and walked down the beach and through the path together . . . I'd have helped you pitch your tent! Why didn't you just come next door?"

"I was trying to be very Hubbard's Point romantic. The drawer had always worked before. I thought you'd have liked it."

"I would have," she said. "You acted so cold afterward."

"I was hurt," he said.

"Spurned?" she asked, her lips tight, and when he nodded, she went on. "I know how you must have felt. For two months I barely heard from you. And then we went to see Elizabeth in that play and everything changed. I just thought it was easier for you to love her than me."

"Rumer—," he began.

"Do you really think it matters anymore? After all this time?" she asked sadly.

Just then the telephone rang. It was Sixtus calling from Lunenburg in Nova Scotia. Outside, the landscaper began hacking down the row of bamboo overgrown with thick honeysuckle vines.

Rumer spoke to her father, sitting down on the love seat by the stone fireplace. Zeb listened to the sound of her voice, soft and happy to be speaking to her father, to know he was safe.

He closed his eyes, wishing she could know how much he wished she had answered the phone when he'd called last fall. He had been so afraid; the explosion had made him look at his life, face the fact that he had made a terrible mistake.

Love is forever, his mother used to say. *When you think you've lost it, come back to our sanctuary. It'll be right here waiting for you.*

Zeb's hands were shaking. Outside, the chain saws roared, cutting into the sanctuary. Rumer spoke softly on the phone, her voice soothing his spirit, touching his heart. When she looked across the room, their eyes met. She kept talking to her father, but she didn't look away from Zeb.

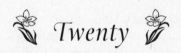

Twenty

ON RAINY DAYS, Foley's store was filled with thwarted beachgoers browsing through books and magazines, children perusing comic books and penny candy, friends having tea, and teenagers playing the jukebox. The message drawer got its greatest use on these days, with one set of friends leaving notes and the next group reading them. The sheets of paper were like movable graffiti.

And over the years, the notes became like leaves on the forest floor. Some settled and became part of the ground; others were retrieved, while still others simply disappeared. Some of the oldest fell apart—the paper folds wearing out, the edges getting caught in the drawer's wooden seams.

Rumer, Quinn, and Michael sat around one of the scarred wood tables. Drinking tea, Rumer watched them do their homework on Act II of *Romeo and Juliet.* Taking a break, they tried to read the old initials carved into the wooden tabletop.

"There's my parents," Quinn said. "LU & MG. And Aunt Dana and her old boyfriend: D&T."

"Here's my dad," Michael said. "ZM—can't be many of those around. But instead of 'EL' it's 'RL'. . . ."

Rumer blushed, stirring honey into her tea. "That was a long time ago."

"RL is you?"

Rumer nodded. "We were old friends, your father and I. You knew that, right? As I remember, he carved our initials together as a joke. It was never serious, Michael."

"Serious enough for him to carve it."

"We had a paper route . . . I think we'd come in for hot chocolate one cold, rainy morning like today. Some boy I liked was probably sitting over there"—she gestured at the counter—"and your father decided to make him jealous. Something like that."

"Mom said you were her biggest rival," Michael said.

"Wow," Quinn said. "A little Shakespeare right here at Hubbard's Point. Two sisters and the same guy!"

"Elizabeth said that?" Rumer asked, stuck on Michael's comment.

Michael nodded. "Yep. She laughed when she did, because obviously . . ."

Rumer reddened deeply. Obviously, her sister meant, Rumer wasn't a contender in any competition with Elizabeth.

"What's her problem?" Quinn asked. "Rumer's awesome!"

"She thinks I'm ridiculously small town," Rumer said, trying to smile. "Right, Michael?" But then, because her nephew was squirming and she didn't want to put him in the middle, she changed the subject. "Have you two left notes for each other yet?"

"Notes? What do you mean?" Michael asked.

"In this drawer," Rumer said, pulling it open to reveal all the folded sheets of paper.

"Lovers," Quinn said, staring into Michael's eyes, "leave messages for each other. It's a Hubbard's Point tradition."

"Good to know," Michael said, taking a pen from his pocket.

"Yes, isn't it?" Quinn asked, taking a pencil from the back of her hair. A notebook lay on the table in front of her, filled with notes about *Romeo and Juliet*. Surreptiously, Quinn began to write, making sure no one could read her words.

Rumer smiled. She wondered who they thought they were kidding. Playing it cool, showing just so much and no more. Lately Quinn had started wearing a new ring made from four strands of copper wire; Michael had a similar one, obviously matching Quinn's.

Watching the kids, she found herself thinking back. As much joy as Zeb's notes had brought her, Rumer knew they had also led to trouble.

One night, back at the beach before her first off-Broadway run had started, Elizabeth had stopped in for a soda, reading over Rumer's shoulder. "Whoa, what's this? My little sister's growing up! And so's our next-door neighbor, from the look of things. . . ." At that time, Rumer and Zeb were nineteen, juniors in college, falling in love.

Looking back, Rumer realized that everything had started changing after that. Elizabeth seemed to regard Zeb in a new way. And, more upsetting, Rumer worried that Zeb would notice. How could Rumer hold a candle to her sister if Elizabeth decided to go after him? Rumer and he still left each other notes in the drawer, but she kept waiting for him to wake up and see that Elizabeth liked him . . . and one day, he did.

"What does it all mean, Rumer?" Quinn asked, back to her schoolwork.

"Mean?" she asked, shaken from her reverie.

"Romeo and Juliet."

"My sister's the actor," she laughed. "I'm just a country vet."

"But you know more than we do," Quinn prodded. "Come on. . . ."

"Yeah," Michael said. "Their families gave them so much grief about being together. It's obvious they loved each other more than anything . . . they were meant to be together."

"Sometimes that's not enough," Rumer said.

"Are we allowed to carve our initials here?" Quinn asked, tracing the table. "I mean, officially?"

"Mr. Foley has never seemed to mind."

Nodding, Quinn took her sailing knife from her book bag. She worked slowly and carefully, making block letters in the wood. Rumer expected them to be hers and Michael's, but instead they were "RM & JC."

"Romeo Montague and Juliet Capulet," Quinn said. "I never want to forget. Two people destined to be together, torn apart by their families."

Staring at the Z and R of Zeb and Rumer, Rumer's eyes swam.

"Romeo and Juliet," Quinn said. "I may be emotionally anorexic, but this is for you."

"Quinn, honey," Rumer said. "You're not—"

"They have a whole play about them to tell their story," Michael said, gently taking the knife from Quinn's hand and starting to score beautiful script letters in one of the few places left untouched on the wide table. "We might have only this little spot to tell ours. And summer's going so fast, we'd better do it soon."

"Because you leave before Labor Day," Quinn said.

"Shhh, don't say that," Michael whispered, getting to work.

Rumer watched him chisel "QG" and "MM," the letters entwined together, and she held herself back from telling them that initials didn't matter at all; neither did the notes they would write and leave. Symbols might last, but unless a couple was really meant to be together—fated and blessed by destiny itself—no amount of carving or writing could make a bit of difference.

Michael's words had reminded her that summer was speeding by. He and his father would be returning to California before long. Rumer shivered as if the first breeze of fall had just swept south from Canada, filling the air with a deep chill.

Tracking the Franklins down took a little doing, but Zeb finally located them. He learned from land records at Black Hall town offices that the Cresthill Road property had been registered under the name Tad's Bedding, Inc. with corporate headquarters located in New Glendale, Connecticut. Speaking with the building inspector, he learned that Tad Franklin had filed papers to request zoning variances on the use he proposed for his property.

Driving north through the Connecticut River Valley, Zeb turned off the windshield wipers. The rain had stopped, but the road was slick. He passed forests, bridges, ponds, and small towns, their white steeples showing through the trees. If there was one thing he could do to keep the promise he'd made to Sixtus, it was to look over Rumer's property and happiness by trying to buy back the sanctuary.

New Glendale was an old manufacturing town originally known for its production of screws. Advancements in the industry had left factory owners unprepared, so the downtown was filled with many abandoned brick buildings, graceful and a century old, their large windows filled with broken panes overlooking the river.

Tad's Bedding was a chain that reached from New Haven to Springfield. Their flagship store stood on the corner of a main intersection between a Burger King and a vacant convenience store. Many storefronts were boarded up, and three men stood smoking outside a pawnshop. Tad's Jaguar was parked on the asphalt apron outside the bedding store.

"In the market for a new bed?" a salesman asked as Zeb made his way around the showroom.

"Not today," he said. "I'd like to see Tad Franklin."

"Ah, the boss," he said, grinning. "Great guy. I'm not sure he's in . . . but if he is, you'd want to go around back to the shipping department. See that sign?"

"Yes, thank you."

Zeb walked past the king- and queen-size beds, the twin beds with Disney character headboards, the wall of bunk beds. When he rounded the corner into the back room, he came upon a receptionist in a cubicle.

"Picking up a bed, sir?" she asked.

"No, I'm here to see Tad Franklin."

"Your name?"

"Zebulon Mayhew."

Nodding, she pressed the intercom just as an inner door opened. Franklin came out as if he'd heard through the walls. His hair slicked back, he was wearing a dark suit; his shirt cuffs, which protruded a perfect inch, were monogrammed. Zeb, wearing jeans and a T-shirt, shook his hand.

"I knew it!" Franklin said, shaking Zeb's hand. "The realtor told me a famous couple had owned before me, and then I saw that TV special, and

I put two and two together—Zebulon Mayhew. I was right! You are the astronaut. Come on in."

Zeb walked into the office. It seemed to have been decorated by a cross between Martha Stewart and the Marquis de Sade. Bedding industry awards plastered the walls, along with autographed pictures of people and their beds. A small seating area of white slipcovered chairs surrounded a low walnut table with a bouquet of roses in the middle. White down pillows were stacked in a corner beside an electric shoe polisher. Paintings of hazy nudes hung on the walls. An Oriental rug covered the floor. Franklin's mahogany desk looked as if it might have once belonged to a king or a president; the wall behind was draped with red satin sheets.

"People like to create a mood," Franklin said, looking around. He had a small worry line between his eyebrows. "It might look like a little too much to you, but I like to try things out before I put them in the showroom."

"That makes sense," Zeb said, staring at the satin sheets.

"They're pretty red," Franklin said. "It seems to be universal: Men love them and women hate them. Last month my wife hung white eyelet up there. Change the balance, she said. She's my decorator."

"That's nice," Zeb said. "You're lucky to be in it together."

Franklin chuckled, nodding. "You might mean the business, but what it really is is life. That's the gift, isn't it? To go through life with someone you like. What else is there? I'm a family man . . . that's what everyone will tell you about me. So. What brings you up here? Not a new bed . . ."

"No," Zeb said.

"It's probably the beach house, right?"

Zeb nodded, and Franklin gestured for him to sit down.

"I bought it for Vanessa," Franklin said. "Her family rented down at Hubbard's Point when she was a girl. She's never stopped dreaming of the place."

Zeb's stomach fell. He'd been hoping it was just real estate, just an investment instead of an emotional attachment to the Point. "I make a lot of money," Franklin said matter-of-factly. "The truth is, I run out of things to spend it on. Nice cars, a new kitchen, private schools for the kids . . ."

"I'd like to buy the house back," Zeb said.

"Whoa, whoa." Franklin laughed. "You want to buy my house?"

"Yes," Zeb said.

"Interesting," Franklin said, frowning.

Zeb sat still, waiting. His gaze took in pictures of another house on the wall, probably where Franklin lived in New Glendale. The colonial-style house itself was new, huge, with fanlight windows in more places than any colonial architect had intended. The landscaping was extremely formal, reminiscent of a professional building, with too-tidy hedges, fake rocks, waterfall, and marble statues.

"Is that yours?" Zeb asked.

"Sure is," Franklin said proudly. "Like I said, I have a landscape architect. This guy is a true artist—a man who takes pride in his work, you know? Look at that waterfall . . . it wasn't easy for him to create. He had to clear the lot and build a rock pool first . . . you'll see. He's doing the same thing down the beach."

Zeb exhaled slowly. He hoped Rumer would never have to see this or any other fruits of the Franklins' landscape architect. Turning his head, he stared straight into the man's eyes.

"So, Mr. Franklin," he said. "Will you sell me the house?"

Franklin's mouth dropped, but he quickly composed himself.

"I'm saying to myself, what's this guy trying to do? You must want it bad. For you to come all the way up here on a rainy day—you know? Look ahead is the way I live my life—for you to come all the way up here, talk to me face-to-face instead of through a real estate broker, you must really want my house."

"I do," Zeb said. He didn't have the energy for bargaining, lying, or beating around the bush. He just wanted to buy the house back for Rumer.

"How bad?" Franklin asked, leaning forward. "That's what I want to know: How bad do you want it? After I just get finished telling you how much it means to Vanessa?"

"Just tell me what you'll take," Zeb said. "I'll pay you."

Franklin slapped the desk in enjoyment.

"You have to play the game with me . . . name a price you're willing to pay," Franklin said gleefully. "Go on. You know what I paid for it?"

"One hundred eighty thousand."

"Did your homework! Not bad, huh? What'd you and your wife sell it for—half that?"

"About," Zeb said, thinking back ten years.

"Well, that's all it was worth—no offense. But the house is ramshackle—that's what the realtor called it. It's surrounded by trees and vines, really clogging up what could be a nice piece of property. And it has animals overrunning the place. So here's what, Zeb: You want the house, you have to pay me what it'll be worth after I'm finished with it."

"What are you talking about?"

"Once I'm done fixing the place up, I'll double or maybe even triple my money."

"You're planning to do all this work and then sell?" Zeb asked.

"Maybe not the first or second year," Tad said. "But sure—eventually.

We'll trade up to a better spot. Maybe a house directly on the water-front . . ."

"I thought you said she loved it," Zeb said, his skin crawling.

"The place—Hubbard's Point. She's not attached to any one house."

You're a fucking asshole, Zeb wanted to say but didn't. Instead, he breathed and began to practice the Zen that had gotten him through so much—the claustrophobia, the isolation, the loneliness of space—and wondered what it would take to get the house now, today, before he cut down all the trees and put in a waterfall.

Franklin opened a drawer and pulled out some plans. He pushed them across the desk toward Zeb. Reading them, Zeb understood what Tad Franklin was going to have to do to the land to get his waterfall.

"Don't do this," Zeb said quietly after a moment.

"It's going to be beautiful."

"You're going to dynamite the rock ledge?"

"I have to. For the pond and waterfall. The town's making me put in a bigger septic system—regulations have changed since your family built the house. These decks will be new . . . one will face the beach; the other will face the rocks. And this new peak"—he pointed at the plans—"will house a hot tub—right on the roof. Can you imagine sitting up there, staring at the view. . . ."

Zeb closed his eyes, thinking of the view from that sagging old roof. He remembered shingling the roof with his father; he pictured the uni-corn weathervane his mother had had made for the family one Christmas. He remembered climbing up with Rumer, sitting by the chimney, naming constellations.

"So, you're planning to tear down the old house?" Zeb asked. "To build this one?"

"I am," Tad Franklin said. "Your friend will love it—she really will. I'm going to be very sensitive to the neighbors . . . I won't block her view in any way. I'm sorry, Zeb . . . may I call you that? But the house isn't for sale. I shouldn't have given you any idea that it was."

Nodding, in shock, Zeb pushed back his chair. Now he wanted only to get down to the Point, back to Rumer.

"You know, I'm getting an idea—an inspiration," Franklin said. "Ever think about doing ads? Getting in front of the camera?"

"No," Zeb said.

"The reason I ask is," Franklin continued, "you'd make a decent spokesperson for a business like mine—you've got name and face recog-nition, but not too much—" He laughed. "Wouldn't cost me an arm and a leg, know what I mean? I thought about asking Paul Newman . . . he's a Connecticut resident—in fact, he was on that same show you were. He lives right up the road from my brother-in-law, drives at Lime Rock now and then . . . but I figure he's priced out of my league."

Zeb moved toward the door.

"So, what would you think? I'd pay whatever you say—just kidding about going cheap with Newman. I'm sure we could work it out. An astronaut selling my beds—I think it would be great."

"I'm sorry," Zeb said. "But no."

"We're not going to have any problems, are we?" Franklin asked, sounding worried. "Because I'm sensing a lot of hostility down there. I was hoping you'd come up here wanting to be friends."

"People love the Point. They don't really think in terms of yards, property lines down there. They love the land," he said quietly, Rumer's voice echoing in his mind. "All the rocks, all the trees—they consider it a sanctuary."

"That's nice," Franklin said, nodding. "I like that."

"It's probably what drew your wife back to Hubbard's Point . . . the thing she fell in love with in the first place."

"Probably so."

"If you start blasting and cutting, all that will change," Zeb said. "You'll change the landscape and kill the animals."

Franklin shrugged. "My wife wants a waterfall and a hot tub," he said. "And she doesn't like vermin. I'm not going to let her down. I've spent a lot of money, and I'm going to spend a lot more."

"Then you're going to upset a lot of neighbors," Zeb said, thinking of Winnie, Hecate, Mrs. Lightfoot, Annabelle, Dana, Quinn, and especially Rumer.

"I'll deal with that," Franklin said, his eyes and the tone of his voice growing cold. Zeb felt the battle lines being drawn. Nodding, he turned and walked out of the office, away from Tad Franklin and his plans.

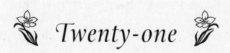 Twenty-one

NOVA SCOTIA WAS the most beautiful place Sixtus Larkin had ever seen in his life—including Hubbard's Point. The landscape informed his very being—the craggy rocks, stalwart pines, and peaceful coves. Childhood memories, good and bad, came rushing back the minute he sailed within sight of the coast. They transformed him instantaneously—from the inside out—as if none of the intervening years had ever taken place.

"It's unbelievable, Clarissa," he said out loud, more to his wife's ghost than to his boat. "I'd forgotten how Canadian I am. Do you think, when I get to Ireland, I'll become more Irish?"

He tacked into Lunenburg, the harbor filled with fishing boats. Bright red and blue buildings filled the boatyards. There was the *Bluenose,* the fishing schooner pictured on Canadian dimes, and there was the Fishermen's Memorial, engraved with the names of those who had drowned at sea. His mother had brought him and his brother here as children. . . .

Giving thanks for his own safe arrival, Sixtus sailed the *Clarissa* straight over to the town pier. His legs were weak and wobbly from the days he'd spent at sea, and he was so exhausted, he wanted to sleep for a week. After calling Rumer from a pay phone to let her know he was okay, he started back down the dock.

"You must be Sixtus Larkin," said a man lumbering toward him. Huge and white-haired, the man grinned and stuck out his hand.

"And you must be Malachy Condon. Considering there's not a soul I know left in these parts. How'd you know it was me?"

"Sam Trevor told me to look out for a pretty Herreshoff, and he was sure right—the *Clarissa* is one sweet boat."

"Thanks, Malachy. Named for a sweet lady."

"Mrs. Larkin, I presume?"

"Yep," Sixtus said.

"Well, from what Sam says, you and I have a lot to talk about. We're both Irish, we're both docked in Nova Scotia, and we're both teachers. How about coming on board my tug for a meal?"

Sixtus hid a yawn. He weighed sleep and hunger, and his stomach won out. "You know, if you're cooking, I'll take you up on it."

"Why don't you grab an hour's sleep? I know you think that's nowhere near enough, and it isn't, but it's a start. I'll give a call when I'm ready for you."

"Sam was right about you," Sixtus said, unable to stop yawning. "You're a good man. See you soon . . ."

An hour later, almost to the minute, Sixtus heard the dinner bell. While not quite rested, he was at least refreshed. Throwing cold water on his face, he changed his shirt and headed down the dock to Malachy's old red tugboat, the *Archangel*.

"I like the name of your boat," Sixtus said. "Fitting for an Irish-Catholic like yourself."

"Refers to my son, Gabriel," Malachy said, offering Sixtus a beer. "He's up in heaven with his mother, looking over me every day."

"That's how I feel about Clarissa," Sixtus said. "How can I go wrong on a boat named for an angel?"

"Well, cheers," Malachy said, reaching over to clink bottles. "Here's to our angels and your voyage."

The men drank beer and ate cold shrimp hauled in the Gulf of Maine. Slitting their shells with his thumbnails wasn't easy for Sixtus's cramped hands, and he caught Malachy taking notice. Throwing the shrimp tails overboard, the men soon attracted a school of fish. The silver fins slapped the harbor's still, dark surface, and then disappeared altogether. Malachy played tapes of dolphins recorded by hydrophone off Big Tancook Island, and Sixtus told how a Minke whale had followed him for the last sixty miles.

"Nothing like being alone at sea," Malachy said, "to clear your head."

"It's true," Sixtus agreed. "I'm retired, and I live with my daughter. She's a veterinarian."

"Ah," Malachy said, indicating the hydrophones used for recording marine mammals. "An animal-lover. A girl after my own heart."

"Yes, she could probably add some insights to those tapes you have. She's brilliant at animal behavior. But feisty and stubborn, just like her old man. I began to feel as if I was squeezing the life out of her—she was so busy going to work and cooking for her old man, she wasn't getting much chance at a life."

Malachy nodded. "Good thinking," he said. "Whenever I catch myself missing Gabriel too much, I have to remind myself at least I'll never saddle the boy with my care—you know, I'm nearly too old and creaky to live on this boat, and if Gabe were settled in suburbia with a nice wife and kids, I just know he'd be offering me the in-law apartment above the garage."

"Creaky—that about covers it," Sixtus said, looking at his hands.

"Arthritis?"

"Yep. Bought the cane last fall. Figure a walker's coming next. Hip replacements, a back operation, a lifetime supply of Advil . . . and Rumer turning into a geriatric-care nurse. No in-law apartment; we share the same house. The same house she's lived in her whole life, if you want to know the whole sorry truth."

"Jay-sus!" Malachy said, scowling as he sucked the head off a shrimp. "What are you trying to do, strangle the poor girl? You want her runnin' a nursing home?"

"I know, I know," Sixtus said, quaffing his beer.

"What is she, divorced?"

"Never married," Sixtus said, slinking down in his deck chair.

"Glory be, man! You set sail just in time. Give the lass a chance. Any prospects on the horizon?"

"Christ, Malachy—I'm not trying to marry her off. Rumer's just fine without any husband. In fact, the last prospect," he said, thinking of Edward, "was so unworthy of her, if I'd walked her down the aisle to him I would have had to stand by just to be ready when the priest asked for objections. The girl is genius at saving animals' lives, but she was on her way to making a muddle of her own."

"Yeah?"

"Yeah."

Malachy chuckled. "So, she needs someone to take care of her for a change."

"She doesn't need taking care of, that one. Rumer's kind and compassionate, but she's sharp as can be too. Graduated from Tufts—hardest veterinary school to get into in the country. She runs a thriving business—everyone on the shoreline brings their pets to her. Very successful."

"No bias or prejudice talking there," Malachy said, pulling out his pipe.

"Of course not."

"So, she's an only child?"

"No," Sixtus said, gazing out over the serene harbor. "She has a sister."

"And the sister isn't one to pitch in, looking after the crippled old father? Not a caretaker like Rumer?"

Sixtus chuckled, thinking of Rumer as a caretaker. Then, picturing Elizabeth, said, "No, no. The sister isn't domestic. Far from it."

"Ahhh. Well, good for her, I say. When people take care of themselves, it's best for all concerned. Survival of the fittest—works in the wild but also in families. An elderly parent can eat a caring child alive. At the very least, keep her from living her life. You're a wise and good man."

"I'll sail off the globe before I do that," Sixtus growled. "You asked if Rumer had someone on the horizon. The answer is yes, she does."

"Someone other than the bloodsucker?"

"Her ex–brother-in-law."

"The plot thickens," Malachy chuckled. "How does her sister feel about it?"

Sixtus considered the personal question. Perhaps it was his exhaustion, or the fact that he was so far from home, or Malachy's warmth, but Sixtus felt like talking.

"Well, to complicate things a little more, Zeb was in love with Rumer first—years before he married Elizabeth."

"Are the girls close?"

"They were at one time," Sixtus said quietly. "Now Elizabeth's divorced, Rumer's alone, and Zeb's back in the picture."

"You want them together?"

"I don't know what the hell I want," Sixtus said. "And I have no business saying. Just before I left, I got him to promise he'd look after her. What do I know?"

"Right. Nothing."

"I'm just the father. Jesus, you have a nice berth here, Malachy. Do I take it you're all alone?"

"Well," Malachy said with a twinkle in his eye. "Most of the time . . ."

"You have a lady friend?"

"That I do. Perhaps you know her—she comes from down your way, in Hawthorne, Connecticut. Lucinda Robbins . . ."

"Sure, I know Lucinda. She used to be the librarian till she retired. . . ."

Malachy nodded. "Yes, that's her."

"You're a lucky man," Sixtus said.

"Amen to that."

Malachy was bringing out a second round of beer and shrimp when they heard someone coming down the dock. She was tall and slim, and she wore a picture hat pulled low over her face.

"Isn't that—" Malachy asked, lowering the plate with a stunned look on his face. "Isn't that that movie star? What's her name—the one who always plays those sexy spies and Shakespeare ladies. . . ."

"Elizabeth Randall," Sixtus said, lowering his beer to the deck and stepping over the rail.

"Yes, Elizabeth Randall," Malachy Condon said, his mouth opened in stunned surprise, watching his guest embrace the movie star.

"My daughter," Sixtus said, grinning into his eldest child's beautiful face.

❧

"Dad, *what* are you doing here?" Zee asked after she'd been introduced to Malachy and walked her father back to his boat.

"I thought that was pretty clear," Sixtus said. "Nova Scotia is my stopping-off point on my way to Ireland."

Zee shook her head, smiling with amazement. Her father was the most hyperbolic person she knew—imagine the audacity of sailing to Ireland! On a century-old sailboat! She was glad she'd shaken the film crew entourage—if anyone, even Bud Stanton her friend and producer, got wind of it, they'd have one of those entertainment shows here on the docks filming news at eleven.

But it was quite stupendous. Zee listened as her father described sailing single-handed from Hubbard's Point to Lunenburg, four days with only a few hours sleep, lashed into the cockpit so he wouldn't be swept overboard.

"The waves were ten foot," her father said. "Bigger than we get in the Sound, that's for sure."

"But nothing compared to the middle of the ocean," Elizabeth said, hugging her father. "My namesake died on a boat in a storm. I've always had premonitions. . . ."

"Get out," her father said, sounding delighted. "You? My practical Zee?"

"I know, I know, don't tell anyone. I'm the hard-boiled New Englander . . . thank God Abigail Crowe paved the way for sensible women in Hollywood. But yes, Dad. I've grown up thinking of Elisabeth Randall drowning off the Wickland Shoal, so I'm highly sensitive!"

"In other words, don't go?" her father asked, laughing.

"You got it, Papa."

Her father yawned, his sunburned face creasing into a million wrinkles. He rubbed his bleary blue eyes, and Elizabeth shook her head fondly. She had seen her father exhausted so many times: staying up late to correct papers, to finish reading a book, to check on Zee's baby sister. Working the steps of AA had allowed her to make peace with her past, with the deep resentment toward her father that she had held for so long.

"You need to sleep," Elizabeth said, pointing her father toward his

208 · Luanne Rice

bunk. "I don't have call till tomorrow. I'm going to sit on this deck and give praise for the fact I don't have about fifty P.A.'s running all over me while you go get some shut-eye. But when you wake up, I want the whole story."

"What whole story? About the whales and sharks I saw out at sea? About the filigree clouds over the horizon? About steering by the stars at night?"

"Jesus Christ, no. Rumer's Nature Girl, not me. I want all the dirt, Dad. Every detail about Zeb's great return to the homeland that you can think of. Okay?"

Her father shook his head. He looked very slightly amused but mostly sad. He had never approved of gossip, and he certainly believed that Zee should lay her marriage to rest and let everyone get on with life. She believed it too, but she couldn't stop herself. Steps or no steps, the subject of Zeb back at Hubbard's Point with Rumer close by was too tender to just drop. Especially with Michael right there.

"Let it go, darling," her father said. "Do us both a favor and drop it. Now let me sleep, and we'll talk later."

" 'Rest now, little father,' " Zee said, quoting Garbo in *Ninotchka*.

She prowled around the deck for an hour—wound up, adrenaline flowing. She had always been this way, as long as she could remember. As calm as her sister was, Zee was that hyper. She would have made a great executive: She wanted to know all, oversee all, control all—even from across the country. Just seeing her father was wonderful—in spite of the fact that he had aged greatly, that he'd gotten so hunched over— but it was the specter of Zeb and Rumer that had really gotten her thoughts flowing.

In spite of that, the peace of Lunenburg soon overtook her. The air was so clear, the harbor so clear and calm. Sitting in the cockpit, she found herself lulled by the rocking of the hull. She hadn't escaped the set in weeks; it was wonderful to not have hair, makeup, wardrobe, producers, the director, all wanting her for something. Before she knew it, she fell asleep.

When she woke up, it was dawn, and her father had covered her with a blanket. He sat across the cockpit, Bible open on his lap, drinking coffee.

" 'There's no use trying to save me, my good man,' " she said, glancing at the Bible.

"Ah, a daughter who quotes James Thurber at first light," her father said, grinning. "I knew I was a lucky man."

She smiled, remembering how she and Rumer had pored over their mother's copy of Thurber's *Men, Women and Dogs*. The book had been a Hubbard's Point fixture, and Zee and her sister knew it by heart. Her father brought her a cup of black coffee, and she hiked up on one elbow to accept it.

"I must look a fright," she said, watching her father move slowly. Everything was soaking wet from the morning mist, especially her hair.

"I'm your father, not your leading man. I've seen you looking much worse."

"Well, thank you. Coming from you, I'll take it as a compliment."

They drank their coffee in silence for a few minutes. The day was clear and fine with that Canadian seaside luminosity Zee had come to know after the many movies she'd filmed up here. The sky was bright blue, yet golden at the same time. The rising sun was just crowning the horizon, solar fire with rays of gold shooting into the sky.

"Seriously, Elizabeth," her father said after a while. "It's wonderful to see you."

"Didn't think I'd come, did you?"

"You do tend to stay away. . . ."

"Only from home, Dad. Too many ghosts."

"Your sister, you mean. She knows you too well, and she can call you on just about anything."

Elizabeth just stared across the harbor. He was partly right, but there was more. He didn't understand the guilt that ate at Elizabeth regarding Rumer. Making amends was a large part of how she stayed sober a day at a time. Although Rumer's name was right at the top of Elizabeth's list of amends to be made, she had so far lacked the courage it would take to actually attempt them.

"We're filming in Laurelton and Halifax," she said, changing the subject. "Just down the road."

"Two very familiar places to me." Her father nodded. "As a boy, I spent time in both."

"Really? I remembered you lived in Halifax. . . ."

"Yes, but I know Laurelton too," he said. His expression darkened, and Zee assumed it was from remembering how it felt to grow up poor, without a father. Her father and his brother had started working when they were very young; he had put himself through college by delivering milk.

"Laurelton is lovely," she said. "It's like a New England sea-captain's town. Graceful white houses, long lawns sloping down to the harbor, yachts on moorings, white picket fences, and geraniums in window boxes. Very Edgartown, very Nantucket—our story is a period piece, a whaling story set in Nantucket. Laurelton is as pretty, and our cheap money people love the price of filming in Canada. . . ."

"It might be pretty, but . . ." her father said, scowling. "Never mind. How long do you have?"

"My next call is four today. We can spend the whole entire day together, Dad. Isn't that wonderful? Now, start talking!"

Zee contented herself with hearing about the boat, the Point, Winnie, Hecate, Mrs. Lightfoot, the Campbells and McCrays, and Dana's wedding.

"Oh, that must have been a *Dames de la Roche* extravaganza if ever there was one," Zee said wickedly. "One of their own getting married. And to a younger man! Much younger, from what I hear . . ."

"They're very happy," her father said. "Sam adores her, and he's a wonderful father to Quinn and Allie."

"The Grayson girls . . ." Zee said, shaking her head with resentment. "Horrible, what happened to their parents. Dana stepped in to take care of them?"

"It's not unheard of," her father said softly. "An aunt loving her nieces—or nephew—that much."

Elizabeth flinched, thinking of how hard she had tried to poison her son's mind against his aunt Rumer. How could she not? When Rumer had been so good, and Elizabeth had been such a fuckup?

"Anyway, *mirabile dictu,* he's enrolled in summer school, doing wonderfully."

"How did that happen?"

"I'd like to say it was my influence, but to tell the truth, I think it was a combination of Rumer and Quinn."

Zee blinked. She swallowed hard, not wanting to show her emotions—which were so strong and overwhelming, she couldn't quite believe it. How could she be feeling this much fury for something that was good for Michael?

"Who . . ." she began, her head spinning. "Why didn't anyone tell me?"

"Well, we knew you'd be happy," her father said. "I guess we just decided to go with the flow, see where it took him."

"Rumer could have called me," Zee said quietly. "Zeb could have."

"I think Rumer tried," her father said. "When she called to invite you to my going-away party."

Zee breathed steadily, the way she had been trained, to keep from turning red. Yes, Rumer had called. Repeatedly. Zee had gotten messages on her voice mail, from her agent, from the production office . . . she had called back once, to decline breezily, when she'd known Rumer would be at the office.

Exhaling steadily, Zee forced a smile onto her face. She did a mental somersault, changing direction in order to keep her composure. "Anyway . . ." she said, her smile growing more radiant. "Dana really robbed the cradle, didn't she?"

"Be careful," her father said. "Zeb was a younger man. Your little sister's age, precisely."

"Low blow," Zee said, the smile evaporating.

"I'm sorry."

"You think I'm insensitive. You're giving me a taste of my own medicine."

"Maybe."

"Well, hit me with the rest of it. How *is* Zeb? He's a reformed celebrity from what I hear. Cast his career aside to drive across country with his son—when I'm sure it was the last thing Michael wanted."

"I hope you don't encourage Michael in that. The boy needs his father."

"I don't try to stop it, Dad."

"Elizabeth, I learned the hard way that carrying a grudge against a parent does nothing but destroy you from the inside out. You seem to have forgiven me for all my mistakes. . . ."

"I love you, Dad," she said. "And you never really made that many."

"Well, it's the same for Michael," her father said. "We Larkins seem to be a long line of imperfect parents—my mother, me, maybe even you and Zeb. . . ."

"Especially Zeb," she said stubbornly, although she knew he was right.

"I know a lot of this dates back to the time your sister went out to visit and blew the whistle on your drinking. She got Zeb very worried that she'd take Michael away if you didn't clean up your act."

"I should be grateful to her," Elizabeth said. "And in some ways I am. But that was not a fun time. . . ."

"I can imagine."

"Zeb was like the police, watching over me. And when he did have a mission, he'd hire extra baby-sitters and nannies so Michael would never be alone. He made me feel as if I could hurt my own child. . . ." She trailed off because, as she had come to accept during her eleven years of sobriety, she very well could have.

"He could have been more diplomatic, I suppose," Sixtus agreed. "But he was worried about his son. Your marriage was falling apart. Nerves were raw."

"And I was in and out of rehab," Zee said, shaking her head. "You want to know about raw. . . ."

"Anyway, he's spending time with Michael this summer. Trying to set him on the right road to a good education."

"Only a diehard teacher would care *that* much about education."

"I became a teacher to help children," Sixtus said softly. "That hasn't changed."

"You became a teacher because you got the whole summer off," Zee said, laughing and shaking her head. "You know that's true, Dad! And I admire you for it! Look at this gorgeous summer day—let's take a ride and enjoy it, okay? And you can explain to me why I shouldn't be upset with Rumer for taking over my son's life . . . she's not his mother, you know."

"I think she's aware of that," her father said.

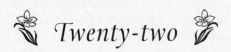

Twenty-two

To celebrate the kids' summer school progress reports, Rumer and Zeb took them out to dinner at Lobsterville. The great old family restaurant was located in Mount Hope, a thirty-minute drive from Black Hall. Zeb pulled into the wide gravel parking lot, and everyone admired the view of fishing boats, robber barons' mansions, and the bridge across the bay. Zeb glanced over at Rumer. The cool breeze had raised goose bumps on her bare shoulder, and the sight nearly stopped his heart.

"This is a celebration restaurant," Quinn said. "My parents brought us here when we were little . . . my father had just bought his new office, I think."

"Everyone has happy memories of Lobsterville," Rumer said. "We used to come here when we got good grades . . . my parents would make a reservation for a window table, and we'd get to order anything we wanted."

"Cool," Quinn said. "I'm having steak."

"At Lobsterville?" Rumer laughed.

"Sure. Lobster is my job, my line of work, my daily bread . . . I need a break!"

"You sound like someone from Nova Scotia," Rumer said. "My father told me lobster's so common up there, farmers used to use it for fertilizer—just plow it into the fields. The inmates at the prison were eating it five nights a week. They got so tired of it, they went on a hunger strike."

"No hunger strike for this girl," Quinn said, rubbing her hands together. "I'm having beef! Extra-extra rare—if they don't cook it, it's okay. This is so nice! You didn't have to do it . . . it's not even for a report card—just a progress report."

"But you did get all A's," Zeb said.

Michael said nothing but got out of the car and walked around to stand by Quinn. The last time he had gotten A's, he had been in eighth grade. He had to be bursting with pride for his achievement—just like his father.

"How do you like this place?" Zeb asked, walking beside his son, on the opposite side from Quinn.

"Looks okay."

Zeb nodded. He and Zee had taken Michael to some of the most sophisticated restaurants in the world. Taillevent and l'Ambroisie in Paris, la Tante Claire in London, Chanterelle and Nobu in New York, their old standbys Orso and les Deux Cafés in Los Angeles. For oceanside experiences, they went to Ivy at the Shore in Santa Monica or their favorite biker's bar, Neptune's Net, in Malibu. Michael tended to be jaded about dining; Zeb just hoped he didn't say anything to hurt his aunt's feelings. Rumer had chosen this place with pride and delight.

"They're supposed to have good seafood," Zeb said.

"I know. It's fine, Dad." Holding Quinn's hand, he pulled her ahead and left Zeb and Rumer walking together. Their feet crunched over the gravel mixed with crushed clamshells. Rumer put her arm around him.

"It's really going well with you and Michael," she said.

"Yes," Zeb said. "It is."

The moral support felt good, but what really preoccupied him was the weight of her arm—small, light, but with enough substance to send serious energy running down his spine.

They gave their name to one of the Keatings, the restaurant owners, and then went into the bar to wait. The bartender offered the adults whiskey sours—the house special drink—but all four of them ordered iced teas. Zeb glanced at Rumer, wishing she would touch him again.

"You never drink, Aunt Rumer?" Michael asked.

"Not too often," she replied.

Michael nodded, satisfied.

As the kids jostled each other, joking about lobsters and homework, Zeb tried to work his way closer to Rumer. He wanted to brush her hand, to feel her skin. He wanted to lean close to her, slide his arm around her, touch her. Her blue eyes were bright and filled with happiness. Was she as happy as she looked? To be having dinner with him, Michael, and Quinn? Was it possible that this was all it took?

Hearing their name called over the loudspeaker, Zeb followed everyone to the dining room. A beautiful young lady greeted them and led them to a table by the window. She wore hearing aids and spoke as if hearing impaired, and she beamed when Rumer conversed with her in sign language.

"How do you know how to do that?" Quinn asked.

Rumer glanced at Zeb, and he felt himself redden.

"Tell her, Zeb," she said.

"We learned when we were young," he said. "So we could talk to each other at night, across the yards, after everyone else was asleep."

"From your windows?" Michael asked.

Zeb nodded, staring at Rumer. Candlelight flickered from an amber hurricane lamp, lighting her blue eyes, warming her pale gold hair; Zeb felt stirred by her beauty and the memory of learning a new language just to be able to talk to her.

"She's deaf," Quinn said to Rumer, "and you know how to talk to her. I'm not, but I used to be in a world of my own. You've always known how to talk to me too. When no one else did."

"It was easy," Rumer said. "Talking to you."

"Rumer's always been like that," Zeb heard himself saying.

"What do you mean?" Michael asked.

"She cares about everyone around her. It's what makes her a good vet."

"You're turning my head," Rumer joked.

But she felt that he meant it, and she liked that he knew her so well; Zeb saw the color rise in her cheeks. For so long—since marrying Elizabeth—he had felt like a hermit in a cave. Hidden away, all alone, communicating with higher forces instead of loving the people around him. Yet here he was, surrounded by his family, and he had never felt so right. The thought of leaving, returning to the West Coast, hit him hard, and his gaze went to Rumer. How could he go away from her again?

"Maybe I'll become a vet," Quinn was saying. "A vet for birds and animals of the shore. Or a teacher, like Sixtus. A lobstering teacher. Or a teaching lobsterwoman."

"You'd need college," Michael said.

"And graduate school," Rumer said. "A master's degree . . . but don't worry. You're on the right track . . . those A's you got on your progress report are the first step. I'm so proud of you both."

"Yes," Zeb said, focusing on the conversation instead of on Rumer's eyes, looking at Michael. "So am I. What about you, Michael?"

"Me?"

"Well, say Quinn does want to be a vet or a teacher . . . how about you?"

"I might like to teach," he said quietly. "Like Grandpa. Or be a lobsterman."

"We could lobster along all sorts of different coasts," Quinn said. "And see the world."

"Yeah." Michael grinned at Quinn, the softness in his eyes going straight to his father's heart. "How far can we get in your boat?"

"It can handle any weather," Quinn said, smiling back. "But we need more range—we'll have to add another engine to get very far."

"Whoa . . . are you two planning to run away together?" Zeb asked, exchanging glances with Rumer.

"If we wanted to," Michael said, "we wouldn't do it in front of you."

"Not for a few years, Mr. Mayhew," Quinn said. "I think we have to go to college first."

"Anywhere she goes, I'm going," Michael said.

Zeb turned to smile at his son, but what he saw in Michael's eyes now made his stomach lurch. Michael was dead serious.

A waitress came over, smiled, and asked if they wanted to hear the evening's specials. Someone must have said yes, because she began to tell them about scallops and lobster sautéed in butter, but Zeb barely heard.

His son was on his way. The rockets had fired, blastoff had occurred, and Zeb hadn't seen it coming. The waitress was taking orders; when she got to Quinn, Michael held Quinn's hand and said, "She'll have the steak. She likes it rare—extra rare. If you don't cook it, it's okay."

"Oh, Michael," Zeb said under his breath just as the waitress got to him and, pencil poised, flashed her most welcoming Lobsterville smile.

Zeb was overcome with the fact—for better or worse, wherever it led—his son could know and trust his own mind so well. Rumer sat so close; her presence was so strong. Why hadn't he trusted himself—and Rumer—enough to know that they had always been meant to be together? That it was only his pride that had been hurt when she'd stood him up that one time, that one night, that had changed the course of their lives.

He sat there, staring at his child, until Rumer said softly to the waitress, "Will you give us just a minute more?"

Driving out of Lunenburg, Sixtus asked Zee to take him by Blue Rocks. It was a ghostly spit of land with just a few fishing shacks standing on stilts above the tide. Rich brown sargassum weed covered the rocks, its distinctive smell filled with salt and decay. No matter how clear the day was, a thin vapor always held on here, softening the contours of the boulders.

"My brother and I used to go fishing here," Sixtus said. "When our mother was working."

"But I thought you lived in Halifax."

"We did."

"That's miles away from here!"

"I know. But work was hard to get . . . she had to take the jobs she could find. We'd come out with her, spend the night so we didn't have to be alone."

"What did she do?"

"She cleaned houses for rich people . . . that led to her taking care of them when they got sick . . . from there, she met a doctor, and he hired her to look after newborn babies, sort of like a nurse's aide."

"In people's homes?"

"No, darling. Not in their homes." Weary again, perhaps from the pounding his body had taken on the long blue-water sail, Sixtus looked at Elizabeth. She was a true beauty, with the wide-spaced brown eyes and glamorous square smile of her mother. Her straight brown hair fell in a chin-length bob, and her high cheekbones were sharply shadowed. How blessed his children were: intelligent, beautiful, loved.

This was the chance for Zee to change the subject. Menial labor wasn't something she knew or cared anything about; Sixtus was surprised she'd stayed on it this long.

"Dad?"

"I'll take you there, sweetheart. I'll show you where your grandmother used to work, if you'd like to see. It's in East Laurelton, just down the road from the town where your movie's set."

"Okay," she said. "I'm game. Climb in." He did, with difficulty. Perhaps it was visiting the land of his youth that made him feel so old.

They drove east along the coastal road. Glimpses of small bays and pristine coves filled Sixtus with nostalgia. Some of the houses looked familiar, and he wondered whether any of the old employees' families had descendants still living in the neighborhood. Whitewashed Victorian houses, tall and sturdy, built to withstand the strong sea wind, lined the streets.

"Slowly, now," he said when they drew closer. He recognized so many things: the post office, the enormous pine—even taller now—that he and his brother used to climb, an old toolshed where they had played hide-and-seek.

"What's that place?" she asked, noticing his stare.

"That's where the Cuthberts lived."

"Who are they?"

"Jean and Richard Cuthbert. They ran the place where my mother worked; the Cuthbert Children's Home."

"Oh . . . a home for unwed mothers?"

"Yes, Elizabeth. It was."

"What did your mother do there?"

"Well, like a lot of the Irish girls who came over, she was a domestic—a cleaning lady and nanny. She loved children—she was a wonderful mother to us, and she tried her best to mother those girls who came here to have their babies. Some of them weren't much more than children themselves."

He paused, glancing over to see how his daughter was taking this. Elizabeth looked uncomfortable, still staring at the house.

"She was there to sweep the floors and scrub the toilets, but she wound up ministering to a lot of those girls. She got a lot of midwife training over the years; she was present at a good many births."

"Sounds like a lot of hard work," Zee said.

"She liked her job."

"I don't see how."

"Well, she liked helping . . . it gave her a lot of satisfaction."

"Must be who Rumer inherited her saintliness from."

"Well, she was a saint," Sixtus said with a lump in his throat. "That's true enough."

Sixtus leaned back in the comfortable leather seat, his gnarled hand gripping the door handle. The sports car was small, compact, barely big enough for two bodies to fit in. He had never imagined having this conversation with Elizabeth—Rumer, maybe, but not Zee.

"She was only one person," he said. "As loving as she tried to be, she couldn't do enough for all those babies."

"No?" Her expression was wide open, reflecting her curiosity in the story, but when she saw her father's face, she darkened.

"Many babies were born here," Sixtus said as if she hadn't spoken. "Their bassinets were arranged in rows, like food shelves in a grocery store. I remember walking through the aisles with my brother, looking at the infants . . . our mother would sneak us in when the weather was too inclement to go fishing at Blue Rocks."

"That doesn't sound so bad."

"She couldn't do it every day. We were young ourselves; we wanted our mother. But we needed the money . . . she took all the hours she could get. The more she worked, the more she'd get attached to the babies."

"What did you do?"

"Well, we took care of ourselves the best we could. We played at the shore, on the rocks; my brother skipped a lot of school. Got in trouble more than I did—I did my best to steer him in the right direction, but he wanted to get her attention."

"Your mother's?" Elizabeth asked, stiffening. Was she thinking of herself and Sixtus? Or, perhaps, herself and Michael?

"Yes. She'd come home exhausted—from trying to do so much. The kids were all ages. Infants, toddlers . . . not to mention the young mothers."

"So your mother did it all."

"Like I said, she needed the money. And she had a huge heart."

"Sad," Zee said, her lips tight. Sixtus looked across the seats. He sensed her closing down hard and fast. This was too sensitive for her. She began to shift into drive, but Sixtus put his hand over hers.

"Wait," he said. "There's more."

"It's crummy, Dad," she said. "I know it happened—I've always known you had a hard childhood, and I'm sorry."

"No excuses, honey. I turned into a shutdown father all by myself. I passed my own pain onto you, and that's something I live with now."

"Don't worry about it."

"You can say that, but I do worry. I'm so sorry, Elizabeth. I wasn't available enough when you were a little girl, and I know it—"

Elizabeth blinked hard, as if she could drive the memories away.

"My mother started to drink after work here," he said. "Just a little sherry before bed at first—to help her relax and go to sleep. She used to cry, telling us about the infants who were sick, premature . . . those were the worst, the ones she most wanted to help."

"Michael was premature," she said, trailing off into memory.

Sixtus nodded. He remembered when Elizabeth had gone into labor seven weeks early. They had whisked Michael straight from the delivery room into the neonatal ICU, and he'd stayed there for several weeks. During that time, not a day went by without Sixtus thinking of his mother's charges, the other babies, the ones who didn't make it; praying for his brand-new grandson, he had also prayed for them.

"Drinking stole her soul," Elizabeth said bitterly. "The way it stole mine."

"I think I pushed you into it," Sixtus said, his eyes tearing as he fumbled for her hand. "All the trouble you've had—I think my neglect made you start. . . ."

"No one can 'make' someone drink," she said, her mouth set, driving faster. "Why did you bring me here?"

"I wanted you to know, Zee," Sixtus said, picturing his oldest daughter, standing on the rocky headland at home, reaching out her arms as if she could pull her father back from sailing out to sea. "Our family has something we need to put back together. This is the summer for it."

"What do we need to 'put back together'?"

"There've been rifts between you and me, you and Rumer. I'm getting old, Elizabeth. I want to see my daughters getting along. And I want to know that you and I can forgive and forget."

"Nothing to forgive," Elizabeth said dangerously. "Although I'm not sure Rumer would agree. She blames me for everything."

"She's working it out," Sixtus said. "Isn't that what life's all about? Making peace with the past, trying to get along happily in the present?"

"Your trip . . . is that it? Making peace with the past?"

"Partly," Sixtus said, flexing his hands. "And partly, it's just a big adventure. I've always wanted to sail home—to Canada."

"And what about Ireland?"

Sixtus laughed. "Maybe once I get there, I'll throw myself on the mercy of the Irish Brothers, or some other order. Get them to take care of me in my old age instead of your sister. One thing I don't want is to be a burden to her."

"I'm sure she wouldn't see it that way," Elizabeth said quietly.

"Perhaps not," he said. "But I do."

"What did you mean before, when you said Rumer's 'working it out'?"

"Well, with Zeb and Michael," Sixtus said, smiling. But catching the look in his older daughter's eyes, he could see he'd stepped into—or set—a booby trap.

"What's she doing with them?"

Sixtus took a deep breath. "She has a relationship with them, Elizabeth. As long-lasting as your own."

"They're not her family."

"How can you say that? Michael's her nephew. Zeb is her oldest friend."

"They're *my* family, Dad."

Sixtus rubbed his eyes wearily. "How did you ever get the idea that there's not enough to go around? They can be yours, but they can be hers too. She's been hurt over the years—when you wouldn't let her see Michael. She has strong feelings about this, Elizabeth. Whether you like it or not."

"Right," Elizabeth said. "I cause pain and then drink to forget it; Rumer's the saint."

"No one's a saint, Zee."

"Oh, come on. She's such a saint, you have to sail to fucking *Ireland* so she won't feel obliged to take care of you."

"That's not it. . . ."

"Fine, Dad."

Elizabeth's mouth was a thin line. She wanted him out of the car, Sixtus could tell. He thought of his two daughters, one who had a boundless ability to give and heal, this other girl, who'd been shut down so long ago.

"I have to get back to the set," she said.

"Elizabeth . . ."

"How much longer will you be here?"

"Just a few days," he said. "The summer's passing by so quickly; I have to leave soon to make it to Ireland before the fall storms start." But even as he spoke, pain gripped his knuckles, as if the cold north sea air were seeping into them.

"Hmmm."

"And you? How long are you filming here?"

"Not long. A day or two at most. We wrap very soon, and then I'm taking a few weeks off. You know, I hope I can see you again, but I'm not sure. I'm really in demand most of the time, Dad—Zeb could tell you. When I'm on set, everyone wants me. This day off has really been an aberration."

"I didn't mean to upset you," Sixtus said, watching her eyes.

"It's not your fault," Elizabeth said. "I'm keyed up. This is a really challenging production, and I hate the fucking director. And then, thinking of Saint Rumer down there, wooing back my husband and son, taking my place . . ."

"She's not wooing anyone."

"Whatever you say."

"I love you, Zee."

"You too, Dad."

"Can you come back later? Or tomorrow maybe?"

"If I can."

But somehow he knew he wouldn't see her again on this trip. Oh, the mysteries of being parents, of being children. Sixtus, in his seventh decade, had just begun to feel it unravel, just started to figure it out.

When she dropped him off at the dock, he limped slowly back to the boat. He thought of sailing across the sea, how much smoother a passage it was. His heart ached, and his throat was full. Turning to wave good-bye to his oldest girl, he saw her car speeding away. He raised his hand, squinting into the bright sun. She couldn't possibly see him, but he stood there anyway.

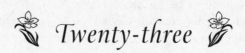 *Twenty-three*

THE SUMMER DAYS lasted so long. Sunlight reflected off the last high clouds and lingered in the sky, captured in tree branches and weathered shingles, until the evening star appeared in the west and seemed to dangle from the boughs.

Heading home after dinner at Lobsterville, everyone felt full and happy. Driving under the trestle to enter the Point, Rumer felt a sense of enclosure: the ultimate feeling of safety and home.

Familiar old trees arched above the winding road, branches interlocking to form a canopy overhead. Zeb dropped the kids off at Quinn's house—having celebrated their excellent interim grades, tonight they had more studying to do. Rumer waved good night and said she'd see them tomorrow.

"There go the future college students," she said when she and Zeb were alone in the car. Their eyes met, and her heart sped up.

"Can you believe it?" Zeb asked, not looking away. "From dropouts to kids with a mission in one summer."

"Never underestimate my nephew—or Quinn," Rumer said, trying to have a conversation while her mind went crazy wondering what was going to happen next. Zeb's hand slid across the seat to take hers.

Zeb pulled up to the stone wall at the bottom of her hill. Rumer turned—to thank him for the wonderful evening or invite him up to the house, she wasn't sure, when she caught Zeb looking past her, over her shoulder, his mouth wide open with shock.

"Rumer . . ." he said.

"What is it?" she asked, turning.

"The trees," he said.

"Oh, Zeb," Rumer breathed, touching her heart.

Together they climbed out of his car. The smell of pine tar and freshly cut wood filled the air. It wasn't what *was* there, but what was not: Something enormous was missing. Looking south toward the point, there was too much sky. Although night was falling, Rumer's yard was too bright. At first she thought it was one tree—one big tree.

"I can't believe it," she whispered, beginning to realize.

"He clear-cut the yard," Zeb said, and then she knew.

"They're gone," she gasped. "They're *all* gone."

Running ahead of Zeb, she burst into his old yard. While she, Zeb, and the children had been gone, someone had cut every single tree down to the ground. They lay in logs—not yet split, six feet long—like the spoils of a lumberyard, waiting for the saw. The sky yawned overhead, a gash filling with stars. Rumer ran from spot to spot, where the trees had stood: the big cedar, a white pine, the huge oaks, the sassafras, the catalpa, the oak and pine saplings. White disks remained on the ground—markers of where the trees had been cut—oozing with sap.

"How could they have done this?" she cried. "All the trees!"

"It's unbelievable," Zeb said, sounding shocked.

"They didn't save even one. They're all gone!"

"I didn't think they'd move so soon," Zeb said. "I thought we'd have time."

"Move so soon . . ." Rumer listened to his words. Had he known this was going to happen? "What are you talking about?"

"I saw the plans."

"You *knew*? And you didn't *tell* me?"

She threw herself at him, shoving his chest with all her might and gasping for breath. Catching her wrists in his hands, he shook her. "Rumer, stop! Listen to me—I had no idea. To go this far? I never believed he'd do it—a few trees, maybe. Some bushes blocking his view. But not this!"

"Oh, Zeb," Rumer said, leaning into his body. "He just went through with a chain saw—he didn't pick and choose—he didn't take any time to decide."

"No, he didn't. He didn't care at all. They were just in his way, and he got rid of them."

Rumer felt a sob rise in her chest, and Zeb held her tighter. She was in shock, as if she'd just witnessed a terrible accident. She cried her heart out, letting Zeb soothe her, feeling his hand on the back of her head.

Night was falling quickly; the Mayhews' old yard had been so overgrown with brambles, trees, and vines that they were part of the landscape and she was used to seeing vague shapes everywhere. Growing along the curved stone steps were—or had been—old roses and hydrangeas.

Suddenly, something inside her shifted. Rumer's years of treating the Point as one big family property were over. This land no longer belonged to Zeb; it no longer, in any sense, belonged to her either. The realization stabbed her heart, and she hunched slightly, drawing inward to protect herself.

Rumer knew that this was the last time she would set foot in this yard. The split-trunk oak was gone, and so was the azalea bush. Zeb's mother's rare lilies bloomed along the rock outcropping—the only green left in sight. Rumer looked around for the rabbits and wondered where they could be—there was no longer anywhere for them to hide.

"We could relocate them," Zeb said, reading her mind.

"I don't know," Rumer said, staring at the flat rock that marked the opening in the ledge, the hole leading to their warren. "This is their home."

"Rumer . . ." he began.

She hadn't thought the pit in her stomach could get any bigger, but it did. He was watching her so vigilantly, his blue eyes taking in her reaction, and she felt her heart clutch.

"What?"

"I didn't want to tell you right away—I hoped I could do something to stop him . . . but Franklin has filed plans with the town."

"What's the difference?" Rumer asked, her voice catching. "He's not going to wait for the hearing. The trees are gone—nothing will bring them back!"

"The ledge, Rue," he said.

"What are you talking about?" she asked, not understanding.

"He's filed for a permit to dynamite the rock ledge. He wants to put in a hot tub, and he needs a huge septic tank for that. Because there's so much ledge, he has to go down pretty deep. You see, Rumer?"

"It's bedrock," she said, leaning down to touch the earth, to feel the craggy rocks under her fingertips. They were warm, heated by the day's sunlight. Zeb was joking; he had to be. No person—not even someone like Franklin—could just come in and destroy the backbone of Hubbard's Point.

"He's going to blast it."

"Why would he even want to? Why would he buy a place here if he wanted to obliterate what makes it beautiful in the first place? This isn't a development; it isn't a suburb . . . it's different than any other spot in Connecticut. It's like Maine, or Nova Scotia—it's glacial moraine. . . ."

"I know," Zeb said softly. "From space, you can see the cut. I mean, you can see the contours where the rocks of Hubbard's Point would merge with the coast of Africa. It's incredible."

"He can't wreck that," Rumer said. Zeb's calmness was making her feel desperate—because she knew that he meant what he was saying. "He can't just change what's been here forever—move it to suit him!"

"But he already did," Zeb said.

"The trees," she whispered, looking at the blank, dark sky where branches should have been.

"The rabbits, Rumer," Zeb said, holding her shoulders.

"What?"

"We might not have another chance before he blasts. Do you want to try to move them?"

She cried, not wanting to accept the truth of what Zeb was telling her. It can't happen, she wanted to scream, he can't just destroy tons and tons of pre-Cambrian rock ledge, but she knew he could: This morning there had been two-hundred-year-old fifty-feet-tall trees standing there, and now there were none.

"The rabbits won't want to leave their warren."

"I know. But if anyone can help them relocate, it's you."

Rumer swallowed. She thought of the hutches in the mudroom; they were all empty right now. "We can keep them inside till we figure something out."

"Exactly. Come on, Dr. Larkin."

Crouching down beside the hole, Rumer rested her hand on the flat rock. Zeb saw and reached underneath: The hidden key was still there. He pocketed it—it belonged to him after all.

"I'll get something to hold the rabbits in," Zeb said, hurrying next door to her house.

While he was gone, Rumer put her face close to the hole. She tried to peer inside but saw only blackness. As a child, holes in the ground had scared her. She had thought of scary things hiding inside: gnomes, trolls, poisonous snakes. Right now she felt more like that little girl than the veterinarian she had become. Closing her eyes and summoning up the grace of her mother, grandmother, Mrs. Mayhew, Clarissa Randall, and all Quinn's mermaids and unicorns, Rumer worked her arm into the hole.

Her fingers touched soft fur.

"It's okay, don't be scared," she whispered.

Perhaps the rabbits had been so terrified by the cutting that they were frozen with fear. Zeb had returned with an empty pillowcase, and Rumer pulled the rabbits out one by one and put them inside: seven altogether, including five infants.

Overhead, without leaves to rustle, the breeze sounded empty. It whistled through the sky, beneath the stars. Holding the pillowcase, they started toward Rumer's house. Suddenly an engine rumbled down the road; headlights pierced the night.

The lights swept the land, revealing a barren moonscape: a treeless hillside of craggy gray rock. As the truck drove past, and the motor's rumble dissolved in the distance, the tall oaks and pine trees shimmered in a ghostly apparition. Had they ever been there at all?

Rumer closed her eyes, to preserve the memory of all those trees she had loved to climb, of the graceful limbs that had sheltered generations. Then, taking a breath, she opened them, and followed Zeb and the rabbits into the house.

&

Looking out the window the next morning, Michael couldn't believe his eyes. Across the street, the hill around his father's old house was as bare as a rock. In fact, it *was* a rock: a huge pile of granite topped by his family's dark green cottage. His father had gotten up early; lying awake, thinking of Quinn, Michael had heard him make the coffee, lay out his papers and photos for the work he was doing.

Pausing in the hall between his room and his father's desk, Michael tucked in his shirt. He saw his father sitting there, head bent as he looked over some pictures.

"Dad?" Michael asked.

"Good morning, Michael. Sleep well?"

"Yeah. What happened outside?"

"You mean up on the hill?"

"The trees are gone."

"The new owner decided to cut them down," his father said, and from his clipped tone, Michael could tell he was upset.

"It looks weird," Michael said. "Not like it's supposed to."

"I know. But it's his right."

Michael's chest squeezed. Why did his father have to talk to him like this, like a kid? Of course Michael knew it was the man's right—but wasn't that beside the point? Michael could see his father felt bad—he could only imagine how Aunt Rumer was feeling, and what Quinn would do, and he wanted to say something, to help somehow.

"Still, he shouldn't have done it," Michael said.

"The laws of man and the laws of nature don't always go hand in hand," his father said.

"Huh," Michael said, mulling it over yet wondering why his father always had to talk as if he were narrating a *National Geographic* special. He took a few steps closer to look over his father's shoulder. The black-

and-white photos were grainy, hard to interpret. Michael saw large areas of muddy black, washed-out gray, dots of white, and he felt upset, uneasy: Seeing his father work reminded him that they'd be leaving Connecticut soon.

"What are those?" he asked.

"They were taken from space," his father said. "Last winter."

"What do they show?"

"Aunt Rumer's house."

"Really?" Michael asked, leaning over.

His father traced the picture with his finger. "This is the Atlantic Ocean."

Michael nodded at the huge black area to the right, realizing that the white dots were wave tops—whitecaps. The ocean flowed into Long Island Sound, narrowing into Winnie's cove.

"There's the Wickland Rock Light," Zeb said, pointing. "With better resolution, you can see where the *Cambria* sank, where your mother's ancestor died. But this particular shot is a little murky. There's the Point, that's Winnie's house . . . there, across the street, is our old place, and that's Aunt Rumer's—"

"There's Quinn's," Michael said, and his father gave him a funny look.

"Yeah," his father said. "There's Quinn's."

"What's it for?" Michael asked.

His father was silent for a moment, staring at the hills and hollows, the many trees and few houses that made up Hubbard's Point. His concentration was intense, as if he were overseeing the entire planet, the whole universe. Shoved under the local photos were others that Michael had seen lying around, satellite photos of forest fires in Montana taken last summer, thick smoke following the west wind.

"I'm looking at the land," his father said finally. He traced the Point itself, the outcropping of glacial rock that jutted directly out into Long Island Sound, like a finger of God pointing straight out to sea.

"Why?" Michael asked.

"Because I'm in awe," his father said softly, "of what man thinks he can do."

"What good does it do to look?" Michael asked.

His father seemed not to hear him. Tapping the table with his fingers, he wouldn't respond. Michael exhaled—it was seven-thirty, time to meet Quinn and go to school.

"I'm not sure, Michael," his father said, suddenly turning his head to look Michael in the eye. "I really don't know what good it can do."

"Why look, then?"

"Because I'm trying to learn something," his father said.

"Learn what?"

"How to be a better—"

A better what? Michael wondered. Everything about space reminded him of how his father liked to fly off, disappear, and watch the world from far away. Here he was, still doing it: Sitting on the Point, the rocky land right at his feet, his father would rather look at pictures of it taken from above. Michael shrugged, backing away—he had to see Quinn right now, as soon as possible, to warn her, before she saw what had happened.

"Have a good day at school, okay?" his father said, stopping him in his tracks.

"I'll try," Michael said, struck by the father-and-son-ness of the moment.

"I'm proud of you, Michael," his father said, turning to look at him. "That progress report was really something. Keep it up."

"Thanks, Dad. I will," Michael said, grabbing his books and walking out the door.

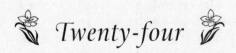

Twenty-four

THE NEXT DAY, rabbits filled the mudroom. Mathilda had come over to help Rumer line the hutches with straw and leaves, cantilevered rocks against the sides to approximate the warren they had left, and left the bright fabric covering the cages themselves.

"Not as quiet as most summers," Mathilda said.

"No," Rumer replied, "I guess the neighbor figured chain saws don't fall under the scope of the hammer law."

Next door, the workmen were busy. With Labor Day just a week off, they were preparing to begin working full force. A demolition team was taking measurements with a yellow tape. Builders had removed the house's white shutters and stacked them by the road like garbage, to be picked up in Monday's collection.

Rumer had immediately moved the pile of shutters from the bottom of the hill into her house. She couldn't bear to see them thrown away—the white panels, solid wood, pine trees cut out for decoration, had framed so much of her heart. She knew she'd think of something to do with them.

"Hey, anyone home?" Zeb asked, knocking on the door.

Glancing up from the hutch, Rumer smiled. He wore jeans and a white T-shirt, his arms tan and strong from all his rowing around. He started toward her quickly, his eyes bright and intense, before catching sight of Mattie there beside her.

"Oh!" he said, stopping short.

"Zeb, this is Mathilda Chadwick," Rumer said. "Mattie . . ."

"Hello, Zeb," she said, smiling. "I'm just helping Rumer make the rabbits a nice little home."

Zeb laughed. "Well, I think I've found a spot to relocate them. Up here on your hill, Rumer—the other side of the house from mine—I mean, the Franklins'—between the rocks and the herb garden. . . ."

"By the roses?" Rumer asked, trying to picture the spot. Her mother had loved beach roses, and she had planted a huge garden of them in the middle of the upper yard.

"Yes," Zeb said. "There's a tunnel into your ledge; it's not as hidden as the spot under the azaleas, but it's similar. There's a lot of honeysuckle and wisteria growing up around the cedar trees there; maybe we could pull some of the vines down and use them to cover the opening."

Rumer nodded, smiling. Zeb inched toward her as he spoke, as if he wanted to close the distance between them. He was so close; if Mattie weren't there, Rumer was sure he'd kiss her.

But when a truck from New Glendale Pest Control pulled up next door, her reverie slammed to a halt. She, Zeb, and Mattie filed outside. Quinn and Michael stood there, interrogating the driver, who told her that Mr. Franklin had hired him to spray poison down the rodent holes and eradicate "the whole problem."

"That seems like a shortsighted solution," Mathilda began. Rumer and Zeb stepped forward to intervene, but Quinn beat them to it.

"The whole problem?" Quinn screamed. "The whole *problem* is that assholes like him think rabbits and squirrels are rodents! Maybe to some-one else they are, but to us they're like family! Like pets! Didn't you ever have a dog, buddy? Or a cat, or a hamster?"

"Are you crazy?"

"Don't you dare call me crazy," Quinn said.

"Back off," the man said, pointing the nozzle of his silver can at her. Mathilda shrieked.

"And don't you *dare*," Quinn said evenly, "aim that thing at me."

Before Rumer could stop her, Quinn had disabled the man with a karate move and taken his spray can. She ran down the right-of-way to the beach and her boat and let Michael block the man's way, leaving him swearing into his cell phone.

"What was that?" Zeb asked, his eyes wide with surprise.

"You've never seen her in action before?" Rumer asked as he took her hand. His touch weakened her knees, and she had to hide her smile from the exterminator.

"Who says girls don't have the power?" Mathilda asked.

"She's awesome," Michael said.

"How the hell did a girl from coastal Connecticut learn moves like that?" Zeb asked as if shocked, but Rumer heard quite a bit of respect and admiration in his tone. The exterminator, shaking his head, continued to yell into the cell phone.

"Girls from coastal Connecticut are vastly underrated," Mathilda said.

"My boss is calling the cops," he said as he disconnected and walked over to them. "She's in big trouble—big fucking trouble."

"Watch your mouth," Zeb said.

"That psycho goes ninja on me, steals my can of poison, and *you* tell *me* to watch my mouth?" the man spat out.

"I think we're clear on that," Zeb said.

"Fuck you," the man said. "Fuck you all! My boss says you've been nothing but trouble since he bought this place. Well, hang on to your seats. He's a great guy, the nicest guy you could want to meet, but cross him, and—"

"We have a ninja to protect us," Rumer said, smiling.

"Yeah, rabbit-killer," Michael said, standing right in the man's face, his red bandanna blazing like a battle flag.

"You were too late anyway," Mathilda said. "We have the rabbits under protective custody. Your trip here was in vain."

"She'll pay," the man said. "And pay big. That stuff is hazardous waste—whatever she's planning to do with it, she'll be in huge trouble. She could go to jail for it, and don't think my boss won't send her. Little bitch."

At that, Michael lurched forward, but both Rumer and Zeb grabbed his arms.

"Are you her parents?" the man demanded.

"Why don't you get out of here?" Zeb suggested—not with rancor, but for the man's own good. His face was scarlet; he was apoplectic.

"I want her name, I want her address, so I know where to send the cops. Are you her fucking parents? Jesus, she's a nutcase. She oughta be locked up. I'll see to it that she is—I'll testify! Who's responsible for her anyway? You? You her parents, or what?"

"I'm responsible for her," Michael said.

"Michael—" his father began.

"I'm responsible for her," Michael repeated, shaking himself free of his father and aunt, standing tall before Quinn's accuser. "She's my friend. Anything you have to say to her, you can say to me."

"Fuck you," the man said, laughing. He shook his head and climbed into his truck and drove away.

When the coast was clear, Quinn ran up the steps from the boat basin. She was holding the exterminator's silver can, and she put it down to run into Michael's arms. "I heard you defending me," she said, holding him tight. "Thank you, thank you."

"We need to talk," Zeb said sternly.

"First," Quinn said. "We have to get rid of that." She pointed at the can.

"I thought about taking it out to sea and dumping it—there's that hazardous waste dump marked on all the charts of Long Island Sound, just south-southeast of the Hunting Ground. What's a little more poison? But that's what *they* would do. I'm not going to kill one more fish in the sea."

"We could call poison control," Rumer said. "That's probably the best thing. Or the police—head this guy off at the pass and let them deal with it."

"We could explain the whole thing," Mathilda said.

"What would we explain?" Zeb asked.

"What I did," Quinn said. "And why. The important things in life. Where we are. Who we're with. Hubbard's Point, each other . . . those are the important things of life. In Shakespeare, *Romeo and Juliet,* people are always dying for what they love and believe in: Right, Michael?"

"Right," Michael said.

"Well, those are the things I love and believe in. The things I'd die for. We could explain that we love this place . . ."

Zeb nodded.

"Enough to die for," Quinn reminded him.

"You're some girl," Zeb said.

Rumer was silent. Growing up at the Point meant everything. It gave kids—and grown-ups—a sense of belonging, lifelong friends, and a place to come home to. It had brought her and Zeb together once, and it had brought them together again.

"Thanks," Quinn said.

"You like nature, don't you?"

"Every bit of it."

"Maybe when you finish school, you could come out to California and work in my lab."

"Really?" she asked, and Michael stepped forward, looking interested.

Rumer's heart fell. Zeb had always said he was going back to open the mission center. But Mattie caught her eyes, gave her a supportive, calming look.

"Sure," Zeb said. "You're just the kind of avid researcher we're always looking for."

"Wow," Quinn said, beaming, considering the possibilities.

Rumer stood still, taking it in. People grew up here and left: It happened all the time, every year. As unthinkable as it was now that Quinn would ever want to move away, it had been just that hard to imagine Zeb at her age leaving. Rumer was the aberration—the person who stayed her whole life. Just then a town police car drove up. Two officers got out, looking stern. Behind them, the pest control truck came to a screeching stop.

"That's her," the man sputtered, pointing. "She assaulted me and stole my can! Ran away, down the hill, probably threw it in the water or something. Little freaking vandal! Ask her where she put it! Go ahead—ask her!"

"Officer, the can of poison is right there," Rumer said, stepping forward.

"You're Dr. Larkin, right?" one cop asked. "The vet?"

"Yes, she is," Mathilda said.

"We're all upset," Zeb said. "If anything, Quinn picked up on my anger. It's been rather volatile here, considering—"

"I appreciate what you're saying," one cop said calmly, "but we do have to question the young lady."

"No," Michael said, stepping in front of her.

"It's okay," Quinn whispered tenderly.

Rumer took in Michael's furrowed brow, Quinn's loving gaze. She and Zeb were standing close together—they were all united. Closing her eyes to preserve the moment, Rumer wondered, like a child, why such closeness couldn't last forever.

"I'll be fine," Quinn said.

Michael nodded.

"Young lady?" the policeman asked.

"I'm right here," Michael said, looking into her eyes as she turned toward the two cops.

"Arrest her!" the exterminator said viciously.

"Be careful," Zeb said in a low, grave voice straight to the policeman.

"I wish Sixtus were here," Quinn said, letting out a sob. "Everything at the Point's changing! He wouldn't let this happen. He wouldn't let someone cut down the trees and poison the rabbits. . . . I wish he were here!"

"So do I," Rumer said, moving to Quinn and holding her, looking into Zeb's eyes.

"So do we all," Mathilda said as the policeman stepped forward. While Quinn answered his questions, Rumer and Zeb flanked her. Rumer felt Zeb's closeness and heard her own loud heartbeat. Glancing across Quinn's head, she saw Zeb's eyes glitter dangerously.

His gaze had nothing to do with the Point, with police, with Quinn in trouble: It was all about Rumer, about wanting her, about another reason they had to wait.

∾

The tugboat rocked from side to side in the wash of a big fishing trawler heading out to sea. Sixtus sat in the deck chair beside Malachy, dangling his drop line over the side. Mackerel were running, and the two men were pulling them in as fast as the fish could swim by. The school looked black from the top, but canting over, they showed a flash of stripes, like shiny silver tigers swimming underwater.

"Another one," Sixtus said, yanking the fish aboard.

"What's that, seven now? Almost enough for dinner."

"Yes? What are you going to eat?"

"You're saying you can eat seven mackerel yourself?"

"They're small."

"Still. Seven?"

Sixtus nodded. He thought of another long stretch of sailing, of arriving in Ireland; he wondered how the cooking would be in Irish nursing homes. Although he had eaten well here in Nova Scotia—dining with Malachy, with Elizabeth, and by himself on some of Lunenburg's best fish and lobster—he was hungry for Rumer's cooking.

Hungry for Hubbard's Point tomatoes, Silver Bay corn, Black Hall lamb, Quinn's lobsters: He was hungry for home.

"Well, I guess we'd better keep fishing if you think seven isn't enough. Got to fatten you up for the long, lean spell ahead." Malachy checked the bait on his hook, dropped it back over the side. "What's your departure date anyway?"

"Tomorrow," Sixtus said.

"Ireland's waiting," Malachy said. "Been there all these centuries, but don't waste another minute getting there, eh?"

"Right," Sixtus said. "Eighteen days across the Atlantic from here . . ."

"Someone else might scarf up your bed in the rest home."

"Well, I probably won't check myself in just yet."

"No, bears some investigation, hmm?"

"Exactly. Besides, that's not the main purpose for the trip. It's my sabbatical, you see. Mine and Clarissa's."

Malachy just nodded gravely, smoking his pipe.

"Nice seeing your daughter?" Malachy asked.

"Elizabeth? Yes, it was."

"She's a beautiful girl," Malachy said. "I go to all her movies."

"She'd be glad to know that."

"So, you toured the island together a bit? Went in search of your roots?"

"I'm a big tree," Sixtus said. "Got roots everywhere."

Malachy nodded. "Don't we all?" he asked. "A person can't get to our age without sending out a root here, a root there."

"Spreading ourselves thin."

"You think so?"

Sixtus shrugged, watching the black and silver fish flash by the bright red hull. The *Clarissa* was waiting for him, just down the dock, ready to go.

He had thought he had a greater destiny—his journey into the past, but also a way out of Rumer's hair forever. But coming here, seeing Elizabeth, had brought something back: the deep love that existed between all generations of his family. He knew he would give anything to see his mother again. And he knew he didn't want to die an ocean away from Rumer.

Suddenly, sitting on deck with Malachy, Sixtus felt the wind go right out of his sails.

"Aaah," he said.

"What's that?" Malachy asked.

"I'm not sure," Sixtus said. "I feel as if I might have just figured something out."

"At your advanced age?"

"You mean at our age there's nothing left to learn?"

Malachy chuckled, biting his pipe. "Jaysus! For a schoolteacher, you're a little dim if you think such a thing. Surely you know that now is when the real learning starts—we've gotten all that youthful crap out of the way."

"Youthful crap . . ." Sixtus said, turning the phrase over in his mind.

"You know what I'm saying, man. All that ego, bravado, machismo, positioning, manipulating, maneuvering, traveling, trying to get the girl, the promotion, the research grant. Get my drift?"

"I do," Sixtus said. "Except you left out guilt and resentment. Getting rid of guilt and resentment."

"Two of the biggies—my mistake."

"Do you believe, Malachy," Sixtus began, "in the sins of the fathers—and mothers?"

"Absolutely."

"And do you believe that children have to answer for them?"

"Interesting question. Why—are you referring to your daughters?"

Sixtus thought of Rumer and Elizabeth, then down a generation to Michael, then back to his own parents. His father had died in Galway, and his brave mother had moved their twin sons right here to Nova Scotia. She was buried in Fox Point, just a few miles from the Cuthbert Children's Home.

"My daughters," Sixtus said. "And myself."

"Fathers and daughters," Malachy said. "Mothers and sons. The good Lord was working overtime when he invented those complicated relationships. Frankly, that's why I enjoy working with dolphins so much."

"I want to visit my mother's grave," Sixtus said. "And then I think I'll be ready to leave."

"Well, I'll drive you, of course," Malachy said. "Unless your daughter—"

"She's busy," Sixtus said softly.

"Ahh. Well, whenever you're ready. After you eat your seven mackerel. Then you're off to Ireland?"

"You know those roots we talked about before?" Sixtus asked.

"Sure do. Nova Scotia, Galway . . . yours are all over."

"Well, every tree has a taproot," Sixtus said. "That's the important one. The one that makes it live or die. My taproot—" He stopped, momentarily too choked up to continue.

"Is in Connecticut," Malachy said gently. "At Hubbard's Point, with Rumer. Of course it is. I've known that all along. Why go searching for the capillary roots when you've already located the main one? You're going home, aren't you?"

"I am, Mal," Sixtus said. "I am going home."

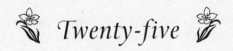# Twenty-five

ON HER SECOND night in Rumer's house, the mother rabbit stopped feeding two of the babies. Rumer sat still, quietly observing: The mother continued nurturing the others, but she turned her back on the two smallest and left them abandoned in the corner of the cage.

The sun hadn't yet come up; Rumer had been awake, on edge, wishing that Zeb would appear. The anticipation made her dizzy. He was so physically near, just down the street, and she pictured him lying in bed. She wondered whether he had slept as badly as she, whether he was feeling the connection between them—not quite brand-new but not like anything they'd ever had before—glowing like a golden thread.

Sighing, Rumer packed up the rabbits and drove over to her veterinary office on Shore Road. Years ago, a dark brown barn had stood on this bend in the road, housing a brown and white pinto horse that Sixtus had jokingly called "Old Paint" whenever they drove by. Rumer had always loved horses, and that pinto had been one of the first.

Rumer had bought the barn and surrounding land, but in her second year of ownership, a big storm knocked the barn down. She remembered it now, and for some reason her gaze went uneasily to the place it had occupied. Timbers of barnboard stood naked, like an abstract sculpture.

Unlocking her office, Rumer grabbed a small bottle and some boxes of infant animal formula. On her desk was a note Mathilda had left at the end of the day yesterday: "Edward called."

Rumer jammed the note into her pocket. She wrapped one baby rabbit in a washcloth and fed it from the heated bottle. She fed the others, then made rounds of the patients—a post-op Border collie, two spayed cats, and a dehydrated beagle.

She finished at seven, an hour before Mattie was scheduled to arrive.

Stretching, she felt the pent-up energy of waiting for time alone with Zeb—every time it seemed about to happen, some new cataclysmic event would occur to interrupt. Felled trees, aggressive exterminator: What would be next?

Knowing of only one thing that could relieve the tension she felt, Rumer climbed into her truck and headed north to see Blue. She would have just enough time to ride Blue and talk to Edward before returning to work.

Reaching Peacedale Farm, she drove up the stony driveway. Edward was nowhere to be seen—he was always up at this hour—but the first-floor windows were open, the cotton curtains blowing lightly in the breeze. Petting some of the barn cats, she walked straight across the yard to the stone wall where Blue stood waiting.

"Ready for a good ride?" she asked. "A nice early ride down by the river . . ."

"Rumer?"

At the sound of her name, she turned around. Edward stood there, hands in the pockets of his old khakis. She swallowed, remembering their last night together, the way she had behaved after seeing Zeb at Dana and Sam's wedding.

"Hi, Edward," she said, walking toward him. "How are you?"

"Well, I'm fine," he said in his slow New England twang. "And you?"

"I'm fine too."

A look of worry crossed his brow, and Rumer stopped smiling. She could see that he had bad news to deliver. "What is it, Edward?"

"Haven't seen you in quite a while."

"I know."

"Seems you've been pretty busy. Blue's been wondering . . ."

"I'm never too busy for Blue," she said. "I've been up here every day."

"Just at times when you know I'm not likely to be around?"

"Oh, Edward," she said.

"Spending lots of time with Zeb?"

"Not lots," she said. "But some."

"That's unavoidable, I would think. Considering your history together. I've finally realized that."

"There's a lot to talk about," she said.

Rumer watched the sun break through the trees across the meadow, butterscotch light pouring across the stone walls and gray rocks. She thought of how wrong Edward was about their history, how much it had gotten in the way.

"I've been seeing someone new," he said. "Annie Benz."

"Yes, I saw her here the other day," Rumer said. "I'm glad for you, Edward."

"How good of you," he said. "To be glad for me."

Rumer stood still. She felt Edward's tension, waiting for her to rise to the bait of his sarcasm. She wore the old clothes she'd fed the rabbits in, and she was covered with patches of shed fur and drops of spilled formula.

"I left you a message at the office," he said.

"I know—I came instead of calling back."

"I've been thinking . . ." Edward said, the pain returning to his eyes. "I must ask you to find a new home for Blue."

"For Blue?"

He nodded, gray hair falling across his lined forehead. His eyes crinkled in the sun from the brightness. "I'm sorry, Rumer. But it makes Annie uncomfortable to have you here. We're very new, you know? I don't want anything to upset her. And she knows what you meant to me. How I had one day hoped things would be more serious. . . ."

"This is Blue's home," Rumer said, stunned. "I just . . . I just never thought of him living anywhere else."

"I could offer to buy him from you," Edward said. "But I know how you feel about him. You can keep him here for as long as it takes; I know you'll find someplace good to board him—Black Hall Stables maybe. Or River Farms, over in Hawthorne."

Rumer held herself together and nodded stiffly. "I'll find something, Edward," she said. "As soon as I can."

"I'm sorry," he said. "It's complicated. I've spent a long time waiting for things to be different between us, but since that doesn't seem to be happening, I need to get on with my life. . . ."

"I'm sorry it didn't happen," Rumer said.

"Are you really?" he asked.

Rumer swallowed but didn't reply.

"I didn't think so."

Edward sounded cool, and his eyes were grim. Regardless of how she defined their relationship—friends, almost lovers—this was a breakup, which by definition meant that it couldn't be easy. Still, Rumer felt a lightening of spirit, as if a huge weight were being lifted from her shoulders.

"You've been wonderful to let me keep him here all these years."

"It meant I got to see you every day. And please feel free to ride him now, anytime, until you find a new place."

"Edward—I'm sorry . . ."

"So am I."

He kissed her on the cheek, stood back, and waited.

Rumer nodded. Edward's eyes filled with sadness and some last traces of lingering hope. She looked around: There was a red barn filled with black and white cows. Stone walls crisscrossed rolling fields of green. The white house was old and stately, and the flowers blooming in the gardens were descended from flowers his mother had planted. Life here would be a dream for almost any woman.

A woman whose first love hadn't been Zeb Mayhew, she thought.

Finally, Edward turned and headed for the kitchen door.

Walking toward Blue, Rumer's heart sank. Were his eyes as bright as before? Was his coat as glossy? She knew how sensitive he was, and she could swear he knew he was losing his home. Without bothering to saddle him, Rumer mounted Blue and rode away.

Riding down the trail to the river, Rumer felt her heartbeat keeping time with Blue's hooves on the rocky ground. She thought of how short life was, of how easily mistakes were made. The message seemed to be everywhere, in the leaves rustling overhead and the river current splashing through reeds growing from the silty banks.

Rumer held Blue's mane, her thoughts racing. Without any prodding, Blue took off in a canter. He tore along the path so that Rumer had to keep her head down, away from the low branches whipping overhead. She couldn't tell where she ended and Blue began. She had had that connection with only one other creature in her life. Zeb.

She thought of Zeb, back at Hubbard's Point, having come such a distance: from California, from the stars, all the way from the far-off past. Cantering along the wide river, she watched the web of sunlight spreading across to Hawthorne's distant shore. She thought of the ties that bind people together, and she knew that there were only two that counted: love, and the magical golden thread that reached all the way from childhood into the future.

Wheeling Blue around, Rumer rode for home.

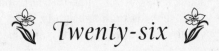 Twenty-six

KNOWING RUMER WOULD be working all day, Zeb had rowed to Wickland Rock Light and back. He returned at dusk, and he found a votive candle burning in the shed where he stored his oars, along with a note: "Come." Her handwriting was unmistakable.

Salty from rowing, Zeb didn't stop to shower. He cut through Hecate's property, stepping over the wall into his old yard. The contractor had marked the rock ledge for blasting; he had left bundles of shingles and a load of lumber for construction to begin immediately after Labor Day. The rabbits' warren smelled of pesticide; the old gardens had been yanked up by the roots, and dying plants and bushes lay piled beside the outdoor stone fireplace.

Zeb's throat constricted as he passed through. He thought of all the years he had stayed away from this place, trying not to care. Yet every important memory, all his strongest emotions, were centered here. He hated seeing his mother's plantings discarded like trash, the small fireplace—built by his father of beach stones, the site of so many family cookouts—marked for demolition.

Zeb glanced over at Rumer's house. She had candles burning in every window.

Although they were past blooming this season, his mother's hybrid lilies were planted somewhere along here. Peering though the darkness, he found the graceful green leaves, now smashed and trampled into a filthy mat. Digging with his bare hands, he felt the tubular roots with his fingers. Planted close together, they were easier to locate than he would have imagined. One, two, three . . . he retrieved twenty-five lily roots altogether before giving up. They would bloom again next summer—russet, deep gold, and dark red. He carried them into Rumer's yard and, kneeling down, planted them around the opening of the stone tunnel he hoped would become the rabbit's new home.

"What are you doing?" Rumer was standing at the kitchen door.

Zeb looked up, wiping the hair from his eyes with dirty hands. "Brought you some flowers," he said. "I'm giving my mother's lilies to someone who will appreciate them."

"Oh, Zeb . . ." Was that her voice breaking? She was backlit by the kitchen light, her face in shadow. She came forward, and as she crouched down, he could see that she was smiling brightly. Tears glimmered in her eyes. He inched over to give her room to dig, and she pitched right in, getting her hands in the dirt.

Her cotton dress was stretched tightly over her body; Zeb could see how thin she was, and he found it almost unbearably sexy to watch her digging in the earth. Her left wrist was weighed down with a big watch; she kept pushing it up out of her way. She smelled of verbena and lavender—or maybe that was just the heady scent blown by the sea wind off the herb garden.

"The flowers are beautiful, Zeb."

"Well, they will be when they get around to blooming next summer."

"You got my note?"

"I did."

"I waited for you all day," she said. "Left work."

"What made you do that?"

"Well, Blue got kicked out of his barn."

"What?"

"Edward's falling in love with someone new, and he decided it was time to move on. So he asked me to move Blue out. . . ."

"What will you do with him?"

"I'm not sure. I could rebuild the old barn that used to stand near my office—do you remember it?"

"Where Old Paint lived."

"Yes," she said. "That old horse."

"You used to want to sneak over and ride him," he said.

"First horse I ever loved," she said. "And first loves count for a lot."

"They do," Zeb said, his heart pounding. "How do you think Blue feels about that?"

"Blue understands," Rumer said. "He's the best. He's true blue; I've had only one other friend like him in my whole life."

"Who would that be?" Zeb asked, turning to look at her. Their eyes met; hers were dark blue, flashing in the starlight, the color of a northern cove. Before he could help himself, he'd reached up to stroke her cheek with a dirt-covered hand.

"You," she whispered. "My true-blue friend . . . Zeb."

"Your friend has made so many mistakes," he whispered. "That he can't forget."

"Everyone has," Rumer said, kissing his hand.

"The only mistake you've ever made," Zeb said, leaning closer to her face, "was caring about me in the first place."

"You're wrong," she said. "It's the truest thing in my life. I realized it this morning, after Edward told me I had to move Blue. I came flying back here—I couldn't wait to see you. Everything changes so fast in life, Zeb. I want to grab on to the only thing I know is true. . . ."

Rumer's head was tilted back. Her eyes had looked wild a minute ago, when she'd told him about Blue, but now they filled with peace and comfort and deep, deep understanding. Leaning closer, he brushed the wheat-silver hair from her eyes and kissed her.

The stars came down. All his years of blasting off, flying into space looking for faraway worlds, seemed false: The important stars were right here in the sky over Hubbard's Point. Zeb had wanted this for so long, his whole life. Rumer was the love of his life, and there was no going back. They kissed as if there were only tomorrow, as if all the rest had already been forgiven.

When they stopped, the night was silent except for crickets in the honeysuckle and locusts in the oak trees. Rumer held him so tightly, kneeling in the dirt, and he never wanted her to let go.

"I tracked you from space," he whispered. "I never stopped . . . even while I was with Elizabeth. I've watched for you all this time."

"That whole time while I was here at the Point, while I was taking care of animals . . . while I was riding Blue, I was missing you."

On her delicate wrist was an old watch of her father's. Gold with a black leather strap, it had been given to him as a retirement gift from the Black Hall teachers: Zeb remembered seeing it in the newspaper article about Sixtus.

"Your father let you wear this," he said, brushing the dirt off the band with his hand.

"Yes," she said steadily. "He wore his chronometer on his trip, to help him navigate."

"He wanted to leave a part of his heart behind," Zeb said, looking into her blue eyes. "Because he loves you."

"I know," Rumer whispered.

"Well, it's the same with me," Zeb said, feeling the breeze off the water. "Only instead of leaving a part of myself behind, I was sending it ahead. Straight from my heart, all these years . . . I was sending it from where I was, up there, down to you. At the speed of light . . ."

"Thank you," Rumer said, sliding her hand behind his neck.

"Only I was so far away," Zeb whispered, kissing her again, "it's taken till now for it to arrive."

In some deep and unshakable way, Zeb felt as if he had dwelled here his whole life. They helped each other up off the ground, and Zeb led Rumer through her own kitchen door.

Rumer turned on the water, and together she and Zeb washed their hands at the old enameled sink. He had a vague memory of being very young, just up from the beach, sitting on the counter beside Rumer as her mother washed the sand from their feet in this sink. Kissing her now with hot water running over his hands, Zeb felt the blood rush through his body.

They walked through the dining room, past the windows overlooking his old house, shutterless, bereft. Passing through the living room, he clutched at the sight of Elizabeth's photos on the wall, posters advertising her performances in *Romeo and Juliet, A Midsummer Night's Dream, Hedda Gabler,* and *The Wild Duck.* Rumer hesitated.

Zeb took her by the shoulders and kissed her again.

"It will always be between us," she whispered. "The fact that you and my sister were married."

"We can't change the past," he said, staring straight into her eyes. "If I could, I would. You're the one, Rue. You always were. . . ."

"But you loved Elizabeth," she said. "You can't say you didn't."

Zeb closed his eyes, stroking the back of her head. No, he couldn't say that. Was she asking him to? His love for Elizabeth had been a shooting star: wild, bright, streaking through space, burning itself out fast, dying into nothingness.

"It lasted so short a time," he whispered into Rumer's ear. "It was real, I can't lie and say it wasn't. It brought me Michael, Rumer. And in a way it kept me connected to you. It was a meteor; you're a star. You're forever, Rue."

"I know," she murmured. "Because that's the way I feel about you."

Holding hands, they went up the stairs. The wainscoting in her house was warm, golden brown in the lamplight. It glowed like a jewel box. The stairs led to a landing, then doubled back to the second floor. Zeb, after all his years living next door, had been up here only a few times. Making it to the forbidden upstairs of the Larkin girls' house—even, or especially, now—bowled him over with excitement.

Rumer led him into her bedroom. It faced the beach out one window, Zeb's old house out the other. Everything about it was sheer Rumer: Although the walls and floor were dark wood, the rest of it was white. The simple wood furniture had been whitewashed, then hand-painted, with brighter white shelves.

A bookcase held schoolbooks and texts, volumes of poetry, novels, and a guide to the stars. Shells, driftwood, and skate and channeled whelk egg cases lay on the bureau top. Several photos of Michael at various ages were stuck into the frame of the mirror. A framed picture of Zeb and Rumer doing their paper route stood on the bedside table.

But the thing that caught Zeb's heart, took his breath away, was her bedstead. Instead of the brass or iron he remembered, she had arranged the white shutters from his old house behind her bed. They looked perfect—as if they had been there forever. The dark walls gleamed through the pine tree cutouts; Zeb looked from them into Rumer's blue eyes.

"You did this?"

She nodded. "I couldn't let the builders just throw them away. . . . I wasn't sure what to do with them; I wanted them somewhere I'd see them every day."

"So you made them into a bedstead."

Rumer smiled. "Watching over my dreams," she said.

Zeb took her into his arms. She felt so small and soft, but his feelings for her were explosive. Holding himself together, he laid her gently on the double bed as they kissed each other with passion that had been building their whole lives.

A salt breeze came through the open windows, blowing the white cotton curtains. Zeb remembered sitting in his own room, just next door, crazy with desire at the sight of these same curtains. He had imagined them touching Rumer's body, blowing across her bed, and now he was right there.

She slid her hands beneath his T-shirt, pushing it up. Her hands felt smooth on his chest, tracing his skin, making him shake inside.

Very slowly, he began to unbutton her dress. The buttons were mother-of-pearl, iridescent in the moonlight slanting through the side window. They came from shells, from the sea, as much a part of nature as the woman wearing them. With each button, he kissed her skin again and again.

"Zeb," she whispered, shivering in the breeze.

When his hand brushed the front of her dress, he discovered the gold lighthouse pinned to the collar. He unclasped it gently and laid it very carefully down on the bedside table. As he did, the beam of the lighthouse itself swept across the room. He thought of the ships that had been saved—and the ship that had been lost—while following its light. The question moved him immeasurably; holding Rumer's face between his hands, he thought of how long they had been lost to each other.

"What are you thinking about?" she whispered.

"Home," he said.

"California?"

He shook his head, brushing the wheaten hair from her eyes. Home: It was nothing so simple as a place. It wasn't a state, a town, or even a house. It wasn't the rabbits' tunnel or Blue's pasture; it wasn't Los Angeles, or the space station, or Hubbard's Point.

"That's just where I live," he whispered. "My home is here."

"At the Point?"

"With you. Wherever you are."

"But you have to go back."

"I know," he said.

"I can't bear to think about it tonight," she whispered. "Every day that goes by is closer to the time, and we're just beginning. . . ."

"I know, Rue."

"Shhh, then, Zeb. Don't talk about it now."

He couldn't have even if he'd wanted to. With all the love flowing between them, there was that one cold fact: He had a lab to run, with too much riding on it for him to back out now. And the idea of Rumer anywhere but here at Hubbard's Point was beyond comprehension.

She moaned slightly, and he slid down beside her in the double bed. The springs creaked beneath their weight; oak branches scratched the roof, and the pine boughs murmured in the sea wind.

Her skin was as incredibly soft as he remembered it. She kissed him on the lips, her mouth hot and passionate. Her fingers traced his backbone as they helped each other out of their clothes.

He had seen her naked as a little girl, but no memory could prepare him for the exquisite beauty of her body. He gasped, kissing her shoulders, her collarbone, her breasts.

Because she was sometimes shy in life, he had expected her to be shy in bed. Perhaps it was her love of nature that made her seem so comfortable and natural. Or maybe it was the fact they had been building up to this their whole lives.

Touching her stomach lightly, he hit a sensitive spot and made her laugh. He laughed too, letting go of the tension. Then their eyes met and held, and the laughter stopped with one flash of the lighthouse beam. They held each other tightly, rocking with the rhythm of the wind and sea. As if they were on a boat, moving gently with the waves, he entered her and felt the most intense heat and wetness he'd ever known.

"Can it really be like this?" she whispered.

"It can, because it's us," he whispered back.

"I never knew."

"Me neither."

He held her close, one hand around her back and the other cupping her face. They kissed without stopping, barely breathing as the waves got bigger and harder, and their boat began to shudder. They were breaking up, hitting the rocks, crashing through a storm, and holding on to each other all the time.

"Don't let me go," he whispered as she trembled beneath him.

"I couldn't," she breathed.

She shivered, sighing as he held her more tightly than he had ever held anyone. They were one, they shared a skin, and her heat was his heat. His heart beat so hard, like a rocket thudding in his chest, blasting him off to somewhere he'd never been before.

But there was Rumer with him, guiding him all the way.

"I have you," she whispered, her hands so gently and firmly on his shoulders. "I love you, Zeb, I've always loved you."

"Rumer," he whispered, exploding inside her, shaking as the enormity of his feelings for her came pouring out. "I've always loved *you*."

They held each other, rocking for a long time. The words hung in there, true and pure. They merged with the wind, became part of the Hubbard's Point air. Zeb breathed them in, feeling Rumer's body solid and strong against his. He felt as if they were more than together: as if they were one.

"I've always wanted you. Always wanted you to bring me home," he said, staring into her blue eyes, filled with the conflict of their separate lives. "A reason for me to want to be here on earth."

"Don't leave, Zeb," she whispered. "Stay here in Hubbard's Point. Don't go back to California."

He couldn't speak, thinking of the lab, the projects, all the expectations everyone had for him.

"Come to California with me," he said, grabbing her hands. "You've looked after this place for so long—your father, Quinn, everyone on the Point. Let me look after you for a change, Rumer. I love you—come with me."

"I can't. I belong in Hubbard's Point, Zeb. Like Quinn said, it's my place."

"Be with me, Rue," he said. "Let *that* be our place—wherever we are, together. . . ."

But she didn't reply. The sound of waves on the rocks and beach lulled them, and he wondered whether she heard them telling her to stay, not to go.

He bowed his head, letting the emotion flow as she stroked his back for a long time. The lighthouse beam passed back and forth, back and forth; he lost track of the hours. Rumer held him, and they listened to the sounds of the beach. Waves lapped against the sand, stirring him up inside again. He drifted in and out of sleep, but every time he looked at Rumer she was wide awake, her blue eyes open and gazing out the window. He wondered whether she was thinking about what he'd said.

"I want you with me, Larkin. Here, there: What does it really matter?" he asked finally.

"It matters," she said, feeling a trickle of sadness because she knew the summer would end and he would return to his brand-new space observatory, just as he had left so many years ago.

"Rumer . . ."

"It matters to NASA," she said. "Even if you wanted to stay here, wouldn't they have something to say about it?"

He didn't want to think about it now. He had Rumer in his arms, gulls were crying across the dark water, the waves were hitting the beach. Zeb closed his eyes because he had never been this happy in his life.

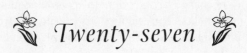 Twenty-seven

THE HOUSE WAS almost perfect. Huge, shingled, with three chimneys, wraparound porches, and lawns sloping down to Long Island Sound, it positively screamed summer, Zee thought. Girls in white dresses should be swinging on swings, boys with cowlicks should be toting home freshly caught fish, and lemonade should be flowing from spigots in the kitchen. *Tra-la.*

Inside, the owners had gone a little decorator crazy. There was chintz everywhere, but *everywhere.* Elsie de Wolfe leopard print rugs that would have worked in a Manhattan apartment ten years ago looked moderately absurd here in Evesham now. Portraits by the Black Hall Impressionist Hugh Renwick—and this was amusing—not of the owner's family, but of other people's families, bought at auction.

"Needless to say," said Marnie McCray Campbell, who had come to help Elizabeth settle in, "these are not the original owners." The two old friends stood gazing at the portraits.

"Something told me . . ."

"It's happening all over the shoreline. People keep these beach houses for generations, and suddenly one heir wants the money, and they have to sell. At least these owners bought Renwicks for their walls. I wonder whether they even know that he lived at Firefly Beach. . . ."

"Just across the river," Elizabeth said, looking toward Hubbard's Point.

"I'm sure old Mr. and Mrs. Bowen would roll in their graves if they could see the marble bathroom. It was so shabby and divine up until it sold . . . but what are you going to do? I'm just glad the new people kept the ratty wicker porch furniture."

"Yes . . ." Elizabeth said. "I can sit out here, sipping tea and gazing at Abigail Crowe's house for inspiration."

"That's it, across the way," Marnie said, pointing at the rambling white house surrounded by scrub pines, nestled in the hollow between beach and marsh. "Our two Connecticut movie stars, right here in the same place. Do you really think Barbara Walters will come to interview you here?"

"Maybe," Elizabeth said, although she knew she would not. The notice had been too short; Elizabeth had felt slightly scalded by the fact that Barbara couldn't rearrange her schedule to accommodate Elizabeth Randall's film commitments. Not wanting to reveal her true feelings to Marnie, she stretched and said, "This leaves me plenty more time to play with my sister and son."

"Zeb's still in residence at Winnie's guest house, you know," Marnie said.

Elizabeth yawned. "You don't say?"

"Was your divorce . . . amicable?" Marnie asked, reddening at her own intrusion. Although they had been friends their whole lives, Elizabeth's status put the question into a tabloid perspective.

"We're friendly," Elizabeth said. "I'm not sure we'll make it to friends."

"He seems awfully happy to be back at the Point."

"Hanging around with Rumer, is he?" Elizabeth asked, nearing a tender spot.

"Yes, quite a bit."

"It shouldn't surprise me. He went on a real woman tear right after our divorce. Everyone in L.A., it seems, wanted to date an astronaut. Nothing lasting: To me, it looked as if he was afraid he wasn't going to get sex, and they were afraid they weren't going to get him to propose. One liaison after the other, you know? He's finally worked his way out here to the East Coast."

"Oh, Elizabeth," Marnie laughed. "He's not like that! Especially not with Rumer. After everything, she means too much to him."

"Hmmm," Elizabeth said. Her marriage had not been a success, yet she had lost ten years of her life to it anyway. God only knew where her career would be now if she hadn't let herself be so divided—trying to be a wife and mother instead of a woman: Like Abigail Crowe, she might have three Academy Awards instead of one lonely nomination. Yet, hearing Marnie's words brought up old, poisonous feelings of jealousy for her sister from deep inside.

"You and Rumer are still close, aren't you?"

"The more time that passes, the less we have in common," Elizabeth said. "I think she mourns the suburban fantasy that passed her by—matching bedsteads and the newest Pathfinder."

"Oh, I don't see her that way," Marnie said. "I think your sister is the happiest person I know."

"She's a lonely woman who talks to cats and dogs," Elizabeth said.

"Oh, Elizabeth," Marnie said, laughing. "She's the best vet on the shoreline. Isn't it wonderful, the way you both made your dreams come true? You're both so accomplished in your fields . . . and everyone always knew you'd be famous, just the way we always knew Rumer would work with animals. *Les Dames de la Roche* are very proud of both of you."

"Well, they're a touch on the clueless side," Elizabeth said, and then she saw the expression on Marnie's face. "Present company excepted, of course . . ."

"Anyway," Marnie said, taking one last look around, packing the rental agreement into her bag. "You're all settled in now. If you need anything, just call. In any case, I know I'll see you at the Point."

"You will," Elizabeth said, gazing across the serene water.

While the kids were preparing for exams and Rumer was off scouting out stables to board Blue, Zeb planted lilies along the border of Rumer's and the Franklins' yards. He thought of the questions he and Rumer had asked each other in bed, and he wondered whether she would be here next summer to see them bloom. He'd been thinking that if he had his way, she'd be out in California with him. They could make time in the summers to come back to the Point, always.

Last night he had gone to bed with West Coast thoughts: Rumer relocating her practice and horse to California, of a fresh start in his new lab, of Michael surfing the waves at Dana Point. But this morning he had woken up smelling the Atlantic salt air—so different from the Pacific salt air—hearing the local seagulls—their cries different from Dana Point seagulls—and feeling that he could never leave, or take Rumer away.

Zeb had woken up with the feeling that he was right where he belonged: back home, with Rumer, in Hubbard's Point. He was part of the landscape, just like the rocks and trees and lilies.

The Connecticut state flag hung from the Winnie's flagpole; bright blue, it bore a white shield showing three grapevines and the Latin motto *Qui Transtulit Sustinet*: "He who transplanted sustains us." Although it referred to the first settlers, transplanted from Massachusetts in the 1630s, Zeb considered his own life as a serial transplant. First to New York, then to Los Angeles, then to Houston, then to space, then to Dana Point.

It felt so good to be home.

The earth here smelled so fine; it felt warm and rocky as he dug new holes to plant the lilies. He remembered seeing his mother crouch in the dirt just a few feet away from where he now dug, weeding around the tall, graceful stalks, as if she wanted to know every inch of her land as intimately as she could. Elizabeth never had; in the years she had owned the house with Zeb, he couldn't remember seeing her garden once.

Zeb had never done much gardening, but he thought that he might just get used to it. He liked the sense of being close to the earth, rooted in the soil. It was the opposite of how he had spent his entire life, and at that moment he looked up at the sky and couldn't believe that he had once stayed up there for sixty-three consecutive days. Although he could never give up his dreams, he knew that the stars meant nothing without Rumer.

"Well, the things you see when you haven't got a gun," came the voice from down below.

Glancing at the road, Zeb spotted Tad Franklin climbing out of his Jaguar. He wore pressed gray pants, a white dress shirt, and a maroon cardigan sweater. Zeb wondered why he was always so dressed up.

"Pretty close to the property line," Franklin commented.

"You want some?" Zeb asked, his hands covered with dirt, holding a handful of his mother's lily roots.

"Look like garbage to me," Franklin said. He waved his hand and made a face. "What are they anyway?"

"Just old plants," Zeb said, wondering whether Franklin could hear the irony in his voice.

"Thanks anyway. My landscape architect is going to really make this yard a showplace. Everything old's gonna go. There'll be all new plantings—fantastic stuff. He's not just some yard mower, in case I haven't mentioned it before. He's a certified landscape—"

"You've mentioned it," Zeb said.

"While I have your ear, let's talk about the other matter."

"What other matter?" Zeb asked, feeling the kick in his gut. Could Franklin have reconsidered his offer? Even without the trees, with the destruction of all the old gardens, Zeb would jump at the chance to buy the place back. No matter what happened, he wanted to spare Rumer—and himself, and all their friends at the Point—having to watch Franklin blast the rock. And then it came to him swift and sure: They could use this yard for Blue's new barn.

"The girl. The little thief."

Quinn, Zeb thought, waiting. Even as he listened, he was seeing the property in a whole new light: the barn, a small pasture, a trail down the bluff to the beach . . .

"She made a mistake," Franklin said. "And I'm not sure what to do about it."

Zeb looked up. Was Franklin asking his counsel? "What are your choices?"

"Her aunt's an artist," Franklin said. "A real bohemian, like half the other people I see around here. I don't have much experience with gals like her. She really doesn't seem to get it—says the girl has apologized, that they're 'handling it at home,' and that's all there is to it."

"Quinn's grounded," Zeb agreed. And he knew, because Michael was in torment over the shortage of their time together. She could no longer meet him before school, hang out after class, go to movies on the beach, or sit around Foley's. Dana allowed Quinn to go lobstering—just because Quinn had invested in all the pots and bait at the start of the summer, and to leave them baited and unchecked would be harmful to the lobster population—and she permitted her one hour of study time with Michael every day.

"You consider that sufficient?" Franklin asked. "The girl steals rat poison, and she gets grounded?"

"First of all," Zeb said, never looking away, "she didn't steal it. She hid it—for about ten minutes. She knows it was a lapse of judgment, and she's sorry. Second of all, if the cops thought it was more serious than that, they'd be pursuing the case."

"You're admitting it's a case, then," Franklin said.

"No, I'm not. I—"

"I get the distinct feeling people are trying to sabotage me around here. First you, coming to my office. Now, some might think your intention was to insult me and intimidate me. . . ."

"It wasn't," Zeb said. To his surprise, Franklin looked hurt—his dark eyes bruised. "I wanted to offer to buy the land back from you."

"You made that clear."

"Then sell it to me."

"No. If you want it so bad, it must be worth more than I think." Franklin chuckled, peering at Zeb. "What is it—treasure buried underground?"

"Not the kind of treasure you understand."

"What's that supposed to mean?"

"The treasure's the land itself," Zeb said. "And the way some of us love it."

"You certainly let me know you don't like my plans."

"We don't have to, do we?"

"We?"

"Well," Zeb said, pushing the hair out of his eyes, temporarily giving up his vision of Blue's stable in his old yard. His gaze shifted down the hill in Rumer's yard: Would there be room behind the garage? "It's a lot for the people around here to handle—seeing you change the landscape so completely."

Franklin's mouth narrowed as he surveyed the other yards. His eyes flicked over the scrub pines, the gnarly oaks up and down the dead end . . . was he wishing he could cut them all down and start over, beautifying the entire Point with his landscape architect?

"It is my right," Franklin said, folding his arms across his chest.

"That is so."

"My wife has always dreamed of having a summerhouse here. . . ."

Zeb nodded. Way back, that had been his grandparents' dream. It had been Rumer's grandmother's as well, and together they—like the grandparents of many of their friends—had settled the Point. "It's a good dream," he said.

"I expected a different reception," he said. "I thought we'd be more welcomed."

Looking at his expression—hurt and bewildered—Zeb actually felt sorry for him. The man was spending hundreds of thousands of dollars to make his property stand out—while he thought he was buying admiration, all the neighbors could see was the hubris of ruining the land.

"You will be," Zeb said to the man getting ready to bulldoze his old house and build something better.

"Doesn't seem like it."

"This is a special place," Zeb said quietly. "We care about each other here."

"Then someone ought to take control of that kid—my exterminator was just doing his job. Regardless of what she thought should happen . . . I was paying for a service. I want her punished."

"When people make mistakes, we don't hold it against them for long. There are lots of kids here—they tend to make mistakes. It's the nature of the species. The age. Think back. . . . Know what I mean?"

Franklin scowled.

"You say you wanted to be welcomed," Zeb said. "I'm sure you will be as time goes on. But maybe if you understood the way things are here, you could feel like part of the place right away. I wanted to buy your land back from you to save it."

"Save it! Jesus Christ—what's so almighty terrible about a person improving their property?"

"Look—as you said, it's your right—your land, your right. If you'd like, I'll show you satellite photos of the rock ledge, the glacial moraine that corresponds with its counterpart across the Atlantic. It's the backbone of Connecticut, and you're going to blow it up."

"Goddammit! That's what this is about? I've had just about enough of you and the rest of you crazies—"

Emotions were boiling out of Zeb, and all he could think of was clocking Franklin.

"It is about Quinn," Zeb said quietly, fighting down the urge to leap across the property line and mess up the guy's dressed-up clothes, knocking him into the next nebula.

Franklin gasped, as if sensing the danger. Straightening his shirt and sweater, he took a big step back. Regarding him, Zeb centered himself, getting his animal desire to rip the guy apart under control.

"You can't just come into a place like Hubbard's Point," Zeb said, "make changes like this, and not expect to get people upset."

"That's their problem," Franklin said, "if they're upset."

Zeb actually smiled. He wasn't happy, but he felt flooded with Rumer's compassion; to his surprise, it was directed at Tad Franklin. "You'll learn," Zeb said. "After you've been here a while. Once everyone forgives what you're doing to the land, they'll accept you as one of them. It might take a decade or so, but that's just the way they are here.

"If they're still alive, Sixtus Larkin will invite you sailing, Winnie Hubbard will make your wife an honorary *Dame de la Roche*—even though you're going to blow up all your *roches* . . . Rumer will take your kids under her wing and teach them to make lists of all the birds they see . . . you might even meet the unicorns and the ghosts. It's a goddamn magical place."

"You're crazy," Franklin said, backing away.

"Yeah, well," Zeb said, watching him go. "What can I say?"

Just then he heard the purr of a sports car; looking down the street, he saw a vintage Buick convertible followed by a Suburban driving along Cresthill Road. The vehicles parked at the foot of Franklin's hill and discharged a pack of teenagers. The driver and passenger of the Buick— twin boys, fair and small—cast proprietary glances over the property.

"You really *do* have a beach house, Bart," one of the girls piling from the Suburban called. "Hi, Mr. Franklin!"

"Yeah," one boy said laconically, ignoring his father. He and his twin dressed like preppys the same way Tad Franklin did: as if they were new to it, as if they had bought the image out of catalogues. "It's nothing like it's going to look. We're tearing that green shack down and building something decent."

"Nothing less than a mansion for Bart and Lance Franklin!" The girl giggled.

"Got that right," one boy said. Going to the trunk of the car, he removed towels and chairs. His friends did the same from the back of the Suburban. Dressed for the beach, they carried a stack of pizzas.

"Those your sons?" Zeb asked in a low voice.

Franklin, still pale from their encounter, ignored the question, and Zeb couldn't blame him.

"We have a private way down to the beach," one twin said with studied indifference. "Right down this path to the steps . . ."

"Strictly speaking, it's a 'right of way,'" Zeb said to him. "It's not really private. Everyone gets to use it, but it just runs through your yard."

The kid gave Zeb a look as if he were gum on the bottom of his shoe.

"I know," Zeb said kindly. "I lived here when I was your age."

The boy didn't acknowledge the comment; he didn't stop to introduce his friends to his father, and Tad seemed conscious of his behavior. Feeling bad, Zeb wished he had held back.

Franklin turned his back and walked away. Gathering up the lily roots he'd dropped, Zeb felt high and happy. Someone had a worse relationship with his sons than Zeb had with Michael. He and Michael were getting better every day. He had defended Quinn, and he felt good about that. Michael kept saying he was going to marry her, and although Zeb thought it was a terrible, impossible idea at their ages, he was managing to hold his tongue.

Space, bedding stores . . . it didn't matter where you worked. A million miles away, or just down the street: Everything depended on what was inside, right there in your own heart. Zeb was learning, and Rumer was teaching him.

Winnie's flag snapped in the wind, the azure blue blending with the sky, the white banner waving, catching Zeb's eye: *Qui Transtulit Sustinet . . .*

The question was, who was going to transplant where? Rumer to California or him back to Hubbard's Point? One of them was going to have to pull up roots and move, because Zeb knew they wouldn't survive another winter apart. As he sat there, watching the Connecticut flag blow in the sea breeze, he felt a lump in his throat. Because although he loved it here more than anywhere else on earth, he had made his life in the stars, and NASA had built him a lab.

In California.

None of the stables Rumer visited were right for Blue.

They were either too far away—forty minutes along back roads, across the Connecticut River on the little ferry, on the far side of Hawthorne—or they were too run-down, with rickety firetrap barns and sour old straw. As she drove through the towns, she found herself thinking about how much she loved this part of the world: how beautiful she found southern New England.

The huge maples, the white churches, the red barns, the glimpses of the river flowing by, sailboats rocking on their moorings. She knew the names of all the wildflowers growing along the sides of the road, and she knew the best farm stands to buy tomatoes and peaches. She saw names of former students stenciled on mailboxes: Many of them had grown up and settled right here.

This was Rumer's place, wasn't it? When her father completed his journey, he would return here and expect her to be waiting at home. He was old. They didn't talk about it, but Rumer had always known she would be there for him in his declining years, for every year that she could spend with him. There would be no nursing home, no assisted living facility for Sixtus Larkin. He was staying right where he belonged, at Hubbard's Point.

And Blue loved it here. He was a Connecticut horse: He relished the rocky fields, the salt air, the stone walls, the low-flying owls that hunted the pastures every night.

But as she drove along, she began to get the feeling she was talking herself into something. Because no matter how much she tried to tell herself that she could never leave this corner of the world, her heart was in total conflict. Hubbard's Point would always be her home, but how could she stay here knowing she had passed up the chance to be with Zeb for the rest of their lives?

When Rumer parked her truck at the bottom of the hill, she saw Zeb standing in the top yard, and her heart jumped. Walking up the stone steps to him, she went into his arms. He held her tight, kissing her hair, and for the first time all day, she felt calm and right: No matter what was happening, if she had Zeb, she was happy.

"What did you find?" he asked.

"Nothing right for Blue. The barns were all too far from the sea." She smiled, because that summed it up as well as anything else.

"Do you think he'd mind?" Zeb asked.

Rumer nodded. "Yes, he's very particular about his sea breezes."

"Ahhh," Zeb said, kissing the side of her neck, sliding his hands down her spine and making her arch her back. "We have an ocean in California. Do you think he'd like Pacific breezes?"

"I don't know," she whispered.

"I think your father would say he would."

"What makes you think that?" she asked, and Zeb just smiled.

"Still haven't heard from Sixtus?" he asked.

Rumer shook her head. She had expected a call from him forty-eight hours ago, telling her he was leaving Nova Scotia to sail to Ireland. If he called, she thought she'd talk to him about Zeb's idea. She could ask him how he'd feel about her going to California for a little while. Maybe she'd take a sabbatical herself—one year off from being a vet; she could always return. When she didn't hear from him, she called Malachy Condon's number and got an answering machine: "I'm out now. Leave a message."

Simple, to the point, just like her father. Was it possible she wouldn't hear from him for eighteen or twenty days, till he reached Galway? That was so uncharacteristic of Sixtus Larkin.

Rumer felt off balance, unsettled about her horse and her father, unable to convince Zeb to stay yet unsure she could leave. Rumer had been this way as a child: She liked to know that everyone she loved was safe, cared for, in a place where she could find them. Over the years, life had educated her in the fine but difficult skill of letting go.

She had had to let Zeb go first: off to Columbia, on his way to the wild blue of sky and space. She had forced herself to let him go even more when he married Elizabeth and became—instead of her best friend—her sister's husband. She had learned to let Zee go—into the stratosphere of Hollywood—taking Zeb and Michael with her.

As time passed, she had let her mother go to heaven, rehabilitated animals go back to the wild, her father go to sea, the trees next door go to ground. She had learned—by degrees—the ability to accept what life was handing her instead of what she wished for.

But how could Rumer live with letting Zeb go again? After asking her to come with him—what if this were their last chance to be together? She thought about the uncertainty of where Blue would live, of when her father would reach the Irish coast, but nothing compared with the terror of leaving Hubbard's Point, even to be with the man she loved. To follow one dream, did she really have to give up another? On the other hand, how could she ask Zeb to walk away from his lab, the culmination of his life's work?

"You've been digging," she said, coming back to the present, noticing the dirt under Zeb's fingernails.

"Planting a few more lilies," he said. "The rabbit hole is nearly covered. I think, when you're ready, we can try releasing them."

Rumer glanced next door. She saw Tad Franklin standing in the sun, examining blueprints. The sight—knowing what was coming, the old house about to be demolished and a mansion raised in its place—sent a chill through her. Staring at the bare spot where the azalea bush had so recently stood filled her with sorrow.

"I wonder whether the poison is still active," she whispered. "If the rabbits try to go back to their old hole, they could die."

"I blocked it with a rock," Zeb said. "The night we took the rabbits out."

She swayed in his arms; she hadn't known. So busy gathering up the pitchers and cups, carrying all the rabbits inside in their gunnysack, she had missed seeing Zeb take that extra precaution. What else had she missed? Sometimes she thought she was the only person taking care of her life, the Point, the creatures she loved—but she wasn't. Not by a long shot.

"If only Blue could come here," she said. "And live at Hubbard's Point."

"Why couldn't he, at least temporarily?" Zeb asked. "We could turn the garage into a barn."

"There's not enough land," she said. "He's used to endless pastures. . . ."

"He could have the whole beach," Zeb said. "And the trails beyond— over to Little Beach, the Indian Grave . . . at least till winter comes."

"And then?" she asked, wondering where he—or they—would be this winter.

"We'd have to decide," Zeb whispered.

"Zeb . . ."

"You'd love Dana Point, Rumer. So would Blue—high cliffs over the Pacific, whales and dolphins passing by. My lab is just down the road from the house—I'd be home every night. We could fence in the yard, and you could ride Blue all day long. And we'd always come back to the Point for the summers, for holidays."

Rumer smiled at the vision, but she didn't have time to reply.

Just then they heard voices coming up the path from the beach, angry and belligerent. Rumer heard Zeb chuckle and say out loud, "Back already?"

"What?" Rumer asked.

"Listen—" Zeb said.

Tad Franklin rolled up his blueprints and took a few steps toward the pack of teenagers trudging up the stairs.

"What's wrong?" he asked.

"This place sucks!" a short blond boy said. "First some lady told us we weren't allowed to play ball on the beach, and then the security guard came over."

"Did you tell them you're a property owner?" Tad asked.

"Yeah, of course! But they didn't give a shit. We're out of here," said a different but identical blond boy.

"What do you mean, you're 'out of here'?"

"We're going to Watch Hill," the boy said. "Where the houses are all decent, not like these shitboxes around here. You should've bought there, Dad. I *hate* it in this fucking place."

"You're going to love it, Bart. Wait till you see the plans. . . ."

"Come on," the boy said to his friends. "It's late, but if we hurry, we can get some beach time."

"How far is Watch Hill?" a girl asked.

"Half an hour," Bart said. "Forty-five minutes at the most."

"Go right back down those stairs and fight for your right," Franklin said sternly. "I've worked my ass off my whole life to buy you a beach house, and you're going to damn well enjoy it."

"Forget it, Dad!" the boy said sharply. "Don't you get it? This place *sucks!*"

As he and his twin climbed into an amber convertible parked in the road, he gunned the engine and gave the finger out the window. Was it to his father, the Point, or the universe? Rumer wasn't sure. Standing still in the shadow of the big oak tree, leaning into Zeb's body, she found herself actually feeling sorry for Tad Franklin.

"Don't waste your energy," Zeb whispered into her ear as he held her tight.

"What do you mean?"

"I'm reading your mind, Rue. You're thinking, someday they'll love it here."

"How could they not?" she murmured.

"Not everyone loves what the Point has to offer," he said. "When someone comes in wanting to change everything that's here, it's not a good start."

"We have to live with him," Rumer said. "In awfully close proximity."

"That may be so," Zeb said. "But it doesn't change the sad fact that he's an asshole."

"Maybe he'll realize it's not for them," she said, "and sell it back to you. . . ."

"I don't think he will, Rue. Not in time anyway. He's too proud for that. But promise me one thing—no matter how much I want to make my son happy, don't let me buy him a vintage convertible, okay? When you're riding Blue through the hills—of Dana Point or Hubbard's Point—tell yourself you don't want to live with a jerk who'd spoil his kid that way. . . ."

Rumer wasn't sure whether to laugh or cry. She turned to kiss him on the lips, and was in the midst of doing so when she heard the throb of a car's big engine. The twins must have forgotten something—or perhaps they were returning to apologize to their father.

The car door slammed—but at the bottom of her hill, not the Franklins'. Leaning back, she saw a familiar face frowning up from the road.

"Uh-oh," she said, blushing as if she'd just gotten caught red-handed.

"Zee," Zeb said quietly.

"Hello, you two," Elizabeth called, getting her expression in order and smiling as she marched up the steps. "I've come to celebrate my son's eighteenth birthday . . . is he around somewhere?"

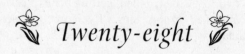

Twenty-eight

"Looks like the new neighbors went a little saw crazy," Elizabeth said, reclining on the faded old sofa in the living room and gazing out the window. "What happened to the trees?"

"They're all gone. The new owners want water views and a huge septic tank," Rumer said, sitting in the old rose armchair.

"The new status symbol—a jumbo-size septic tank," Elizabeth said wryly, gazing out the window at the new owner, walking his property.

Rumer didn't reply. Zeb had gone home—fled, Elizabeth thought. Coward. Rumer sat quietly, probably trying to hide her feelings but failing utterly. Elizabeth could see she was flooded with emotions. The sisters had played hide-and-seek behind the furniture they were sitting on. Their mother had told them—more than once—while sitting in this very room, "You'll have many friends in life, but only one sister." Elizabeth could see all of that history behind her sister's eyes, passing like storm clouds across her bright face.

"We're really hitting a new low," Elizabeth said. "I can't quite remember the last time I sat around with my fellow actors, cursing our neighbors and discussing their septic systems."

"Guess you had to come home for that," Rumer said darkly. "We get down to basics pretty fast here at the Point."

Elizabeth stretched, then smiled. "You're not getting defensive already, are you?"

"Defensive?"

She laughed. "Guess you are . . . even the way you ask: 'Defensive?' As if you're on guard. Relax, Rumer. This isn't a fencing match. Unless . . . you want it to be?"

"I don't want it to be," Rumer said, taking a deep breath as if willing herself to be civil. Elizabeth could practically see the gears turning in her head. "It's just that we haven't talked in so long. Tell me everything, Elizabeth. First of all, how was Dad?"

"Dutiful daughter, of course that would be your first question. I'm surprised you've held it in this long. He was . . . Dad."

"What do you mean?"

"You know—scholarly and earnest. Sailing away, as usual."

Rumer's face remained passive, obviously hating Elizabeth's characterization of their father. It made her angry, but even more, it caused her pain. But she let it pass. "Was he all right? In good spirits?"

"Reasonably. He took me on a strange tour down memory lane. A little minidocumentary of his life in Nova Scotia. He seemed to be visiting old ghosts, planning his next step in life."

"What next step in life? He's sailing to Ireland, then turning around and coming home—right?"

Elizabeth shrugged. "I guess so. He's aged a lot."

"It just seems that way because you haven't seen him in so long," Rumer said, holding Elizabeth's eyes with her gaze. The better to drive in the knife, Elizabeth thought, smiling as she responded.

"I've had the gift of a busy life. I'm surprised you let him on the boat. He's very stooped over—arthritis, right?"

"Right, but I didn't want to stop him," Rumer said. "It seemed to be such a huge dream of his. But why do you think he didn't call me before he left on this leg—for Ireland?"

Elizabeth shrugged. It felt so bizarre to be here in her family's old house. The whole Larkin dynamic came flooding back; it shouldn't surprise her that Rumer was still, forever, being the family caretaker—wanting to keep minute track of everyone. It so often felt as if their birth order was reversed, with Rumer taking the role of the older, responsible one, leaving Elizabeth to pick up the slack as the selfish, self-absorbed younger child.

"I think he had things on his mind," Elizabeth said.

"Like what things?"

"Darling, I'm not a mind reader. Dad was never one for confiding in me before taking a powder to the nearest high seas. Okay?"

She wanted to get off their father and onto the subject of Zeb, but she had to tread lightly. It really did seem strange, the fact that Rumer didn't seem more guilty; in spite of the divorce, because of their son and their marriage, Elizabeth would always have the primary claim on him and she thought her sister should acknowledge that fact.

But Rumer just sat there, staring out the window at Long Island Sound, as if their father might miraculously sail into view.

Elizabeth cleared her throat. "You seem upset."

"No . . . just concerned. Worried, maybe."

"He's a grown man."

"I know, but . . ."

"He's allowed to keep some things from his daughters. He's not required to check in—maybe he wants his freedom. Just because he lives with you doesn't mean he can't have his own life."

"I know that," Rumer said, a dangerous cloud of anger veiling her eyes.

Elizabeth bit her lip; she couldn't quite understand why she was pushing her sister this way. Her chest hurt from her own anger simmering inside.

"I'm sorry," Elizabeth said tensely, quietly. "It's just that you can come off as so smothering sometimes."

Rumer stared, two red dots appearing high on her cheekbones. Elizabeth had to stifle a laugh; she could push buttons that made her little sister react just as she had when she was a child. Now, taking it back, she leaned forward to touch Rumer's hand.

"It's probably what makes you such a veterinary genius," Elizabeth said.

"That I'm smothering?" Rumer asked.

"Well, bad word. Sorry. Perhaps I should have said 'vigilant' instead. You know, watching all the little doggies and kitties to see what ails them. Especially since they can't talk on their own . . ." Elizabeth smiled. "You've always been so good at drawing the innermost feelings out—in people and animals."

"Look," Rumer said, getting upset. "Never mind any of this. Now I'm really worried. He must have said something—I'm beginning to wonder about why he went in the first place."

"I'm sure he'll tell you when he gets back." Standing up, Elizabeth swept around the big open room and looked at pictures, books, and shells. Every object brought back memories—of her parents, of her and Rumer, of Zeb.

"When will he get back?" Rumer asked.

"When he's ready, Rumer," Elizabeth said with exasperated patience.

"You saw him," Rumer said. "Dad's getting old; what if something happens to him?"

"Oh," Elizabeth said evenly. "It seems to me as if you've found someone to take your mind off Dad."

Rumer sat silently, the red spots getting brighter. Elizabeth couldn't help noticing that her hair was completely natural: She was letting the silver melt in with the light brown. Elizabeth couldn't think of one close friend—in California, New York, Europe—close to her age who was just letting her hair color alone. The irony was, instead of making Rumer look older, the silver gave her the look of a wise child.

"Zeb?" Rumer asked, her blue eyes full of motion and passion.

"That'd be my ex-husband," Elizabeth said. "Yes. Zeb."

"I've been waiting for this."

Elizabeth laughed, her heart in her throat. Controlling her younger sister had always been one of the things she did best. A well-timed look: a frown, a go-ahead smile, and a stop-right-there shake of the head. Disapproval in the voice, encouragement in the hug . . . all had been effective over the years. But right now the sisters were staring each other down, and Rumer was winning.

"Waiting for what?" Elizabeth asked.

"For you to ask me about Zeb," Rumer said. "That's why you're here, isn't it?"

"I'm not allowed to come back to my own home? Without it being about Zeb?"

"You never have before," Rumer said, ignoring the last question.

"Well, seeing Dad made me nostalgic for family and home. It's my son's birthday, he's here, and I decided to surprise you all."

Rumer drew in a deep breath, as if pulling herself together. Then, reaching forward, she grasped Elizabeth's hands in hers. To Elizabeth's surprise, her heart was racing and her mouth was dry with emotion and apprehension.

"I'm glad you did," Rumer said. "No matter what has ever been between us, I love you. And I'm glad to see you."

Elizabeth laughed—she was exquisitely trained, and in her stage and film work she often had to react to comments she didn't really find funny. She found herself doing that now, using technique to communicate with her sister just to avoid the true, painful feelings that were coming up inside.

"Really?" she asked. "Because, when I walked up the hill and saw you kissing Zeb, I would have thought the opposite."

"You're divorced, Elizabeth. I'm not worried about that anymore," Rumer said softly, squeezing her hand before letting it go.

Then, going into the kitchen to make them some tea, Rumer left Elizabeth alone in their family living room. Elizabeth stared straight at the spot where their mother always put the Christmas tree and—out of nowhere—tears came to her eyes.

Gazing out the window, she looked at the beach. Many families were down there now, with their blankets and brightly striped umbrellas. Memories were flowing fast now, of her and Rumer and their parents there on a Sunday, trying to build the biggest sand castle ever; of her father buying them Good Humors; of watching Rumer and Zeb—twelve years old—go crabbing and feeling left out; of the swans on their island in the boat basin.

Wiping her eyes, she focused on the boats in the boat basin. They looked bigger than she remembered, and then she realized that the bridges leading out the creek to the Sound had been raised—to accommodate the larger sizes. More money, gaudier tastes: That explained the grossness next door as well as the bigger boats. She thought of that saying she'd seen emblazoned on the bumpers of yacht transporters—The only difference between men and boys is the size of their toys.

Staring at the boats, she did a double take.

There, lying athwartships a really hideous old lobster boat, was her son. She would know him anywhere: his long, lanky build, his golden brown hair, his California tan, his trademark red bandanna.

"Michael," she whispered.

"He's always there," Rumer said, coming in with a small silver tray holding mismatched blue and white china cups and a sugar bowl and milk pitcher covered with cabbage roses.

"On that disgusting boat?"

"Well, more like with the girl who owns it."

"Who's that?"

"Quinn Grayson."

"Lily's daughter?"

"Yes."

"She has to be pretty messed up, losing her parents like that. . . ."

"Zee—don't stir up trouble," Rumer said softly. "She's a wonderful girl. I think she's been awfully good for Michael too. He's doing very well in summer school, talking about college; they're down there doing homework together right now. See the book?"

Picking up the binoculars, Elizabeth stared at the two teenagers. Yes, there was a book open on the seat between them, but all she could really see were their fingers interlaced, their mouths moving incessantly as if there were endless things to say to each other.

"What's he doing?" she asked.

"Elizabeth, they're in love," Rumer said, laughing—Elizabeth thought—quite wickedly.

Elizabeth felt a black veil come across her spirit. She didn't need to hear this from her sister the same day she'd seen her kissing Zeb. Filled with rage, she turned on Rumer and stared her down.

"You don't have children of your own," she said.

"No. . . ."

"Michael's just your nephew—not your son. We went through this already when I was in rehab. You tried to take him over then, just the way you did right after he was born."

"I've always loved Michael," Rumer said simply.

"One thing you've never gotten right, Rumer," she said, "is boundaries. They probably don't matter as much with horses, but with people, you really have to pay attention. He's my son."

"I've never thought otherwise."

"And Zeb married me."

"I never forget that," Rumer said solemnly, her gaze steady and dignified.

"Good," Elizabeth said, feeling a shockingly primal hatred for her sister, wanting to rub the dignity right out of her face. She felt like the wicked stepmother, like an evil fairy, and she knew she would do anything in her power to tear Rumer and Zeb apart. And to take what was hers. Michael.

"Think about it. I'm going down there to see my son."

"Mom—what are you doing here?" Michael asked, shocked to look up from where he and Quinn were sitting in her lobster boat in her slip at the boat basin.

"My God," his mother said, holding out her hand. She was in her Queen of England mode. Imperious, royal, larger than life. "When did you grow six inches?"

Michael stood to take her hand and lean forward to kiss her. At first he thought she wanted to come aboard, but when he realized she was trying to pull him onto the seawall, he slid his hand free and went back to Quinn.

Quinn looked frozen, the way she got when something unexpected happened. She'd scrunch her neck down like a turtle trying to hide in its shell, and she'd give a severe frown as if trying to scare the person away. Right now her frown was wavering, trying to become a smile, wanting to make a good impression on Michael's mother.

"Well," his mother said, flashing Quinn her megawatt movie-star smile. Not a good sign, and Michael's stomach fell—his mother had an ax to grind here, and Michael was starting to guess what it was. "Now, you look familiar. Whose daughter are you?"

"Lily Underhill Grayson's," Quinn said. "I'm Quinn."

"Oh, my heavens. Aren't you all grown-up!"

"Thank you," Quinn said. Michael slid his arm around her protectively—she was relaxing, thinking his mother meant well, but something was coming. Michael wanted to be happy to see his mother—he had missed her this summer—but she had a strange, angry energy going, and right now he wanted her to disappear.

"I'm sorry about what happened to your parents," his mother said, her voice laden with sorrow. Quinn accepted the statement with awesome dignity; she bowed her head, and then faced out toward the Hunting Ground, where her parents' boat sank ten years before.

"Thank you," Quinn said again.

"Too much tragedy."

"Yes, it is."

"Mom?" Michael asked, wanting to move her along. He knew her so well; she was building to a big dramatic statement. Maybe she'd let rip some embarrassing story about Michael's childhood.

"What's that you're studying?" she asked, craning her neck.

"Shakespeare," Quinn replied.

"Romeo and Juliet," Michael supplied.

"Oh, my God. I was Juliet the summer your father and I started dating," she said. "Get him to tell you about it—it's just about the most romantic story you can imagine."

"I've heard it," Michael said.

"What was it?" Quinn asked.

"I'll tell," his mother said. "I was appearing at the Lark Theater. Your father had come to see me with Aunt Rumer, but she left early . . . to take the train back here."

"To Hubbard's Point?"

"Of course," his mother said to Quinn. "Romances flourish here, that's for sure," his mother said, smiling tenderly, and for a minute Michael thought it was all going to be okay. "Something in the air, in the water, the breeze . . .

"Winnie says it's an aphrodisiac," Quinn said.

"I'm not sure Winnie should be saying that to children. . . ."

"We're not—" Michael began, but his mother silenced him with a smile.

"Anyway, your father had brought me roses. . . ."

"With Aunt Rumer," Michael said. "They'd bought them together, right? Before she left to go home on the train?"

"Oh, maybe. But anyway, on my way to the theater, I'd been wearing my lighthouse pin—the one my mother had made for me. It was my good luck piece; we're very superstitious in the theater, Quinn, and I never went onstage without touching it three times. That night on my way to the theater, I lost it. I had to skip my ritual. And I was *very* upset."

"I can imagine," Quinn whispered. "I'd die if I lost a pin my mother gave me."

"Well. After the show, it was a lovely warm night . . . the crowds were strolling the Village streets, listening to music, on their way to restaurants . . . and as Zeb and I were walking along Great Jones Street—and I swear, I didn't even remember walking along that way earlier—" His mother gave a radiant smile, looking straight into Michael's eyes. "Go ahead, Michael," she said. "Tell your friend what happened."

"My dad found the pin," he said quietly.

"Really?" Quinn asked, eyes sparkling.

"Yes," his mother said, nodding at the sky. "Zeb just happened to look down, and there in the gutter along with you-can-only-imagine-what was my lighthouse pin."

"That your mother had made for you," Quinn breathed.

"So you see," his mother said. "*Romeo and Juliet* has special significance for our family."

"I like it too," Quinn said, her voice full of awe.

"Where are you staying?" Michael asked, staring at her. People walking past had noticed her, pretending not to. It happened all the time, and he could see his mother eating it up.

"I was thinking, maybe I'd stay with you and your father."

Michael's stomach dropped. Was she kidding? What about his father and Aunt Rumer? He had seen them walking down the street last night, holding hands. And the other morning, when he was walking Quinn over to Aunt Rumer's for their ride to school, he could have sworn he saw his father coming down the stairs, tucking his shirt into his pants.

"Uh . . ." he began.

"Why, Michael? Don't you want me there?" she asked.

How could he tell her that he liked things the way they were right now? His father was a different man: funny, nicer, more relaxed than he'd ever been. He and Michael ate dinner together, and Michael didn't even mind. In fact, one night when his father had gone over to Aunt Rumer's for clam chowder, Michael had missed their time together.

"Never mind," his mother said briskly. "I can tell from the look on your face that you don't."

"It's not that, Mom. . . ."

"A girl knows when she's not wanted, right, Quinn?"

Quinn was back to frowning, frozen, not understanding the weird dynamics of life in the Mayhew family.

"How sweet that you've found each other again," his mother said after a few moments, gazing thoughtfully into the marsh.

" 'Again?' " Quinn asked.

"Mom?"

"Darling, you played together when you were children. Now, Amanda never knew him at that age. They were all grown-up. . . ."

"Hey," Michael said, shaking his head to stop her.

"Amanda?" Quinn asked, frowning, looking at Michael for answers.

"Michael's friend," Elizabeth said. For some reason, calling her his friend instead of girlfriend just made things worse. Quinn looked stunned, then devastated as her shoulders began to cave in on her chest.

"What do you mean, all grown-up?"

"Well, there are childhood friends and grown-up friends," Elizabeth said.

"You knew Dad when you were kids," Michael shot out. "And you married him."

His mother laughed. "Actually he and your aunt were the childhood friends—I kind of watched them from afar, till the time was right. A little like you and Amanda. She's heartsick this summer, I hear."

"Why?" Quinn asked. "What happened?"

Michael wanted to grab the starter cord, pull as hard as he could, drive the boat far away and leave his mother talking to herself. His heart was hammering in his chest, and his hands were cold and clammy. He knew Quinn wasn't his mother's kind of girl, and he knew that the story had more to do with that than anything else. "Mom, don't," he said quietly.

"She misses Michael," Elizabeth said. "She can barely get through the summer without him. Her father's a dear friend of mine; he asked if Amanda could come east to visit, and I said I didn't see why not."

"I didn't know you were seeing someone else," Quinn whispered, reaching for Michael's face, going pure white.

"No, Quinn," Michael said, leaning forward. "Only you."

"Are you sure?" Quinn begged, grabbing for his hand.

Michael held her, his heart pounding out of his chest, his mother standing right there, staring at them. Why would she try to do this? Just because she'd screwed things up with his father, she thought everything about Hubbard's Point was bad. Soothing Quinn, feeling her shake in his arms, Michael suddenly felt the truth about love come flooding in.

It wasn't about what you wanted, or what you thought should happen, or what everyone else judged was best: Love was about what *was*. It was bigger than anything Michael had ever imagined. It had nothing to do with Amanda's beauty or his mother's friendship with her father or the rightness of their being together.

Love was much different than any of that. Michael had learned this summer that the real truth was often different from the stories told about it. Watching his father with Aunt Rumer, he had seen him happier than he ever had before—and that totally contradicted the things his mother used to tell him. And Michael knew, because holding Quinn, he was also holding his own true love in his arms right then, at that moment, and he never wanted to let her go.

As he looked up at his mother, he could see that she knew she'd made a mistake. She had thought Michael was playing around—that this was puppy love or something, that it didn't matter. Her eyes had a dawning look of upset in them, as if she wanted to reach out and pull her words back from the air.

"Michael?" she asked, staring at him, but Michael closed his eyes—not to shut her out but to let Quinn in.

"Quinn," he whispered into her wild auburn hair. "Don't cry. Don't be afraid. I love you. . . ."

But Quinn tore away, scrambled up onto the seawall and ran. And Michael ran right after the girl he loved, leaving his mother standing speechless and alone.

After Elizabeth went down to see Michael, Rumer met Zeb behind the privet hedge. She felt as if they were a pair of illicit lovers stealing a few minutes together. They kissed with mad abandon, and they couldn't keep out of each other's arms. No one could see them from the street or beach.

"Why is she here?" Zeb asked when they stopped for a minute.

"For Michael's birthday."

"No, that's what she says. There's another reason."

"How do you know?"

"You know it too, Rumer. She heard about us—maybe your father told her, or a friend mentioned it. Or even Michael."

"How could she know about us?" she asked, stroking the side of his face. It was lean and angular, cleanly shaven, and felt wonderful to her hand. "*We* didn't even know about us."

"The rest of the Point did," Zeb said. "Your father, Winnie . . ."

"Mattie," Rumer said, agreeing.

"I'm worried," Zeb said, his gaze direct and hard-edged. "About what Elizabeth being here will mean to us."

"I want to say it won't matter," Rumer said. "But obviously it will. It feels very complicated. She's my sister, and I want to love her. I want to have a relationship like Marnie has with her sisters; like Dana had with Lily and Quinn has with Allie. I want us to be the kind of sisters I always thought we were, the kind our mother wanted us to be. That's what I've always wanted my entire life. And it's how we were as children . . . but not now."

"Don't let Elizabeth change what's between us. It's ours, Rumer. Ours alone—don't let her have anything to do with it."

Rumer pulled back to look Zeb in the eyes. They were blue and clear, the same eyes she'd known her whole life.

"I won't," she said fiercely.

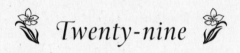 Twenty-nine

CRASHING THROUGH THE narrow path at the end of the beach, Michael could hear Quinn up ahead. He ran up the crooked rise into the woods where Fish Hill, the old hunting lodge, once stood. Here the trail grew narrow and dark, encroached upon by bushes and vines growing in from the sides. Past the offshoot path leading to the Indian Grave, straight on to where the woods stopped and Little Beach began.

Michael knew where she was going; Quinn had showed him once, a few weeks earlier, the spot where she had buried her diary long ago, the summer after her parents were lost. Slowing down, he looked around.

"Quinn?" he called, coming around the big rock. The paint had almost faded, but there were big shark jaws painted on the rock's surface.

He could hear her crying, and he followed the sound. She lay curled on her side, on the dry sand just above the high-tide line—shells, seaweed, and driftwood marking the gateway to the sea. Kneeling beside her, Michael looked into her eyes.

"Quinn?"

She covered her face, unable to speak. Michael gathered her onto his lap as if she were a child. She sobbed hard enough for both of them. Michael felt like crying himself; seeing his mother had affected him strangely. Although he had started off feeling angry about what she'd said—that stuff about Amanda—now he felt sad, sorry for her, and lonely. Trying to figure it out, he just rocked back and forth with Quinn in his arms.

"I'm sorry I acted like that in front of your mother," she whispered after a long while, when she could keep some control of her voice.

"Don't be," Michael said. "She was being a jerk."

"Your mother hates me, it's obvious."

"She doesn't, but it wouldn't matter if she did."

"I don't like being hated," Quinn said. "A lot of people feel that way . . . it's because I'm so different. Your mother just wants to protect you. . . ."

Rocking her gently, Michael just listened as her voice merged with the sound of the waves.

"When you came," she said, gulping, "I expected you to ignore me. There are so many beautiful girls here—they wear shorts and bikinis and things, not kimonos or their father's old shorts. They use fingernail polish on their nails, not to paint numbers on their lobster buoys. They wear jewelry instead of fish scales and rope bracelets. Like Amanda, I bet . . ."

"Well, Amanda's not too keen on fish scales, that's for sure."

"Who is? Except me."

Michael smiled down at the top of her head.

"I know I'm weird," she whispered. "I can't help it. I think I told you once. . . ."

"You said you were a changeling."

"Yes. I'm intense and strange, and it got worse after my parents drowned. I look at Allie—so cute and normal—caring about things like lip gloss and the right color socks, and my head spins."

"Maybe she gets to be that way because you're the way you are," Michael said.

Quinn looked up with one eye, her head still buried in his lap.

"Because you feel enough for both of you," he whispered.

"I do feel a lot," Quinn said, her voice thin, stretching, as if to the sky. "When it first happened, I'd sit right here—in this same spot—and wait for the mermaid to come. I thought she was my mother . . . to this day, I think she was. I'd leave her white flowers, and I'd feel her singing to my broken heart."

"You had a broken heart?" Michael asked, the words piercing his whole body.

"Yes. I did. I do."

They sat very still, holding each other as the tide came in, every wave a little closer, licking the bottoms of their bare feet.

"Broken hearts never grow back together," Quinn whispered. "They never really get fixed—don't let anyone tell you they do. But I believe that if you're lucky, you find the right things in life to let you live with one."

"Like what?"

"Like Hubbard's Point . . . the people, the lilies, the rocks and roses, the rabbits, the lobsters, Rumer, Winnie . . . you."

"Me," Michael whispered, his throat aching.

"When you came here this summer, and you liked me so much," Quinn said, "I couldn't believe it. I thought it had to be a mistake. Like out of the blue I was going to get a message from God: *Sorry, my mistake.*"

"You won't be getting that message."

"I just can't believe it," she said, shivering in his arms. Now, reaching up, she gently traced his cheek with her fingertips. "Why do you like me when there's someone like Amanda?"

He laughed. "You don't even know Amanda. . . ."

"Sure I do," Quinn said stubbornly. "She's like the perfect girls at school, I'll bet. Ashton or Megan or Isabella. The ones who look like models, who never eat, who get the best grades, whose mothers take them shopping every Saturday . . ."

"I could be wrong," Michael said, "but it sounds like you're making generalities. They might not be half as happy as you are."

"Why do you think that?"

"Because you know who you are," Michael said. "I saw that in you the first day we met."

"What good is that?"

"It's everything."

"Well, you know who you are," Quinn said, tracing his face with her hand.

"I'm getting to," he said. "I didn't use to. But I used to try. . . ."

"Like how?"

"Well, like wanting a scar," Michael said, spinning into the past. "My dad has some—from falling out of trees, crashing off the roof, training exercises, stuff like that. I thought if I could have one, it would make me more like him."

"You don't need a scar for that," Quinn whispered.

"Yeah, but I used to think I did. I thought it had to be a mark, a grade—something to prove I was rough and tough like him. I thought he'd like me more."

"You thought he didn't like you?"

Michael shrugged. "Kind of, I guess. This summer, I see it differently."

"How?"

"Well, he was pretty unhappy himself. Their marriage wasn't so good. My mom's drinking, and the way she always blames him—"

"But it's not his fault," Quinn said.

"No."

"It's probably not hers either."

Michael looked into her face, waiting.

"Even though she wants you to go back to Amanda," she whispered, smiling.

"There's no chance of that." Michael played with her hair for a while, leaning over to kiss her.

"She doesn't like it here, does she?" Quinn asked.

Michael shook his head. "She said we'd never come back to Hubbard's Point—and we almost never did. Even though we kept the house till they got divorced, we started taking summer vacations other places . . . Hawaii once, a ranch in Montana, the Oregon coast, Europe . . . Aunt Rumer would sometimes come out to be with us. I remember missing her, and Blue."

"Her horse . . ."

"Yeah. She brought me a stuffed horse that reminded me of him. I named him Blue . . . but one night I went to sleep, and when I woke up, he was gone."

"What do you think happened?"

Michael closed his eyes, playing with her hair some more. "I know what happened. My mother took him away."

"Why?"

"The same reason she wants me with Amanda," Michael whispered. "Because that's the way she knows . . . the closer I get to here . . . Hubbard's Point . . . the farther away it feels to her."

"But this is her home. Just like it's Rumer's and your dad's."

Michael shook his head. "No, it's not like that for her," he said. "I don't know why, but it never was. She couldn't wait to get away, never wanted us to come back. She doesn't even want me here now."

"But I'm glad you are."

Holding her even tighter, Michael kissed her head, her ear, the side of her face. "You and I are meant to be together."

"Maybe your mother will try to make us break up."

"No one can make us," Michael said fiercely, holding Quinn tightly to his chest as the cool white tops of the waves touched their feet, their ankles, coming higher. Their rings of copper wire glinted in the sun. The rocks around them were silver—bare, bald rock as white as clouds against the bright blue sky behind them.

He touched her face, kissed her cheek. She smelled warm and sweet. The waves lapped their feet. They were on a boat together, just the two of them, steering a magical course. Michael didn't know where they'd end up. But he'd gotten the idea from watching his father and Aunt Rumer that an early shipwreck could ruin entire lives.

So with his eyes open, Michael just pulled Quinn closer, kissing her lips, knowing he'd never look away from the horizon or let go of the wheel, no matter what happened.

The *Clarissa* surfed the Gulf Stream home, and Sixtus Larkin and Malachy Condon were having the time of their lives. By night, bioluminescence streaked along the hull—sea fire created by their speed through the plankton-rich waves. By day, humpback whales and bottlenose dolphins swam just out of sight, revealing themselves just enough to tantalize Malachy into dropping his hydrophone over the side or grabbing his video camera for a scant chance at capturing on film a glossy black back, a sharp dorsal fin.

"You're trying to get yourself a show on the Discovery Channel," Sixtus said, hand on the tiller.

"The hell I am," Malachy said. "I'm too goddamned serious a scholar to bother with such nonsense."

"Nope," Sixtus said. "You're after your own show. 'Malachy the Whale Tracker' . . . something like that. Like the guy who hunts down poisonous snakes, or the one who travels the world's reefs in search of great white sharks."

"Bad men, they are," Malachy said, biting harder on his pipe stem. "Stirring up the public to loathe and revile the species . . . no, Sixtus—I am simply doing my small part, feeding the river of knowledge about cetaceans. As a teacher, surely you understand the value of that. Enough drops in the bucket fill the bucket. . . ."

"You're right, Mal. And I respect you for it."

"Besides, Lucinda thinks knowledge is sexy."

"Well, she would. She's a librarian. Think she'll be pleasantly surprised when you show up in Hawthorne?"

"Hell, I hope so. I'm not given to much impetuosity these days, but when a fellow Hibernian offers me a ride south on his Herreshoff, I figure I'd better go along with him. Besides, I haven't seen my Lucinda in a good month." He smoked his pipe for a while as Sixtus steered their way. The *Clarissa* sliced through the water, waves peeling off her sharp and lovely bow.

Sixtus gazed ahead at the sun making a path along the open sea. With all the wide open blue, he was steering straight along the golden waves as if they were calling him home. He thought about dreams, how all his adult life he had wanted to sail solo transatlantic—man versus nature. He had taught *Moby Dick* to more classes than he could remember; he had always wanted to go in search of spiritual riches, family knowledge, and the white whale himself.

"Do you ever think, Malachy," he asked, "about how alone we are?"

Malachy, sitting to leeward so he could be closer to the waves and the creatures swimming within them, trailed his fingers in the swiftly passing water and nodded. "Every day. Isn't that what this is all about?"

"This?"

"Your quest? This trip?"

"I'm not sure."

"You're testing yourself, Sixtus," Malachy said. "Seeing the limits of what you can take."

"Into the abyss, as it were," Sixtus said, "I got to thinking about Zeb. About all those trips to the stars, into the sky, alone in his space suit with the sound of his own heart pounding in his ears. Sometimes it's easier to see the mistakes of the younger generation than it is to see our own."

He pictured Zeb, trying to make up for lost time with Michael, spending the summer at Hubbard's Point trying to establish a footing here on earth instead of off searching the stars for his dreams. He hoped Zeb had taken him good and seriously, that he was looking after Rumer. And that she was looking after him.

"And what did the younger generation's mistakes teach you this time?"

"That everyone needs an eye to look into."

"An eye?" Malachy said, cocking a bushy white eyebrow.

"Sure. Even Ahab—out at sea, staring into the nothingness, he found Moby Dick. He found a white whale, and by chasing him till the moment of his own death, he found a way to not be alone—an eye to look into."

"You *are* a goddamned teacher, aren't you?"

"Sorry to say, it's a quality that dies hard."

"Okay. I'll humor you. Say I have Lucinda as my eye to look into. Ahab has Moby Dick. How about you?"

Sixtus held the tiller, squinting into the sunlight ahead.

"You got to thinking about Ireland, didn't you? Staring into the eyes of strangers. Nurses, aides, the occasional podiatrist . . . maybe the doctor would look in once in a while. That's what you were thinking, weren't you?"

"Yup."

"And those aren't the eyes you want to look into, are they?"

"They're not."

"So tell me, Sixtus: Who are they?"

Sixtus swallowed, peering into the golden light dancing ahead on the waves. As a child he had had his brother and mother and, through this trip to Nova Scotia, he had just regained them. As a young man, he had found Clarissa, and she had given him two daughters—he still had them. But mainly—as much as any of it—he had Hubbard's Point. Rumer, Quinn, *les Dames de la Roche,* and—for as long as they stayed this summer—Zeb and his grandson, Michael.

"My friends and family," he said huskily. "At Hubbard's Point."

"Glad you figured that out before you stuck yourself in Shady Acres, or whatever Irish rest home you'd have discovered over there."

"Guilt's a weird thing."

"Guilt?"

"Yes. I feel guilty for having a daughter who cares about me. Cares enough to let me stick around."

"You never stop to figure she might like her father, do you? Sure, you're old and annoying, but we all are."

"I'm the luckiest man in the world."

"By any scientific definition available," Malachy said with utter seriousness, "along with the empirical evidence at hand, I would say that that is most definitely so. With yours truly running a very close second."

"Amen, brother," Sixtus said as they cleared the elbow of Cape Cod and turned right toward home.

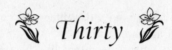 Thirty

Despite her resolve, with Elizabeth nearby, Rumer wasn't sure how to be around Zeb. It made her act shy and feel foolish, more becoming to a young girl than a seasoned woman. But whatever they had started was gaining force, and the sudden distance between them only made it feel more powerful. They were all supposed to get together that night, at Rumer's house, to celebrate Michael's birthday. Rumer was dreading it.

"How is it, having Elizabeth home?" Mathilda asked as they were scrubbing for early morning surgery on an aged Jack Russell terrier.

"Difficult," Rumer said, scouring her wrists and forearms.

"Were you always known as the Larkin girls? My sisters and I were always known as the Metcalf girls. Isn't it a shame that we spent half our childhoods wanting to claw each other's eyes out for borrowing clothes without asking?"

"Strange you should mention that," Rumer said, drying her hands. "Elizabeth told me I don't pay enough attention to boundaries. *Boundaries*." She pronounced the word as if it were in a foreign language.

"Well, who's the one who ignored the boundary line first? Weren't you in love with Zeb your whole life? And didn't your sister walk right in and take what she wanted?"

Rumer put the stethoscope against Danny's—the patient's—chest. His breathing was shallow, his heart strong. His owners, the Robinsons, had loved the terrier as if he were their own child since first getting him sixteen years earlier. Rumer took a deep breath and picked up the scalpel.

"Yes," Rumer said. "She did. But it feels so low, fighting with a sister over a man."

"It's not low at all," Mattie said, looking her in the eye. "It's only your life. If it takes a fight to find happiness, then isn't that worth it? You're wise, Rumer. When it comes to pets and pet owners, you're the doctor. When it comes to me, you're my guru and guide. But when it comes to you . . ."

"I can't see my way clear," Rumer said, taking a deep, even breath.

Rumer smiled, and then turned her full attention to Danny. She consulted the X rays again, then made the incision. Playing with his owners, Danny had swallowed a golf ball. It had lodged in the upper end of his large bowel, causing him much distress. To make matters worse, the golf ball had been chewed first, and the inner core of rubber string was coming unraveled.

As she worked, Rumer thought of the nobility of life, the ignominy of swallowing a golf ball. She thought of the difference between being a movie star and being a veterinarian. Although one was more glamorous, the other got to give a family back its dog. Rumer knew what was important, and she knew that there was more than one way of being pinched from the inside. Fighting with her sister over a man wasn't so low; as Mattie had said, it was only Rumer's life.

She closed up Danny's incision and made surgical notes in his record. She still had to make calls about new stables for Blue, and that night she was hosting Michael's birthday party. She had thought about canceling, backing out, just so she wouldn't have to see Zeb and Elizabeth in the same room together.

She hoped it wouldn't come to a fight, but if it did, she was ready. She still hadn't heard from her father, and it was making her crazy. It wouldn't take much to push her to the edge, and this time she wouldn't back down.

❧

Rumer set the old oak table with her mother's Blue Willow china. She and Quinn polished the silver and washed the crystal till it sparkled.

"His mother hates me," Quinn said. "I don't think I should be here."

"Michael invited you," Rumer replied.

"He doesn't have to," Quinn said. "I can see him later. . . ."

"It's his eighteenth-birthday dinner," Rumer said, sliding her arm around Quinn and squeezing. "How do you think he'd feel if you weren't here? Don't worry about his mother. Leave her to me."

"Were you and she like me and Allie?" Quinn asked.

"Yes, we were," Rumer said, and the question made her sad because it brought back such vivid memories of being close to her sister as children and how much she had missed that connection, felt its loss.

"She's very different from you," Quinn said, looking worried.

"That's true. Does it bother you?"

"Just that I always think sisters should be exactly alike. But they're not—at all! Sometimes it seems we're not even from the same family, and that's how it looks with you and Elizabeth. See, I want to be like you when I grow up, but I'm afraid I'll be like your sister."

"Why do you say that?"

"Well, Allie and I are as different as you guys. We have totally separate personalities. . . . She's the nice one—just like I bet you were the nice one when you were our age."

"You're nice," Rumer said. "Among other things."

"Yeah, but she's the Nice One—that's what people say about her. There's a difference."

Rumer glanced over at an old photo of her and Elizabeth. "That's the thing about sisters," Rumer said, "that I wish were different. Why does there have to be such separate 'territory'? As if only one can be the nice one, one the pretty one, one the smart one . . ."

Quinn cocked her head, watching Rumer. "I'll bet that your sister was 'the pretty one' when you were little."

"She was," Rumer said, feeling surprisingly hurt.

"Yeah, well now you're the beautiful one," Quinn said. "Your sister's still pretty, but you're beautiful. I'll bet she knows it too."

"I don't think she sees it that way," Rumer chuckled.

"Oh, I do. She can't miss it. Her prettiness—I don't know how to say this . . . or even if I should."

Rumer laughed. "Quinn, you've never been one to hold back. Don't start now. Go ahead."

"Well, her prettiness is all in her face. In her skin, eyes, nose . . . on the surface. Yours is a lot deeper. It's in your eyes. I know it's weird, me noticing that about you, but I can't help it. It's just so there—and Mr. Mayhew sees it too."

"He does?"

"Oh, yeah. He stares at you like he wants to drink you in."

"Well, Quinn," Rumer began.

"He does. He's in love."

But just then Elizabeth drove up, climbing out of her Porsche with an armload of presents, and began to walk up the hill.

Zeb and Michael came in from the terrace, where they'd been setting up the telescope Zeb had given him as his big gift.

"It's amazing," Michael said. "It's computer run, with a motor that keeps it following the stars all night. You can set it on Saturn and watch till the sun comes up. Practically as cool as the one he's going to have in his new observatory."

"See the rings and everything?" Quinn asked.

"Certainly," Zeb said. "Wait till dark, and we'll show you."

"What about opening *my* presents?" Elizabeth asked, walking in. She spilled them on a side table and pulled Michael over.

Rumer had set white candles in her mother's crystal and brass candlesticks; the flames flickered in the breeze. While Michael sat in Sixtus's armchair, Rumer felt a pang for her father. He should be there for his grandson's eighteenth birthday—and to see his daughters here together.

"Should we call the Coast Guard?" she asked, drifting toward the window.

"Why?" Elizabeth asked. "Dad's a great sailor. Let him have his adventure."

"Aren't you worried?" She looked around the room.

Michael and Quinn both nodded. Elizabeth busied herself with arranging the pile of presents. Zeb said nothing, but Rumer saw him glance over. He caught her gaze, his blue eyes holding her with humor and something else—a sort of teasing that sent goose bumps up her arms.

"Zeb?" Rumer asked. "What do you think?"

"Tell her, Zeb," Elizabeth laughed. "That he's a big boy."

"I think he's fine," Zeb said quietly, still staring at Rumer with eyes filled with heat.

Elizabeth laughed smugly.

Rumer's stomach clenched. She knew that Zeb wasn't siding with her sister, but Elizabeth thought so. Rumer shook it off and glanced at the phone. Maybe she'd call the Coast Guard on her own; if she still felt this way in a little while, she'd make the call regardless of what her sister and Zeb thought. Her father had promised he would phone before leaving for Ireland; while she didn't think he was midway across the Atlantic without checking in, she did wonder about his reason for staying silent so long.

Elizabeth placed her hands on Michael's shoulders.

"We've waited long enough," she said. "The suspense is killing me! Open your gifts . . . which package do you want first?"

"Quinn's," he said, eyes gleaming as he looked at her.

"Well, mine's kind of little . . ." Quinn said, handing him a small package.

"Isn't that cute?" Elizabeth said wryly.

"I was thinking you could open it later," Quinn said.

"Do you want me to?"

Zeb still hadn't looked away. Was he thinking of them at that same age? Rumer shivered, thinking back, recalling how many young birthdays they had shared together—she remembered Zeb always standing by her side to help her blow the candles out on her cake.

Quinn nodded. "It's . . . personal," she whispered.

"Keeping secrets," Elizabeth said in a funny, displeased voice.

"Mom—" Michael warned sharply.

"Fine, fine. I'm just the mother! Okay—which present first?"

"This one," Michael said, choosing Rumer's package. Opening it, his eyes lit up to discover a fountain pen and a bottle of ink. As Rumer showed him how to fill it, she kissed him on the cheek.

"It was mine in college," she explained. "My parents gave it to me my freshman year. I used it to write papers for a while, but it was a little too distracting—I'd get sidetracked trying to do calligraphy—but I did use it for my journal, my life list of birds, letters home . . ."

"Oh, God, Rue—" Elizabeth laughed. "It has your initials on the side! RGL."

"What's wrong with that?" Michael asked.

"Just . . . it's so *used* looking."

"I like it," Michael said, feeling the pen's weight in his open palm. He grabbed a piece of paper and started to write, practicing on the name Quinn, but his mother took hold of his wrist and gave him a killer smile.

"There's time enough for your memoirs," Elizabeth said with dark humor.

"It's a love letter," he said, looking her straight in the eye.

"In any case, pick another package. One of mine!"

Michael reached for one off the top of the pile. Working his way down, he opened a Tag Heuer watch, a set of studs, and monogrammed cuff links, "for when you take me to Jeffy's Oscar party," his mother joked—a new laptop computer, and a black lambskin jacket.

"Wow, thanks, Mom," he said, reaching up to hug her.

"Good thing your father thought to drive out from California," his mother said. "In a big car—so you can haul all your loot back home."

Quinn let out a small squeak, and Rumer watched Michael attempt to suppress a smile. The harder he tried, the bigger it got.

"More secrets," Elizabeth said. "It's not very polite to leave everyone else out in the dark—you're hurting my feelings. Quinn's gift next."

Zeb smiled, casting a reassuring glance Quinn's way.

"It's nothing much," Quinn said quietly as Michael slowly, carefully, untied the bow. "I made it myself."

"Homemade presents are the best kind," Zeb said.

Elizabeth's lips thinned as she glanced at the stack of gifts Michael had dutifully opened yet left lying on the table. He hadn't even tried on his watch; Rumer felt a burst of sadness for her sister.

The ribbon was rough twine and the wrapping paper was actually a section of newspaper. Peering over Michael's shoulder, Rumer saw it was the front page of the *New London Day.*

"From June 16," Quinn whispered.

"The day we met!"

"I had to go through all the papers in our garage to find it; luckily Aunt Dana was so busy getting ready for her wedding, she forgot to recycle."

Now Michael's fingers moved faster, breaking the tape and untying the twine. He got it open, and the paper fell away, revealing a brown diary.

"What have we here?" Elizabeth asked as Michael guarded it in his lap.

"Maybe it's private," Rumer said softly, watching Quinn's eyes.

"Nonsense," Elizabeth said. "Right, Quinn?"

"It's private and public at the same time," she whispered. "The thoughts are mine, even though I didn't write them."

Rumer, knowing what an avid diarist Quinn was, felt eager to see what was inside. Zeb had stepped back from the table to circle behind everyone else and slide his arm secretly behind Rumer's back. She tingled under his touch, and from the anticipation of what was in Quinn's book.

Now, slowly, Michael opened the front cover.

Quinn had drawn several scenes of stick figures: Michael—unmistakably him because of his red bandanna—pulling lobster pots with Quinn—unmistakably her because of her frizzy hair—at the helm; the two of them sitting side by side, reading books; on an airplane flying over the ocean, their faces in one window; and last, most tenderly, the stickgirl bending over to kiss the forehead of the stick-boy.

"It's us," Michael whispered, taking her hand.

"But there's more," Elizabeth said, reading over his shoulder. "Words . . . from the Bard . . . oh, my God!"

"What is it?" Michael asked.

"My dear!" Elizabeth said. "It's Juliet! Act Three, Scene Two—my favorite in all of Shakespeare! 'Gallop apace, you fiery-footed steeds,'" she sang out.

"Blue," Zeb whispered in Rumer's ear.

"It doesn't say that, Mom," Michael said. "It says—"

"I know what it says, dear. I know exactly what it says—I was just giving you the lines that precede it in the text. Do I know this scene, or what, Zeb?"

"You know it," Zeb said quietly.

"*Romeo and Juliet,*" Elizabeth said, her eyes sparkling. "Our finest hour . . ." She touched the pin on her collar. "Remember when you found this for me? In the gutter! Of all the streets in all of New York; when I think of the hours it had been lying there . . . and you just bent down and picked it up as we passed by."

"I remember," Zeb said. "Amazing coincidence . . ."

"Meant to be," Elizabeth laughed. "Losing it that night, I thought I'd never see it again."

"But Dad found it," Michael said as if the story were an old and precious family legend.

"I'm still wearing it," Elizabeth said, glancing down. "How 'bout you, Rue? Do you still have yours?"

"Of course," Rumer said.

"Our special pins. They're different from each other; one of them has a secret. . . ."

"What's the secret?" Quinn asked.

"I don't know. Our mother always said she'd tell us someday," Rumer said. "But she died first; she never did."

"Show Quinn," Michael suggested. "She'll get it, I bet."

While Rumer went upstairs to get her pin, she heard Elizabeth take the book Quinn had made and start reading. The scene, Juliet in the orchard, was intense, passionate, filled with the anticipation and excitement of waiting for Romeo. The words stirred Rumer, reminding her deeply of how it had felt to wait for Zeb—as children, teenagers, all through her life.

The thing was, she couldn't bear to face her sister acting it out now, downstairs, as if she were speaking of Zeb—with him standing right there. It felt like an arrow through her heart—and she couldn't get away from it. Zeb's body and Elizabeth's body had joined together and produced Michael—eighteen years and nearly nine months ago today.

Elizabeth delivered the speech masterfully, her voice ringing through the old house as if she were standing on stage at the Lark Theater. Her skin crawling now, Rumer remembered the night when she and Zeb had gone to see her perform.

Returning downstairs with the gold lighthouse pin in her hand, Rumer was just in time to hear her sister get a huge round of applause. Quinn was clapping the loudest, her face radiant with the joy of hearing such beautiful words read by Michael's mother.

Rumer's stomach dropped, remembering how Elizabeth had given that speech at the Lark Theater; listening in the audience, Rumer had thrilled to it, feeling it was about herself and Zeb. Yet by the end of the night, while she was on the train home, Zeb would have found Elizabeth's pin in the gutter, and the two of them would have become lovers.

"Bravissimo!" Quinn called, still clapping.

Walking over to her, Rumer put the lighthouse pin in her hand. Quinn smiled into her eyes, her hand chapped and rough from lobstering.

"Look at Mom's too," Michael said.

Quinn looked from one pin to the other. Rumer had long since stopped wondering what made them special, different from each other. Perhaps her mother had just bestowed particular blessings—one for each of her very different daughters—on the jewelry the day it was made.

Each pin was about an inch high. The lighthouse looked exactly like the Wickland Rock Light—made of bricks, straight and narrow, with four small windows, one over the other, rising to the lens on top. The rock island spread out from its base, made of individual tiny gold nuggets.

"The island looks so real," Quinn said, tracing the surface of each pin with her index finger.

"What makes us think Quinn will know the difference between these two pins?"

"Because Quinn is very good," Rumer said, her hand on the girl's shoulder, "at seeing the truth of things. She always has been. As far as I know, she's the only one who's actually encountered Mom and Mrs. Mayhew's unicorn."

"I have," Quinn said quietly. "On foggy nights."

"You said I saw one," Michael said. "The day of your aunt's wedding."

"Don't tell me you've started smoking pot," Elizabeth said to her son, but no one reacted. Everyone was watching Quinn, but no one—besides Rumer—recognized the moment when she discovered the secret. Not even Michael.

But Rumer had known Quinn since she was born. All her years of science had taught her to observe the moments—big and small—of discovery. That single instant when the click occurs, when all the facts fall into place, when everything suddenly makes sense. In the biology lab, in the field, in her surgery.

A blush spread up Quinn's neck into her cheeks. Blinking, she shook her head, handing the two pins back to their rightful owners. "I'm sorry," she said softly. But as she did, her eyes met Rumer's and flashed with excitement. Rumer saw Quinn's gaze flick toward Zeb, and the blush increased even more.

"Well. You gave it your best try," Elizabeth said. "Okay. What about cake?"

"Not yet," Michael said. "One more thing . . ."

"Anything, darling. You're the birthday boy."

"I want Quinn to read her present to me."

"Read it?" Quinn asked, smiling.

"Yeah. The lines . . . Act Three, Scene Two," Michael said, smiling back.

Elizabeth laughed. "Out of the mouths of babes," she said. "Not to blow my own horn, but you did just hear the Juliet-to-end-all-Juliets . . . tell them, Zeb."

Zeb ignored her, watching Quinn, nodding with encouragement. "Go on, Quinn."

"I can't follow such a wonderful performance," Quinn said.

"Sure you can," Rumer said. "Let it come from your heart, just like when you copied the lines into the diary."

"You can do it, Quinn," Zeb said, passing the girl Rumer's lighthouse pin. "You can wear this for luck."

Although she didn't pin it on, Quinn held the pin in her hand. She closed her eyes, and Rumer could see her drawing strength from the gold, the love, and the nearness of Michael. Rumer felt the anticipation that sometimes precedes a stunning performance, and she knew even before Quinn opened her mouth that it was going to be great because it was going to be true.

Come, night; come, Romeo!

The passion in her voice shook Rumer to the core. Quinn continued, speaking straight to Michael:

Come thou day in night;
For thou wilt lie upon the wings of night,
Whiter than new snow upon a raven's back.
Come gentle night, come loving black-browed night,
Give me my Romeo, and when he shall die,
Take him and cut him out in little stars,
And he will make the face of heaven so fine,
That all the world will be in love with night.

As Rumer wiped the tears from her eyes, she expected to see Quinn doing the same. But her attention was caught by Michael instead. He was gazing at Quinn with bright eyes and all the love the heart of an eighteen-year-old man could hold.

"You're awesome," he said.

"That was for you," Quinn replied, grinning.

"Little stars," Michael said. "I'll give them to you when we get married."

"What?" Elizabeth asked.

"We're getting married," Michael said.

"You're out of your mind," his mother said, her voice rising.

Zeb stayed calm. He watched the drama unfold, tension in his face. But right now his son had a new and different seriousness of purpose about him, as if the first order of business of being eighteen was going to be marrying Quinn Grayson.

"Talk them out of this," Elizabeth said sharply to Zeb. When he didn't respond, she turned to Rumer. "Do you hear me? Tell them they're wrong—it's illegal."

"Marriage isn't illegal," Rumer said.

"When you're this young it is!"

"Young?" Zeb asked.

"Yes! Let them court for as long as they want. Beach movies, boat rides, Little Beach, messages in the drawer at Foley's, the Indian Grave . . . innocent things that won't ruin anyone's life."

In the midst of her tirade, Elizabeth looked Rumer straight in the eye, and then she looked sharply away. Mystery filled the air. Rumer's heart began to speed up, and she knew it was time for her to see the truth of something she'd always wanted to hide from. Elizabeth's glance had hit Rumer like a knife, and it took all her effort to breathe normally.

Michael and Quinn held hands, huddling together by the chair. Rumer watched them, so wrapped up in their own love that they couldn't hear or see what was going on. She listened to her own blood pounding in her ears, and she held herself with arms crossed over her chest.

"Happy Birthday, Michael," Rumer said.

"Thanks," he said.

"Maybe you and Quinn would like to be by yourselves for a while," she said.

"I'm his mother." Elizabeth smiled. "I'm not quite ready to break up the party. . . ."

Michael hesitated, not sure what to do.

"Maybe we should try to get Grandpa on the radio—give him a chance to say happy birthday to you. Or, since Aunt Rumer is so worried about him, maybe we should give the Coast Guard a try. I know he wouldn't want to miss your birthday. . . ."

"Maybe we should call them," Quinn said, looking upset.

"He's safe," Zeb said softly, looking at the kids. "You two run, okay? Have a good night. We'll see you later."

"You're sure he's okay?" Michael asked.

Zeb nodded. "Yes, trust me. He's fine."

Holding hands, the kids grabbed Quinn's brown diary and they slipped away. Rumer heard their voices fade as they hurried down the path to the boat basin. A few moments later, she saw them start up Quinn's boat, turn on the running lights, and head into the Sound for a ride—to get away from the adults and be alone.

"He's safe," Zeb repeated.

"How can you know? Is it just because you've done this sort of thing—flown alone—that you know?"

"No, it's not that."

"Then, what?" Rumer asked. "Sailing to Ireland is too big a thing for him to do . . . without saying good-bye. I'm worried, Zeb—he might be in danger, he might—" She broke off, everything too much to consider.

"He's on his way home," Zeb said, putting his arms around Rumer.

"Excuse me?" Elizabeth asked. "I don't see how you can say that. I saw him last, and he was getting ready to sail to Galway—don't humor her, Zeb. Let her grow up, accept the fact her father has a life."

"He's coming through Buzzards Bay right now," Zeb said. "He'll be rounding Point Judith before midnight if he holds his course."

"How do you know?" Rumer asked.

"I'm tracking him," Zeb said.

"Tracking him—"

"Did you think I'd let him set off for Ireland without keeping track? Navigational aids work both ways; the signal he sends out to find his position can also be used to locate him from above. I sent his data to one of my satellites, and I've been looking over him from the sky."

"Zeb . . ."

Now, closing her eyes, Rumer remembered what he had said: that he had watched over her from above all these years.

"I wanted to let him surprise you," Zeb said. "I figured that must be the reason he hasn't called to tell you he's coming home."

The moment had left even Elizabeth speechless. She stood there just staring from Rumer to Zeb and back again.

"I'll run over to the cottage," Zeb said. "And get the printout . . . to show you, so you don't have to worry anymore."

"Thank you," Rumer whispered. "For looking after him."

"I did it for you," he said. "Will you be okay? I'll be right back."

"I'll be fine," Rumer said evenly, turning toward Elizabeth. "My sister and I have something we have to say to each other."

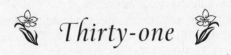# *Thirty-one*

"YOU'RE NOT GOING to break them up," Rumer said softly now, stepping toward her sister.

"Excuse me?"

"You did that to me and Zeb back when we were their age."

"You know, I've had about enough of Hubbard's Point to last me the rest of my life," Elizabeth said, snatching her shawl.

Rumer grabbed her wrist. Her pulse racing, she pulled her sister back.

"That summer," she said, feeling as if she'd been punched in the gut. "Before you did *Romeo and Juliet* at the Lark Theater . . . before you lost your pin and Zeb found it . . ."

"What about it?"

"He and I were falling in love," Rumer said.

"So much so, he married me!"

"You saw it," Rumer said. "You read the notes we were leaving for each other at Foley's; I know, Elizabeth—don't pretend you don't know what I'm talking about—I was sitting right there, and you mentioned them. You saw what he wrote to me, and you knew that everything was changing between us."

"You've lost your mind."

"Something clicked," Rumer began, her head throbbing. She felt a tremendous whoosh inside, as if her body contained a tornado. She wanted to grab Elizabeth's hair and yank, just whirl her around like a small object in the funnel's path.

"What do you mean, something clicked?"

"Just a few minutes ago, when you were speaking about Quinn and Michael. It's what the young people around here do, isn't it, Zee? Leave each other love notes in the drawer."

"So what?"

"You reminded me of that day when you and I were sitting there and you read what he had written."

"I don't remember. . . ."

"We were falling in love," Rumer said. The words came spilling out. "I was with him, he was with me . . . everything was changing. We were about to lose our virginities to each other."

"That's a detail I didn't need to hear."

"Well, it didn't happen," Rumer said, the feelings surging up—old, violent, unbearable grief for the love she had lost. "You knew it; you could feel it—and I think you decided to do something about it."

"I have no idea what you're talking about!"

"Yes, you do," Rumer said sharply. "Because I told you. We were so close back then. You knew all the boys I liked; I told you everything."

"You were madly in love with Zeb your whole life," Elizabeth said. "Like a little puppy dog—what was I supposed to do about it?"

"We were kids," Rumer screeched. " 'Puppy dogs' together. But we were growing up; everything was changing. We'd been best friends, but we loved each other! You hear me, Elizabeth?"

"Love?" Elizabeth asked, raising her eyes as if she thought it was laughable. "You and Zeb?"

Rumer stepped forward, the force inside taking her over, a band of pain constricting her heart, her head, and she raised her hand and slapped her sister. The sound was like a crack of thunder filling the room. Elizabeth cried out, palm against her cheek.

"How dare you?" she screamed, twisting her hands in Rumer's hair. "How dare you hit me?"

"You deserve it," Rumer said, pushing her back with a hard shove. "For laughing about me and Zeb. And for everything you did."

"What's wrong with you?" Elizabeth asked, tears pooling in her eyes as she sprawled onto the blue chair.

Rumer stood back. Her body was buzzing with energy, with everything she had held inside for so many years—the fury, hatred, grief, sorrow. It had all come to rest right here, where it had all started so long ago. Had she really done it—slapped her sister across the face? Her palm stung to prove she had.

Slowly, as if sleepwalking, she went into the kitchen. Removing a clean cloth from the dry sink, she ran it under cold water. Then, returning to the living room, she handed it to her sister. Without looking, Elizabeth accepted the cloth and pressed it against her bright red cheek.

"He was our next-door neighbor," Elizabeth said, softening her tone as if she were spinning back in time. "Over the years, he had crushes on both of us. On you one summer, me the next. Remember how he fell off the roof trying to see me through the window? You were right there to watch him do it!"

"He fell off trying to save me," Rumer said.

"I'm sure you loved him," Elizabeth said, pressing on. "I don't doubt it. In fact, my heart has always ached for you. It really has, Rumer. Because I know how much it hurt to see us—Zeb and me—together."

Rumer closed her eyes.

"My drinking didn't help. I was on a crash course, taking everything in my way. I'm sure I could have been more sensitive to you. Maybe, if I'd been sober back then, I wouldn't have gone after Zeb in the first place. I would have recognized how you felt about him and just let him go."

"Just like that," Rumer said.

"Yes. Why not?"

Rumer tried to breathe steadily. No matter how her sister was trying to justify what had happened, Rumer knew it was real, and it had torn her apart.

"The drawer," she said quietly.

"Oh, so we're back to Foley's again?" Elizabeth asked, bringing her hand down hard on the table.

"Because that's where it started."

"Notes left in a drawer," Elizabeth said derisively. "In a stupid drawer."

"At first, when we were eighteen, nineteen, they were the best Zeb and I could do . . . we were both too shy to say those things face-to-face. But when you saw the way he wrote to me, you decided to go after him yourself. You read his words, and you set your cap for him. It took a while, but you saw your moment."

"Don't be an idiot—even if I did, if your great love for each other was so great, don't you think it would have survived my *flirting* with him? Whether I did that or not, even if we did get together in New York that time, or whatever you're saying happened—couldn't you have talked about it and straightened everything out?"

Rumer closed her eyes, thinking back. It had been the spring equinox . . . late March. While Zeb was at the Indian Grave, Rumer had been waiting to hear from him. She had come home from college—she would have done anything.

And Elizabeth was spending her last two days at home before starting previews of *Romeo and Juliet*. For years, Rumer had tormented herself with the question: If she and Zeb had met as planned, would he and

Elizabeth have gotten together? Rumer had messed up—left Zeb waiting and feeling so humiliated, he couldn't look her in the eye.

"What I want to know is," Rumer said, "did you really love him at all? Or was it just so I couldn't have him?"

"That's a terrible thing to say. I always loved you."

"As long as I was less than you," Rumer said clearly. "Not as pretty, not as successful, just a veterinarian—not an actress, taking care of animals instead of starring in *Romeo and Juliet.* . . ."

"Think what you want," Elizabeth said, shrugging.

"Just tell me," Rumer said. She felt frantic, the rage building again. It gathered force, like a wave. She felt it crashing toward shore, the crest curling, the edge silver and knife sharp.

And then, suddenly, the wave broke. She got it: She understood. This conversation was no longer about her and Zeb; it was about Rumer and Elizabeth. Rumer felt herself let go as stinging tears sprang to her eyes.

Taking a deep breath, she reached for her sister's hand. Trembling, her own fingers laced with Zee's. The sisters' eyes met and held. Rumer's heart raced as she stared into Elizabeth's beautiful wide brown eyes— they flickered, looking away. Up, down, out to sea.

"You and I were so close," Elizabeth said. "You say that I was beautiful, I was the actress. . . ."

"You were."

"But you were the one, Rumer. Mom and Dad were so proud of you— all your achievements. Every day a new award. Remember how Miss Conway used to give out gold stars for excellence?"

Rumer nodded, recalling.

"Well, every day you'd come home with papers covered with gold stars. Mom would hang them on the refrigerator till there wasn't any more room. Dad would hang them on his bulletin board. Stars everywhere . . ."

Rumer blushed, picturing her gold stars. It had felt so good to make her parents proud; she had never known that it bothered her sister.

"I wanted stars too," Elizabeth said.

"So you became one."

"Who cared about being pretty? I'd stare in the mirror and wish I were smarter—then I'd be as good as you. Sometimes I felt like the stepmother in *Snow White.* You were natural—no makeup, never time to fix your hair . . . everyone loved you."

"They loved you too."

"I knew Zeb had a crush on me," Elizabeth said quietly. "Over the years, I could see it coming up. I was the older girl next door; he thought it was sexy. I'd catch him watching me through the window . . . I'd take my time putting on my bra. Sometimes I wouldn't put it on at all. You were his little friend—you had the paper route together, you went crabbing, childish pastimes. . . ."

"But our feelings were real," Rumer said.

"You were inseparable—you left me out of everything. Maybe I was jealous—not of you, but of *him*. Zeb's hold over you."

"I loved him."

"I know you did." Raising her eyes, Elizabeth tried to smile. "I thought—I could have this one thing Rumer doesn't."

"Zeb?" Rumer asked, feeling her stomach drop out, hearing this admission.

Her sister nodded. "Not just him, but his adoration. You know? In a way you didn't have it. But then . . ."

"That last spring," Rumer whispered.

Elizabeth shrugged, her face twisted. "I felt it changing. The things you told me, and—the way I saw him look at you. In a new way. The way I'd seen him look at me over the years. And his letters in the drawer . . ."

Rumer waited, holding her breath.

"I'd been in the theater for a couple of years by then. Living in New York . . . I knew about all the jerks in the world. There was this producer . . . he was married, and we had an affair." She glanced up as if to gauge her sister's shock. "I know—you would never have done that."

Rumer just listened, knowing that her sister was right, that she never would.

"I thought—he'll leave his wife to marry me. We'll have babies; we'll start a stage company; we'll live happily ever after. He didn't leave her . . . none of them did."

"None of them?"

"He wasn't the last producer . . . or the last married man. Eventually, I got the role as Juliet. I was empty inside—a big metal drum. I couldn't imagine what reserves I'd find for Juliet. To act such love and passion— when my heart was dead."

"But you were brilliant," Rumer said.

"I'm an actor," Elizabeth said. "I pulled it out of somewhere. . . . I conjured up a vision of Juliet—a modern-day real-life Juliet who stood on her balcony and waited for Romeo—and made her part of myself. You want to know who inspired that vision?"

"Who?"

"You," Elizabeth said.

Rumer couldn't speak, staring at her sister.

"Standing on the screened porch, waiting for Zeb. Not just that year, but all our lives. You were this young girl just *inhabited* by love for the boy next door. You lived and breathed it. . . ."

"I did," Rumer whispered.

Elizabeth nodded, tears rolling down her cheeks. Remorse creased her forehead, and she reached for Rumer's hand. "I've carried this for a long time," she said. "This particular secret."

"You can tell me," Rumer said. "I want you to."

"That night in New York . . . I never thought we'd get together. I knew he was in love with you. He sat through my performance, watched you leave. I swear, all he could think of was calling you. But then, that thing with the pin . . ."

"Mom's lighthouse?"

"Yes," Elizabeth said. "You're wrong about what you think—I didn't plant it there. It just fell off. Amazing, I know. The clasp was broken, and it slipped off on the corner of Great Jones and Lafayette . . . by the time we walked back, it was nearly hidden under a crumpled-up candy wrapper. I was so afraid, all through the performance, that I'd never see it again. You were gone, and Zeb was walking me home."

"And it was still there," Rumer said.

"Yes. So much luck," Elizabeth said, her voice catching. "I tripped as I came off the curb: What are the odds? That I would happen to trip on that curb, at that moment . . . with Zeb right there? Typical actor's legend material . . . especially because I'd just given the performance of my life. Inspired by my little sister, Juliet to Zeb's Romeo."

Rumer couldn't speak; she could see that Elizabeth was still enthralled by the enormity of coincidence.

"When Zeb picked up the pin, I threw my arms around him and let him think I owed him everything: my luck, my talent, my place in the theater . . . and I made him believe it, Rumer. I swear, I behaved as if the fates had thrown down thunderbolts. Perhaps they did—who knows? It *was* quite incredible. I convinced him it was a great miracle, a moment of truth that would go down in the history books of the American theater."

"That was the night you . . ." Rumer whispered.

"We got started," Elizabeth said bitterly.

"Started with a moment of truth . . ." Rumer trailed off. "Him finding your pin."

"Yes, I suppose you're right," Elizabeth said, staring into Rumer's eyes. "But before that truth there was something else. In a way, a bigger way, Zeb and I started with a lie. . . ."

"What lie?"

Elizabeth closed her eyes and finally, slowly, let out a sigh so filled with pain that Rumer felt it in her own bones. Rumer's handprint still showed on her cheek, hot and red.

"Come with me," Elizabeth said finally, rising and taking her sister by the hand. "There's something I want to show you."

❧

The sisters went into the garage and pulled out their bikes. Elizabeth hadn't ridden hers—or any bicycle at all—in many years. They pedaled off, down Cresthill Road, out of the Point's cul-de-sac. Fragrance filled the night air: jasmine, honeysuckle, roses, pine, and salt. Elizabeth, who owned a large house on the beach in Malibu, knew that she had the Atlantic Ocean in her blood, that she was herself tonight in a way she hadn't been in years.

When they hit the winding hill behind the tennis courts, Rumer put her head down to achieve maximum speed. Zee knew the moment this would happen—she and her sister had ridden this route perhaps a thousand times. They slowed at the stop sign, curved around Rainbow's End—the cottage with the most beautiful gardens—and through the sandy parking lot.

Pebbles crunched beneath their tires. Zee pedaled harder, pulling away from her sister. Although this was the long way to their destination, she wanted to smell the marsh—the rich, thick, decaying smell of low tide—and the sea—fresh, bright, salty, full of life.

Rumer followed, staying close, her front wheel drawing even with Elizabeth's back one. With Zeb's constellations blazing overhead, the sisters swerved ahead of and behind each other, crisscrossing and zigzagging in a bike-riding ballet they remembered from long ago. Elizabeth had a lump in her throat, remembering how easy it had been to get Rumer to follow her, to do anything she ever said.

You'll have only one sister.

How true it was, Zee thought, and how badly she had fouled it up. In all these years, how often had she wished she could call Rumer? With the happy news that followed good notices, the time she had worried about a mammogram, all the little things Michael had said and done.

Elizabeth's throat closed tighter, knowing that she had kept Michael away. He could have spent summers here in this magical place, but her guilt had made her keep him from his aunt. As they rode closer to Foley's Store, Elizabeth knew that her moment was here—that no matter how Rumer reacted, Elizabeth would soon be free. She had paid a great price for the relief she would get tonight.

The store was right in the middle of Hubbard's Point. Cottages spread out from it on all sides—to boundaries formed by the beach, the railroad tracks, the marsh, and the cove. The cemetery, where their mother and Zeb's parents were buried, lay just north, around the bend. They parked their bikes—no need to lock them here. Silently asking their mother's forgiveness, Elizabeth took Rumer's hand and walked her up the cement stairs.

"Remember when you were little," Elizabeth said, "and I'd take you here to buy penny candy?"

"You held my hand then too," Rumer said.

They walked past the single checkout counter—with a summer girl, probably one of their friends' daughters, reading a magazine as she waited for customers. A few people wandered the aisles, baskets on their arms. The soda fountain was filled with kids, and Elizabeth remembered sitting there with her friends. The walls were stained from decades of salt air; the wide-board floors were scuffed and splintered from generations of Hubbard's Point feet.

A few people noticed her. She heard them whisper, saw them tug their companions' sleeves, try to point discreetly. Her heart hurt: She was famous. Her wish had come true, made all those years ago in the shadow of her little sister's award-winning school papers: Elizabeth was a star.

"What do you want to show me?" Rumer asked.

"Oh, I think you know," Zee said softly.

Still holding her sister's hand, she led her to the table with the drawer in the middle. Pulling out one chair for her sister, Elizabeth sat beside her. Her breathing was hard, as if she'd just run a marathon. The ceiling fan turned overhead, and wisps of fog came through the open window.

What if it wasn't here? Twenty years had passed. What if an employee had swept it away long ago? Or what if the owners had put down tile or linoleum? Somehow Elizabeth had known that none of those things would have occurred. Nothing had changed at Hubbard's Point in so long, she knew what she would find.

Rumer opened the drawer and absently shuffled through the papers inside as if magically—after all this time—she would find the note Zeb had left for her. It was almost impossible: Layers and layers, years and years of notes had been added, taken away, sifted, rearranged. Many of the oldest notes had found their way into scrapbooks or photo albums; the newest belonged to kids the ages of Michael and Quinn.

"It's not there," Zee said.

"What's not?" Rumer said, still not getting it.

"You never even knew it existed, did you?"

Rumer stared at her, an expression of shock in her eyes. Elizabeth's heart pounded; her blood scalded her veins. She had never felt this nervous, not on any opening night in her life.

"This . . ." Elizabeth whispered. Reaching down beneath the scarred oak table, she worked her fingers under the floorboard. It had been loose then, two decades ago, and it was loose now. Mr. Foley still hadn't gotten around to banging in a nail to secure the plank. Her hand shaking, Elizabeth felt around until she felt the wadded-up paper.

Without reading it, she passed it across the table to Rumer.

At first sight, Rumer's eyes filled with tears.

"I found it by mistake," Elizabeth said, her voice low. "I'd come here by myself to have tea and think about the play . . . when I opened the drawer, I recognized his handwriting. And I read the note."

"Zeb's last note to me," Rumer whispered. "He told me he'd written one. . . ."

"I'm sorry, so sorry," Elizabeth said.

She watched her sister cry, reading the words he had written so many summers ago; the words had haunted Elizabeth all this time, and she knew them by heart:

> *Rue,*
> *Will you meet me tonight at eight? I think you know the place—*
> *the Indian Grave. I'm bringing my tent and I'll set it up in the little*
> *valley. We'll be safe there—together. I can't wait to see you.*
>
> *Zeb*

"You found it, and you hid it," Rumer said.

"Yes," Elizabeth murmured. But when she looked up, to her amazement, her sister's eyes were shining. They were filled with pain, but over it all Elizabeth saw sparks of old love. The way they had always been— sharing magic, secrets, and the love of two beach girls who would have many friends but only one sister.

"I'm sorry, Rumer," she said.

Rumer nodded. Her gaze fell to the note, and she read it again.

"I used to tell myself it shouldn't make a difference. If you two were really meant to be together, you would find a way. I didn't think it would honestly matter in the long run."

"Everything matters," Rumer said. "Everything adds up."

"What do you mean?"

"Life, Elizabeth. I've wondered about this forever—not just the note. All of it—why life turned out the way it did. Every single thing that happens in it counts. This counts, Elizabeth."

"This?"

"The fact that you're showing me now. That you've given me back the note." Rumer took her hand. "Thank you."

"Our lives would have been different, you know," Elizabeth said, wiping her eyes. "You would have married Zeb, not me."

"We'll never know. Don't think about it anymore," Rumer said, her voice cracking as she reached across the table. "I love you, Elizabeth. You're my only sister. If you hadn't married Zeb, there would be no Michael . . . I fell in love with Michael the minute I laid eyes on him . . . he has your smile and his father's eyes."

"He's the best thing Zeb and I ever did together," Elizabeth said.

Rumer lowered her eyes, nodding.

"You're a good aunt to him, Rumer. Take good care of him till summer's over."

"What do you mean? You're just across the river, in Evesham. . . ."

Elizabeth shook her head. "I'm going home. To L.A."

"Connecticut's your home too."

"Not anymore. It's too hard . . . too much water under the bridge."

"I don't want it to be," Rumer said, frowning. "I don't want to drive you away."

"You're not. I just have to go."

Elizabeth pushed back her chair to leave, and Rumer stood too. Bowing her head, Elizabeth let the sorrow wash over her. Not because she regretted losing Zeb, but because she had never loved him enough in the first place. She thought of the years he and Rumer had lost. The years she had lost with her sister. She had been in so many plays and movies about complicated women—fearful at heart but evil in deed. It hit her like a ton of bricks, standing right there in Foley's, that she was one of those women.

"Elizabeth, I love you," Rumer whispered.

"I don't deserve it."

"After today you do," Rumer said, still holding the yellowed note. She was smiling and crying at the same time. "I feel as if you've just handed me back my life. Thank you."

"Oh, my little sister," Elizabeth said, gulping on a sob because Rumer was so willing to forgive and because Elizabeth knew that when she left Hubbard's Point that night, she was never coming back.

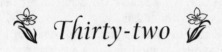

Thirty-two

SIXTUS LARKIN MISSED seeing his two daughters together by twelve hours. Just as Elizabeth was driving out of Hubbard's Point on her way to pack up her things and leave Evesham, Sixtus was sailing the *Clarissa* around Brenton Point in Newport, Rhode Island.

Zeb tracked him the whole way. Via transmitter, he was able to register Sixtus's position on a chart on his laptop, watch as the green speck blipped closer and closer. Michael, Quinn, and Rumer sat with him, quietly reassured by the "beep-beep-beep" that was Sixtus Larkin returning home.

Although Elizabeth had offered no explanation for her sudden departure, Zeb had not expected one. He was used to the impetuous comings and goings of his ex-wife; it was Michael he was worried about.

"Didn't she say anything?" he asked Rumer the next morning when everyone had gathered to wait for Sixtus and to talk about the kids' plans. He kept his arm around her and held her very close. Once, on a sudden impulse and in spite of the kids standing there, he kissed the back of her head.

"She said to watch out for Michael," Rumer said, keeping quiet about what had gone on between her and Elizabeth.

"What else?"

"I'll tell you, Zeb, I really will," Rumer said, reaching for his hand. "She was my sister even before I knew you. We go back so far, so strong, I sometimes forget that."

"And you want to hold on to it for a while?"

Rumer nodded. Her clear eyes, her slim shoulders, the scent of her hair, all filled Zeb with a sense of longing that rattled his bones and made him feel drunk on the day.

"It was good," Zeb said, shaking himself out of it, "that your mother came for your birthday."

"Yeah," Michael said, sitting beside Quinn.

"I was embarrassed," Quinn said. "Reading my Juliet lines in front of such a famous actress."

"You were better," Michael said.

"No," Quinn said. "She was."

"Do you think she left because we want to get married?" Michael asked, and Zeb looked over at Rumer.

Part of him wanted to give his son every ounce of blessing he could muster—reach into the sky and bring down the sun, moon, and stars—to ensure that he and Quinn would have a happy life together from now on, save the long years that Zeb himself and Rumer had wasted. When time interfered, people made separate lives—sometimes on two different coasts. But just because their hearts were finally ready to be together didn't mean that practicalities would allow it.

But another part of him didn't want Michael to sell himself short— what if he decided he wanted to study something that would take him far away from Quinn? Or what if he learned—next week, next year—that he wasn't ready to settle down with one woman, that he wanted to see the world by himself first?

Or what if Quinn did?

Clearing his throat, trying to decide what to say, he watched Rumer cross the small room and sit down between the two kids. She smiled, looking from one to the other, and then across the room at Zeb. The sight of her made his blood boil. He wasn't letting her go ever again. This was it for him and Rumer Larkin. Whether she knew it or not, she was his from this day onward.

"I'm your aunt," she said to Michael, "and your friend," she said to Quinn.

"For my whole life," Quinn said.

"Are you going to try to talk us out of this?" Michael asked. "Because you can't."

"Have you spoken to Dana and Sam?" Rumer asked them.

"Not yet," Michael said defiantly. "I'm going to ask for her hand in marriage though."

"And what do you think they'll say?" Zeb asked.

"Believe it or not," Quinn said sagely, without wavering, "they will say yes."

"Do you think so?" Rumer asked, still smiling, taking Quinn's hand.

Quinn nodded. Her brow was wrinkled, and she had started to frown. Tears were just behind her eyes; she blinked to keep them back.

"They want me to be happy," she whispered huskily.

"I want them to know how much I love her," Michael said.

Zeb tried to breathe. There were times when he could hardly believe that this was his son. How strongly Michael believed in himself, in his love for this young woman! Where had he gotten this much confidence and courage?

Zeb thought back on the last year, the months, the events in space. He thought of exploding stars releasing energy so destructive that all that was left in the end was a black hole. A vortex, a huge cosmic whirlpool, sucking everything into nothingness. That was how Zeb had lived his life. His marriage to Elizabeth had been so wrong, so apocalyptically wrong, he had lived his life like a black hole. Without Rumer, nothing else had much mattered.

Zeb wasn't going back into space. He wasn't taking off again—not for anything. He was a grown man, and it had taken him until now to know what he wanted from life, that all that really mattered was right here— Rumer and Michael. His dreams of the sky were still there, and always would be. But he needed to stay here, near Rumer, to find them.

"Can I tell you a story?" Rumer asked.

"As long as you don't try to talk us out of it," Michael challenged.

"When I was very young, younger than you are now," Rumer said, "I fell in love with a boy here at Hubbard's Point."

Zeb leaned against the doorjamb leading to the screened porch. The laptop's blue screen beeped intermittently, indicating that Sixtus was getting closer—past Napatree Point at Watch Hill, along Fishers Island, past Ledge Light. . . .

"We thought it never could end . . ." Rumer said, but she had to stop to gather herself together. Her eyes glittered, looking back and forth between the kids. "And I wish I could tell you that it never did. . . ."

"It did?" Quinn asked.

Rumer nodded, careful not to look at Zeb.

"I thought this was going to be a story with a moral," Michael said, "telling us that if it's meant to be, it will last forever."

"You know the story," Rumer said softly, taking her nephew's hand in her free one, "because that's the moral."

"Which was?" Zeb asked, needing to hear.

"Which was that our love was there the whole time."

"But you stopped being friends?" Quinn asked.

"We each had things to do. Important things—going to school, finding out that we wanted to go further, to get graduate degrees . . . we had to get jobs. . . ."

"One of you had to get married," Quinn said. "And have a wonderful son . . ." Her eyes flicked to Zeb.

"I don't want you to marry someone else," Michael said, looking scared.

"Or you . . ."

"When you close your eyes," Quinn said, staring at Rumer, "and look into the future . . . thinking about me and Michael . . . what do you see?"

"She's not Hecate," Michael said.

"I know," Quinn said. "But I trust her. . . ."

Closing her eyes, Rumer sat very still, her hands balanced on her knees.

"Well," she said. "I see you holding hands."

"Are we married?" Quinn asked. "Have we been together this whole time?"

Rumer gave a slight shrug. "I don't know, Quinn. I don't have that sort of gift. But I definitely see you together—it's not a big mystery. It's just that anyone can see you love each other."

"You're not clairvoyant?" Michael asked.

"No."

"Was your mother?" Quinn asked.

"Not really," Rumer said. "She was sensitive. She saw the unicorn, and she believed in ghosts . . . but she couldn't really see the future."

"Then how did she know, when you were a little girl, that you would be together with Zeb—Mr. Mayhew?" Quinn asked.

"Excuse me?" Rumer asked.

"Your pin," Quinn said quietly with deep love in her blue eyes. "That's the secret that makes it different from your sister's. Your mother knew that you belonged with Zeb."

"How can you tell?" Rumer asked, her voice shaking as if she knew at some deep level that Quinn was right. Hand trembling, she reached up to her lapel and started to undo the clasp.

"Elizabeth's lighthouse was plain," Quinn said, examining the tiny gold nugget rocks, distinct bricks, deeply scored windows, and light lens. "It was just the lighthouse itself. . . ."

"What makes mine different?" Rumer asked. "I still can't see—"

"Look in the wall," Quinn said, pointing. "Just below the top window."

"It's just tiny bricks," Rumer said. "Laid one on top of each other."

"With mortar between them," Zeb said, beginning to see. "All made of gold—the scoring is deeper to show where the cement's supposed to be."

"Right there," Quinn said, tracing several bricks whose mortar seemed to be deeper, darker.

"Oh, my God," Rumer said with a little cry.

"It says something . . ." Michael said.

"Read it," Quinn said. "Two letters . . ."

"Z-R," Rumer said, her voice cracking. "Zeb and Rumer."

"Your mother knew," Quinn said. "From the time you were very young, when she had the pins made, that you would be with Zeb."

"We weren't fooling anyone except ourselves," Zeb said, holding Rumer's hand and kissing it. This was the moment—he felt it deep inside, and he read it in her straight posture, the quiet certainty in her blue eyes.

"And this is supposed to convince us we should wait?" Michael asked. "Because it's not doing a very good job."

"I get their point," Quinn whispered, holding his hands. "Your aunt just looked into our future, and she can't imagine us not together—like her mother with her and Zeb. And guess what? The most convincing thing of all?"

"What?" Michael asked, frowning as he gazed into her eyes.

"They're together, Michael. We can't deny that—"

Michael couldn't answer. Zeb watched him clamp down, not giving an inch. *Fight for it*, Zeb half wanted to say. *Don't give up. Don't let go of her even for a minute.*

"How are you as a carpenter?" Zeb asked.

"Not bad," Michael said, scowling as if he couldn't believe how badly his father had missed the point.

"I hear you did a good job building a barn at your mother's house."

"It was a tack room," Michael said. "That we added onto her stable. That's all. But, yeah, I helped."

"How would you like to build your aunt a barn?" Zeb asked. He felt Rumer's eyes on him, shining with tears.

"What do you mean?" Michael asked. "When?"

"This week. Right now. She needs a place to put Blue."

"But I still have school—" Michael said, frowning.

"After school. You can help me," Zeb said. "Because that's what I'll be doing. Building a barn for Blue. Right by your aunt's office, in the field where Old Paint's barn used to stand."

"Zeb," Rumer said. She moved closer. She was crying, and she rubbed her eyes as if she thought she might be dreaming. "What about California?"

"We're not going," Zeb said, pulling her into his arms right in front of the kids, not caring about anything except that they loved each other, that she understand that he'd do anything for her.

"What about your new lab?"

"Someone else will run it. I'll find a place out here. Don't worry. That's my past," Zeb said, his lips nearly touching hers.

"And this is our future?" Rumer asked.

Zeb looked around. The house was filled with old things: faded slip-covers, wicker warped by years of salt air, black-and-white photographs of both families, baskets of shells gathered when the girls were small. The air swarmed with ghosts. Memories bounced off the walls. He pictured the glass and chrome and stainless steel of the brand-new research center on the California coast, and it drifted straight away.

"Yes," Zeb said, lifting Rumer right off the floor into his arms. "This is our future."

❧

By the time Sixtus had taken his first hot shower in a week and had dinner with Rumer, the sun had made its day's transit and started down over the trees beyond the golden marsh. It was dark now, but he still felt the shock he'd experienced upon seeing what the new neighbors had done to the property next door.

"Home again," he said, sitting beside her on a bench in the kitchen.

"I can't believe you're here, Dad," Rumer said. "Instead of halfway to Galway."

"Well, neither can I. This isn't quite the way Clarissa and I planned our sabbatical."

"What happened?"

"Ah, change of heart," he said. "Guess I got homesick."

He watched as Rumer adjusted the baby rabbit—the latest to be rescued from the yard—in her hand, trying to get it to take more formula. The sight gave him a pang—Rumer was always taking care of something. He shifted in his chair. His joints ached. His bones creaked. But he was awash with the joy of being home, of being with his daughter.

"Elizabeth was here," Rumer said, her voice low and steady.

"I know. Michael told me. You think Elizabeth might have mentioned it to me herself."

"She made the decision to come on the spur of the moment."

"After I told her about Zeb," Sixtus said, feeling sad. The byzantine workings of his eldest daughter's mind never failed to dismay him.

"Well, she and I had some things to work out," Rumer said.

"Ahhh," Sixtus said.

"What is it, Dad?" Rumer asked, looking worried.

"Nothing," he said, rubbing his eyes. "Just tired from my trip."

"Was your trip okay?" she asked. "Was it everything you hoped?"

"In a way, more," he said. "Which is why, perhaps, I decided not to continue."

"I thought you always wanted to sail across the Atlantic. . . ."

Sixtus smiled, watching the way Rumer finished feeding one infant rabbit, let it down on the floor, and walked out to the hutch for the other.

"Yes. But I wanted to sail home more. I'm gone just a couple of weeks," he said, gesturing, "and my house is overrun by rabbits."

"I'm sorry, Dad," Rumer said, smiling. "Zeb and I rescued them from the house next door. Everything is changing so fast. I hate to think of you coming home to it all."

"They clear-cut the lot," Sixtus said. "Steering home, into the cove, I looked for that tall, tall pine, and it wasn't there. I've navigated by that tree for thirty years, from the time it had grown taller than any other. . . ."

"It's all going to change," she said. "On Tuesday, the day after Labor Day."

Sixtus felt the bottom drop out of his stomach. Like sailing through high seas, he felt as if he'd just fallen off a ten-foot wave. "It's too much," he said. "Next, you'll be telling me you're moving back to California with Zeb."

"We love each other, Dad. We always have, but it took us until now to realize that it's more alive than ever. It's not going away."

"No, of course it's not. . . ."

"I can't leave you, Dad," she said. "Or the Point."

Sixtus swallowed. His hand was shaking too much to reach for hers—if he even tried, he'd blow the whole thing—of course she had to go. So he clasped his own wrist to hold it steady and took a deep breath. "Oh, but you have to," he said in a low, deep voice. "You can't lose each other a second time."

"I'm not leaving."

She was talking about sacrifice, Sixtus thought. His beloved daughter wanted to give up her own happiness in favor of staying here, looking after him. Edward, her father, her animals . . . When would she be happy? When he was dead? When all the *Dames de la Roche* were gone?

He thought of his own mother, of the sacrifices she had made for Sixtus and his brother. She had held on so tight—to her sons, the babies, her livelihood, everyone's well-being but her own. It had eventually destroyed her . . . Sixtus knew, with all his heart, what he had to do.

Touching Rumer's shoulder, he led her outside. They stood in their yard under the canopy of summer stars. A whippoorwill called from down the hill, across the marsh, and locusts rasped in the oak trees.

"Do you trust your mother?" Sixtus asked after a moment.

Rumer looked up, tried to smile. "Of course."

"Then listen to her."

"Dad . . . she's gone."

"Sweetheart, if you really love this place the way you say you do—if you really think it's the place of love, spirits, and eternity that you claim to—then you know your mother is right here. Right now, Rumer! Tell me what you think she's saying."

"That I should be with Zeb . . ."

"Ahh, Clarissa," Sixtus whispered.

"Right here, Dad. Zeb knows it too. He's building me a barn—right in the meadow beside my office. He's having plans drawn up; he's already ordered the wood. He and Michael are going to build it together."

"Zeb's staying? He doesn't want you to go away with him?"

"No, Dad. We couldn't. This is our place."

"After all this time," Sixtus said, amazed at the magic of life.

"I want to be with him, Dad," Rumer said. "It's what I've always wanted."

"Dreams need to come true," Sixtus said, "when you've been dreaming them all this time. . . ."

"I have," she said.

Sixtus nodded. They stood quietly on the rocky ledge at the top of their yard. Sixtus had come to this home—the place of Clarissa's childhood—nearly four decades ago. She had welcomed him, made him feel like a part of the place from his very first day.

"Do you know how much I love it here?" Rumer whispered.

"I think I do," he said. "I've watched you nearly every day of your life."

"I wish Elizabeth could feel the same way."

Sixtus took a deep breath. Summer was ending, but he had the fall—with leaves to rake and pumpkins to carve. Then winter, with dustings of snow to cover the yards and trees and rocks and beach. Then spring, when it would be time to clean out the gardens and sand and paint the *Clarissa*, get it ready for another season of sailing. There was all that time for him to think about what he had seen and felt in Canada, for him to reach out to Elizabeth, love her a little more. The rhythm of Hubbard's Point would get him through it all.

"Forgive her, Rumer," he said softly, reaching out to touch his daughter's face.

"I already have, Dad," she said.

Sixtus felt a lump in his throat. "That's good," he said. "Forgiving your sister will set you free. Now—let me be, will you? I had a long, hard voyage, and I'm glad to be home."

"I'm glad you are."

"Do you have plans?"

"To meet Zeb," she said. "We have a long overdue date tonight. . . ."

"Ahhh. That's good," Sixtus said. "Very good."

"Is there anything I can get you before I go?"

"Just a hug and a kiss, Rumer," he said. "Like when you were my little girl."

"I still am," she whispered as she put her arms around him. She was such a good person; she was patient. She had waited all these years to be with the man she'd always loved, and she'd made an amazing life for herself.

Sixtus wished his mother could know Rumer. His chest filled with pride.

Standing on the rock, Sixtus looked up at the stars and reached into the sky. He closed his eyes and thought of Clarissa, and he pulled her down against his chest, straight into his heart. Clutching his wife, he stood very still. He gave thanks for everything: his family, his love, the fact that he had made it safely home. Eyes shut tight, he saw meteors streaking through the purple-black sky. The stars were in motion tonight.

Joints aching, not caring, Sixtus Larkin began to move. The music of the spheres propelled him. Gently holding his wife, feet gliding over the gray rocks of their hilltop in Hubbard's Point, they danced beneath the dark star-filled sky.

Thirty-three

To get to the Indian Grave, Rumer crossed the beach. The night was clear, with just the smallest hint of fall: a chill lay just beneath the soft breeze. Her feet made footprints in the wet sand, and the waves washed them away. Her father's words played in her head, making her rush faster—she had to see Zeb. They had made this plan that morning, but it had been twenty years coming.

The water felt warm. It frothed around her ankles, and Rumer thought of a nighttime swim she and Zeb had taken when they were sixteen. The sea had surrounded their bodies, exciting and scary in the dark, holding them afloat, side by side. Treading water, their feet had brushed each other, and they had held hands and looked into each other's eyes as they stayed afloat.

Rumer had felt the water streaming around her body, the intermittent bump of Zeb's knees and thighs against hers. Their hands were clasped at the surface, and small waves broke around them, filling their eyes and mouths with water.

The Wickland Rock Light beam had passed over their heads, and Rumer had thought of her ancestor dying in a shipwreck just a mile away. She had wondered whether the captain had held Elisabeth's hands, whether they had held hands and tried to help each other to shore.

"If this were a shipwreck," she had said to Zeb, her eyes stinging with saltwater, "I'd save your life."

"Funny you should say that," he said, gripping her hands harder, "because I'd save yours first."

"Good thing I know lifesaving," she said, "because I'd get you in a rescue hold and pull you to shore."

"Like this?" he asked, putting his arm around her neck and in a sidestroke swimming them both to shore. Underwater, a big fish scraped her leg, and she shrieked. But Zeb didn't let her go—he just kept swimming till he had her safely on the sand.

Hurrying down the beach, Rumer remembered how it had felt to be held by him. Playing around, it had always been so easy to touch each other. Life at the beach had always been so physical—swimming, climbing trees, playing football. Zeb was always giving her a boost, carrying her down the sand, pulling her through the water.

Swimming that night, had he thought of kissing her? She had wanted him to. A week later, the kiss had come to pass, and it had turned her inside out.

But that leap from being best friends to something more had been more daunting than any big fish swimming past in the deep darkness. Rumer hurried now, knowing that Zeb was—finally—waiting for her up ahead.

In pitch darkness she climbed the steep path by the fallen tree, past the ruins of Fish Hill, through dense oak woods, and right across the culvert in the deepest and swampiest creek in the marsh.

She had brought a flashlight. It dipped and bobbed as she walked along the sandy trail, trying to avoid the thickest hanging vines and drooping branches. Mosquitoes seemed attracted to the flashlight's beam, and they hovered in front of her like a filmy and buzzing gray cloud.

Out at sea, just past the breakwater, the more powerful beam of the Wickland Rock Light swept the sky. Back and forth, keeping ships on course. Overhead, stars hung in the late summer sky, the constellations ready to march forward through September, into autumn.

Spiders had spun their webs everywhere: connected to branches, tall grass, cattails, and a dead tree. Rumer felt the silk across her nose and lips, hands and shins. Wiping them off, they stuck to her fingers. By the time she reached Zeb, standing on the small rise where the Indian was buried, Rumer was laughing.

"Now you know what it's like to be an earth scientist," she said.

"Give me a black hole any day," he said, taking her into his arms.

They kissed, and then stepped back to wipe more spiderwebs from their cheeks. More swamp bugs hummed in their ears. When the lighthouse beam split the sky, it caught a bat zooming through the trees.

"Spooked, Mayhew?" she asked.

"No way, Larkin. This is my turf as much as yours."

"Isn't this romantic?" she asked, steadying herself.

"Yes, Rue. I was just thinking—no wonder we've both suffered so much over the years, missing this the first time around."

"Why do you think all the young lovers of Hubbard's Point have been making tracks here for so many years?" Rumer asked, hearing something slither through the reeds, splashing into the tidal creek.

"Because it's scary," Zeb said, pulling her close, "and it makes people press up against each other."

"I didn't need to be scared to want to do that," Rumer said, tilting her head back and kissing him. They held each other for a long time, ignoring all the buzzing around them, completely lost in how far they had traveled to get to this place.

When they stopped, she stood peering at him in the starlight. Her heart was beating so fast, she felt as if she had swum a mile. Zeb's blond hair was mussed, and his blue eyes were vigilant, as if he were ready—at a moment's notice—to pick her up and carry her away from the mosquitoes or anything else. But it was his T-shirt that endeared him to her most ferociously.

"Camp Courant," she read, shining her flashlight on it. The *Hartford Courant* had sent them each a T-shirt one year, thanking them for being such fine newspaper deliverers. Dark green, emblazoned with the paper's distinctive lettering and an image of enthusiastic children enjoying camp, the shirt was faded and torn.

"You kept it all this time?" she asked.

"I stuck it in a trunk," he said. "And left it in Winnie's garage. Hubbard's Point things that I didn't want to throw away but couldn't quite see taking to California."

"Because you always knew you would come back," she said, touching the frayed, holey green fabric stretched across his chest, brushing his skin underneath.

"I suppose I did," he said.

"I never thought I'd see this shirt again—" she began, but had to stop for a minute and make sure her voice wouldn't break. "Actually, I never thought I'd see *you* again. When Winnie told me you had rented her cottage, I was shocked. I lay awake night after night, wondering what I would say to you when I saw you again."

"You didn't want to see me at all."

"No, I didn't," she agreed.

"So we needed safe topics," Zeb said. "Michael, your father . . ."

"Stars," Rumer said, looking up at the sky. "I thought we'd talk a lot about the Milky Way, and what it was like for you to be up there and look down here."

"Watching you, Rumer," Zeb said. "Flying through space, I was keeping track of you. I used to wonder what you were doing, whether you had met someone new. I'd picture you riding the horse Michael told me you'd gotten, Blue, and that made me think up a new constellation."

"What is it?"

"A girl on a winged horse," Zeb said.

"Like Pegasus . . ."

"Yes," Zeb said. "Only this horse flies very low. He keeps close to the ground, just clearing stone walls and privet hedges. Rabbits can feel the wind in their ears as he passes overhead. The girl loves him. She takes him on amazing adventures—over the sea, across the Wickland Shoal, up to the Indian Grave—and every night she steers him home."

"Where is home?" she asked.

"Hubbard's Point, of course."

Rumer swallowed—of course. The only home she had ever known . . .

"It's changing," she said, feeling a tug in her throat.

"Because of Franklin?" he asked.

She didn't reply, because she couldn't quite trust herself to speak.

She took Zeb's hand, and as if she were the girl steering the star horse on their nightly adventure, she began to lead him across the narrow stream. Marsh grass tickled their legs. Rumer had bare feet, and her toes sank into the soft, warm mud. The ground grew hard, and rocks were everywhere. Making their way up, they held hands.

The Indian Grave stood on top of the hill. Climbing the last few feet, Rumer and Zeb looked down on it. Legend had it that the man buried there had been a member of the Nehantic people. His family had been some of the natives from this beautiful area; his ancestors had hunted and fished here, lived in tepees set up on the Point.

Moved inland to a reservation, the natives had spent less time here by the sea. This man—Uncle Lote, according to the gravestone—had worked for one of the wealthy families at Tomahawk Point. Rumer remembered coming here on a walk with Zeb's mother once; gazing at the grave, she had grown solemn. When Rumer had asked why, Mrs. Mayhew had said because it was sad Uncle Lote had had to work for people who had stolen the land that was rightly his.

"Tad Franklin should come here," Zeb said quietly, staring at the granite headstone. "We can introduce him to the spirit of Uncle Lote. Maybe he'd learn something about loving this part of the earth . . .not just owning it."

"I wish you could have talked him into selling."

"I tried, Rue," Zeb said, holding her face between his hands.

"He's too proud. He'll never be happy here, but he won't give us the satisfaction of selling it back."

"I tried and tried, told him I'd pay him twice what he paid. Anything. Even without the trees, I thought it would be worth it. If it made you happy . . ."

"I know how to be happy," she said.

"How?"

"Being with you . . ."

"We'll have a house here," Zeb said. "Maybe just outside the Point . . . what would you think if I built us a house by your office? There's so much land there. Walking around, trying to site the barn, I started thinking. . . ."

"It's not in the Point," Rumer said.

"No, but it's not very far away. We'd have our privacy—you know, your father's gonna watch my every move till I prove myself to him."

"Not to mention *les Dames de la Roche* . . ."

"Exactly, Larkin. See? This is going to work out perfectly. I give up my job at the lab, and I find work as a builder. The barn, our house . . . what do you think?"

"I can't believe you want to give up your career," Rumer said, holding his arms, looking into his eyes. "Why are you doing it?"

"Because I want to be with you."

"But to throw away this amazing chance—are you sure?"

Zeb pointed up at the sky. He slung his other arm around her shoulder, and she watched the way he squinted into the night, as if mapping out the routes he'd always dreamed of traveling, from one star to another.

"They're not going anywhere," he said. "The stars are up there to stay. There are ten satellite photo specialists all lined up to take my place in California. No problem filling my spot. What my bosses don't know is that I have even bigger plans for the East Coast."

"What do you mean?"

"A nice new observatory somewhere between here and Providence, Rhode Island. You and I will have to scout the location. Mattie will have to be on call—because once I get the house finished, I'll be dragging you off on lots of day trips. I'm going to have a lab, and it's going to be within driving distance of here."

"Here . . . Hubbard's Point?"

"Our place, Rumer. Wherever you are."

And then, holding her hands, Zeb knelt down on the ground, in the dirt by the Indian Grave. With the scent of the earth rising around them and all the stars blazing overhead, Zeb pulled her down.

"I love you, Larkin," he said as her knees sank into the damp earth.

"Same here, Mayhew."

Rumer blinked, wondering why Zeb had chosen this place—with all the beautiful spots at Hubbard's Point—for them to come together. Twenty years ago, this was where they would have made love for the first time—why here? Why was it so important to them? Swatting the bugs away, she stared up at Uncle Lote's proud grave.

It was right there, in front of her eyes, clear as the day. This man had loved the Point—the wildness, the location, the heritage—as much as Rumer, as much as Zeb. If the legend was true, he had served those whom he could have hated—for stealing this incredible, beautiful land. Zeb had said it himself: Uncle Lote had known about loving this place, not just owning it.

"Thank you, Uncle Lote," she said out loud, holding Zeb's hand as he pulled her up.

"For what, Rumer?" he asked. "Why are you thanking him?"

"Because he taught us all," Rumer said. "All the Hubbard's Point kids who know about him . . ."

"Taught us what?"

"You know," she said, kissing Zeb. "That we never really leave this place we love. No matter what happens, no matter where we go."

"Is that the part I missed twenty years ago?" Zeb asked.

"Not at all," she whispered. "You knew it then. And you're back, aren't you?"

"And I watched you from up there, all this time. . . ."

The lighthouse beam slashed the sky, obliterating all stars. Rumer thought about her ancestor, the first Clarissa's mother, Elisabeth. She had missed that part too—sailing away with Captain Thorn. They had sunk, drowning within sight of the land that could have saved them.

"The bulldozers come tomorrow," Rumer said, choked up with the knowledge that the Franklins' yard, the face of Hubbard's Point, would change forever, and there was nothing she and Zeb could do to save it.

"I know."

"You tried so hard to keep them away. . . ."

"But it wasn't enough," Zeb said, holding her tighter. "Come on," he said, tugging her hand.

"Back home?" she asked.

"To the green house," he said. "My house . . . one last time."

They ran, flying through the woods as if Uncle Lote himself were carrying them along. Sliding down the path, Zeb blocked her from falling. Across the hard silver sands of the main beach, their feet pounded steadily. Holding hands, they raced over the footbridge and up the narrow stairs that led to the right-of-way through Zeb's old yard.

The green house stood there, naked on the hill. Where once it had nestled in pine and oak trees, now it stood bare, under the starry sky. Rumer's heart lurched once again—it probably would every time she saw the trees gone, for a long, long time.

Zeb walked over to the flat rock before remembering that the ancient brass key was gone—the locks changed. Glancing down at the road, he and Rumer made sure none of the Franklins' cars was parked there. The house was dark, with no lights burning inside.

Standing beside the north side, Zeb grabbed hold of the chimney. It was crooked, with small steps—formed as the bricks cut in from a wide base to a straight, narrow column. Pulling himself up the first five feet to the lowest foothold, he glanced over his shoulder.

"Can you make it?" he called to Rumer.

"I'm an old hand at this, Mayhew," she called back. "Do you have any idea at all how many mornings I used to climb up here to knock on your window when you overslept for our paper route?"

"I know, Larkin," he said. But even so, he held his hand back and let her grab on so he could pull her up.

One brick at a time, they climbed the chimney. When they reached the roof's lowest level, Zeb stood aside to let Rumer go first. She scuttled along like a crab just below the dormer windows, keeping her footing as she scrambled up to the second tier. Grasping the top of the dormer, she swung herself onto the very peak.

Zeb was right behind her. Sitting side by side, they caught their breath. A steady breeze was blowing off the water, keeping all mosquitoes away, down on the ground, over by the marsh and the Indian Grave. Rumer held Zeb's hand, thinking of all the promises they had kept tonight.

She gazed through the open space where trees had been, staring with love at every single rock and boulder in the yard. The smell of freshly cut lumber was still strong. Pinesap scented the air, as sweet as honeysuckle nectar. *We belong here*, she thought. *I'm the ground, he's the sky. I pull him to earth, and he flies me to the moon. No matter where we go, this is where we began.*

"This is my home," Zeb called up to the stars.

They twinkled overhead—white fire in the velvet black. Rumer recognized Orion, Ursa Major, Arcturus, and the Pleiades. The stars had cradled Zeb all these years, then sent him back to her. She sent them silent prayers of thanks, and then turned her attention back to the ground.

"Your home," Rumer said.

"This house, this rooftop," Zeb said, staring down at the yellow bulldozer, the crane with its wrecking ball, standing in the street below, "will be gone tomorrow."

"I can't believe it," Rumer said. All the love she felt for Hubbard's Point came welling up, and it poured out of her as Zeb took her in his arms. The chimney guarded one end of the roof, the unicorn weathervane the other. Tears sprang into her eyes as she thought about what they had and what they were about to lose.

"It's give-and-take, Rue," he whispered. "That's the truth of life. . . ."

"Why is it too much to ask to be able to keep the things that should last forever?" she asked. "Trees, rocks . . . this old, old house . . ."

"We'll be together," he said. "And we'll never forget. Let it all in, Larkin: Feel it now, so we never have to forget."

"Never forget," Rumer said. Wiping her eyes on Zeb's sleeve, she glanced through the window next door and caught sight of her father asleep in his chair. His feet were up, a book balanced on his lap.

She thought of Sixtus Larkin's teachers' manual, and the words rang in her mind: Recognize that every child needs a sanctuary.

This was Rumer's sanctuary. Hubbard's Point, and these overgrown old yards. She had learned who she was here—a woman who loved animals enough to become a veterinarian. The Point had been her classroom, and these yards, as Mrs. Mayhew had said, her sanctuary.

"Up there," Zeb said, pointing overhead, "is the new constellation I was telling you about. I wish I could give it to you, Rumer."

"The girl on the winged horse," she said, and as she stared up, she could see the horse galloping through the sky, the girl's arms around his neck, crouched low, just flying over the rocks, bushes, and rabbits. "Are they just beginning their night's adventure? Or ending it?"

"Beginning it," Zeb said, kissing her head.

"What's it called?" Rumer asked. "The new constellation?"

"Well, there's only one possible name. Since it's you and Blue flying home to me," Zeb said, "I think it has to be True Blue. My true-blue friend, Rumer."

"You're mine, Zeb," she said, flinging her arm around his neck. "No matter what happens," she said. "Let's always love this place."

"That goes without saying."

"And each other."

"Forever, Rumer," he said, pulling her close and kissing her hard. "Like always."

When they moved apart, they heard voices. Keeping still so they wouldn't be seen, they saw a cluster of people gathering down in the road. Voices murmured, and then there came the sound of matches being struck, lighters clicking into flame. One white candle was lit, then another and another.

"What is it?" Zeb whispered.

Rumer, in awe, couldn't speak.

They watched Michael, holding a burning candle, run up the hill to Rumer's house. He ran in without knocking, and they watched him shake his grandfather awake. Rousing himself, Sixtus shook the sleep from his eyes and let Michael pull him out of his chair.

"Where's Aunt Rumer?" they heard Michael ask as he led his grandfather down the hill.

"Off somewhere with your father," Sixtus said.

More candles had been lit, and in their orange-gold flames, Rumer could see the faces of all *les Dames de la Roche* and their husbands, sons, and boyfriends: Annabelle, Marnie, Charlotte, Dana, Allie, Sam, Quinn, Michael, Sixtus, Hecate, and even reclusive old Mrs. Lightfoot. Someone must have called Mattie, because her old Volvo rattled down the road and she climbed out to join the gathering. Every candle burned brightly as they spread along Cresthill Road in a silent, mournful, yet somehow joyous ceremony.

"What's going on?" Zeb whispered.

"I think it's a candlelight vigil," Rumer said. "For your house."

They had no candles, matches, or lighters, but in sorrow and celebration they joined hands and raised their arms toward the stars. When Winnie strode out in a pure white caftan—as bright and white as her upswept hair—and began to sing, everyone listened in silence.

"What a summer to come back home," Zeb said.

"What a summer to welcome you back," Rumer said.

"Tomorrow this house will be gone forever," he said, clasping her hand a little harder, "but you and I and Michael and Blue—"

"Will still be here," Rumer said.

They kissed, bracing themselves so they wouldn't tumble off Zeb's steep roof. The women and men of the Point sang below, and Rumer knew they would stand there all night, till their candles burned out, till the wrecking ball began to swing.

"I'm home," Zeb bellowed out, his voice carrying across the sky, down to the people standing in the street that they loved so well.

"Who's up there?" Annabelle called.

"You know exactly who's up there," Winnie scolded. "It's Rumer and Zeb. Who else could it be?"

"That you two?" Sixtus called, his face glowing in the light of his candle.

"It's us," Rumer said, her voice carrying on the sea breeze.

Quinn and Michael hooted once, and then Quinn let out what could only be called a ninja howl. Once the echoes finished reverberating against the granite ledges, the others' singing resumed. Rumer Larkin, who still ruled the earth, and Zebulon Mayhew, who still owned the sky, joined in. Although they had no candles to hold, they reached their arms up until they could each grab hold of a star. And the starlight shone down, making the rocks and roof and even the terrible yellow bulldozer look beautiful, as if lit from heaven.

The lighthouse continued to shine, guiding mariners home from the sea. It illuminated the sky, the sea, the marsh, the Indian Grave, and Foley's store. It passed over the osprey in his nest, the *Clarissa* at her dock, the Larkins' old yard, and Blue's new pasture. Its transit illuminated the yards, throwing magical threads of gold over every tree. The light's beam shone upon the Mayhews' old green house, high on the hill, on its last night on this earth, and it shone across the expanse of the roof, upon two best friends in love.

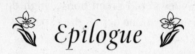

Epilogue

THE LETTER ARRIVED just past dawn the next day, delivered by messenger. Written on cream vellum stationery, it came with a sheaf of documents sealed and notarized. Although the messenger went first to the Larkins' kitchen door, he found Rumer standing by the oak tree at the edge of Zeb's old yard.

"What is this?" she asked.

"Just sign for it," the messenger had said. "The sender wants confirmation of receipt by seven A.M., and it's almost that now."

Rumer felt tired and frayed.

The vigil had been long.

Some neighbors had lasted the night, others had drifted home, falling into an uneasy sleep. Candles burned down or blew out. Michael and Quinn huddled together by the stone angel, wrapped in a blanket against the damp sea air. Rumer and Zeb came down from the roof at dawn, relinquishing the green house to its terrible fate.

Signing the register, Rumer accepted the envelope.

As she held it in her hand, feeling its weight, she noticed the workmen arriving next door. At seven o'clock, the precise moment that the wrecking ball was scheduled to start swinging, the crew started up their heavy machinery. Rumer smelled the exhaust and prepared to hear that first sickening smash.

"What is that?" Zeb asked, looking at the envelope.

"I don't know," Rumer said, her attention on the green house. She hardly cared, but she knew she had to open it. Slitting the flap, she pulled out a single sheet of thick paper embossed with her sister's monogram.

"It's from Elizabeth," she said.

"Read it out loud if you want," Zeb said, putting his arm around her for support.

"*Darlings,*" Rumer read.

By now you will be exhausted and limp, after your sleepless night. Yes, I know you: You will have stayed awake till sunup, worrying about the little green house. I'm so sorry I couldn't have spared you that, but the wheels of real-estate transaction grind so slowly, even when it is I turning them.

Yes, it is true: I have purchased the house. The green house and, I might add, the treeless property upon which it sits. Although the trees you climbed are gone forever, new ones can now be planted. And the rocks you love so dearly will never be blasted.

Tad Franklin, although quite as loathsome as advertised, was really rather reasonable. Of course, he wants us to believe that money is no object, but, in fact, it is. Money is always an object to people determined to make you believe it isn't. So I offered him plenty of it, along with a promise to appear in one—one single—Tad's Bedding commercial.

It was the 'single' that convinced him. Had I gone overboard, offering to do a whole series of them, he might have sensed my duplicity and balked. However, I used restraint—I'm not a Shakespearean actor for nothing, darlings—and thus prevailed.

Sadly, for Franklin, my agent will soon be informing him that TV spots really are not my bailiwick, that I can't be permitted to follow through on my impetuous and genuine—if ill-advised—promise.

Never mind. All will be well. Everyone is now happy. I offered Franklin the graceful way out of what would obviously be a hellish existence at Hubbard's Point. I offer the green house a chance to stand. I offer the bedrock a chance to remain, and I offer you—my dears, Rumer and Zeb—the dream you've always deserved.

These legal-looking documents are just that.

I've quit-claimed the house and property to the two of you. Consider it my early—or belated, depending on how you view it— wedding gift to you. Bedrock is bedrock.

What can I say?

With love always,
Elizabeth

Rumer squeezed her eyes tight. Then, as she opened them again, lifting her gaze from the paper to Zeb's face, as he looked back in disbelief, the bulldozer next door kicked into gear.

Rumer nearly shouted—what if they hadn't gotten the word and destroyed the old house that Elizabeth had just saved? The charges might already be set, the dynamite ready to go off. But before she could say a word, the workmen put away their tools and began to walk down from the hill to the road.

One by one, the trucks began to turn around.

And finally, the big yellow bulldozer began to rumble down Cresthill Road. Holding the letter in her hand, Rumer threw her arms around Zeb's neck.

"It's ours, Larkin," Zeb said.

"It's really ours, Mayhew," Rumer whispered.

Watching the bulldozer drive out of sight, feeling the tremor in her bones, Rumer knew that Elizabeth Randall—Hollywood star, artist extraordinaire—was Sixtus and Clarissa Larkin's daughter. She was Michael's mother.

But even more, most of all and forever, Elizabeth was Rumer's sister.

About the Author

LUANNE RICE is the author of *True Blue*, *Safe Harbor*, *Firefly Beach*, *Dream Country*, *Follow the Stars Home*, *Cloud Nine*, *Home Fires*, *Secrets of Paris*, *Stone Heart*, *Angels All Over Town*, *Crazy in Love* (made into a TNT Network feature film), and *Blue Moon* (made into a CBS television film). Her next novel, *The Secret Hour*, will be published by Bantam Books in February 2003. She lives in New York City and Old Lyme, Connecticut with her husband.